SPARK THE FIRE

Book One of The Dragons of Mother Stone

MELISSA MCSHANE

Night Harbor Publishing

For Teleri,
who not only read with enthusiasm but contributed so much of her personality to
Lamprophyre

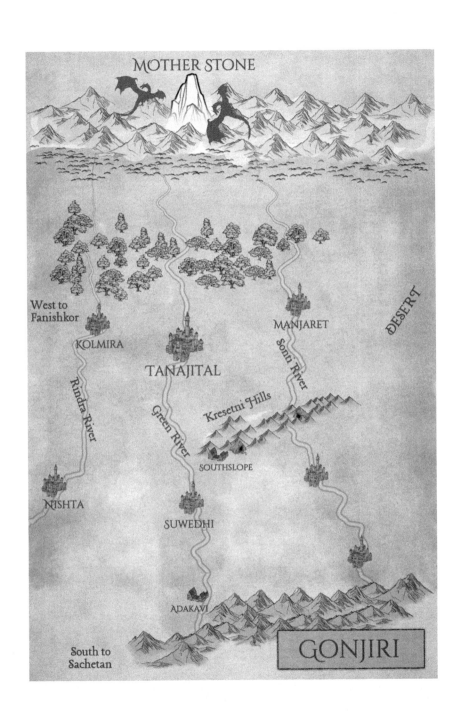

AUTHOR'S NOTE: ABOUT DRAGONS

Dragons have six fingers on each hand, and the number twelve is semi-religious to them. They measure the passage of time in twelvedays as well as seasons and years, and frequently count by dozens as well as more conventional base ten numbers (thanks to having ten toes on their feet).

Dragons measure time of day by the position of the sun: dawn, morning, mid-morning, noon, mid-afternoon, late afternoon, dusk/sunset. Time of night is measured by relation to midnight: dusk/sunset, evening, late evening, midnight, the dreaming hours, pre-dawn, dawn.

Dragons take approximately thirty years to reach adolescence and are considered adults at age fifty-five, though it can take another ten to fifteen years for a dragon to achieve her full adult size.

Dragon time and distance measurements are inexact and based on the average dragon body. The basic unit of time is the heartbeat, or beat. A dragon's resting heart rate is about twenty-five beats per minute, so a single beat is the equivalent of two and a half seconds, a hundred beats is a little over four minutes, and a thousand beats is almost forty-two minutes.

An adult dragon is approximately the same length and height (not including wingspan) as a double-decker bus, but slimmer. Their basic unit of distance is the dragonlength, which is somewhere between twenty-five and thirty feet long (counting from tip of the nose to tip of the tail). For smaller distances, they use the handspan, which is approximately twelve inches long. For long distances, they are more likely to measure by the length of time it takes to fly somewhere rather than how far it is in drag-onlengths. A dragon standing erect is sixteen to twenty feet tall.

Adult dragons weigh between 4000-5000 pounds. An active dragon will eat, on average, 250-300 pounds of meat per day, plus a quantity of stone equaling another 8-10 pounds (sometimes less depending on the "richness" of the stone). Dragons generally eat twice a day, though in lean times a dragon will gorge herself on available food and then not eat again for several days.

An adult dragon can fly up to 120 miles per hour.

CHAPTER ONE

The sun had barely peeked over the distant horizon when Lamprophyre took to the air above the nook where she'd spent the night. Six, seven, twelve sure strokes of her wings to gain altitude, and then she coasted along the updrafts that coursed through the mountain heights, maintaining speed with minute twitches of her wingtips.

In only a dozen dozen heartbeats, she descended from the rocky crags where only dragons and the hardiest of birds survived to the lower slopes, covered with a mossy scruff and the occasional scraggly pine. Here, small animals lived, rock hares and slender black birds and the goats who leaped fearlessly from cliff to sharp-edged cliff as if they, like the dragons, would fly and not fall if they missed their step.

She spiraled downward past the rocky slopes to land on the foothills, which were gently rolling rather than proudly stark, with soil and grass covering them like flesh laid over the bones of the mountain. The air of the lowlands, humid and heavy even just after dawn, weighed on Lamprophyre's wings and the delicate scales surrounding her eyes and mouth.

Three days of hunting with nothing to show for it wore on her soul in a different way. Not for the first time, she considered turning back. It wasn't as if anyone in the flight knew she'd intended anything but an extended search for game, and none of them would know she'd failed. But *she* would know, and that burned more fiercely than her physical or emotional pains.

She crept over the gentle slopes of the foothills, crushing green plants whose names she didn't know—what was the point of knowing the names of such transitory things?—and sending up more thick, heavily-scented drafts of air that choked her if she breathed too deeply. Ahead, where the ground flattened out, trees grew in clumps thick enough to hide a dragon, if she had to hide. Far better to conceal herself by blending with her surroundings, turning her bright blue scales mottled green and brown and furling the copper membranes of her wings. But it didn't matter, because there wasn't anyone to see her.

She blew hot air through her nostrils in exasperation. The creatures she sought had plagued the dragon flight for weeks, and now they were nowhere to be seen. Stupid humans with their stupid, incomprehensible desires and their stupid encroaching on dragon territory.

Lamprophyre clambered over yet another rise and saw no movement beyond a flock of birds busily pecking the ground of the wide, grassy plains. They looked like a scattering of dark pebbles against the rich green. It was a lovely color, she had to admit, deep and bright and—

Lamprophyre scowled. The same green as Coquina, Stones take her. Coquina who could do no wrong, Coquina who was always two steps ahead of Lamprophyre, two wingbeats above. Lamprophyre's intentions hardened into granite resolve. She would succeed, and then Coquina would be the one eating Lamprophyre's dust.

The thought of eating dust made Lamprophyre consider taking to the air. She'd certainly have a better view. But that meant the humans would be more likely to see her, however she concealed herself against the sky, and for this to work, she needed surprise. She continued creeping along the hills, casting her mind out for a stray thought that would reveal her prey.

The sun climbed higher, its edges fuzzy as it burned through the morning mist. Lamprophyre came out of the foothills and crossed the grassy plains to the first clump of trees. The birds scattered as she drew near, not soon enough, as three of them found. Lamprophyre crunched their bones happily between her back teeth. She much preferred cooked food, as any rational person did, but sometimes a couple of raw morsels stirred the blood. She wiped her mouth and pressed on, finally taking a rest in the shade of the tall, skinny trees, lush with leaves and the buds of orange flowers.

A thought brushed her mind, the faintest breath of a mental breeze: ... *never going to find...*

Lamprophyre sat up and cast about her. Her range for intercepting thought was only average, which meant the thinker couldn't be far away, no more than thirty dragonlengths. She slunk around the side of the copse and strained to hear more thoughts.

She caught the next one just as she saw motion off to her left: ... *outpaced us already...*

Lamprophyre flattened herself to the ground and watched a double column of riders come into view. They were a muddy streak against the vibrant green, brown horses, brown clothes, brown skin. All had white hair —no, those were caps covering their heads and hanging low over their necks. The jingling of metal chinking against metal reached her ears, but no speech.

Lamprophyre watched the humans, examining each. She didn't know enough about humans to be able to interpret their expressions, but she could tell who their leader was by the way she rode ahead of the columns, how she held her head alertly, searching for danger. Humans weren't so different from dragons in that respect. Finally, Lamprophyre had a target.

She scooted back behind the trees and flapped her wings once, twice, gaining just enough altitude to put herself above the leafy canopy. Concealing herself against the sky was difficult and couldn't be maintained long, but Lamprophyre was the best in her clutch, far better than stupid Coquina. Her body tingled as the concealment spread over her scales, turning her a misty yellow-gray to match the morning sky. Then she spread her wings and shot upward, resisting the urge to shout for joy as she flew. There was nothing in the world to beat that sensation.

She spiraled upward to get a better view. Before her, the plains spread out into the distance, gradually changing from verdant green to a muddier olive. Behind her, the foothills marched on to where they rose to meet the mountains, their greenery fading into dusty brown and gray. And beyond *that*, Lamprophyre's mountain home stretched to meet the sky, surrounding Mother Stone and her rocky slopes, white with snow year-round. It was so beautiful it made Lamprophyre's chest ache with longing —but she had a purpose, and finally she could achieve it.

She glided down toward the columns of riders, counting: seventeen in all. It wouldn't matter to her plan, but she did wonder idly whether that was a lot, or a few, for whatever purpose they had. Some of the other dragons had encountered humans in much larger groups. They'd scattered them, sent them fleeing out of dragon territory, regardless of the size of the group, but it was curious.

The female at the head of the columns had called a stop and was looking around intently. If she had detected Lamprophyre's approach, she was smarter and more observant than Lamprophyre had imagined a human could be. The female's intelligence wouldn't save her in the end, but it might mean the success of Lamprophyre's plan.

Lamprophyre furled her wings and dropped, snapping them open at the last minute with a crack like thunder, but not dropping concealment. The horses shifted restlessly, raising their heads and tossing their manes, and the humans turned in their seats, exclaiming over thunder out of a clear sky. Their thoughts were a wild tangle Lamprophyre blocked easily, not wanting the distraction. She glided past overhead, maddening the horses, who smelled danger even though their riders could not.

The leader shouted something and waved her hand, keeping a firm grip on the reins with the other. Lamprophyre curved into the sky and hung, flapping her wings to stay aloft. Then she let her concealment fall, blue and copper bleeding across her scales and wings, and dove.

They didn't see her at first, preoccupied with looking for a terrestrial enemy. Then the leader shouted and pointed, and the columns disintegrated into a mass of horses and humans, screaming and fumbling for weapons. The leader stayed outside the melee, sawing at her horse's reins to get it to stay put. Just as if she knew what Lamprophyre wanted and was actually cooperating.

Lamprophyre smiled and flexed her hands. She swept low over the leader, slowed her flight just so, and plucked the leader off her horse as easily as snatching a roe deer from the herd.

CHAPTER TWO

I nstantly she beat her wings hard to gain altitude, leaving behind the screaming mass. The leader struggled, but Lamprophyre had expected that and gripped her tighter. "Don't fight me, or I'll drop you," she shouted over the sound of the wind in her wings. "I wouldn't even do it on purpose."

The leader froze. "You speak my language," she said.

"No, *you* speak *mine*." The female was heavy and awkward even now that she wasn't fighting, and Lamprophyre was breathless and not interested in conversation. Explaining that humans had learned to speak from dragons, far in the distant past, was more work than she was willing to do at the moment. "Hold still," she warned again, but the warning was unnecessary, because the human clung to Lamprophyre's arms and pressed her face against the dragon's chest.

She swept along northward for more than a thousand dragonlengths until she was deep within the foothills. Then she descended slowly, alit in one of the valleys, and gently set her prize on the ground. The female staggered, but remained upright. Her cap had fallen off somewhere in their flight, and her short, dark brown hair was disordered and her eyes wide. She dropped into a crouch and put her head between her knees, breathing heavily. Lamprophyre calmed her breathing as well, concealing her excitement. It had worked! The first part, anyway. Now to see if she could pull off the rest.

The human rose from her crouch, then dropped to one knee, bowing her head. "My lord Katayan," she said, "please, spare my life."

Lamprophyre settled back on her haunches. "I'm not your lord. My name is Lamprophyre."

The female didn't raise her head. "Aren't you Katayan, that which the Immanence gave shape to rule all dragons?"

"No. I've never heard of that. There's no such person as Katayan. Get up—I want to see your face."

The female slowly stood and raised her head. Her dark eyes met Lamprophyre's fearlessly. "Then I ask that you kill me quickly," she said, "and spare my men your wrath."

"I don't want to kill you," Lamprophyre said, feeling irritable. She thought about pointing out that if she'd wanted the female dead she would have killed her immediately, decided that would ruin any chance of them reaching accord, and added, "I'm taking you to meet someone you can explain yourself to. To tell what you humans are doing invading our territory."

"Me?" The female sounded so startled Lamprophyre felt a twinge of uncertainty. "Why me?"

"I could tell you're the leader of those humans. We're tired of scaring you people off. I want you to talk to Hyaloclast and see if we can't come to an agreement."

"But I—who's Hyaloclast?"

"The dragon queen. Now, do you want to ride, or should I carry you again?"

The female took a few steps backward, and Lamprophyre was about to lunge for her when she stopped and examined the dragon. "Why would you let me ride?"

"I thought it would look better. More noble. You *are* sort of an emissary of your people."

The female said nothing.

Lamprophyre started to feel nervous. She had thought the human leader would leap at the chance to speak with Hyaloclast, but this female wasn't behaving at all as Lamprophyre had expected. Again that twinge of uncertainty shot through her, and she suppressed it.

Finally, the female said, "I'll ride, if that's allowed."

Lamprophyre crouched low and rolled her shoulders toward the female. Awkwardly, the human climbed up Lamprophyre's arm and shoulder and fitted herself into the notch just ahead of Lamprophyre's wings. "Can you see where to hold on?" Lamprophyre asked.

"It's as if you were made for human riders," the female said.

Lamprophyre sat up abruptly, and the female clung to the ridge of scales at the base of her neck. "Never say that again," she said. "We're not human servants."

"Sorry," the female said. "I just meant it's surprisingly comfortable. I would never dream of you as a servant of any kind. You're magnificent."

The compliment embarrassed Lamprophyre. To cover her embarrassment, she shrugged her shoulders to settle the human more securely in the notch. She'd never been this close to a human before, and even though she knew from stories that humans had once ridden dragons, she hadn't been able to guess how it would feel to have a person perched there at the scruff of her neck, like a fly she couldn't reach to swat. "Hold on, then," she said, and leapt into the sky.

The strain on muscles that hadn't flown far in three days had ebbed, and Lamprophyre felt powerful, ready to catch the air currents and soar high above the smelly green ground. She had to remind herself that she had a passenger—how awful if she lost her to a roll or a dive! "What's your name?" she called back over her shoulder.

"Rokshan," came the reply, faint and blown about by the wind. "And you said you are...?"

"Lamprophyre."

"Lamp—that's a mouthful."

"Not much harder than Rokshan."

The female said nothing for a few breaths. "And you want me to negotiate with your queen," she finally said.

"It's been centuries since humans set foot in dragon lands," Lamprophyre said. "And now you're all over the place. I want you to explain why."

"I see," Rokshan said. "But—"

"What?"

"Nothing. It's nothing."

They flew in silence the rest of the way through the foothills, where Lamprophyre banked low to follow the river that cut through the mountains. Green gave way to brown and then gray as they climbed to the lower slopes of the mountains, covered this early in the year with pale green scruff that felt so peculiar underfoot.

A splash of red and a speck of gold far below, tucked into the curve of the river, showed where Nephrite guarded his nest. He looked up as they passed, but gave no wave of recognition. The eggs of this year's clutch were within a twelveday of hatching, and their fathers were even more dili-gent than usual in keeping contrary thoughts from damaging their young. In a few years, Lamprophyre would bear an egg, and her mate, whoever that would be, would take Nephrite's place. The idea bothered her. She had no interest in any of the flight as a potential mate and no feeling that that would ever change.

She rose higher along the slopes. In the distance, she saw the cliffs and caves that were the flight's home. Brightly colored draconic shapes clung to the outcroppings, sunning themselves. The air was cool and fresh and invigorated Lamprophyre. She drew in a great lungful and slowed her speed, swooping around the long way to give everyone a glimpse of Rokshan perched on her shoulders.

When she alit on the shelf outside the caves, she pretended not to notice all the attention, or hear the gasps as one by one the nearest dragons saw the human. She leisurely crouched to allow Rokshan to dismount, then gave her a hand when she staggered.

"By the Stones, Lamprophyre, what is *that*?" Scoria exclaimed. The elderly dragon clambered arthritically down from her perch and put her nose right up next to Rokshan. "You brought a human here?"

"I did," Lamprophyre said. "And she's going to stop the humans from invading."

Grass-green scales slithered up and over the ledge. "*You* captured a human," Coquina said. Her tone of voice, dismissive as always, made Lamprophyre want to push her back over the edge.

Higher up the slope, bronze Leucite rose into the air with a few lazy flaps, then descended to the ledge and disappeared into the biggest cave. The royal cave. He was going to fetch Hyaloclast. Lamprophyre's heart beat faster. It was what she wanted, what she'd hoped for, but now that the moment was here, she couldn't quite believe it was happening.

Coquina cleaned her teeth with her sharp sixth claw. "There must be something wrong with it," she said lazily, but Lamprophyre knew her clutchmate well enough to recognize when Coquina was jealous.

Rokshan had backed away from Scoria's nose, which was emitting gentle bursts of smoke—well, Scoria was old and not always in control of her second stomach's fiery emissions. The human pressed against Lamprophyre's haunch, but didn't otherwise seem nervous. Lamprophyre thought about patting Rokshan's shoulder in reassurance, but wasn't sure that was a gesture that translated across species.

Heavy footsteps signaled Hyaloclast's arrival. The great dragon queen emerged and unfurled her wings, and Rokshan pressed even harder against Lamprophyre's leg. Lamprophyre couldn't blame her for being nervous now. Hyaloclast was a third again the size of Lamprophyre, her scales pure black and gleaming like obsidian, her eyes and the fine membranes of her wings the red of a blood ruby. She stood at her full height and looked down on Lamprophyre and Rokshan both.

"So," she said, her voice rumbling like a distant avalanche, "you have brought me a human, Lamprophyre."

"Yes," Lamprophyre said, sitting up tall even as she was conscious of Rokshan's body against hers. "She is the leader of the humans."

"And what will I do with a human leader?"

Lamprophyre met her bloody gaze fearlessly. "The humans have encroached on our lands with no explanation," she said, "and I have brought this female here for you to treat with. You can send our demands and make the humans leave."

Hyaloclast cast her gaze on Rokshan. "Interesting," she said. "I don't know where to begin. This was your plan?"

The way she said it, as dismissively as Coquina ever dreamed, made Lamprophyre's stomachs churn. "Yes, but—"

"How did you know this human was their leader?"

"I...it was obvious. The way she moved, the way she spoke to the others—"

"And it didn't occur to you that the humans might have more than one leader? That they don't all have the same goals?"

"Well..." This was all wrong. "Even if there are many—"

"You don't even know," Hyaloclast said, "that this is a male."

Hot blood rushed through Lamprophyre, tinting her scales violet with embarrassment. She ignored Coquina's laughter and said, "It doesn't matter if he's male or female. Isn't it better that we try to find a permanent solution than to keep scaring them away? Maybe there are lots of human groups, but this is a start!"

Hyaloclast transferred her attention back to Rokshan. "What's your name?"

"Rokshan. Son of Ekanath." Rokshan stepped away from Lamprophyre. "He is the king of Gonjiri."

A jet of smoke escaped Hyaloclast's left nostril. "So Lamprophyre got lucky."

"I guess he did," Rokshan said.

"I'm *female!*" Lamprophyre exclaimed. Laughter rippled through the watching crowd, which had grown to include practically every member of the flight. Lamprophyre was sure she was nearly purple with humiliation.

"It seems you have a mutual inability to identify each other's sex," Hyaloclast said, her eye ridges rising to echo her sarcastic tone. "Now that we've gotten that all straight, where does that leave us? Oh, yes. With a royal hostage."

Lamprophyre's head whipped around and she stared at the dragon queen. "Hostage?" she said. "But that's—he isn't a hostage!"

"I could be, if the queen insists," Rokshan said. "I hope your honor won't allow you to take advantage of Lamprophyre's mistake."

"Dragons do not deal dishonorably, but they take advantage when it's given to them," Hyaloclast said. "What do you offer, your highness?"

"Information," Rokshan said. "Didn't you wonder why there were humans in the northern wilds?"

"What humans do is of little interest to us," Hyaloclast said. "But I admit it's a curiosity."

"It was a prophecy," Rokshan said. "Jiwanyil—the Immanence made human flesh—told our ecclesiasts that human destiny lies in the northern wilds. We did not know dragons lived here. All our legends say the dragons were killed in a great catastrophe, hundreds of years ago. So we followed the prophecy. Human settlers, and the bandits who prey on them. My company was pursuing bandits when Lamprophyre captured me."

"I see." Hyaloclast settled back on her haunches. "And if you'd known there were dragons here?"

Rokshan gazed at her without a trace of fear. "We still would have come," he said. "We don't ignore prophecy. We've learned to our sorrow what happens when we do."

"I see," Hyaloclast repeated. "Lamprophyre. In your cunning plan, what did you anticipate I would do?"

Lamprophyre ducked her head. "We can't solve our problems if we don't know what's causing them. I hoped you could talk to the humans and convince them not to intrude on our lands."

"Bold words from someone who has made a terrible mistake. Didn't you think, if you did manage to capture someone of rank, that other humans might see that as an act of war? It's irrelevant that humans can't hurt us—think how many innocents might lose their lives if we're forced to defend Mother Stone."

Lamprophyre ducked her head lower. "I didn't think of that."

Hyaloclast let out a deep breath. "Take the prince back where you found him. Then return here, and we will discuss the consequences of your mistake. And you, young prince—" Hyaloclast leaned over so her face was level with Rokshan's. "Tell your royal father if humans persist in entering our territory, we will defend it. And we will not be so gentle as we have in the past." She turned and stumped back into the cavern.

The laughter had stopped. Even Coquina was silent. Lamprophyre crouched low and wordlessly leaned over so Rokshan could mount. Then, with a tremendous push from her hind legs, she launched herself into the sky.

CHAPTER THREE

S he flew straight up for a time, aiming for a point past the morning overcast, welcoming the chilly air caressing her hot flanks and cheeks. She'd forgotten she had a passenger until Rokshan said, "I'm cold."

"Oh. Sorry." She backwinged, hovered for a moment, then spiraled down gently until the air wasn't knife-edged with cold. Spreading her wings, she coasted southward, staying well above where the flight might reasonably be. She couldn't bear to look any of them in the eye.

"I'm sorry," Rokshan said.

She tried to look at him and could only see the curve of her shoulder. "*You're* sorry? You're not the fool who nearly started a war!"

"I mean they shouldn't have laughed at you. It wasn't a bad plan." Rokshan laughed. "I can't believe I'm saying this, but...that really was remarkable, snatching me off my horse and all that."

"Don't patronize me."

"Sorry."

They flew on for several dragonlengths before Rokshan said, "What will Hyaloclast do to you?"

"Lecture me," Lamprophyre said. "Give me penance duty. I'll probably fly a lot of long patrols to teach me humility."

"That doesn't sound so bad."

"It's not." The worst part would be the mockery, the sidelong glances and the whispered comments. It would be years before the flight let her forget about her stupid mistake.

She saw Nephrite again in the distance, that same blotch of red, very still against the banks of the river. She thought about veering to the side to avoid him, but that was pointless, since it wasn't as if he could know what she'd done. And he wouldn't come after her, abandoning his egg, for any reason. So much for Lamprophyre laying an egg any time in the next twelveyear. As if anyone would want to mate with her now. Small comfort that she'd already mentally rejected all of the males in the flight.

She swept past Nephrite, glancing down at him and the nest that held his and Fluorspar's egg. He was so still she could almost imagine—

With a gasp, she furled her wings and dropped like a stone. Rokshan let out a shout of surprise, and his hands gripped her ruff more tightly, but all her attention was on Nephrite. She landed a dragonlength away and ran toward him, not caring that she was far too close to the unborn dragonet. Rokshan clung to her against her uneven lope.

She skidded to a halt and grabbed Nephrite's chin, tilting his head toward her. The dragon's nictitating membranes were closed over his silver eyes, making them cloudy, and although he was now staring directly at the golden spot that was the sun behind the haze, his eyelids didn't blink shut. "Stones," Lamprophyre breathed, and twisted to propel Rokshan off her shoulders. He stumbled, caught his balance, and put a hand on Lamprophyre's arm.

"Is she dead?" he asked.

"He," Lamprophyre said, but she wasn't really paying attention to the human. No coherent thoughts came from Nephrite, even as close as she was to the dragon. She pressed her ear against Nephrite's chest and covered her other ear with her hand, blocking out distractions. After what felt like forever, she heard the distant thrum of his heartbeat, far too slow and far too quiet, but at least it was there. "He's alive."

She sat up and looked around, wishing madly for inspiration to strike. Nephrite moaned, drawing her attention back to him. "What happened?" she demanded.

Nephrite blinked, and his nictitating membranes drew back. His silver eyes were unfocused, the pupils bare slits in an argent field. "The birds break water under the moon," he said.

Lamprophyre sat back. "What?"

"Open the chasm into the last of the geode." Nephrite blinked again and swayed upright. "The fall eats its young."

"You're not making any sense," Lamprophyre said.

"Lamprophyre," Rokshan said, "is this a nest?"

Lamprophyre turned, releasing Nephrite to fall back against the stony cliffside. She scrambled over the stony riverbank to where Rokshan knelt, examining the pile of soft dead grasses and shards of eggshell. "Yes," she said. "The egg is gone."

"It didn't hatch?" Rokshan picked up a thin piece of eggshell, gold on the outside and tawny cream on the inside, then dropped it hastily.

"No. Dragon eggs have very thick shells when they're laid, and layers of shell fall off gradually until the shell is thin enough for the dragonet to break through. It's too early for it to hatch, and there'd be a lot more shell if it had. Someone stole the egg."

Lamprophyre stood and turned in a slow circle. It was impossible. No dragon would steal an egg—you couldn't even call it theft, because the eggs belonged to the whole flight. Dragons had no natural predators. That left humans. Lamprophyre knew practically nothing about humans—she'd just proved that spectacularly in public—but she'd never heard of a human being able to hurt a dragon the way Nephrite had been attacked.

"I have to tell the flight," she said. "They'll be able to find the ones who did this."

"There's no time," Rokshan said. "By the time you rouse them to action, the bandits will be long gone, and you'll never see that egg again."

A vision of the egg hatching in some distant human stronghold, surrounded by horrible humans thinking terrible thoughts, struck Lamprophyre to the heart. "All the more reason to hurry."

"I can track them," Rokshan said. "You go. Follow me when you can."

"What? I'm not going to let you go after those thieves alone! Why would you?"

"Look," Rokshan said, turning on her, "you were right about one thing. Humans and dragons need to be able to understand each other. If I can help restore this egg to your people, maybe that will convince your queen that that's possible. But we have to move *now*. I can't tell how long they've been gone—"

"Not long. The egg was here when we flew past on the way—I mean, I remember seeing it before."

"I can see the path they took. They can't be far away, but they're headed for the river, and if they have a boat, that could take them anywhere. We can at least see where they end up, and then, if you and I can't get the egg back, you can bring the dragons in force."

Lamprophyre glanced at Nephrite, who was drooling saliva mixed with thin black acid from his second stomach. "We can't leave him like this."

"He doesn't seem to be in any danger. And wouldn't he tell you to rescue the egg over tending to him?"

"I want to know what they did to him. If it's permanent—"

"Let's worry about that later." Rokshan hauled himself up to his seat and gripped her ruff tightly. "How close to the ground can you fly?"

"Not too close. We might be better off walking, except that's so slow."

"If you can stay about six feet off the ground—I mean, about as far as I am tall—that should be enough."

It was hard going, staying low enough that Rokshan could follow their tracks, fast enough not to drop but slow enough not to lose the trail. Lamprophyre's wings and shoulders ached, and her rear end was tense from keeping her tail from dragging. They followed the rocky foothills along what Lamprophyre could barely call a trail. "Are you sure you're following them?" she asked. "I can't see anything."

"I'm an experienced tracker, and I don't think they expected anyone to follow them," Rokshan said. He leaned well to one side, with a single hand on her ruff for balance. "Why was that dragon so far away from your home? Isn't that dangerous?"

"No animal would attack a dragon. And dragon fathers have to stay well away from other sapient creatures, so they don't hurt the egg with their thoughts."

"Their—I don't understand."

Lamprophyre's nerves were keyed to the breaking point as she strained to see any trace of humans or egg. "Dragons can hear the thoughts of intelligent creatures," she said, hoping to calm herself. She'd do the egg no good if she were too tense to react properly. "A dragonet in the egg can't shield herself from those thoughts. So they have to be kept away from everyone except their fathers, who are experienced at thinking the right things. Language. History. Traditions."

"So that dragonet is in danger from those bandits' thoughts."

He was quick, Lamprophyre had to admit. "Yes. We have to get her free soon, and hope she isn't damaged."

"What happens if she is?"

"I don't know. It's never happened before, not so I'm aware. There are stories of eggs gone wrong, but they're just stories."

Rokshan leaned out far enough to make Lamprophyre flap harder so she wouldn't overbalance. "Turn here."

The new path took them more southward, out of the foothills and into the plains. Ahead, Lamprophyre saw the glint of flowing water. A river, wider and slower than the one near her home. Now even she could see the trail left by the bandits, the grass crushed by the passage of many feet. She alit near the trail and leaned to let Rokshan off.

"At least ten humans, and a pack animal," Rokshan said. He crouched near the trail as if he could smell the bandits and track them as a fox would. "We have to be careful now."

"Humans can't hurt dragons," Lamprophyre said.

"What about what they did to your friend? They have *some* weapon," Rokshan countered. "Once we've spotted them, you distract them, and I'll grab the egg."

"That's a terrible idea," Lamprophyre said. "What if the egg is hidden? You'd be in danger the whole time you searched for it."

"All right, what do you suggest?"

"Let's find them first."

With Rokshan once more mounted, Lamprophyre launched herself into the sky, beating her wings for altitude. From that height, the river was a thread of blue against the fields of new growth, lined with bushy trees whose leaves were a dustier green than the grass. A breeze had come up, stirring the heavy air and fluttering the leaves so their white undersides flashed, dark-light-dark. The motion drew Lamprophyre's eye to the river-bank, and to a different kind of motion, this one heavier and slower.

"I see them," she said, just as Rokshan said, "There they are, under the trees."

Lamprophyre rose higher and circled above her enemy. At that distance, wispy traces of the bandits' thoughts brushed her mind, hard and cruel and filled with thoughts of gold—not the warm, living gold of the egg, but cold disks spilling out of cloth sacks. She understood very little of what she saw, but coin was something all the oldest stories contained. Apparently they were right about how much humans loved it.

"What is that thing in the water? Is that a boat?" she asked. Boats were something else from stories of the past, something humans used to travel on rivers. She'd never understood why they didn't just swim. Maybe they were as awkward in the water as dragons were.

"Yes, and it looks like they're loading it. The trees are in the way, so I can't tell more than that." Rokshan sounded frustrated. "If they get the egg on board, that's the end of this chase."

"Why? I'm faster than any boat. And—" Lamprophyre's lips curled in a smile. "I think I know how to stop them."

CHAPTER FOUR

They hid behind the trees on the far side of the river. Lamprophyre couldn't keep still, she was so agitated. Every moment that passed was one more moment for the egg to be corrupted. But her plan called for the bandits to cast off from the shore—a phrase Rokshan had taught her —so she waited, impatiently, and watched the bandits through the trees. She hissed when she saw one of them carrying a wrapped bundle the size and shape of a dragon egg, then felt embarrassed about her lapse into barbarity. Then she considered whether barbarity might not be needed in this case. She certainly intended to wreak havoc on the kidnappers.

Beside her, Rokshan laid a hand on her arm. "It's almost time."

"Then mount up." It was getting easier, and Rokshan's weight no longer bothered her, though she was still aware of him perched above her wings. The last bandit jumped from the bank to the boat, someone else gave a shove with a long pole, and the boat drifted into the river's current and picked up speed. It was as fast as a fish, with a thick pole sticking up from its center that had a sheet of coarse fabric attached to it. The fabric caught the breeze as a dragon's wing would and propelled the boat along.

Lamprophyre scrambled on hands and feet parallel to the shore, pacing the boat until it was fully in the center of the broad river and well away from either bank. "Hold on," she told Rokshan, and pushed off from the spongy ground.

This time, she didn't bother concealing herself, depending instead on speed and surprise to get the advantage of the bandits. She rose a few dragonlengths into the sky, hovered briefly to get her bearings, and as the first cries of alarm rang out, she dove at the boat and spat a great blast of fire.

As she'd intended, it missed the boat by the barest margin and made the water on its left side steam. Screams of terror, and the sound of feet pounding the boards, warmed her heart. She drew in another breath and sent more fire over the right side of the boat, brushing its side and sending up a stink of charred wood with the cloud of steam.

She landed near the pole and spread her wings wide as Rokshan tumbled off and away. In her deepest voice, she roared out, "*Thieves!* Give back what you stole!" It was for drama's sake rather than because she believed her order would make them obey, but drama was deeply satisfying.

A female, heavier-set than Rokshan and with dark black hair concealing the lower half of her face, hauled herself out of a square hole in the boat's floor some distance away. She shouted, "Archers! Kill the beast!"

Archers. That was another word Lamprophyre knew. She shut her nictitating membranes, making the world go slightly dim, as arrows plinked away at her impenetrable hide. Shoving off, she flapped a few times and dove at the female who had given the order. The female didn't have time to move before Lamprophyre had her pinned with one of her deadly sharp claws at her throat. She instantly stilled. Lamprophyre wished she knew how to interpret human expressions to tell if she was afraid or angry. It didn't matter. She was Lamprophyre's prisoner.

"Tell them to give me the egg, and I'll spare your life," she hissed, giving in to ancient instincts.

Sweat beaded on the human's forehead. "Give it the egg," she shouted, her voice much deeper than Rokshan's. "It's not worth my life."

"Good choice," Lamprophyre said with a smile.

Something slapped Lamprophyre's right haunch. Instantly the dim world turned rosy pink, and a flock of birds winged past, laughing with the voices of a hundred dragons. Lamprophyre turned her head to follow them and saw the moon hanging low in the sky, full and heavy and tinted orange. It looked like a fat orange, pebbly and rough, close enough to touch, so she reached out—

"*Lamprophyre!*" Rokshan shouted.

"I need to pluck the orange," she said, reassuring him.

Something cracked against the side of her face, a heavy blow that rattled her brains and made her teeth feel loose. She jerked away, blinking both sets of eyelids, and then flattened herself to the floor as the bandit chief swung a length of wood at her head again. The moon was gone, the sky was faded pale blue, and all she could hear was the rush of water past the sides of the boat and the shouts of angry, frightened humans.

"Ow," she said, and rose up from the floor to tackle the bandit chief. She caught the chief's arm and wrenched the wooden beam from her grip. Tossing it aside, she threw her to the floor and put a heavy foot on her chest. The female gasped for breath, scrabbling at Lamprophyre's foot and ankle with both hands.

"Lamprophyre, help!" Rokshan shouted.

She turned, not letting up on the bandit chief. Rokshan was wrestling one of the bandits for another length of wood. This one was finely carved and had a chunk of uncut sapphire half the size of Lamprophyre's fist strapped to its tip with strips of leather. Other females—males?—circled the two, and one bandit looked like she was preparing to attack Rokshan.

"Stones," Lamprophyre cursed. She shoved the bandit chief hard into the floor and leaped for the bandits. Her tail whipped around and caught the nearest one, the one approaching Rokshan, below the knees, sending him to the floor. She reached for the stick Rokshan and the other bandit were fighting over.

"Don't touch it!" Rokshan said. "It's a weapon. It will hurt you. Go get the egg!"

Lamprophyre had no idea where the egg was. This plan had failed even faster than the first one had. Instead, she snatched the bandit grappling with Rokshan and shook him until he loosed his grip on the stick, then flung him overboard to sink screaming beneath the water.

Something struck her hindquarters, and she turned to see the bandit chief once more holding the length of wood. "You're a fool," she said, and breathed out fire to engulf the female.

The bandit chief screamed and dropped to the ground, beating at herself to put out the flames. Lamprophyre sneered. "That was a warning," she said. She kicked the bandit's weapon over the side of the boat and grabbed the bandit chief by her ankle, hauling the female up to dangle in front of her nose. "My fire can burn much hotter. Now. Last chance. Where is the egg?"

The bandit chief appeared incapable of speech, but she waved her arms in some kind of signal. Lamprophyre looked over her shoulder. Rokshan stood behind her, brandishing the sapphire-tipped stick—that little thing, a weapon?—in a stance that said he was ready to attack anyone who approached. One of the bandits dropped into the square hole in the floor and clambered out holding the fabric-wrapped bundle. Lamprophyre took it with her free arm and shoved the wrappings aside with her nose. Golden eggshell gleamed.

"Don't try this again," she said to the bandit chief. She dropped her on her head, making her cry out once and then go still and silent. Lamprophyre found, looking at the innocent egg, she didn't much care if she'd killed her. How much damage had these humans done to it? And she didn't dare burn the ship for fear so much death terror would mark the dragonet for life.

"Stay close," she murmured to Rokshan. She slowly turned in a circle, her tail held ready for an attack, until she was facing the rest of the bandits. "Now mount."

It was fortunate Rokshan no longer needed help in mounting, because the bandits looked poised to attack her again. That they were more afraid of losing the egg than they were of dying at her claws surprised and frightened her. To cover her fear, she said, "Whatever you had in mind, forget it. You won't take us by surprise a second time." Tucking the egg securely under one arm, she leaped into the sky.

"You need to kill them," Rokshan said. "Those men and women have killed so many humans, and I'm sure they would have killed us—couldn't you perceive their thoughts?"

"I was blocking them so I wouldn't be distracted. And if I burn them, the dragonet will sense their deaths, and that could..." She didn't want to finish that sentence. It might already be too late for this egg.

"They'll come after you again. You dragons, I mean."

"We'll be ready for them." That, Lamprophyre was sure of.

CHAPTER FIVE

Nephrite was gone when they returned to the nest. Lamprophyre settled on the river bank and bent low to drink water from her cupped hand. She hadn't realized she was thirsty until she tasted the delicious, cool water. Rokshan knelt by the river and scooped up a drink for himself. When he finished, he wiped his mouth and said, "What now?"

"We can't leave the egg unattended, and I don't dare bring you back to the flight. I'm in enough trouble as it is. I'll return you to your people and then take the egg back."

"Won't that be dangerous?"

"It's already been hurt. A few hundred beats exposed to our thoughts can't make a difference." She eyed the stick, which lay on the ground near Rokshan's feet. "And what am I supposed to do with that?"

"It's not safe for the dragons, and I don't think humans should have it either. But breaking it could be a bad idea."

Lamprophyre resisted the urge to kick it into the river. "Why is that?"

"Artifacts like that one are full of magical energy. Breaking it might release that energy explosively. It needs to be safely drained and then broken." Rokshan picked it up and put a hand over the sapphire, squeezing it as if it were a fruit he could crush for its juice. "I don't know why it doesn't work on me. Somebody made this to hurt dragons. But

22

nobody knew dragons existed until a few months ago, so why would it exist at all?"

"Will it hurt me if I touch just the stick?" Lamprophyre held out a hand.

Rokshan extended it toward her as if he expected it to discharge a pulse of magical energy that would kill them both. Lamprophyre closed her hand around the wooden shaft. "I don't feel anything," she said. "So it's just the stone that does the damage."

"That still makes it dangerous."

"Less dangerous for us to keep it where we can see it." She knelt for Rokshan to mount. "We should hurry. Princes are important, yes? So we don't want your people getting upset and starting a war."

"I'm not that important. I'm the youngest of my father's children and therefore redundant."

Lamprophyre shot into the air. "Your *father's* children? Do human males give birth?" Rokshan had sounded uncharacteristically grim just then.

"No, I meant that my father has had two wives. Elini died in a boating accident when her youngest was only a baby, and Father married my mother Satiya shortly after that. She had two children, and I'm the youngest."

"You sound as if that's a problem."

Rokshan laughed, though it didn't sound very cheerful. "My father and I don't get along. Look, I think I see my company—there, to the left."

Lamprophyre thought about pressing Rokshan for more details, but decided it was none of her business what humans did in their families. How much better to be part of the flight, with your parents having no more or less influence on you than anyone else. A pang of ridiculous homesickness flashed through her, and she hugged the egg closer to her chest and thought calming thoughts. She wasn't as effective as the egg's father would be, but she had to be better than nothing.

She alit a dozen dragonlengths from the humans and leaned over to let Rokshan off. "Thank you," she said. "It wouldn't have worked without you. I'll be sure to tell Hyaloclast that."

"Good luck," Rokshan said.

He waved a farewell as she leapt into the sky. Another gesture humans and dragons had in common. Language, gestures, some memories of a distant past...Hyaloclast was right; none of that was enough to give them a shared foundation to work from.

Lamprophyre wheeled and flew off toward home. She thought Rokshan might still be waving, but she didn't look back to find out.

~

A TWELVEDAY LATER, LAMPROPHYRE RECLINED ON THE ROCKY CLIFFSIDE outside the caverns and soaked up the sun, so comforting in contrast to the brisk wind blowing across her scales. She needed that comfort to ease the tension that pulsed through the flight like a living thing, a snake gripping each dragon in its coils. Fluorspar and Nephrite's egg had begun hatching before dawn, and while no one would intrude on their joyous moment, everyone longed to know who this dragonet would turn out to be.

Lamprophyre felt inappropriately guilty every time she thought of the dragonet. If not for her and Rokshan, it would be lost to the flight entirely, but suppose she'd taken too long, and the bandits' corruption wouldn't have taken hold if she'd been faster? What if her passing overhead had been the distraction that had left Nephrite vulnerable to the magic stick? They were all nonsensical thoughts, but she still burned with humiliation over the incident that had brought Rokshan to the flight, and inappropriate guilt seemed part of that.

She heard someone scrambling rapidly up the cliffside, climbing rather than flying, and opened her eyes to see Bromargyrite of her own clutch pull himself over the ledge and disappear into Hyaloclast's cavern. Bromargyrite was the new dragonet's sibling, Fluorspar and Nephrite's previous egg, and while he wouldn't have been allowed to be present for the hatching, he would have been close by. Lamprophyre sat up and unfurled her wings, focusing on each muscle to keep from leaping into the air and flying to where the dragonet was.

Hyaloclast emerged, followed closely by Bromargyrite. She walked to the edge and stepped off, extending her wings before she hit the ground and swooping away. That was the signal for the rest of the flight to follow, at a respectful distance, of course. Lamprophyre lagged behind. If something was wrong with the dragonet, she didn't want to know about it until she had to.

The hatching cavern was the largest one in the mountains, big enough to hold twelve dragons at a time and high enough that a dragon could fly from one end to the other without so much as brushing a wingtip against the walls. Its mouth, on the other hand, was too narrow for more than one dragon to enter at once. Lamprophyre, waiting outside with those of the flight too slow to find a place inside, reflected that it would be easy to trap dragons inside the hatching cavern with a few well-placed boulders. It was a thought she wouldn't have had before facing humans and being touched by their terrible weapon.

She'd explained the magic stick to Hyaloclast as best she could without demonstrating it on anyone; the effect had been so terribly disorienting she couldn't bring herself to inflict it on others. Hyaloclast had listened without saying anything until Lamprophyre had started repeating herself, then said, "I will warn the others, and put it where no one can easily reach it."

"But suppose humans find it again?"

Hyaloclast had regarded her with amusement. "No human will ever get that far," she had said, and that was the end of the conversation. Lamprophyre wasn't sure the queen's confidence was totally warranted—humans had to have made the stick, because it wasn't something that had sprung fully-formed out of the earth, and who was to say they might not make another?—but she knew well that dragons were more than a match for ordinary human weapons, and she didn't feel like arguing with the dragon queen.

A couple of dragons emerged from the hatching cavern, and Lamprophyre leaned forward, eager despite herself. Neither of them looked concerned or afraid, but they also didn't have the cheerful expressions of dragons who'd just welcomed a new addition to the flight. Lamprophyre subsided. That wasn't so awful, if they weren't upset. The dragonet probably wasn't deformed, or mentally deficient, or—she made herself stop going over the list of possible ailments she'd generated and refined in the last twelveday.

More dragons filed out, making way for others to enter. Chrysoprase stopped near Lamprophyre. "She's not what anyone expected," she said, "but it's not so bad. You saved her, Lamprophyre. We're all grateful for that."

"She's not corrupted?" Lamprophyre asked.

Chrysoprase frowned. "I wouldn't call it corrupted, exactly. But nobody expected her to be completely untouched by her experience. Just remember how many twelvedays she was under Nephrite's influence alone. A few thousand beats spent with humans, even vicious humans, isn't enough to completely negate that." She patted Lamprophyre's shoulder. "Go on in. See what you think."

Lamprophyre hesitated in front of the cavern until a few more dragons emerged. Before she could let fear stop her, she ducked her head and entered the cavern, folding her wings closely along her back though there was plenty of room. A moment of darkness, as her body blocked the sunlight, and then her eyes adjusted to the luminescence filling the chamber. Two dragons came toward her, murmuring to each other. Lamprophyre stepped aside to let them exit, then walked forward to the cavern's far end, where a hollowed-out platform of stone rose above the smooth floor. Fluorspar and Nephrite flanked it, settled back on their haunches as if the hatching had exhausted them. Hyaloclast sat nearby, towering over the new parents. Her body obscured Lamprophyre's view of the stone nest, but she seemed relaxed.

A high-pitched chattering echoed off the distant walls and ceiling, rapid like birdsong. It took Lamprophyre a moment to realize she was hearing speech. Mesmerized, she walked forward until the words became clear:

"...and I want to see the trees and the birds and the rocks and the everything, yes, Mama and Papa? There are so many trees and they grow taller than us and they're green, and not many dragons are green, they're red and blue and purple and bronze and black like that dragon, she's really big, bigger than Mama. And Mama is bigger than Papa and Papa is smaller than that one—"

The dragonet was no bigger nor smaller than any other dragonet. Her scales were an unsurprising gray; her adult color would fade in over the first ten years of her life. She looked up at Lamprophyre with eyes that were pure liquid gold, and her flood of words cut off. Lamprophyre gazed at her, speechless.

Finally, the dragonet said, "I remember your thoughts. Blood and death and fire. You killed humans."

It felt like a blow to both stomachs. "I thought I hadn't," she said. "I'm sorry."

"I remember death," the dragonet said. "It hovers over me and if I talk it floats away like a boat—what is a boat?"

"It's...a human thing that floats on water like a leaf, but it's made of wood."

"I thought it was a living thing." The dragonet yawned. "If I sleep, will I still hear screaming?"

Lamprophyre felt like screaming herself. "I don't know."

"I hope so. The screams are like a song." The dragonet clambered over the lip of the hatching nest and snuggled between her father's knees. She yawned again and lay still, a little gray ball that blended with the stone floor.

Lamprophyre looked at Hyaloclast, her eyes wide. "I'm so sorry," she began.

"Her memories will dim as time passes," Hyaloclast said. "Already she thinks of her experiences as a bad dream, though a vivid one. I don't think the effect will be permanent."

"I swear I tried not to kill them. I really don't remember—"

"Enough, Lamprophyre," Hyaloclast said. "The blame lies with the humans who stole her. But you will need to stay well away from young Opal until she heals. Contact with your memories will lengthen her recovery."

"Of course." Lamprophyre dared to look at Fluorspar, who regarded her with the look of a parent who sees a threat to her child and wants it gone at any cost. "That makes sense."

She hurried back outside and took to the air, with no particular destination in mind, just filled with the desire to fly and fly and never come down to earth again. They were right, it wasn't so bad. Opal would live. She might even turn out sane. If Lamprophyre had only been able to eliminate those bandits, everything would be...well, not perfect, but better than all right.

She soared over the peaks toward Mother Stone, who rose endless and mighty over the lowlands. If she dared, she might fly higher, where the air was too thin to breathe and the cold could freeze your eyeballs. She might find the final resting place of all dragons, where the old and sick journeyed at the end of their lives. But that would mean the end of her own life, and she wasn't so discouraged and low as to want that. She flipped a lazy roll in midair and headed for home.

As she neared the flight's caverns, movement on the lower slopes caught her eye. She swooped lower to examine it—a large deer, or a mountain lion, perhaps? Whatever it was moved steadily in the direction of the caves, and no animal would do that. Then she gasped, and dropped out of the sky to land near Rokshan. "What are you doing here?"

"Wishing I had the wings of a dragon," Rokshan said. "Will you give me a ride? I didn't realize how long a journey this would be." His normally brown skin was flushed ruddy with exertion, and the hair over his brow was matted and damp with sweat.

"Give you a ride where? Rokshan, why did you come here?"

Rokshan squatted and drank from a waterskin at his hip. "I told my father about you. All of you," he said. "About how we're wrong to simply come into your lands, prophecy or no. That we should treat you as we would any other kingdom, with respect. He's authorized me to bring our requests before Hyaloclast."

"She won't listen. You're wasting your time."

"Lamprophyre," Rokshan said, tilting his head to look up at her, "I have to take that chance. You don't understand our position. The last time humans ignored a prophecy of this nature, thousands died. We don't want to impose on you, but we *must* move north. I'm counting on being able to explain this to her."

Lamprophyre regarded him steadily. Rokshan's expression was as incomprehensible as ever. "Fine," she finally said. "But I still say you're wasting your time."

"Then I waste my time. But if it means spending more time with you, I can live with that." He hauled himself into the notch before her wings.

"With me? Why would you care about that?" Lamprophyre launched herself into the sky.

"Because you're interesting. Because we've fought together, and saved each other's lives. Among my people, that makes for a bond that isn't easily dismissed."

"You're strange. I'm a dragon. You're a human. How much in common can we have?"

"We both want humans and dragons to live in peace," Rokshan said.

That startled her. She'd been so intent on impressing Hyaloclast she hadn't really cared *how* she might impress her. Solving the human problem had simply been a means to that end. But after meeting Rokshan, and fighting those bandits...humans weren't just a faceless mob anymore. And she discovered she agreed with Rokshan: their two peoples needed to learn to live together, not humans invading dragon territory or dragons scaring humans away.

"Did the dragonet hatch?" Rokshan asked.

"This morning. She's...well, she's not entirely well, but she'll recover. It's better than death, or whatever fate those bandits had in mind."

"I'm glad. I took my men hunting those bandits, but they'd already fled downriver. Probably went to ground in Kolmira—that's the next big city to the south along the Rindra River. I'm sorry we couldn't catch them."

Ahead, the ledges of the flight's caves loomed. It reminded her so much of that day a twelveday ago when she'd brought Rokshan so triumphantly to meet Hyaloclast she almost veered off and flew away. The thought of being humiliated once again curdled her second stomach. She could already feel Hyaloclast's disdain. This was idiotic. She would never listen to Rokshan, might even decide to kill him, and his death would be on Lamprophyre's head.

But she knew Rokshan well enough—how strange, to think of knowing a human at all—to realize if she refused to take him, he'd come on his own, and Lamprophyre would be a coward as well as a fool. No, she owed it to both of them, and to all dragons, to see this through.

She settled lightly on the outermost ledge and leaned over to help Rokshan dismount. "Wait here," she told him, and climbed to the royal cavern. As she'd hoped, Hyaloclast had either seen her approach or been warned, and the queen waited outside the cavern for her. She caught a breath of Rokshan's thoughts—*big dragon could crush me like a bug*—before shutting them out. The drifting thoughts of the flight were enough of a distraction.

Hyaloclast regarded her closely, her nictitating membranes half-lidded in deep thought or disdain. Lamprophyre controlled her impulse to grovel and said, "The prince has returned with a request to negotiate."

Hyaloclast looked past her to where Rokshan stood. Lamprophyre risked glancing at him over her shoulder; he stood straight, his head bare and his feet planted securely as if he expected a stray gust of wind to knock him over the edge. It filled her with fear for him, and she resolved in that instant to carry him to safety if this went wrong as it surely would.

"Negotiation is for those who want something," Hyaloclast said. "We have nothing we want from the humans."

"But they want to live in harmony with us," Lamprophyre said. "Our oldest stories say that was once possible. Why can't it be again?"

"Because they have nothing to offer." Hyaloclast continued to stare at Rokshan. "Take him back where you found him."

"No."

Hyaloclast's gaze snapped to Lamprophyre's face. "No?"

Lamprophyre swallowed. "No. You need to talk to him. Maybe there's no chance for an accord, but shouldn't you find that out rather than assuming it's impossible?"

"You dare challenge me?" A jet of white smoke shot from one of Hyaloclast's nostrils.

"It's not about me. It's a reminder of what's true. Of what the queen owes her people." Lamprophyre dropped to her knees, an uncomfortable pose for any dragon. "Please. Mother. Just listen to him."

More smoke rose to wreath the queen's head. "You choose to trade on our relationship for this human?"

"I won't ask for anything ever again. That's how important this is." Lamprophyre's knees ached and her thighs burned with the effort of staying upright.

Hyaloclast looked at Rokshan again. "He has until midday," she said, leaping down from the ledge to land lightly in front of Rokshan. Lamprophyre got to her feet and followed, ranging herself behind Rokshan. She hoped she didn't look too much like she was poised to flee.

CHAPTER SIX

"Young prince," Hyaloclast said, looming over him. She was nearly three times his height, but Rokshan stood unmoving, and that was body language even a dragon could understand. "You come as an emissary from your father the king?"

"Yes, your majesty," Rokshan said. "I apologize for using human terms of respect, but I'm afraid no one in the human world remembers how to speak to dragon royalty."

"Rational creatures do not take offense where none is intended," Hyaloclast said.

"I wish that were true of humans," Rokshan said. "Your majesty, my father asked me to explain our situation and ask for your wisdom in solving our mutual problem."

"I see no problem for dragons," Hyaloclast said, "but I'm willing to listen."

Lamprophyre cast an eye on the sky. It was already past mid-morning, and if Rokshan only had until midday, he had better talk fast.

"I don't know if you know anything about our religion," Rokshan said. "Until I met Lamprophyre, I believed all thinking creatures shared the same faith. But you have to understand something of what we believe for this to make sense. The power that fills the universe, the Immanence that gives life to everything, communicates to our ecclesiasts through Jiwanyil, the Immanence given human flesh. He gives them glimpses of the future that he intends us to act on. About a hundred years ago, there was a prophecy that told the people of one of our largest inland cities to build boats. Boats on dry land. The people scoffed and ignored the prophecy—and were all drowned when their valley was flooded by a dam bursting. No human has ever forgotten that prophecy."

"Interesting. But it has nothing to do with us," Hyaloclast said.

Rokshan shook his head. "Seven months ago, the ecclesiasts received another prophecy in response to my father's request. Tensions are high between Gonjiri and Fanishkor—that's a kingdom west of Gonjiri. He wanted guidance as to how to deal with them. And the ecclesiasts told him he was to begin settling the wild northern lands. Nobody knew dragons still existed or that this was your territory, or we would have acted differently. We began settling, and you dragons scattered us. Reasonable, considering that we came upon you without warning. On behalf of my father and his people, I apologize for that intrusion."

Hyaloclast inclined her head. "I accept your apology, prince. Provided it does not happen again."

"I wish I could make that promise," Rokshan said. "As I said, we don't ignore prophecies anymore. We have to continue settling here."

"That's foolishly confident of you. And when dragons raze your settlements to the ground, what will you think of your prophecy then?"

"That this must be what Jiwanyil intended." Rokshan tilted his head to look the dragon queen in the eye. "We will abide by whatever rules you set. We will pay whatever tribute you ask. We ask only that you allow us the use of parts of your territory. No human will encroach on your mountains or go anywhere you tell us to avoid. Name your price, and we'll pay it."

Hyaloclast's lip curled in a smile. "You are a terrible negotiator."

"Negotiations are for two people who each offer the other something. We come before you as supplicants. What we ask is for your help in saving our people from whatever disaster this prophecy is meant to avoid."

Lamprophyre held her breath. Her fingers twitched in preparation for hauling Rokshan away from Hyaloclast's fire or claws. Hyaloclast gazed down at Rokshan. "You are correct," she said. "You have nothing to offer us. We are stronger, wiser, better armed, and have a good defensive position if humans choose to attack."

Lamprophyre's shoulders ached with tension. Rokshan sagged a little. "Your majesty," he began.

"But that does not mean we cannot treat together as rational creatures," Hyaloclast continued. "We don't worship your God, but we know what it is like to live in the shelter of someone greater, and we understand your predicament. It would be cruel of us to deny you survival." She sat back on her haunches. "We'll allow your people to settle in the lowlands, provided they do not spread beyond the mark I will give you. But the land will be under dragon rule, and their settlement will not be considered part of the kingdom of Gonjiri. This is not a thing I will make an exception for."

"I'll present it to my father. He won't be happy about it."

"If he's truly only interested in the survival of his people, he will accept it. And you will not present it to him. My emissary will."

Rokshan's head came up. "Ah, your majesty, an emissary? You mean, a dragon living among humans?"

"I do. I will insist on one of my people receiving the honors due an ambassador. She will be my voice. And I hope she will begin a new tradition of mutual respect between our peoples."

The moment Hyaloclast said "she" Lamprophyre's heart sank. "Hyaloclast," she said, "an ambassador?"

"You've already championed this relationship," Hyaloclast said. "Are you not committed to your proud words?"

"I am," Lamprophyre said. "But—" She found herself unable to remind Hyaloclast of her earlier humiliation, but that didn't make it any less relevant now. She was foolish, young, brash. Hyaloclast couldn't possibly think she was a good choice for ambassador.

"You have made many mistakes," Hyaloclast said, pitching her voice so everyone could hear. "You were too quick to act and you made foolish decisions based on not enough information. You are also brave, honorable, willing to learn, and decisive. And if the king of Gonjiri is willing to send one of his own into possible death as a negotiator, I believe it is only fair that the dragon ambassador be of my own blood as well."

Lamprophyre thought about arguing. She had no preparation for such a role, was barely an adult, would no doubt make mistakes, some of them potentially harmful. She watched Hyaloclast, who in turn was watching her with a look of anticipation. Hyaloclast was giving her the chance to refuse—a refusal that would reduce her in her mother's eyes, lose her any chance of gaining the queen's respect. And by the look in Hyaloclast's eyes, refusal was what she expected from Lamprophyre. It angered her so much she sat upright and said, "I'll go."

Hyaloclast's eyes gleamed. To Lamprophyre's surprise, she saw satisfaction and pride there. "Join me," the queen said, "while I give you your instructions. You need to know what I intend you to say to these humans."

Lamprophyre followed her into the cavern. Its phosphorescent light turned Hyaloclast's black scales blue and made Lamprophyre seem to glow. "I won't let you down," Lamprophyre said.

"Never mind that," Hyaloclast said impatiently. "I have no interest in treating with humans. Stand firm on the territory issue, and refuse to make agreements on any other subject. That is not why I'm sending you."

"But—Rokshan came here in honor. Shouldn't we respect that?"

"I'm not saying you should lie to them, Lamprophyre. I'm saying they will want treaties with us, mining rights almost certainly, and you are not to give them anything regardless of what they offer."

Lamprophyre wanted to ask how Hyaloclast knew anything about what humans wanted—what the Stones were mining rights?—but Hyaloclast had already moved on. "What I want," she said, "is for you to discover who sent those bandits after young Opal's egg, and who created that foul magical item whose sole purpose is to incapacitate a dragon. Whoever is responsible is in one of their cities, where they will have the resources to do such a thing. And when you have discovered that their king is behind it, bring me word, and we will burn the city to smoldering ash."

"But—" Lamprophyre's jaw slackened. "It might not be the king. We can't make that assumption."

"It's an informed guess. The king might have sent his son to 'help' us retrieve the egg to make us more responsive to his plea." Hyaloclast let out a deep breath that wreathed her head in white smoke. "But I will not act rashly. We will have proof first."

"I want that person found as much as you do. But I refuse to believe Rokshan is involved."

Hyaloclast snorted. "The boy is an idealistic fool. He was probably his father's dupe. But don't trust him. He's not one of us and your loyalty is to your people."

"I understand." She felt profoundly uncomfortable, as if Hyaloclast had asked her to betray Rokshan. It surprised her to discover she felt loyal to him despite his species. Maybe they weren't so different, after all. "I'll find whoever did this."

"Good." Hyaloclast brushed past her out of the cavern. Lamprophyre followed more slowly, dragging her tail behind her. She hadn't even reached the human city and already she was tangled in deception.

Rokshan hadn't moved. He looked completely undisturbed by being surrounded by dragons. Lamprophyre wished she felt as calm at the prospect of being surrounded by humans.

"A fair sendoff for Lamprophyre, ambassador to the humans," Hyaloclast shouted.

Every dragon within earshot sat back on their haunches and snapped their wings open with a crack like thunder splitting the sky. Half of them tilted their heads back, drew breath, and blew great gouts of fire to stream in the wind that chased round the peaks night and day. More fires ascended as the female dragons farther away saw the flames and joined in. The fire tangled with the wind to trace delicate runes before extinguishing.

The heat bathed Lamprophyre's upturned face and for the moment, at least, chased away her disquiet. Hyaloclast had no intention of her succeeding, and had probably chosen her for that reason, but Lamprophyre intended to do her best as ambassador of her people, even if she was a powerless one. And she was even more determined to find the one who had ordered the egg theft and make her pay.

"Thank you," she shouted when all the fires were extinguished. "I'll do my best to protect our interests." She crouched beside Rokshan. "Shall we go?"

"Right now? Don't you, um, have belongings to pack?"

"I don't know what that means. We don't have clothes like you do."

"Well, obviously..." Rokshan gave up and mounted with ease. "Thank you, your majesty," he said, giving Hyaloclast a complicated salute. Hyaloclast inclined her head regally in return. Lamprophyre pushed off from the ledge and dropped a short distance before unfurling her wings and letting the wind carry her away.

They flew in silence for a dozen dozen heartbeats, then Rokshan said, "An ambassador of her blood?"

"We don't have families the way you do," Lamprophyre said. "We are members of the flight first, of our pair-bond second, and of our clutch—all the eggs born the same year—third. Once we're adults, we owe our parents respect for giving us life, our mothers for laying us and our fathers for hatching us, but that's not nearly as important as the respect we owe our queen. So we keep track of parentage and siblings for childbearing purposes, but that's about all. It doesn't really matter that she's my mother." She chose not to mention abasing herself in front of Hyaloclast on his behalf. It was the only time in her adult life she'd called the dragon queen Mother, and would certainly be the last.

"How do you know about our families? We don't know anything about you."

"There are stories from before the Cataclysm. Dragons live long and have long memories. Though I'm sure some of the stories are wrong. Like the one about you living with animals in your caves."

Rokshan laughed. "No, we don't—wait, do you mean pets? I suppose that's true, but it's not like you made it sound. We only make pets of certain animals, and they're trained not to mess indoors..." His voice trailed off. "You know, seeing that from your perspective makes my having once had a dog seem very strange."

"I've never seen a dog."

"There are plenty of them in the city, though if they're anything like horses, you'll probably spook them."

His words brought something else to mind. "Where are we going?"

"To Tanajital. It's the capital of Gonjiri. Which, as I say that, I realize means nothing to you." Rokshan leaned forward, past Lamprophyre's right ear. "It's on the Green River—that one to your right. The wider one."

Lamprophyre banked right until she flew above the wide river. She couldn't see why it was called Green; it was the same gray-blue as every other river she'd seen, and murky with sediment as it swelled its banks with springtime snow melt. "What does it look like? The city, I mean."

"It's big by human standards. You might find it small compared to the mountains. White. Some buildings have brass or copper sheathing on their roofs. I can't think of many streets you'd be able to walk down comfortably, but near the palace the streets are all very wide, and there's the parkland surrounding it. Lots of markets, lots of people buying and selling in the markets. I've lived there my whole life, so it all seems ordinary to me. You'll have a very different perspective."

Lamprophyre squinted into the distance, but saw nothing that resembled Rokshan's description. "I don't know all those words. What is a parkland?"

"A place where trees and grass and flowers grow within the city. Not wild, but tended to. Do dragons grow things?"

"We don't really eat plants—not most plants. I love cherries. The pits are good for digestion. There's a forest of cherry trees about a thousand dragonlengths from the caverns that we take care of so it will yield good fruit, is that what you mean?"

"Yes, like that. Humans plant vegetables and grains and fruit trees and store the excess so we can count on food in the lean times."

Lamprophyre thought about that. It wasn't anything she'd considered doing ever, but it made sense. "That's very clever. I didn't realize humans thought that far ahead. You live such short lives."

Rokshan laughed. The wind carried the sound away so it sounded like the ghost of laughter. "That makes us even more interested in making the most of the time we have."

"I guess that's true." Lamprophyre had hundreds of years of life ahead of her, but it occurred to her now that a human her age was heading into the end of her life. "How old are you?"

"Twenty-five."

"So, are you an adult?"

"Humans are adults when they're sixteen," Rokshan said. "How old are you?"

"Sixty. But for a dragon, that's just barely adulthood. So in a sense, you're older than me."

Rokshan laughed that faint laugh again. "That's an interesting way to look at it."

Lamprophyre surveyed the ground beneath them. They weren't flying very high, and now she saw pale lines against the green ground on which humans on horses, or driving wheeled wooden carts, traveled. She pointed. "Those people are staring at us."

"Nobody's running to hide," Rokshan said. He leaned to look over her shoulder. "Or trying to shoot you."

"Arrows can't hurt me."

"They can hurt *me*, and I don't know that anyone will care that you have a human rider if it's a matter of frightening the scary dragon off." Rokshan touched the scales at the back of Lamprophyre's head, sending an odd twinge through her. "They feel so soft, it's hard to believe arrows bounce right off, except I've seen it happen. What about a sword, or a lance?"

"My scales can't be cut by any human weapon, according to the stories." Lamprophyre dropped lower until she could see her reflection skimming along the surface of the river. "Now that I'm an adult, my wing membranes are too tough to cut. And dragon bones are made of stone, so they don't break. I imagine a bludgeon could hurt me, if you could find one big enough. That bandit leader came close."

"Stone?" Rokshan's voice cracked. "How can you fly if your bones are stone?"

Lamprophyre laughed. "We're creatures of magic, Rokshan. And it's not the kind of stone you're thinking of. It's strong and light at the same time."

"Astonishing," Rokshan said. "I wonder, though."

"Wonder what?"

"Our country is developing a new kind of weapon. It uses magic to create a pulse of force—that's like a bludgeon. But it's meant to be used against a human enemy, so I'm not sure it would affect you any more than that bandit leader's club did. I don't think it's big enough."

Lamprophyre considered this. "Have you seen it used?"

"No. Not my field of military expertise, so I don't know how it works. But we wouldn't use it against an ally, which we want dragons to be." He laughed. "I can't believe you're coming to Tanajital. My sister Anchala will be in ecstasies. She's a student of history specializing in the lore surrounding the catastrophe. When we first learned there were still dragons in the world, she didn't sleep for three days, pulling records from the archives and accosting anyone who got too close with stories of how it meant the ecclesiasts were right and we were intended to make common cause with you."

"I don't know that I'm comfortable being the answer to some other religion's prophecy."

"She's just enthusiastic. Please don't hold that against her. She's not always good with people, but she means well."

"She's your sister. How many siblings do you have?"

Rokshan's grip tightened. "There are five of us. Tekentriya is the oldest, my father's heir. Then Manishi, Khadar, Anchala, and finally me. Do you have siblings?"

Lamprophyre tried to look at Rokshan before remembering that was impossible. "No. Tell me more about your siblings."

"I'd rather talk about yours—or why you don't have any. Unless that's rude."

Lamprophyre blew out a cloud of steam. "My father Aegirine rejoined Mother Stone ten years ago. Cave sickness. Hyaloclast hasn't pair-bonded again. And before you ask, I'd rather fly face first into a glacier than ask her why not. Now, why is it you don't want to talk about your siblings?"

Rokshan pressed his face briefly against the scales at the base of her neck, an odd feeling like having a thumb lightly touching an exposed nerve. "My family—politics is the sea we all swim in, except maybe my mother and Anchala. It doesn't make for warm and loving relationships. Everyone else has a place in the royal household. Tekentriya's the heir. Manishi has her magic. Khadar is an ecclesiast. And I didn't want anything to do with any of it, so I was sent off to the Army."

"What's the Army?"

"It's a group of humans who fight together, as a unit, I mean. They're who's developing that new weapon I mentioned. The Army defends Gonjiri against attackers. If, for example, dragons were to attack Tanajital, the Army would fight back."

"Dragons won't attack Tanajital," Lamprophyre said, feeling an itchy guilty sense that it might be a lie.

"It was just an example. We're more likely to go to war against Fanishkor. That's why some divisions of the Army are stationed on the Fanishkorite border." He hesitated. "There's also a division of the Army on the border with dragon territory. It's mostly to defend the settlers against bandits. I hope your people don't take offense."

"It's all right. You can't hurt us." She didn't want to tell Rokshan that Hyaloclast would probably laugh herself sick over the idea that human armies might do anything except bleed and die if they attacked dragons.

"Anyway, because I'm a prince they made me a commander, as if royal blood somehow confers leadership abilities. But it turned out to be something I'm good at. And as a bonus, it keeps me free from the politicking that goes on in the palace, between Father and Tekentriya and the foreign ambassadors."

"And I'm an ambassador." She hadn't felt nervous about her role until just that moment. Suddenly Hyaloclast's instructions about not agreeing to anything were a comfort.

"Don't worry about it. They'll all be too intimidated by you to try anything sneaky."

Lamprophyre wasn't so confident, but there was no point in worrying about that before she'd even reached the city.

She looked up from scanning the ground and was struck by the sight, unexpectedly near, of what could only be Tanajital. She sucked in a startled breath. Given how small Rokshan and the other humans she'd seen were, she had expected something equally small, but the stones of the human city rose high enough that even at her current elevation, she could fly past and scrape her claws on their pointed tops.

Calling them stones wasn't right, either. She'd never seen anything so obviously non-natural in her life as the human city. The...buildings, she thought the word was...the buildings bore some similarity to crystals in how regular and straight-sided they were, but they lacked the shiny reflectiveness or transparency of a crystal. They were white enough she might have thought them carved of talc, if she didn't know how stupid building with talc would be, and she had no reason to think the humans stupid.

Spots like bits of mica embedded in the buildings flashed white in the noonday sun, and there were blobs of copper or gold set atop the tallest buildings that made no sense to Lamprophyre. It was an alien place, and it made her shiver to look at it.

She sped up, making Rokshan grip her ruff more tightly. "Maybe you should slow down," he called out.

"Why? I want to get a better look." There was a wall, about a dragonlength in height, that hemmed the city in. It sparkled like granite in the bright noon sun, but had an unusual pinkish cast to it she wished she could taste. They probably didn't want her tearing even very small bite-sized chunks out of their wall. She was sure it went all the way around Tanajital. That would be interesting to explore.

"Because they—"

There were humans on the top of the wall, running along the flat ridge of wood attached to the granite. Lamprophyre was too far away to hear any noise they might be making, but she wasn't too far away to see them brandishing curved wooden sticks. No, not sticks, bows, taller than the ones the bandits had had. Before Rokshan could finish his sentence, they'd raised their bows to the ready and sent a hail of arrows directly at Lamprophyre.

CHAPTER SEVEN

Lamprophyre closed her nictitating membranes to protect her eyes and flapped her wings hard to slow her momentum. Too late to conceal herself. The archers' first volley fell short, but that didn't stop them trying again. Shouts drifted toward her from their direction. "I thought they were expecting me," she said.

"Sending you was Hyaloclast's idea, remember? Nobody knows you're coming. And I should have expected that reaction, but I was distracted by our conversation. Fly higher. Let's get past the wall."

Lamprophyre beat the air, driving upward at a steep angle, though not so steep as to lose her passenger. "*Past* the wall? Shouldn't we set down outside the city?"

"It's too late for a peaceful, non-aggressive approach—"

"I wasn't aggressive!"

"You're a dragon. Every one of those soldiers knows by now what dragons are capable of. You're aggressive just by being here." Rokshan leaned farther forward. "The only thing left is to brazen it out. Let's head for the palace."

Lamprophyre blew out steam from both her nostrils. "Just because human weapons can't hurt me doesn't mean I want to be smacked by a sword, or pelted with arrows."

She felt Rokshan twist in his seat as if he were looking behind them. "The Army mostly posts guards at the wall, not at the palace. There's a much smaller force there, and all of them know me and owe obedience to me as a commander. I can talk them down before they attack us. And then we'll talk to my father."

The plan seemed rather thin, but Lamprophyre was willing to trust Rokshan's knowledge of human behavior. She winged higher in the sky, then wheeled and beat the air to hover briefly. "So which one of these is the palace? I assume it's big, but there are a lot of big buildings."

"Keep flying. It's farther east, away from the river."

At the point where the river entered Tanajital, it was dozens of drag-onlengths across and ambled like a well-fed bear through the river valley. The city sprawled on either side of it, though most of it lay on the east bank, making Lamprophyre wonder why it wasn't considered two cities. Or maybe it was, and Rokshan just hadn't mentioned it. The larger, taller buildings were all grouped toward the center of the east bank city. In fact, all the buildings on the west bank were short and unadorned and very close together, adding to the illusion of companion cities.

Boats filled the river, most of them making their way from one side to the other, a few with those scraps of fabric belling out to catch the wind to take them downstream. Lamprophyre thought about swooping low over them to see if any were the bandits, but remembered that had been a twelveday ago and the bandits had been on a different river. If she was to find the culprits behind the theft of Opal's egg, she would have to go about it differently. And she'd probably terrify these humans unnecessarily, anyway.

"There, where I'm pointing," Rokshan said. Lamprophyre twisted her neck to follow the line of his finger. "Past the building with the red arches."

Lamprophyre swooped downward and glided toward the indicated building. "That one with the red arches is large," she said. "What is it for?"

"It's a coliseum. For races, and competitions. A generation ago they held gladiatorial fights there, before people lost interest. The palace is—that's it. The one with all the golden roofs."

Lamprophyre swept past the coliseum and descended, gaping in amazement. She didn't know enough about human buildings to appreciate whether this one was nice, but gold was something any dragon under-stood, and the palace did indeed have a dozen gilded roofs, some angled, some round and curved. The smell of the gold roused her hunger, though gold was more a seasoning than a meal. "That's impressive," she said.

"Most of what makes it really beautiful is on the inside, and you won't fit into the halls to see it. But there's the Great Hall, and the throne room, and a few other places that might be big enough to admit you. Set down there, at the center of the park. Let's not scare the citizens."

Motion below her caught Lamprophyre's attention, a surge and ebb like the flow of colored water. "I think it's too late for that," she said, pointing. Distant, terrified cries came to her ears and were carried away by the wind.

Rokshan followed the line of her arm and said a sharp, curt word she didn't know. "I've been so stupid," he said. "They've seen you."

Lamprophyre halted her descent and hovered about a dragonlength above the fleeing, screaming humans. "Should we leave?"

"You'll have to enter the city eventually if you're the ambassador. We might as well not terrify them a second time. But—" Rokshan said the same incomprehensible word again. "All right. Fly past the park—the trees —and to the right of the palace. We'll land on the training grounds. That will put you within reach of the Army, but better you scare them than cause any more of a riot among the citizens."

Lamprophyre beat the air again and soared past the trees—how strange, the contrast between the natural trees and the unnatural city— and around the palace, marveling at the smoothness and whiteness of its walls. For something that couldn't have been built with dragons in mind, it certainly looked as big as a dragon cavern. The thought made her uneasy. It was one more reminder of how alien humans were, that they lived in places far too large to fit them.

The trees circled the palace, leaving a gap three or four drag-onlengths wide between them and the walls of the palace. That gap widened gradually as Lamprophyre circled the walls until it was the size of a plain, but with the ground hard-packed earth without a single growing thing on it. A series of buildings smaller than the palace, their roofs dull red rather than gold, huddled at its far side, and humans wearing dark blue sleeveless shirts and tan trousers that came only to the knee streamed out of them. Their tangled thoughts nevertheless were filled with images of her, terrifyingly large in the humans' minds and glowing with fire.

"Rokshan," Lamprophyre warned, "they're going to attack."

"We need to get close enough that they can see me," Rokshan replied.

The humans were organizing themselves into a regular pattern of rows and columns, like so many ants. She recognized weapons from the old stories: swords, and javelins, and bows like the ones the humans on the wall had had. "They'll shoot you by accident," she said.

"Not if we're fast enough," Rokshan said. "Get lower."

Lamprophyre plummeted, causing Rokshan to shout—with delight, she thought. Humans were so strange. She landed on all fours at the far side of the plain from the soldiers and shrugged to help Rokshan dismount. Rokshan darted forward as the archers leveled their bows at Lamprophyre, calling out, "Stop!"

Lamprophyre gasped and grabbed Rokshan around the waist, rolling to put one wing between him and the soldiers just in time for dozens of arrows to plink off the tough membranes. It felt like a hail of porcupine needles prickling her hide. "Stop!" she shouted, adding her voice to Rokshan's. "Don't attack!"

Rokshan struggled out of her grip and peered around the edge of her wing. Lamprophyre looked over the top of it. The archers still held their bows at the ready, and the soldiers with javelins were trotting toward them. "I don't think the archers will shoot if there's a chance they'll hit humans," she said.

"Stay here, and try not to look threatening," Rokshan said. He walked around the edge of her wing and ran forward to meet the soldiers. Lamprophyre muttered irritably under her breath. She was about as non-threatening as a dragon could be, since she still hadn't achieved her full adult size, and the knowledge that eventually she could be the size of Hyaloclast was no comfort in the present.

She lowered her wing and sat back on her haunches, dividing her attention between watching Rokshan and keeping a wary eye on the archers, who still hadn't relaxed fully. Rokshan had met the soldiers a little more than halfway across the field, out of earshot, though she could hear his thoughts: *stupid soldiers, need Sajan, where the devil is he?* and *Father will be furious, like always, no point even trying to change that.*

More movement at the far side of the plain caught Lamprophyre's attention. Another dozen soldiers had emerged from the low buildings, these wearing more brightly colored clothes and armed only with sheathed swords. Rokshan's thoughts became tinged with relief. Lamprophyre hoped that meant one of them was this Sajan person Rokshan wanted to talk to.

The new group of humans joined Rokshan without coming any closer to Lamprophyre, which frustrated her. She was tired of not being able to hear the conversation. Instead, she focused on identifying the thoughts of their leader. After a beat or two, she decided it was the female directly facing Rokshan. She had gray hair covering her head and the lower part of her face and wore clothing dyed bright yellow that was covered up both sleeves and its front with golden markings. Lamprophyre had heard soldiers wore uniforms. That uniform would certainly stand out on the battlefield.

The female's thoughts were direct and fearless, though she glanced repeatedly at Lamprophyre in a way that would otherwise have suggested nervousness. Lamprophyre could hear the female mentally plotting ways to attack her, and rather than make her angry, it settled Lamprophyre's nerves. It was a soldier's duty to defend her country, and as far as this soldier knew, Lamprophyre was a threat. So long as she didn't try to implement her plan of attack, Lamprophyre didn't mind her having it, if it made her feel more confident.

Rokshan was gesturing in Lamprophyre's direction, thinking *hope Lamprophyre doesn't get impatient.* Lamprophyre held as still as she could, though her position made her wings tense and uncomfortable.

The female regarded Lamprophyre, thinking *nothing we can do about it, look at the spread of those wings,* and Lamprophyre resisted the urge to spread them more fully. Concealing her ability to hear human thoughts could be useful to her as she set out to discover who had stolen Opal's egg. True, Rokshan knew about it, and he might tell someone, but for now, it could stay a secret.

Finally, just as Lamprophyre's curiosity became unbearable, Rokshan turned, and he and the female approached her together. Lamprophyre relaxed slightly, twitching her wings to relieve the tension.

"Lamprophyre," Rokshan said as they drew near, "this is General Sajan, commander of the Gonjiri Army. General, may I introduce Princess Lamprophyre, ambassador of the dragons."

Lamprophyre opened her mouth to correct him—she wasn't a princess, that was a human concept—but General Sajan stepped forward and saluted her. "Your highness," she said. "I apologize for our poor welcome. We were not expecting you." Her thoughts said *good thing she didn't attack, wonder if they really do breathe fire.*

"I'm sorry we startled you," Lamprophyre said.

"I take responsibility," Rokshan said. "I should have considered how everyone would react."

"You should have," General Sajan said, clapping Rokshan on the shoulder. Her thoughts sounded amused, as if it was somehow funny that Lamprophyre might have started a riot.

This prompted another thought, and she said, "We scared a lot of people when we flew in. I've never been in a riot, but it certainly looked like one. Should I—"

"Not you, your highness," General Sajan said quickly. "I've sent troops into the city to keep the peace. But I'm afraid I have to ask you not to leave just yet. We'll need time to spread word that you're not dangerous."

Lamprophyre stretched her senses to the utmost and heard no sounds of terror, mental or audible. Fearing this just meant the riot had moved farther than she could sense, she said, "How long is that? I can't sit in this field forever."

General Sajan exchanged looks with Rokshan. Rokshan's thoughts were irritated, but not with her; he was thinking how stupid people were to be so afraid. General Sajan's thoughts were more mixed, with fear and admiration and exasperation all tangled together so she couldn't tell what the subjects of those emotions were. Lamprophyre felt a little exasperated herself. All right, maybe humans didn't have many stories of dragons, but surely not all of them featured dragons as the enemy? She hadn't considered, when she thought about Hyaloclast's orders, that she might have to begin by teaching humans not to fear her.

"It's your responsibility, your highness," General Sajan said, addressing Rokshan. Rokshan's lips twisted in a strange, unreadable expression, but his thoughts were even more irritated than before. "What are your instructions?"

"You're my superior officer."

"And you are a prince, and this is a diplomatic situation, not a military one."

Rokshan looked up at Lamprophyre. *Some welcome*, he thought. Aloud, he said, "Is the coliseum in use today?"

"The next races are in two days."

"Then Lamprophyre can stay there for now. It's isolated, for all it doesn't have a roof, and we can keep it guarded."

"I'm in no danger from humans, Rokshan," Lamprophyre said.

"No, but we have to prevent anyone from attacking you. You're an ambassador and that would look bad." Rokshan saluted General Sajan. "Is that acceptable?"

General Sajan nodded. "Give us an hour to post guards and clear the streets, your highness. We'll make it safe for the ambassador. And then you and I—" She leaned closer and tapped Rokshan in the center of his chest— "will have a conversation."

Lamprophyre heard Rokshan's thought clearly: *should have known I wouldn't get out of this unscathed*. She said, "Thank you, General Sajan."

General Sajan bowed. "An hour, your highness," she said, and returned to her soldiers.

Rokshan sagged. "That could have gone worse," he said.

"Nobody died," Lamprophyre said. "And I think she's honorable."

"Who?"

"General Sajan."

"Oh. The general is a man, not a woman. There aren't any women soldiers."

Lamprophyre flushed a delicate purple. "I'm glad I didn't say anything. All the stories say you humans are very prickly about having your sex misidentified."

"He'd have understood. Not many would." Rokshan settled on the ground next to Lamprophyre and folded his legs in a way that would be impossible for a dragon. "And now we wait."

"Shouldn't you tell your father I've arrived?"

"I sent a messenger. The protocol is that an ambassador should approach the king, not the other way around. But you'll have trouble fitting inside the palace. So I told him the essentials and asked his advice."

Lamprophyre settled more comfortably on the ground and blew out a cloud of white smoke. "I didn't think this would be so difficult."

"Neither did I." Rokshan laughed. "I was so amazed at not being killed by dragons that I didn't think about the complications of having one for an ambassador. Our cities aren't made for creatures like you."

Lamprophyre looked over her shoulder at the palace, rising tall and white above her. It certainly looked big enough to hold her, but maybe it was smaller on the inside. There were caves like that in the mountains, with mouths wide enough to admit a dragon that quickly narrowed smaller than any dragon could fit. If all the human buildings were like that one, she couldn't imagine how she could follow through on Hyaloclast's instructions to investigate the egg theft.

She glanced down at Rokshan, who'd propped his elbows on his knees and rested his chin in his hands like a contemplative monkey. Hyaloclast had told her not to reveal her true purpose. She'd also said Rokshan might be complicit, if his father had ordered the theft. But Lamprophyre was increasingly certain there was no way she would ever learn the truth if she didn't trust someone.

She idly listened to Rokshan's thoughts—*have to find something better than the coliseum, what if it rains?*—and felt uneasy. If he were a dragon, she would do him the courtesy of blocking his thoughts unless they were pair-bonded and enjoying sexual intimacy. She didn't think she owed humans the same courtesy, especially since she needed every edge she could get in searching for the truth. But Rokshan was different—he was her friend, and friends didn't eavesdrop on each other.

"Rokshan?" she said.

"Yes?"

She opened her mouth and closed it again. Hyaloclast would skin her alive if she revealed her true intentions to someone who turned out to be complicit with a villain, friend or not. "Am I going to frighten everyone I encounter?" she said instead.

Rokshan shrugged. "I don't know. Possibly. But I believe humans and dragons can learn to live together, and this is part of that. You're not giving up before you've begun, are you?"

"No. But I wish I had a cave to retreat to. Not right this moment, just in general."

"There aren't any caves in the lowlands. We'll figure something out. I want you to be comfortable."

Lamprophyre nodded. They both fell silent, Lamprophyre already regretting her decision not to listen to Rokshan's thoughts. It would give her something to do that wasn't fretting over how stupid this whole idea was.

The soldiers had all disappeared, and the plain was empty but for Lamprophyre and Rokshan. The sun had reached its apex and beat down on Lamprophyre's head and wings, heating the damp air uncomfortably. There was another thing she hadn't considered; she'd have to live in the lowlands throughout the hottest part of the year, when the air was heavy and muggy and burdensome. That kind of weather made Lamprophyre sleepy. She'd be a terrible ambassador if she kept falling asleep when people wanted to talk to her.

Rapid footsteps drew her out of her reverie. She turned her head to see a human wearing a bright green shirt and short trousers that left her legs bare trotting toward them. Her gait slowed as she approached Lamprophyre. Her long dark hair, gathered into a tail like a horse's at the back of her head, bobbed the way a real horse's tail would. Her thoughts were full of confusion and fear, and Lamprophyre's spirits sank lower.

Rokshan stood and dusted himself off. "Come closer, Lamprophyre won't hurt you," he said, his voice deeper than usual. It was a commanding sound, one Lamprophyre instinctively almost responded to. The female, who was smaller than Rokshan, approached very slowly, not taking her eyes off Lamprophyre. Lamprophyre smiled, which startled the female so much she halted.

"Your highness," she said in a high, breathless voice, "the king says...he says if dragons are willing to come this far, he can reciprocate in kind."

"Meaning he's coming here?"

The female nodded.

"Thank you. Please return and tell his majesty—tell my father the dragon ambassador appreciates his condescension, and will await his arrival here."

The female nodded again and ran away the way she had come. Lamprophyre said, "Was that one female?" She wasn't sure about her assumptions. Among dragons, males were smaller than females, but a female was more likely to be given the honor of speaking for the queen.

"Yes, she was female," Rokshan said. "Were you guessing?"

Lamprophyre blushed. "I was. How *do* you tell the difference, for humans?"

"Well," Rokshan said, "most of what makes the difference is hidden by our clothes. Men have...they are..."

"Why are you embarrassed?"

"Because we cover our male and female parts out of modesty, and it's considered crude to discuss those parts. And you're female."

"I don't understand. Don't human females know about their own bodies? How can that be immodest?"

Rokshan was as red as he'd been earlier that day, climbing the mountain. "I mean," he said, "it's especially crude for a male to talk about bodies with a female he's not intimate with."

"Rokshan, don't be ridiculous. It's not as if I care about human sexuality." Lamprophyre blew out an impatient cloud of smoke. "What about the differences that aren't hidden? Why do some humans grow hair on their chins?"

"Oh. Facial hair." Rokshan sounded relieved, as if she'd changed the subject. "Only males can grow facial hair, but not all males do. So if you see someone with facial hair, he's male."

"I see. Facial hair is male. Soldiers are male. Do all soldiers wear their hair cut short? That would make sense, not to have anything flying around that an enemy could grab."

"That's—actually, that does make sense, but really it's that custom dictates men wear their hair cut short. So I guess that's another characteristic."

Lamprophyre remembered the messenger's waving horse tail. "So females have long hair? Why is that?"

"I don't know. It's only custom in Gonjiri and Fanishkor. Other countries have different grooming customs." Rokshan walked behind Lamprophyre, forcing her to turn to keep facing him. "I think that's them coming now. Can you bow? I mean, are you capable?"

"Awkwardly, but yes. Also, I'm not a princess—"

"I guessed as much, but humans will treat you with more respect based on who your mother is, so let's just pretend that's a rank with meaning, all right?" Rokshan wiped his hands on his trousers. "I'll introduce you to Father, and you bow. Then don't speak unless he speaks to you first."

"Why not?"

"Lamprophyre, I can't explain all our customs before they get here.

Just believe me when I say this is good manners." He looked past her at the palace. "Here we go."

Lamprophyre followed his gaze. A crowd of more than a dozen people had rounded the corner of the building, their thoughts tangled together like creeping vines trying to strangle each other. She swallowed, feeling unexpectedly nervous. Time to be an ambassador. It would help if she had any idea what that meant.

CHAPTER EIGHT

The humans were grouped oddly, some out in front widely spaced from one another, the rest tightly clustered behind. They surrounded one male—he had gray hair on his chin the way General Sajan had had, so Lamprophyre felt confident about her judgment—who sat in a strange wooden contraption like a cage without walls. Very large humans, also male because of the short hair, carried the wooden cage by wrist-thick sticks protruding from its four corners. Their gait was so smooth it was like the cage was floating.

The four males in front bore enormous swords sheathed at their hips, curved and wide at the tips, and they wore no clothing on their torsos, which shone as if oiled. Lamprophyre examined them in fascination. Their muscles were more defined than a dragon's, giving them a bumpy look Lamprophyre secretly found amusing. There was nothing else amusing about them, though; they didn't smile, and their gazes flicked in all directions, not just at Lamprophyre. She guessed they were the king's personal guard and therefore concerned about all threats, not just the most obvious one.

Her attention was drawn to the male who, unlike those grouped fore and behind, walked beside the wooden cage. Brown hair cropped close to his ears didn't move at all in the light breeze that had come up, and he lurched with every step, swinging his left leg stiffly wide and setting his foot down heavily. He wore a brightly colored robe over white clothing, and his footwear exposed his toes, which were blunt with flat, close-trimmed claws. "Who's that?" Lamprophyre whispered to Rokshan.

"Who?"

"The lurching one."

"Oh. My sister Tekentriya, my father's heir. Don't stare. She hates that."

"Was she born like that?"

"No. There was an accident five years ago. We don't discuss it."

"You said only males have short hair."

Rokshan shook his head. "I know, but Tekentriya is different in a lot of ways. Just—don't stare."

Lamprophyre turned her attention to the male in the cage. He had to be the king, Ekanath, but why a king would be in a cage, she had no idea. Unless there was something wrong with his legs, too, and he needed to be carried by the four males, also unclad from the waist up, also with muscles bulging.

She glanced down at Rokshan. His clothing obscured his body, so she couldn't tell if his muscles were large and bulging, too. He'd probably be embarrassed if she asked to see. Humans were so odd.

She couldn't see the king clearly because the cage's roof obscured her view, but he wore the same white clothing and colorful robe Tekentriya did and sat in the complicated legs-folded position Rokshan had used earlier. It made Lamprophyre's hips ache just looking at it. Most of the king's face was hidden by his facial hair, but he didn't look like he was smiling. Lamprophyre's discomfort grew. Another thing she hadn't considered was that the humans might not *want* an ambassador from the dragons. If they rejected her embassy, she didn't know what she'd do. Hyaloclast was unlikely to accept a human refusal as grounds for Lamprophyre failing to discover the egg thieves.

The king's guards came to within half a dragonlength of Lamprophyre and Rokshan, then with a couple of long strides they took up wary positions to either side of the cage. The males carrying the cage lowered their burden to rest on four tall wooden legs protruding from its base, but didn't step away from it. Lamprophyre wondered if they, too, were part of the king's guard. They were certainly muscled heavily enough that they could give another human a good fight.

Lamprophyre cast her gaze over the humans bringing up the rear, all of whom wore robes the same style as Tekentriya and the king's, but less colorful. A few of them had long hair hanging loose around their faces and down their backs, and Lamprophyre took a closer look at them, but couldn't immediately see any other characteristics that distinguished them from their male companions. It was all she had time for before Rokshan took three long steps forward and dropped to one knee before the cage, bowing his head.

"Your majesty," he said, "may I present the Princess Lamprophyre, dragon ambassador to Gonjiri."

The king leaned forward to look past the roof of the cage. "Approach," he said. His voice sounded so much like Rokshan's it was eerie. Lamprophyre walked forward until she was even with Rokshan. Carefully, she bowed at her midsection, hoping she wouldn't overbalance and fall on the king.

When she rose, the king was still staring at her, his face unreadable. "Your mother is the dragon queen?" he asked.

Lamprophyre resisted the urge to set him straight about dragon customs. She could pretend to be a princess if that would make humans more comfortable. "She is, your majesty," she said. "She said, if you were willing to send Rok—someone of your own blood to approach the drag- ons, she could return the courtesy."

"Generous indeed," the king said. "We were not expecting you."

Lamprophyre really wished she could read human facial expressions better. His tone of voice had been neutral, but his thoughts were angry in a complex tangle she had trouble deciphering: angry that dragons existed, angry at Rokshan for bringing Lamprophyre here with no warning, angry that she was here at all. One flash of coherent thought surfaced: *need that weapon, Jiwanyil knows what the creature could do to me.* She felt confused, and uncertain, and completely unprepared for this confrontation.

She bowed again. "I apologize for coming on you unawares," she said, filling her thoughts with polite emotions even though she knew the king could not hear them. The practice gave her balance and calmed her. "I'm afraid I was eager to meet you, and let that influence my approach."

The angry thoughts turned confused briefly, and she heard him think *eager to meet me, why?* "Dragons and humans have not interacted well to date," he said. "I assume your arrival is intended to change that."

"We want to live in harmony with humans," Lamprophyre said, hoping Rokshan wouldn't do anything to indicate he knew she was exaggerating. Well, *she* wanted dragons to live in harmony with humans, and as far as the king was concerned, what Lamprophyre wanted matched the intent of all dragons, starting with their queen. "But we can't allow humans to encroach on our territory unchecked any more than you would want dragons settling in your cities. Hyaloclast—the dragon queen—has sent me with her response to your request."

Once more, the king's mind seethed with anger, and this time Lamprophyre had no trouble hearing his thoughts: *letting animals dictate our movement, what are we, weak infants?* and *creature could crush me without a thought, must be polite.* "And that response is?"

Lamprophyre shifted her weight, and the guards flanking the cage came immediately more alert, setting their hands on the hilts of their swords. She chose not to take offense. "You will be allowed to settle in dragon lands according to the limits we will give you," she said, trying to sound formal and official on Hyaloclast's behalf. "But the territory will remain under dragon rule. It will not be part of the kingdom of Gonjiri."

The king recoiled. "Impossible," he said, his voice sharp to match his tumultuous thoughts. "Dragons cannot rule humans anymore than humans would know how to govern dragons. What you demand is unthinkable."

"Your majesty," said Rokshan, "I'm sure that's not what the dragon queen intended. Right, Lamprophyre?"

"This is none of your concern, Rokshan," the king said, gesturing at him sharply.

Lamprophyre heard Rokshan's unspoken *just as I thought, never good enough for him, doesn't matter that I made this happen,* and the humiliation touching that thought made her angry on his behalf. "I said the land would be under dragon rule, not the people," she snapped, not pausing to think about her words, following her instincts. "I believe Hyaloclast's intent was that humans do not have full rights over the land. You wouldn't be able to send your army there, for example. And if humans behave badly, we will expel them."

"What about agriculture?" Tekentriya asked. Her voice was quieter than the king's, but perfectly audible. "They'll have to feed themselves."

"Agriculture—does that mean growing things?"

Tekentriya nodded once. Her thoughts were almost as angry as the king's, but her anger was all for Rokshan: *stupid boy bringing a damn dragon into the city, how much damage did it do, rioting still not under control.* Lamprophyre decided she disliked the strange female.

"As long as the agriculture is kept within the bounds of the human territory within dragon lands, that will be acceptable," she said. "You should arrange for another embassy to speak to Hyaloclast so she can show you where you'll be allowed to settle." There. Put it back on Hyaloclast to handle the details.

The king nodded. "That is acceptable," he said, as if Lamprophyre had been the one to acquiesce. "But none of that requires a permanent ambassador. Did the queen have something else in mind?"

Lamprophyre found herself hoping the king *had* had something to do with stealing Opal's egg, so she could be justified in making him flee in terror. She'd been nothing but polite, and he treated her like a poor supplicant! "Now that humans know dragons exist, we can't live completely separate anymore," she said, once more drawing on formality to keep herself from spitting fire at the cage. It was soft wood and would likely burn easily. "Hyaloclast wants humans to understand dragons better, and for dragons to learn more about human culture. All we have are very old stories of humans and dragons, and old stories can be wrong. She asks that you accept me as ambassador with that end in mind."

The king said nothing, but the anger filling his thoughts ebbed slightly. Lamprophyre waited. Finally, the king said, "You honor us with your presence, ambassador. We look forward to learning more about our neighbors to the north." *Can't get rid of it, might as well keep it where I can watch it.*

Lamprophyre opened her mouth to protest being thought of as "it" and remembered in time she meant to keep her ability secret. "Thank you, your majesty, I feel the same," she said, bowing again.

"The ambassador will need a place to stay," Rokshan said. "She can use the coliseum for now, but that's a very temporary solution."

The king barely nodded in Rokshan's direction. "Mekel, see to it," he said, raising his voice. One of the men in the group behind the cage came forward and bowed, first to the king, then to Lamprophyre. "Did you bring a retinue?" the king asked Lamprophyre.

Lamprophyre had no idea what that was, and by the sound of the king's thoughts, nasty and amused, he knew he'd confused her. "I—"

"Your majesty," Rokshan said, "if I may, I request to be assigned as diplomatic liaison to the ambassador. She will need humans to assist her, since she is built to a much larger scale than we are."

The king's amused, mocking thoughts expanded to include Rokshan: *let him have the thankless task.* "An excellent notion," he said. "A royal prince to attend a royal princess, yes?"

He meant it as sarcasm, but Lamprophyre was too relieved at having a friend stay with her to care. "Thank you, Rokshan and I will suit very well," she said. Maybe that's what a retinue was.

"I will arrange for hiring the ambassador's household help once she has a permanent home," Rokshan said, and now his thoughts were filled with cheerful satisfaction Lamprophyre thought might be unjustified, given that his father had assigned him to her out of spite. Rokshan might not be able to hear the king's thoughts, but Lamprophyre had no doubt he knew his father well enough to know what the king intended.

"Very well. I'm sure the ambassador's household will be well provided for, dragons traditionally being very wealthy," the king said.

That struck Lamprophyre to the heart. She knew humans exchanged coin for goods, but it hadn't occurred to her that they would expect a dragon to enter into similar transactions. "Um, I'm sure we'll figure something out," she stammered. She certainly had no coin and no idea what dragons did have that humans would find interesting. She needed to get Rokshan alone, and quickly.

"And you will want to host a reception once you're settled, to meet our city's nobles and foreign dignitaries," the king continued.

How, *how* could he possibly know just what would discomfit her the most? She almost would have thought him capable of hearing her think. If not for the sound of his thoughts, she might have imagined the king was simply being friendly and helpful. Instead, she could hear his satisfaction at throwing her off-balance. Her dislike of him on Rokshan's behalf hardened into a personal antipathy. What was a reception?

"I look forward to it," she said politely.

The king snapped his fingers twice, and the muscular males at the corners of the cage picked up their poles and hoisted the king into the air. The humans surrounding the cage moved in a complicated pattern that ended with them all pointed in the direction they'd come from, which meant the males and females at the rear were suddenly much closer to

Lamprophyre. All of them were unsettled by her proximity, though she didn't hear any overly fearful thoughts, and one of them, a male with the top of his head showing through thinning brown hair, was more curious than afraid. Lamprophyre realized he was the one who'd bowed. He stayed behind as the king and his companions strode away toward the front of the palace.

The male bowed to Lamprophyre again. "Your highness, I am Mekel, the king's chamberlain. Allow me to serve you."

"Um, yes, thank you?" She hadn't meant that to sound like a question, and cleared her throat. "Thank you. You will find me a better place to stay? That is, I'm sure the coliseum is very nice, but I like a roof over my head."

"Of course," Mekel said, bowing again. "I'm afraid I must ask you to remain in the coliseum until I do, though. We will need time to spread word of your arrival, so you don't...that is, the people of Tanajital are unfamiliar with dragons..."

"We know, Mekel," Rokshan said. "Are you hungry, Lamprophyre? What do you eat?"

She'd been feeling moderately hungry ever since smelling the gold of the palace roofs, and realized in the tension surrounding Opal's hatching, she'd forgotten to eat her morning meal. "I normally eat twice a day, morning and night," she said, "but I feel hungry now. And I usually eat deer or wild boar. Elk, sometimes. Wild horse if there's nothing else, but horse meat is so unsatisfying."

Mekel glanced at Rokshan. "I think a cow, perhaps?"

She'd heard of cows. "That would be fine." Hopefully they were less stringy than horses. "But I'll cook it myself."

"Have the kitchens send a butchered cow to the coliseum, Mekel," Rokshan said, "and something for me as well." He climbed easily onto Lamprophyre's shoulders and settled himself into the notch. "And keep me informed on your progress in finding an embassy for the ambassador."

"Of course, your highness." Mekel bowed again, apparently respectful, but his thoughts were full of awe and dread: *he just climbed right up, no fear, never thought I'd see a dragon in the flesh.*

Lamprophyre waited only briefly for Rokshan to feel secure, then leaped into the sky, beating the air for a rapid ascent. She couldn't help remembering the terrified scattering of humans the last time she'd taken to the skies above Tanajital. She could conceal herself; that didn't last long, but it would be long enough to reach the coliseum. But with Rokshan on her shoulders, that concealment wouldn't be very convincing. Maybe rising high above them and making a quick, nearly vertical descent would minimize her exposure to the humans.

Tanajital from the air was beautiful, she decided, primarily because it was so alien. And yet it made sense to her in a way humans themselves didn't: it was obviously not transitory and would outlast the humans with their brief lives, which made it almost dragon-like in its permanence. She examined the palace's golden roofs once more before diving for the coliseum and making Rokshan cry out with mingled excitement and pleased terror, an emotion she understood from flying blind through storms. Hyaloclast forbade it, which made it even more exciting.

The coliseum, alone among all the buildings of Tanajital, had no roof, just that circular wall topped with red arches, like a tiny city within a city. She alit within the wall and sniffed the ground. It was packed earth like the plain behind the palace, stale and dead and almost rock-hard. She dug her small sixth claw into it and sniffed again. It didn't smell like anything fertile.

"Why earth, and not stone?" she asked Rokshan.

Rokshan stood with his hands on his hips, surveying their surroundings. "It would be expensive and difficult to bring stone all the way from the mountains. And I think the earth is easier on the runners' feet."

"Oh." She patted the dirt back into the groove she'd made. The walls of the coliseum rose taller than she, then ascended in a series of steep stairs to a second, even taller wall that was the one she'd seen upon descending. "Why are there two walls?"

Rokshan pointed. "The space between the walls is the stands, where people come to watch the races. Over there is the royal box, where my family sits so we aren't pressed by others."

With the sloping sides between the two walls, the coliseum felt like a bowl, though human-made instead of natural. Lamprophyre pushed off and flapped slowly to get just enough height to examine the space. The deep tiers had shallower stairs dividing them into neat sections. She flew around the coliseum, pausing at one end to look at the royal box. It didn't look much different from anywhere else in the building, except for having wooden seats. It was open on three sides and fully illuminated by the sun, though its flat roof sheltered it from the worst of the rays. Lamprophyre was starting to feel over-warm herself.

She settled into the narrow strip of shadow on the western side of the coliseum—very narrow, at just after midday, but it was better than nothing—and rested her chin on her folded arms. "I didn't know I would need coin," she said. "There are so many things I didn't anticipate."

"Neither did I. I was so excited—damn him anyway for being a blind fool," Rokshan said. "Dragons in our midst, and all he can think about is his pride."

"He was angry about my arrival."

Rokshan sat beside her head and folded his legs beneath him. "He doesn't like being out of control, and he *hates* having to be a supplicant. So yes, he was angry. Were you reading his thoughts?"

"I don't know what you mean by reading. Dragons hear thoughts and sometimes emotions, if they're strong. Only it's not like hearing with your ears. I've never had to explain it before and I'm probably doing a poor job of it."

"You don't know what reading is?" Rokshan sounded unexpectedly surprised. "But you said you have all those stories."

"Stories we tell each other, yes. Is that what you mean by reading?"

Rokshan shook his head. "We...God's breath, I don't know how to explain reading and writing. We have symbols that correspond to speech." He scratched a few lines and curves in the hard dirt between them. "That's my name written down. And anyone who can read will know what those symbols mean, that they're my name."

"Oh." Lamprophyre peered at the marks. "How convenient. Then it's true human memory is short, or you wouldn't need writing and reading, yes?"

"That's it exactly. If I write your name—don't know how to spell it—" He scratched out a much longer series of marks— "but on paper or stone, it will outlast a human lifetime, and humans hundreds of years from now will be able to read it and know it means you."

Lamprophyre traced the marks that meant her with her sharp sixth claw. "Fascinating." What a concept, that marks could have meaning. "Who invented it?"

"I don't know. After you told me dragons taught humans their language, I sort of thought dragons had taught writing to us, too, but if you don't have a written language, I guess not. It must have been centuries ago, though."

Lamprophyre rested her head on her arms again. "I don't know how to get coin. I understand humans use it to exchange for other things, so I will need it to buy a home, perhaps? And pay humans to take care of it? And I can't go on expecting the king or his people to provide me food. Though I suppose I could hunt."

"That would be a bad idea," Rokshan said. "All the herds around here belong to people. You'd be stealing unless you gave them money for what you hunted."

Lamprophyre let out a puff of smoke from both nostrils. "You see? I don't even know that I don't know things!"

"All our stories say dragons have hoards of gold and gems. I take it that's not true."

"We don't love gold more or less than any other metal, though it is delicious, especially when you eat it with anthracite. And gems. Don't humans prefer certain stones?"

"Diamonds and rubies, emeralds and sapphires," Rokshan said. "Though adepts in magic use certain stones to channel magical energy. Like that wand they used against you. Sapphire must have mind-confusing properties."

"So they care about specific stones, too."

"Yes. But they're not all precious gems. I know my sister Manishi is always buying semiprecious stones, jasper and quartz and dozens of others I don't know the names of. Some of them are very hard to find."

"I love the taste of jasper. It's got so many flavors." The thought of the delicious stone made her salivate. Then the rest of what he'd said registered. "Hard to find, you say?"

"That's what Manishi says. I know she's always dealing with the most disreputable traders from all over Gonjiri and Fanishkor and even beyond."

Lamprophyre sat up. "So do you think," she said, "she'd agree to deal with a dragon?"

CHAPTER NINE

L amprophyre tore into the delicious, juicy meat and rolled her eyes in pleasure. "This is *amazing*," she said. "I've never had anything so good. Why is cow so much better than deer?"

"Because humans carefully tend their cows and feed them things that will make their meat richer and more tender," Rokshan said. He had a couple of small sticks that gleamed like silver, one a knife, though smaller than the ones the soldiers had had, and one with a couple of sharp prongs on the end. His chunk of meat lay on a thin, flat stone that shone with a glossy finish, and he held the meat in place with the pronged stick and cut bits of it off with the knife.

"Dragons need to do that. I want to eat like this all the time. I wonder how hard it would be?"

"You'd have to grow grains first, I think. I'm afraid I don't know much about it." Rokshan chewed his meat thoughtfully. "Or you could exchange valuables for cows. How sure are you that you can find the kind of stone adepts will want?"

"Very sure, if they're willing to tell me what they're interested in." Lamprophyre cracked a leg bone with her back teeth and sucked out the marrow. "Finding stone is as easy as smelling the difference between the dirt and this delicious cow."

"Then I'll bring Manishi here to meet you." Rokshan made a face. "If she'll listen to me. We don't get along."

"Rokshan, you don't get along with your father and Tekentriya, and now you say you don't get along with Manishi. Is there anyone you're related to that you *do* get along with?"

Rokshan chuckled. "My mother. My sister Anchala. It's no coincidence that they're the least political of my relatives. Manishi—with her, it's nothing personal, she's just abrupt and self-absorbed. I don't think she gets along with anyone, especially other adepts. She's very secretive about her work and never works in partnership with anyone, even though most adepts collaborate at least some of the time."

"Well, I don't like your father or Tekentriya. But they don't like me, so I think that's all right."

"Just so you don't share that opinion with anyone else. It's undiplomatic."

Lamprophyre nodded. "I do know how to behave myself. Though I'm not sure dragon manners translate to human manners. I suppose I'll find out."

"Not saying what you really think is probably common to both our species." Rokshan took a final bite and set the stone and the sticks aside. "I should speak to Manishi now rather than waiting. You'll need money soon, though I can convince the kitchens you're an honored guest for a while."

"I'll be fine," Lamprophyre assured him. She set what was left of the carcass on the wheeled wooden platform they'd brought it in by and gave it a small push. She'd only managed half the cow before feeling full. It was considerably bigger than a deer. "Bored, but fine."

Rokshan stood and stretched. "What would you normally do, this time of day?"

"Oh...go flying, probably. Tomorrow is my turn to hunt, so I'd do that. Share stories. Race my clutchmates, if I can stand to listen to Coquina brag about how many times she's won."

"Who's Coquina?"

"I told you dragons are part of a clutch—all the eggs born in a season? She's the only other female in my clutch, and I hate her. She likes to make me feel stupid and small."

Rokshan nodded. "My brother Khadar is like that. I understand. Look, I'll be back as soon as I can. Sorry about the boredom. Soon enough, you'll be able to fly freely."

Lamprophyre watched him run to the exit and disappear beyond it, then sighed and tried to fit more of herself into the strip of shadow. It was wider now, but not by much. She closed her eyes, but she didn't feel sleepy despite her large meal. Still, it wasn't as if she had anything better to do.

Footsteps approaching made her blink and sit up. Four humans, two male, two female, stopped some distance from her, their thoughts a tangle of fear and awe. She recognized them as the humans who had brought the cow on the wooden platform, though at the time she'd been hungry enough not to pay much attention to them. Now, she regarded them with curiosity. They were dressed more plainly than the king's companions, or at least their clothes weren't colorful, and they didn't wear the animal hide armor the soldiers did.

"Did you prepare the cow?" she asked. "I'm glad you skinned it. I hate skinning animals. My claws always feel so dirty afterward, but roasting an animal unskinned makes it taste strange."

Her words made three of the humans take a step back. The fourth, a male with dark hair on his face, said, "I didn't butcher it, my lady ambassador, but I chose the carcass myself, so I'm pleased you like it." *Talking to a dragon, what in Jiwanyil's name am I supposed to say?* he thought.

"Well, thank you. It was delicious," Lamprophyre said. "Did you come to take the rest away? I hope it's not too much trouble. I'm afraid it was too much for me to eat all at once."

"Not at all, my lady ambassador, it's our pleasure. The kitchens are open to you any time."

There was that word again. "What are kitchens?"

"The places where we prepare food."

So they had special places for food just like dragons did. How unexpected. "That's very generous of you."

The male bowed. His thoughts mirrored his words so perfectly Lamprophyre felt more relaxed than she had from the moment the archers on the city wall had shot at her. "My name is Akarshan, my lady ambassador."

"I'm Lamprophyre." Lamprophyre bowed in return, and Akarshan's thoughts became amused, though not in a mean way; she could hear him think *no one will believe this, dragon bowed to ME.*

She looked at the other three, whose fear had diminished as Akarshan spoke to her without being eaten or burned alive or whatever they feared Lamprophyre might do. "Are you all with the kitchens?" she asked.

"I am the chief cook, and these are my assistants," Akarshan said. "They are honored to serve you." *Better be honored, by Jiwanyil, God's breath, it's like meeting a legend.*

"I appreciate your help," Lamprophyre said. "And you don't have to be afraid of me. No dragon has ever harmed one of you." She suppressed memories of fighting the bandits. That didn't count.

The other three humans glanced at each other, then at Akarshan. Two of them relaxed. The third still looked poised to flee, but Lamprophyre was willing to accept three out of four as a victory.

"Rokshan tells me I am your guest until I have an embassy of my own," she said, "and if it's not too much trouble, I normally eat twice a day, morning and evening."

"It is most certainly no trouble," Akarshan said. "We'll take this out of your way now, my lady ambassador, and will see you again this evening?"

"Morning will be soon enough." She'd never felt so well-fed in her life. It occurred to her that the kitchens probably couldn't provide her with stone to eat, and she would need to hunt some for herself as well as to sell to Manishi or some other adept, as Rokshan had called the humans who created magic artifacts.

She wiped her mouth and watched Akarshan and the other humans turn the wheeled platform around and steer it in the direction of the largest exit. She felt more cheerful now than she had since being shot at on approaching Tanajital, between the excellent meal and the friendly conversation. Maybe this wasn't an impossible task, after all.

She stood and stretched, extending her wings fully. Normally, she would go for a flight after a meal to keep from feeling logy, but that was out of the question—or possibly not. She walked around the perimeter of the coliseum's oval floor until she stood beneath the royal box. Flapping gently, she lifted off the ground until she was level with the top of the wooden box. This still put her below the top of the outer wall and out of sight, she hoped, from the city.

With a few more gentle strokes, she propelled herself forward along the inner wall, keeping carefully level with its top. It was a challenge not to drift too far up or down, and she amused herself by using the barest twitches of her wing tips to maintain elevation. After a couple of circuits, she turned and flew in the opposite direction to keep from becoming dizzy. Then she practiced flying as fast as she could from one end of the oval to the other, but that meant coming to a halt against the wooden lower wall, and the first time she left scratches with her non-retractable toe claws, she decided to stop doing that.

She thought about digging up enough dirt for a dust bath, but that would ruin the hard surface, and she was sure nobody would appreciate that even if she put all the dirt back when she was finished. The thought did make her wonder how she would get a real bath. The river was more than wide enough for her to share it with the boats, especially if she went downstream far enough, but that might still not be enough distance to make the humans comfortable. Frustrated, she returned to her strip of shadow and settled herself. Stupid fearful humans.

Flying had made her feel even more alert than before. Unfortunate, since napping would be a good way to pass the time while waiting for Rokshan to return. Until today, she hadn't realized how active a life she normally led. Waiting was stifling and boring and she hated it.

She rolled onto her side and watched the clouds drift past overhead. They were high and thin, not a sign of an oncoming storm, which was as well if she had to live in this roofless oval for a few days. She hoped it was only a few days. Mekel had seemed to understand the urgency of finding her a permanent home, but he was human and presumably had a home of his own. People, or at least dragons, never acted so quickly as when it was their own needs they were meeting. Possibly humans were the same.

The air within the coliseum oval was close and thick and warm, and Lamprophyre's muscles relaxed in response. Maybe she could sleep, after all. She closed her eyes and listened with her ears and her mind. If she held very still and breathed shallowly, she could hear the sound of the city humming along. It was probably the noises of a lot of people in one place, but it was easy, after what she'd considered earlier, to imagine the city as a living creature that tolerated humans within it. Whether it would be as accepting of a dragon, she had no idea.

Distantly, she heard Rokshan's thoughts, just a snatch or two of disconnected words, but she'd spent enough time with him to recognize the way he thought. She couldn't hear anyone else with him. Sitting up, she stretched her wings and then furled them along her back. Maybe Manishi wanted Lamprophyre to come to her, which would be a nice excuse to get out of this boring place.

But when Rokshan entered the coliseum, it was in company with another human. The female's long hair was piled high atop her head in a messy way, with strands escaping to fly in every direction. Lamprophyre had thought Rokshan's dark trousers and blue shirt plain by comparison to the king's rich robe, but this female dressed the way Lamprophyre remembered the bandits dressing, in roughly woven tan clothing with a deep neck that showed more of her brown skin than Rokshan's revealed. She wore nothing on her feet, which were dirty, the claws longer than Tekentriya's, which was the only other measure of comparison Lamprophyre had.

A whiff of sodalite reached Lamprophyre's nostrils, and she inhaled more deeply and scented other stones: citrine, and quartz with a chlorite inclusion, and aventurine. She examined the strange female and saw she wore rings set with those stones on both hands. The citrine was polished, but the other three were rough-cut circles of stone. Lamprophyre took half a step forward before stopping herself. If this was Manishi, it was especially important that Lamprophyre not frighten her.

Rokshan halted half a dragonlength from her, saying, "Lamprophyre, this is my sister—Manishi, wait—" The female hadn't stopped when Rokshan did, but came right up to Lamprophyre and tilted her head back to stare at her.

"You're bigger than I expected," Manishi said. "Bigger, and more brightly colored. Are all dragons like you?"

"I haven't reached my full adult size yet, but almost all dragons are colorful," Lamprophyre said. To her surprise, she heard nothing but a dull hum from Manishi, like the background noise of the city. There were some dragons who couldn't hear thoughts, but Lamprophyre had never heard of anyone whose thoughts couldn't be heard. Maybe it was a human thing. Not being able to hear Manishi's thoughts was pleasant and unsettling at the same time.

"How intriguing," Manishi said. She reached out and brushed her fingers across Lamprophyre's scales. It startled Lamprophyre so much she jerked away. In a dragon, that would be a serious breach of etiquette and a profound invasion of one's privacy. If humans were going to feel entitled to touch her without permission, she would have to do something about that.

"Excuse me," she said, reining in her shock and discomfort, "it's not polite for you to touch me like that."

"No, it isn't," Rokshan said, sounding angry. "Manishi, that was rude. You should apologize."

"Was it?" Manishi said. "I didn't realize. Your scales are very soft." She actually extended her hand to touch Lamprophyre's flank again. Lamprophyre moved away again.

"*Manishi*," Rokshan said with some force. "Stop it. She's a person, not an animal you can pet."

Manishi lowered her hand. "My apologies," she said. Lamprophyre wished she could hear the female's thoughts to know if she was sincere. "Rokshan says you can find specific stones. How does that work?"

Her abruptness startled Lamprophyre. "Oh, dragons have an affinity for stone, and I can feel its nearness. And stones have unique scents that I can perceive. If you tell me what you want, I might be able to find it. We could exchange coin for that, yes?"

"Of course," Manishi said.

Rokshan took a few steps forward. "A *fair* exchange."

Manishi glanced at him and returned her attention to Lamprophyre. "Of course. You don't think I'd cheat a dragon, do you?"

"I think you'd take advantage of Lamprophyre's ignorance."

"I'd never do that."

"Of course you would."

Manishi rolled her eyes. "We can come to a civilized agreement, Rokshan. Can you find opal?"

For a moment, Lamprophyre thought she was talking about the dragonet and felt confused again. "Opal. Oh! No, I'm afraid not. There's no opal anywhere near this place. I've never even tasted it." She decided not to explain how dragons knew about stones throughout the world, even stones they'd never actually seen; it was a religious thing and none of Manishi's business.

"Damn," Manishi said, but without any force behind it. "What about emerald? Having a local source would be invaluable now that we're virtually at war with Fanishkor."

"Emerald? Maybe." Lamprophyre thought for a moment. "I know

there are deposits of garnet nearby, and plenty of jasper. But maybe you already have those."

"We get our garnet from Sachetan, far to the south. But you can never have too much garnet. So many men wanting to breed sons, so many women wanting to avoid pregnancy..." Manishi's voice trailed off. "But it might be even better if you could bring me something no one's ever seen before."

"I'm not sure how I'd know what that was. I don't have any idea what humans already use."

Manishi ran a finger over the rough, jagged surface of the sodalite. "The Parama Mountains have never been mined by humans. There must be any number of stones available there that we've never heard of. It could start a whole new line of research."

It was an interesting idea. "It would have to wait until I can leave the city, but that could work."

Manishi waved her hand in the air, a gesture Lamprophyre was unfamiliar with. "You're afraid of scaring people? Just leave at night, and no one will see you to be scared."

And *that* was a surprisingly useful idea. "That's true," Lamprophyre said, concealing her excitement at the thought of not being trapped in the human city, waiting on humans to come to terms with her.

"So it's settled," Manishi said. "You'll bring me something unique, and I'll pay you a fair rate for it."

"Not good enough," Rokshan said. "If it's something no one's seen before, how can you put a fair price on it? And suppose Lamprophyre doesn't find anything you're satisfied with? Then she'll have put in the effort for nothing."

Manishi's lips curved in a scowl. "All right, what do *you* suggest?"

"You'll pay Lamprophyre to search, just as you would an ordinary explorer," Rokshan said. "And then we'll negotiate a price for anything she finds. *After* I've done some research on fair prices."

"Rokshan, don't be absurd. Merchants mark up their prices once they've bought the stones from the suppliers. I should only pay what I would if I bought from an ordinary supplier."

"I'm not stupid. I'll take that into account." Rokshan turned to Lamprophyre. "Is that an acceptable deal?"

Lamprophyre's excitement about being able to fly freely had faded as the conversation progressed. Manishi struck her as the kind of obsessed person who might create a dragon-incapacitating weapon simply to be able to say she'd done it, and without being able to read her mind, Lamprophyre couldn't prove her guilt or innocence. If Manishi were the one who'd made the weapon, it was a bad idea for Lamprophyre to provide her with stones to make other artifacts, potentially dragon-harming ones.

On the other hand, this deal, as Rokshan put it, put Manishi where Lamprophyre could watch her. She might lead Lamprophyre to the egg-stealing bandits, too. And if it wasn't Manishi behind the theft, she might still provide Lamprophyre with information about other adepts who were.

"I suppose so," she said. "I think reasonable people can always come to agreement."

"You don't know enough humans," Manishi said. "But don't worry, you can trust me."

"Which is what untrustworthy people always say," Rokshan said.

Manishi scowled again. "Just be circumspect when you ask around," she said. "I don't want anyone figuring out that I have a new supplier. You won't work for anyone but me, right?"

"She's an ambassador, not a rock sniffer," Rokshan said. "Anything she does is her own business and none of yours."

"But I won't cheat you," Lamprophyre said. "If that's what you're worried about." People who worried about being cheated usually did so because they were cheats themselves, but it seemed Rokshan knew this about his sister, so Lamprophyre wasn't worried.

"Of course not," Manishi said. "If you happen to find any large pieces of obsidian, I'll pay you double the market rate. See? I'm giving up my advantage so you'll know I'm trustworthy."

"Uh *huh*," Rokshan said. "Fifty rupyas for Lamprophyre to make the journey. In advance."

"Excuse me?" Manishi's eyes widened. "That's virtually extortion. I pay a rock sniffer twenty rupyas to make an exploratory journey."

"But Lamprophyre has skills no rock sniffer can boast, and she can also do her own digging. Fifty or nothing."

Lamprophyre watched the exchange in fascination. How did Rokshan know she could dig?

Manishi eyed Lamprophyre. "All right. Fifty." She dug in a pouch at her waist and pulled out a handful of silver coins, from which she counted several into Rokshan's hand. "I advise you," she told Lamprophyre, "to learn to speak on your own behalf quickly. You don't want to look weak."

"It's not weak to allow others the pleasure of using their strengths on your behalf," Lamprophyre said. "Does it make Rokshan weak that he has to ride my shoulders in order to fly?"

Manishi grabbed Rokshan's wrist. "You've flown on a dragon?" she said in a low, intense voice, as if she were telling a great secret. "How is that possible?"

Rokshan removed his wrist from her grip. "It's a glimpse of the future. If humans and dragons can learn to live together in harmony, who knows what might be possible?"

Manishi regarded Rokshan closely. Then she turned her attention to Lamprophyre. Lamprophyre wished more than ever that she could hear Manishi's thoughts, because the female's eyes were narrowed and her lips set in a firm line. The expression probably meant something, but it was incomprehensible to Lamprophyre. "Who knows," Manishi repeated. "Contact me when you have something." She turned and strode toward the entrance without another word.

"Sorry," Rokshan said. "I told you she was like that."

"It doesn't matter, so long as I can gain coin to pay for things." Lamprophyre squinted at Rokshan's hand. "I thought coin would be bigger. The stories all make it sound so important, and it's just little things." They were small and round, not much bigger around than the stones in Manishi's rings, and had curved dents all across their flat surfaces.

"Vahas are bigger—they're made of gold." Rokshan closed his hand over the rupyas. "This will be enough to make a start. You don't mind me handling your money, do you?"

"Of course not."

"Well, I'll keep careful track, anyway." Rokshan put the rupyas away in his own pouch. "I have to give Manishi credit for one thing—it hadn't occurred to me that you could fly out of here at night. You *can* fly at night, yes?"

"I can see by moonlight, though I've flown under the dark moon a few times. It's scary in an exciting way." Lamprophyre looked at where the half-moon sailed high in the eastern sky. "There should be enough light tonight."

"Don't feel like you have to run Manishi's errands immediately. It will do her good to wait."

"I have to find stone for myself to eat, though." Lamprophyre sank down on her haunches next to Rokshan. "Want to come along?"

Rokshan laughed. "Do you even have to ask?"

CHAPTER TEN

The half-moon hung high in the western sky when the sun set, as if the moon were chasing its brighter sister. Lamprophyre waited impatiently for the color to fade from the distant horizon, then took to the sky with Rokshan clinging to her ruff. Manishi's idea was sound; she heard no cries of fear or distress with either her ears or her mind. Even so, she rose high above Tanajital before winging her way northward. "I didn't realize how much I took flying for granted," she said. "I was only confined to the coliseum for half a day and it felt like forever."

"I think things feel like they take much longer when there's something else you want to do," Rokshan said. She felt him lean far back and grip the ridge at the base of her wings, as if he were looking up at the sky. "Flying in the dark is so strange. It's like night swimming, unable to see what's beneath you and nothing but the stars and moon overhead."

The Green River was a wide, bright snake winding its way across the invisible land below, gleaming in the moonlight. Lamprophyre remembered what she'd thought about needing to bathe. Maybe that was the solution, night swimming. She scowled. Flying at night, bathing at night... she shouldn't have to behave like a sneak thief, skulking about in the darkness so no one would see her to be afraid. "Do you swim in the river, then?"

"Sometimes. Not often. I used to go with Dharan and Baleran, but Dharan lives in Kolmira these days, and Baleran returned to Sachetan when his apprenticeship was finished."

"I take it they're friends of yours."

"The best of friends. I wish they could meet you. Dharan in particular. He's a collector of legends and ancient stories. He'd be in raptures over the chance to interrogate you. In a polite way, of course. He's more proper and correct than any noble I know."

"I thought royalty only had friends among the nobility."

Rokshan was silent. Lamprophyre considered her words and couldn't see anything offensive in them. She said anyway, "I'm sorry if that was rude."

"What? Oh, no, I was just remembering. Dharan is unique in every way. The most brilliant mind of our generation. Taught himself to read when he was three, was studying advanced mathematics when he was seven—that might not mean anything to you, but among humans, it's exceptional. His parents aren't wealthy, just a couple of shoemakers, but they took him to the academy in Kolmira when he was eight, and the scholars sent him to Tanajital for a formal education. That's where we met, at the academy here. I was struggling with one of my classes and the scholars assigned Dharan to tutor me. He taught me mathematics, I beat the stuffing out of the boys and girls who were tormenting him, and we became friends."

Lamprophyre banked right to take advantage of an updraft. "I don't understand most of that. Academy—you go there to learn things? We have stories of humans and dragons learning together, but I didn't know it happened in a particular place."

"Academies are mostly for the upper classes who can afford to pay, except for people like Dharan. They teach scholarly subjects and prepare students who are inclined that way for studying magic and artifact creation. There are schools for the lower classes, but not all of the citizens take advantage of them. I've heard commoners are more likely to learn practical skills." Rokshan laughed. "I'm not sure an academy education is so much greater than an apprenticeship. I learned aspects of mathematics I never use."

"So why did some of the other learners torment Dharan? Was he too proud of being intelligent?" She thought of Coquina and how she wished she'd been in a position to beat her, if only metaphorically.

"Actually, no. He's the most self-effacing man I know. Human children are just like that sometimes. Dharan was poor and small for his age and they took pleasure in making him miserable. People like that still infuriate me." Rokshan laughed again. "But then Dharan grew about seven inches and gained fifty pounds, mostly muscle, and suddenly he didn't look like such a fun target anymore."

Lamprophyre laughed with him, though she had no sense of what human measurements meant in practical terms or by comparison to dragonlengths. "And Baleran was also in the academy with you?"

"A few years later. Baleran was there to study magic. I met him because he was Manishi's apprentice for about a week before he lost patience with her and demanded a different master." Rokshan shifted his weight, rubbing up against the sensitive spot at the back of Lamprophyre's neck and sending an odd twinge through her. "If you knew how unheard of that was, you'd have a sense for the kind of person Baleran is. Changing masters is rare, and a student demanding that change and getting it is almost impossible. Also, the scholars thought they were doing Baleran an honor by assigning him to a princess—apprentices benefit from the resources of their masters, and Manishi could have done much for him."

Lamprophyre snorted, sending up a cloud of pale smoke. "I barely know her and even I know that's improbable."

"Baleran figured it out almost immediately. He put together a truly amazing case for his being reassigned and dragged me into it as a character witness against my sister."

"No wonder you don't get along."

"That would be true if Manishi thought like an ordinary person. She hadn't wanted to have an apprentice at all, but Mother thought it would be good for her. So Manishi might actually be grateful to me for getting her out of it."

Lamprophyre's opinion of Manishi continued to drop. "I thought you and Manishi had different mothers."

"We do, but Mother married Father when Elini's children were little more than babies. I think Tekentriya is the only one who remembers Elini. Mother's certainly always considered all of us her own."

"I see." If Hyaloclast became pair-bonded a second time, her mate certainly wouldn't consider Lamprophyre his child, and she wouldn't think of him as her father. Humans were so different in unexpected ways. "And you and Baleran became friends."

"He's the kind of person who makes up his mind about things and then never wavers. He decided I was interesting, and then he decided we were friends, and then he was just always around me and Dharan. If he hadn't been interesting himself, it would have been annoying."

That made sense. "So do humans have clutches, too? It sounds as if Baleran and Dharan are the same age as you."

"They are, and you may be right, but it's not as formal as I think dragon clutches are," Rokshan said. "For one thing, there are hundreds of children born in a year in Tanajital alone, and that's far too many for us to know all of our age-mates—or am I wrong, and your clutch is large?"

"No, there are seven dragons in my clutch. Which is large for a dragon clutch, but not several hundred large."

"It's more accurate to say humans create their own clutches, if I understand correctly. We make friends among those studying in the same classes, or sharing apprenticeships, things we only do with those of the same age."

Lamprophyre thought about this for a few beats. "I can't decide which way is better. Though there are so few dragons born to a clutch, it's not as if we can avoid knowing each other well. It would be nice not to have anything to do with Coquina."

Rokshan leaned forward. "You've mentioned her before. She sounds like a bully. Does being part of the same clutch mean you're thrown together often?"

"Always. She's bigger than I am, faster, prettier. It feels like anything I do, she gets there first." Lamprophyre knew she sounded petty and didn't care. "We were friends when we were dragonets, but as we got older, she decided I wasn't good enough to be her friend. And because we're in the same clutch, I can never get away from her."

"Until now."

Startled, Lamprophyre craned her neck as far as she could and still couldn't see more of Rokshan than his right foot. "What do you mean?"

"Well, you're the first dragon to have contact with humans, right? Coquina didn't think to approach us. And you're the first ambassador, and the first to fly with a human. It sounds like there are a lot of things you've done that Coquina can't say she did first."

She'd never considered that. "You're right," she said, the bitterness she always felt when thinking of Coquina fading.

"Which dragon was she, anyway?" Rokshan asked.

"The green one. The one who laughed when it turned out I couldn't tell you were male."

"Huh. Well, I don't know what makes dragons attractive to other dragons, but I can tell you your coloring is much prettier than hers. Green and rose aren't nearly as nice as blue and copper."

His compliment warmed her heart. "Thank you."

Rokshan leaned out to one side to look around Lamprophyre's head. "I can't see well in the darkness—is that the mountains up ahead?"

Lamprophyre nodded. She didn't need much light to see clearly in the darkness, and the half-moon illuminated the dark peaks and, beyond those, the higher range of mountains that surrounded Mother Stone. Snow gleamed white on Mother Stone's slopes, making her glow in the moonlight. Lamprophyre had barely been gone a day and the sight still gave her an unexpected pang of homesickness.

She banked right again and headed for the nearest gleaning field. She was hungry enough for a bite of stone she decided Manishi's demands could wait. The cool, crisp night air felt even better after a day spent in the heat of the lowlands, and she glided the last few dragonlengths, welcoming the wind coursing over her body. She alit neatly at the base of the gleaning field and crouched to let Rokshan off.

"This looks like it was carved out of the mountains," Rokshan said. He took a few steps toward where the slope began. "How is that possible?"

"Dragon claws are sharp and strong," Lamprophyre said, "and dragon teeth are even stronger." She climbed up to an outcropping and sniffed the granite. The aroma made her stomachs growl. A protruding knob the size of her fist beckoned to her. "Watch out," she told Rokshan. She traced a guide line with one claw, circling the knob, then dug the rest of her claws in and twisted. A sharp *skree* sounded from where her claws scored the stone, and fragments and dust flew. Lamprophyre dug a little deeper, then loosely held the knob with her left hand and struck it a sharp blow with her right. The knob popped off in her hand, releasing another shower of stone dust.

She turned back to face Rokshan, whose mouth was hanging open. "That's incredible," he said. "I had no idea dragons were so strong."

"It's more that our claws are strong, though I'm sure dragons are stronger than humans because we're bigger." Lamprophyre bit into the knob of granite, chewing blissfully. "I didn't realize how much I wanted this."

"How much should we take back with us? Because strong or not, it did take you a few minutes to break off that rock, and we might be here all night." Rokshan pulled out the sack he had tucked into his waistband and shook it out.

"Oh, I'll take some of what's already been gleaned," Lamprophyre said. "But it's never so fresh as when you take it right from the stone." She gestured at the neat piles of stone, realized Rokshan might not be able to see them, and took the sack from him. "I don't need much."

Rokshan watched her fill the sack halfway. "Once you have money, we can buy stone from the masons in the city," he said. "They might not even charge much if you can eat the waste stone from their building projects. Or leftover marble from a sculptor's chisel."

"Marble's not my favorite, but it will do." Lamprophyre crouched to let Rokshan back on. "Now we'll see what we can find for Manishi."

"She said she would pay double for obsidian, so how about that?" Rokshan said.

"She wants large pieces, and those are very hard to find. I think we're better off looking for something else," Lamprophyre said.

"Garnet, then," Rokshan said. "Is that nearby?"

"Not very far."

A hundred beats took them to where Lamprophyre could smell garnet, in a very small gleaning field. Lamprophyre descended and immediately felt discouraged. "There isn't any harvested," she said. "We'll have to break some off, and garnet is harder to glean than granite."

"Let's leave it for now, and see if you can find anything already free from the stone," Rokshan suggested. "Though it makes me wonder if we're stealing, coming in under cover of night and snatching what the dragons have mined."

"We all take turns gleaning, and all the stone belongs to all of us," Lamprophyre said, though she had had some furtive thoughts along those lines. It was one thing to help herself to food, and another to take stones to exchange for human coin for her sole use. She told herself her needs in Tanajital were essentially those of dragonkind and suppressed those thoughts. "And it's not as if we're depriving the flight of necessary food. They'll harvest more."

"All right," Rokshan said. He still sounded skeptical, but he said nothing more.

Lamprophyre took off again and flew straight up, then hovered, considering her surroundings. Manishi wanted something humans hadn't seen before, which could be anything, and Lamprophyre didn't feel like playing a guessing game. So she decided to visit the nearer gleaning fields and take her chances. Manishi was, despite her other failings, a clever female, and she could no doubt make use of anything Lamprophyre brought her.

They had better luck with the next few sites as Lamprophyre flew higher and higher into the mountains. Rokshan was shivering by the time she settled onto a ledge formed by dragons digging into the mountainside to follow a vein of turquoise. "I didn't think we'd have to fly this high. I'm sorry," she told him.

"My fault for not dressing more warmly," Rokshan said. He rubbed his arms vigorously and stamped his feet. "But we should probably finish anyway, if we're to return before the moon sets."

"I can fly in full darkness, but it's not safe." Lamprophyre scooped a handful of turquoise chunks into the sack. "But I—do you smell that?"

"I can't smell anything. It's too cold."

Lamprophyre sniffed the air. "Wait here," she said, and flew off into the darkness before Rokshan could protest.

She followed her nose to the crisp, clean scent of quartz tinged with something else, something rich and darkly sweet. On a nearly sheer cliffside, she found it: a highly striated bright blue stone embedded within the quartz, striping the cliffside where a recent rockfall had exposed it. She clung to the cliffside with her feet and one hand and brushed the blue stone with her free hand. Kyanite. One of the more popular stones among dragons, sweet to the taste and rich enough that more than a bite led to indigestion. There was plenty of kyanite in the mountains, but this source was closer to the flight's caves than the ones Lamprophyre knew about.

She carefully traced along the lines of the elongated crystals with her claws until she could pop one of them free. She would have to let the flight know about this source, but for now, this would be a nice treat for her. She felt she deserved a treat, what with dealing with terrified humans all day. She broke a tiny nibble off the end of the crystal and swallowed it whole. Delicious.

She flew back to where Rokshan waited. Despite her resolve not to eavesdrop, his emotions were strong enough she could hear his distress at being cold. "I'm sorry," she said, feeling instantly contrite at letting her appetite get the better of her. "Let's hurry down from here." She dropped the kyanite into the sack and, with Rokshan mounted securely, skimmed over the peaks for the lowlands as fast as she dared fly.

Rokshan hunched close to her shoulders and neck, shivering occasionally and making Lamprophyre feel even more guilty. "Are you all right?"

"I'll be fine. You're warm enough it counters the cold." Rokshan pressed himself against her neck and embraced her with both arms. "Next time I'll wear warmer clothes."

"It makes me wonder where humans and dragons used to live if they shared the same territory. Dragons are more comfortable at higher altitudes, and humans can endure the heat of the lowlands better than we can. That doesn't leave much room for compromise."

"Maybe they didn't share territory." Rokshan's voice was loud, his head right next to her ear. "Maybe they went back and forth."

"It's not something the stories mention."

They flew on in silence for a while until Lamprophyre began to worry about her passenger. "Rokshan, are you falling asleep?"

"No, I'm still too cold for that, thank Jiwanyil. I was looking at the stars and finding constellations."

"What are constellations?"

Rokshan shifted and sat up. "Dragons don't know constellations?"

"I've never heard that word before. Is it something in the stars?"

"Yes. Some stars look like the outlines of pictures, and humans tell stories about the creatures and people in the pictures."

Lamprophyre surveyed the sky. The stars still looked like white specks scattered over the black sky. "Humans must be very clever to see pictures in all that."

Rokshan chuckled. "Some of the pictures are a stretch. We believe Jiwanyil put those people and animals into the sky as a reminder to us that God is always watching over us, and that the act of putting them there transformed them, so what we see is their essence rather than their actual bodies."

"That's fascinating. Can you show me one?"

"Maybe." Rokshan extended an arm. "There's the Dragon, that should interest you. Can you see those two stars that are very close together? One of them is reddish?"

Lamprophyre followed the line his arm made and squinted. "I think so. Right between that mountain and Mother Stone?"

"What's—is that what you call Nirinatan? The big mountain?"

"Mother Stone. Yes."

"All right. Yes, those two stars. Those are the Dragon's eyes. Then if you look above them a handspan, there's another, dimmer star where its head is, and then to the right there's a half-circle of stars for the wings, and below that and farther to the right you can imagine a line for its tail—see it?—and then you come back around to its belly and up to its nose."

Lamprophyre followed his directions. "It doesn't look much like a dragon. It's got no arms or legs, for one."

"I did say it's just the essence of a dragon. It's the story that matters."

"All right, tell me the story."

Rokshan blew out his breath. "One day, Jiwanyil and Katayan, god of the dragons—"

"I told you there's no such person as Katayan. Dragons worship Mother Stone."

"I know we have different faiths. But this is how the story goes, all right? Jiwanyil and Katayan were arguing over who was more powerful. Jiwanyil said he was more powerful because there were so many more humans than dragons, and their worship strengthened him. Katayan said dragons might be few in number, but they were individually stronger than the strongest human and that made him more powerful."

"Do your gods bicker like children, then?"

Rokshan stiffened. "That's a rude thing to say."

Stricken, Lamprophyre said, "I apologize. I didn't mean to be critical. It's just that among dragons, Mother Stone is above petty concerns and hatreds, and your gods seem more...human, I suppose."

"I'm not an ecclesiast, so I don't know much about the nature of God. And if dragons worship differently, maybe our stories are wrong. Do you want to hear the rest?"

"I do." Lamprophyre felt embarrassed at having criticized Rokshan, even indirectly, and wished he'd stop sounding so angry.

"All right," Rokshan said. "Jiwanyil and Katayan decided to have a contest to prove which of them was most powerful. They would each select a champion and set the champions a task, and whichever of them succeeded first would prove the superiority of his God. So Jiwanyil chose Dharan, a king of one of the olden time countries—this was before the catastrophe that we believed killed all the dragons."

"Isn't that your friend's name?"

"It's a very popular boy's name in Gonjiri. There were at least three Dharans at the academy when we were there."

"That sounds like it could be confusing."

"Well, one of them went by Dar, and another had the nickname Bruiser because he looked like a side of beef. But Dharan was always Dharan, except to the bullies."

Lamprophyre thought about this. How strange, to be called anything but who you were. "I see. So your friend was named after this king from the olden days. I didn't think humans knew anything about those times."

"We don't have any histories, nothing provable. Just legends like this one. Jiwanyil chose Dharan, and Katayan chose the dragon Parvetil." Rokshan paused. "Now that I know you, I realize that's not a very dragon kind of name."

"No. We're named to celebrate our connection to Mother Stone."

"Anyway, the legend has several different versions of what challenges the gods gave Dharan and Parvetil. My favorite has them instructed to carry a living flower to the top of Nirinatan—Mother Stone."

Lamprophyre laughed. "Even a dragon can't survive that high."

"That's part of the story. Parvetil could reach the top, but the flower died in his hands. And Dharan could keep the flower alive, but couldn't reach the summit. So to succeed, they had to work together, Dharan protecting the flower and Parvetil protecting Dharan. And the gods realized that their real power was in the harmony between their creations. So they put the two of them into the sky as the Dragon and the Traveler. The Traveler is to the left of the Dragon, but it's much harder to make out. I can draw you a picture on a star map sometime."

Lamprophyre examined the constellation again. "That's a lovely story, whether or not it's true."

"It's some of why I want dragons and humans to live together in harmony. That story promises that we will be stronger together than we are apart." Rokshan paused. "But you probably shouldn't suggest the story isn't true. There are people in Gonjiri who believe every one of our religious legends are infallible, and they'd shun you or maybe even attack you if you denied them."

Irritated, Lamprophyre said, "You mean there are humans who would rather believe lies than truth?"

"Yes. Absolutely," Rokshan said. "Are you saying dragons aren't like that?"

"No, we aren't. Living where we do, believing in what isn't true could kill us."

"Well, humans cherish our beliefs, and some of us cling so hard to them that they refuse to accept any proof to the contrary. Not everyone, but enough that you might have a problem dealing with them."

"And what about you?" Lamprophyre asked. "What do you believe?"

Rokshan was silent for a few beats. "I believe God exists," he said. "Until I met you, I believed what we're taught about the Immanence given flesh to govern the Five Peoples. But I knew—still know—that much of our knowledge was lost in the catastrophe, and if aspects of what we believe are false, the true answers might lie in what we're missing. So learning that dragons don't worship Katayan is disturbing, but it doesn't shake my faith."

His calm certainty unsettled Lamprophyre. If he believed in a god Lamprophyre had never heard of, who was to say he wasn't right, and Lamprophyre's faith was the false one? She mentally shook off her disquiet. "I think I understand," she said. "Though I'm confused as to why a human religion might include a god of dragons. Our faith doesn't say anything about you."

"I don't know. You could ask an ecclesiast, if you could find one willing to give you a straight answer," Rokshan said.

"I don't understand."

Rokshan sighed. "All the ecclesiasts I know, starting with my brother Khadar, seem to delight in giving ambiguous answers. If I were more cynical, I'd say it's because they want people to depend on their intercession with God, and ambiguity gets them repeat business. But maybe it's just that the mind of God is confusing enough that ordinary humans can't understand it, even those devoted to worship. I don't know."

Lamprophyre slipped lower to follow the Green River as it snaked through Tanajital. "Mother Stone doesn't talk to us, either," she said. "Maybe our faiths have more in common than I thought."

CHAPTER ELEVEN

The smell of fresh meat roused Lamprophyre the next morning. Yawning, she propped herself on her elbows and regarded Akarshan, who walked a short distance in front of the wheeled wooden platform drawn by three other humans. She normally woke just after dawn, but the sun was a few handbreadths into the sky and she still felt she could sleep a thousand beats longer. Her night flight had kept her up later than anticipated. She yawned again and said, "Good morning, Akarshan."

"Good morning, my lady ambassador," Akarshan said with a bow. "I hope you slept well."

"Yes, it's quite comfortable here," Lamprophyre said. It wasn't entirely a lie; the ground was no harder than the stone of her cave, and the warmth of the lowlands made up for the openness of the coliseum. "Thank you for bringing food. Your cows are delicious."

"You're welcome." Akarshan hesitated. "Ah, my lady?"

"Yes?" Lamprophyre picked up the remainder of the cow by its hindquarters and sniffed it, enjoying the smell of raw meat that was almost as good as cooked meat.

"I was wondering—we wondered—how you cook your meat?"

"Hmm?" Lamprophyre lowered the half-carcass. "With fire, of course."

"I guessed that dragons breathe fire, yes. I meant that, well, we cook meat, too, but we butcher it first and cook the pieces. If you don't mind,

I'd like to observe how you do it, to see whether we might prepare the meat more efficiently."

Lamprophyre wasn't sure it mattered, but Akarshan's thoughts were clear; he cared very much about treating her well, and it warmed her heart that this near-stranger, not even of her kind, might go out of his way to satisfy her needs. "If you want," she said. "But only female dragons breathe fire. Males spit acid from their second stomachs."

She raised the carcass well away from Akarshan and the humans accompanying him, drew in a breath to mingle with the fires in her second stomach, and exhaled slowly. Fire bathed the carcass and licked over her hand, gently warming her scales. The smell of cooked meat rose from the cow, tantalizing and delicious. Lamprophyre turned the carcass to let the fire touch all of it, gently breathing in rhythm to keep the fire burning steadily. When the meat was fully cooked, she patted out the remaining flames with an edge of her wing and set it on the ground.

"Astonishing," Akarshan said, walking toward the cow. "A perfectly contained burn, and you roast the meat without burning it. But I can see it's unevenly cooked in places—I'm guessing you prefer underdone to overdone?"

"Yes," Lamprophyre said, mystified at his curiosity and his sharp, analytical thoughts. "Raw meat isn't as delicious, but it's better than burned. Do humans eat raw meat?"

"No." Akarshan prodded the carcass. "I have an idea, if you'll allow me an experiment, my lady?" Gone was any residual fear he might have displayed. His intent, curious thoughts amused Lamprophyre, not because she thought Akarshan ridiculous, but because he reminded her of her clutchmate Orthoclase, though Orthoclase's passion was for blending stones to achieve new taste sensations. She wished she could introduce him to Akarshan.

"I don't mind if you experiment," she said. "What did you have in mind?"

"I'll show you this evening," Akarshan said. "We'll leave you to eat in privacy now." *Jiwanyil only knows if these three will be rude, it's not like dragons have table manners, or maybe they do and I'm the ignorant one.*

Guided by Akarshan's thoughts about his companions, Lamprophyre waited for the four humans to leave before tearing into the rest of the cow. It was just as delicious as it had been the day before, so that hadn't been hunger making it seem the best meal she'd ever had. She ate contentedly until the cow was a pile of cracked bones and scraps, then cleaned between her teeth with her sixth claw and let out a pleased burp. A couple of bites of granite would round her meal out, but she felt full enough she didn't want to move, even to retrieve the sack she and Rokshan had filled the previous night.

Of course, that was the kind of thinking that led to indolence, and indolence led to laziness, and Lamprophyre hated laziness. With a groan, she got to her feet and stretched her wings to their full extent, then stretched her arms and flexed her tail as well. The sack was half a dragonlength away, only a few steps, and she collected it and began removing her haul. Some of the stones she'd found for Manishi were fragile enough they'd been fractured by being stowed with the more robust stones, but Lamprophyre figured if Manishi didn't want them, they would make a nice snack for her.

She entertained herself by sorting the stones into piles until Rokshan arrived, out of breath from running. "Is something wrong?" she asked.

"No, I'm just later than I wanted to be after visiting the market—that's a lot of stone. I didn't realize we'd found so much." Rokshan crouched to pick up a chunk of emerald between thumb and forefinger. "I think I have a sense for the value of these stones. This would be valuable to an ordinary lapidary, even without its potential for magic."

"I wish I knew what Manishi could do with it."

"You mean, what if she does something terrible? Manishi is off-putting, abrasive, and rude, but she's not evil." Rokshan set the emerald down and picked up a piece of turquoise, roughly pyramidal in shape. "What's this?"

"It's turquoise. Haven't you seen it before?"

"No. Manishi might have. I mentioned she buys stones from all over the world." He rubbed rock dust off its rough surface. "I bet this would look amazing if it were polished."

"All I know from the stories is that humans cut stones into shapes they find pleasing. I'd never seen a polished stone until I met Manishi and saw the citrine ring she wears." Lamprophyre ran a claw along the kyanite crystal and licked the scrapings gingerly, careful not to cut herself on the sharp edge and tip of the claw. "And the sapphire attached to that wand was rough-cut, so at least some magic doesn't require shaped stone."

"I asked Manishi to join us this afternoon." Rokshan tossed the turquoise in the air and caught it. "This morning we're going to see about a permanent home for you."

"Mekel found something?" Lamprophyre felt a twinge of embarrassment at having thought poorly of Mekel, even in such a sideways manner. "That was fast."

"I know." Rokshan tossed the turquoise again. "I hope it's not a warehouse. You deserve better than that."

"What's a warehouse?"

"A big building for storing things. Food, or lumber, or fabric, anything humans need only part of the time, or intend to sell. They're usually rough and in less savory neighborhoods."

Rokshan's explanation made less sense the longer he talked. She didn't know half the words he'd just used. "I don't need a fancy place," she said. "I'm used to my cave, and that's not decorated with colors and metals the way the palace is."

"Yes, but you'll meet with other ambassadors and nobles in your home, and they will judge you based on what it looks like."

"They will? That's ridiculous!"

"It's the way humans are. Don't worry about it. I'll make sure wherever you end up is suited to your dignity."

Lamprophyre snorted laughter. "You make me sound as old as Scoria, sleeping in the sun all day and being brought food instead of hunting. I'm not sure how much dignity a dragon my age has."

"Ambassadors always have dignity no matter their age." Rokshan tossed the turquoise chunk to lie in a pile with the others. "How old is Scoria?"

"Three hundred and seventy-three."

Rokshan's mouth fell open. "God's breath," he said. "I didn't realize dragons lived as long as that."

"She'll probably live to be more than four hundred. The oldest dragon I ever knew was Pyrite, and he rejoined Mother Stone when he was four hundred and forty-seven." Pyrite's stubbornness in refusing to make that final journey until his last tooth fell out was as legendary as his age. Lamprophyre had been afraid of him when she was a dragonet, his milky eyes and his tendency to drool acid if he wasn't careful making him seem not quite a true dragon.

"That's almost older than Tanajital," Rokshan said. "It's hard to imagine."

Lamprophyre remembered Rokshan was only twenty-five and felt a pang at thinking he would be old in only a handful of years while she would still be young. "Does it bother you?" she said. "That you don't live very long?"

Rokshan's shoulders moved up and down in that peculiar gesture Manishi had used. "My dog Surana only lived twelve years," he said. "I know people who don't want a pet because of that. Because of seeing them grow old and die. But I think being with them even for that short time is joyful enough to make it worth the eventual pain. We don't know how long our lives will be, so we make the most of what God gives us."

"That's very wise." Lamprophyre thought of Aegirine, her father, who had rejoined Mother Stone before the age of two hundred. "Are you sure you're only twenty-five?" she teased, feeling a need to lighten the conversation.

"My mother says I'm wise beyond my years. I'm not sure how true that is, but it's a nice compliment." He smiled. "Are you ready? I'll show you where to go."

"Flying? Are you sure? I can conceal myself for a few hundred beats, but that's not much."

"Conceal yourself?" Rokshan said curiously.

"Blend in with my surroundings. It's how I surprised your company when I snatched you."

Rokshan took a step back. "I remember. You seemed to come out of nowhere. I thought it was just confusion, but—you make yourself invisible?"

Lamprophyre shook her head. "No, it's—let me show you." She examined her surroundings, the dull red wood of the inner wall, the darker rust of the packed earth, and let her awareness shiver over her, making her body tingle pleasantly. The bright blue of her scales and the copper of her wing membranes shimmered once, and then a rusty hue bled across them, dulling their shine. Lamprophyre blinked at Rokshan, then closed her eyes to hide their copper brightness—not something concealment could disguise.

She heard Rokshan take in a quick breath. "That's astonishing," he said. "Can you do it anywhere?"

"It's easier against a solid background. And it doesn't last long. Mostly we use it while hunting animals that don't have a good sense of smell." Lamprophyre shook her body as if that would make the color bleed away faster and watched her hands return to their normal blue color. "But I wouldn't be able to conceal you, if you were flying with me."

"No, I can see that." Rokshan still stared at her as if expecting her to vanish again. "It's all right, though. The news of your presence here has spread throughout the city, and while I'm sure people are still afraid, they aren't terrified, and you won't surprise them. They have to get used to you sometime, Lamprophyre. Unless you want to be stuck in the coliseum forever?"

Lamprophyre shuddered. "I just don't want to start another riot. I felt terrible about the first."

"You won't." Rokshan nudged the emerald with his toe. "Should I post guards? Or I suppose we could take the stones with us to protect them."

"There are all those guards surrounding the coliseum," Lamprophyre pointed out. "Besides, it's not as if I can't get more."

"True, but you shouldn't have to," Rokshan said. "And we don't want people thinking you're vulnerable to theft."

Lamprophyre crouched to give Rokshan an assist up. "I think they're more likely to be too terrified of what I might do to a thief. Really, it will be all right."

Rokshan settled himself into the notch. "You make a good point. Up, and to the north. Mekel said to look for the big blue roof."

Lamprophyre nodded and pushed off from the rusty earth, smiling at Rokshan's shout of excitement. Flying was so much better with a rider who appreciated it.

CHAPTER TWELVE

L amprophyre rose higher, flapping leisurely and scanning the ground below. An empty space wide enough for her to stretch out in circled the coliseum, with smaller streets leaving it at random intervals to connect with other streets in a drunken web covering the city. "Nobody's screaming," she said, relieved.

"They're also not coming close to the coliseum," Rokshan said. "I can't tell if anyone's noticed you."

Lamprophyre swooped northward, surveying the streets. "A few," she said, her keen eye picking out movement as humans pointed upward and nudged their neighbors.

"You must have very good eyesight," Rokshan said. He leaned out and added, "I see the blue roof. The one not as bright as you? Ahead, and to the right a little."

Lamprophyre tore her gaze from the humans. The blue roof was much bigger than those next to it, and was dull as if the weather had worn at it for years. She wished she knew more about human buildings to be able to guess what this one was for, if it could be repurposed for a dragon.

The narrow streets converged into one larger one that pointed at the blue roof as if guiding Lamprophyre there. She dropped lower as she approached, looking for a place to land. *Now* the humans were pointing and staring, and the city's voice grew louder, rumbling like oncoming thunder. But no one fled, no one screamed, and Lamprophyre swept past them to alight at the center of a round, empty space next to the blue roof. She hoped it didn't belong to someone who might object.

From the ground, the blue roof's shape looked strange, angled sharply down on both sides from a broad ridge Lamprophyre might be able to perch on. By comparison to the other, more shallowly inclined roofs, it looked like a dragon's wings half-folded after a long flight. A narrow opening, arched at the top, gave access to the building beneath the odd roof. The opening was taller than Lamprophyre and wide enough for her to enter if she kept her wings tightly furled. It would barely be big enough to fit Hyaloclast. For all its odd shape, the building was certainly big enough to hold her, assuming it opened up past the entrance, and her curiosity increased.

She turned away from the building, keeping her tail well off the ground so she didn't run into Rokshan, and faced the wide street that ended where the circle of bare ground began. Humans filled the street, motionless except for a few very small ones she guessed were children, struggling in their parents' arms. Children and dragonets seemed the same when it came to anything new; they were so small and inexperienced, everything was equally fascinating to them. Lamprophyre thought of Opal and the rest of the newest clutch and wondered what they might think of this crowd of strange creatures.

"Good morning," she said, pitching her voice to carry past the first rank of humans. "Rank" was a good word for more than one reason; the humans smelled strongly of sweat and meat and a sweetish odor she didn't recognize. She hadn't smelled anything unusual on Rokshan and guessed it was having so many of them together in one place that did it.

Several humans stepped backward when she spoke and ran up against others who hadn't moved, and a few people gasped, but no one fled or screamed. Their thoughts were a mad tangle of fear and curiosity at war with one another, and Lamprophyre, feeling a little overwhelmed, blocked them out. She bowed awkwardly and added, "My name is Lamprophyre, and I thank you for your welcome. Your city is very nice." It hadn't actually been much of a welcome, but politeness was the sort of thing expected of an ambassador.

No one spoke. Rokshan walked forward and said, "Lamprophyre is the daughter of the dragon queen and an ambassador of her people to humans. You don't need to fear her. I hope Tanajital will make her feel welcome."

A scream rang out, causing the crowd to turn and sway as an unseen something moved toward Rokshan and Lamprophyre. A very small human burst through the crowd, laughing as it ran. A larger human with long hair pushed after it, crying out, "Stop!"

Rokshan took a few rapid steps forward and snatched up the child, who struggled in his grip and stretched out its arms toward Lamprophyre. The female chasing the child stumbled to a halt beside Rokshan, staring up at Lamprophyre with her mouth hanging open. Lamprophyre squatted so she didn't overtop the humans and said, "Is this your child? I've never seen a human child before. They aren't much smaller than a hatchling dragonet."

The female reached for the child, her eyes never leaving Lamprophyre's. Lamprophyre considered asking to touch the child, but decided that was too much to expect. After all, she wouldn't touch a dragonet she wasn't related to. But she examined it closely. It had thick, short dark hair and wore only a cloth wrapped around its midsection, and its brown skin was lighter than Rokshan's. It laughed again and waved at Lamprophyre. Lamprophyre waved back, causing its mouth to fall open to match its mother's.

Rokshan handed the child off to the female. "As I said, you have nothing to fear from Lamprophyre," he said, loudly enough that his voice echoed faintly off the surrounding buildings. "And if any of you would like to speak with her, that can be arranged."

The crowd shifted again, but this time Lamprophyre heard someone saying, "Excuse me...please step aside...if you wouldn't mind, I'd like to pass." The crowd parted for Mekel, who looked slightly disheveled, his thinning hair in disarray. Lamprophyre was surprised, if Mekel was the king's representative, that the humans didn't show him as much respect as they would have the king. One more curiosity she didn't understand.

Mekel bowed to her. "My lady ambassador, thank you for meeting me here," he said. "I have investigated a number of royal holdings here in Tanajital, and I'm sorry to say none of them are immediately satisfactory as a dragon embassy. But I believe this place may be remodeled to your satisfaction, if it proves large enough." He gestured at the arched opening.

Lamprophyre half-turned, then faced the crowd again. "It was nice meeting you," she said, "and I hope to be a good ambassador to your people." She bowed, shallowly because she was off-balance, and turned to follow Rokshan into the blue-roofed building.

She'd been right about the size of the opening; she passed through easily so long as she furled her wings tightly along her sides. There were caves with mouths as narrow back home. Within, the space opened up wide enough to allow her to stretch her wings to their full extension, which she did.

The only light came from the opening, but Mekel handed a strange metal contraption about the size of Lamprophyre's fist to Rokshan, saying, "If you wouldn't mind, your highness?" Rokshan crossed to Lamprophyre's left side and did something with the contraption that made a spark, and then a tiny flame grew to a bright light inside a metal and crystal box attached to the wall. Lamprophyre examined it closely. The box was half the size of Lamprophyre's head and had sides of crystal clearer than any Lamprophyre had seen before. It smelled of burning oil and gave off a nice warm glow. She tapped the crystal with her sixth claw, expecting to hear a clear *ting*. Instead, there was a dull click, and a crack spread across the crystal.

"Careful," Rokshan called out from the far end of the room when she exclaimed. "The glass isn't very thick."

"Glass?"

Rokshan came back toward her. "Glass is something humans make. It lets light pass through—we use it in lanterns like these, to keep them from burning too high from the wind, or in window openings so we can see out without, well, the wind blowing through our houses."

"I know what glass is. Female dragons make it out of sand when we're young. Like a game. But I've never seen glass like this. It looks like crystal, but finer." Lamprophyre started to tap the glass again, but thought better of it. It was the first human thing she'd seen that she could call an improvement on what dragons had. Imagine a sheet of this glass blocking the western winds that always brought cold rain with them!

"I should take you to visit the glassblowers. They'd be fascinated to compare experiences."

Rokshan turned away to join Mekel at the center of the hall. Mekel had lit many more lanterns all up and down the right-hand wall, and Lamprophyre examined her surroundings more closely. The floor was packed earth like the coliseum, but less red, and her toe claws made the barest of scratches on its surface. The roof rose to a sharply angled crease that matched what she'd seen of the blue roof, but it was more than twice as tall as Lamprophyre and didn't make her feel claustrophobic.

Down low, between the lanterns, were slabs of wood set into the wall, about as tall as Lamprophyre's leg and placed at regular intervals. Small sheets of metal the size of her palm were attached to the walls above each slab, and the curved and straight lines Rokshan had called writing were carved into each one. Curious.

There was something strange about the walls where they met the ceiling. Patches of pale brown tinged here and there with light blue made a dark contrast to the walls, as if someone had smeared dirt over those places. She wanted to investigate, but as broad as the room was, it wasn't big enough for flying, and the high ceiling was out of reach.

Lamprophyre decided to ignore it for now and walked to the far end of the room, where another archway matching the entrance stood. This one had wood filling it. Lamprophyre inhaled the dusty, warm scent of damp wood and was transported to the cherry orchards south of her mountain home.

"What is this place?" she asked Mekel.

"It was a customs house twenty years ago, before the new one was built at the landing," Mekel said. "From when more trade came through the overland route."

Very little of that made sense to Lamprophyre. She grasped the one thing that did make sense and said, "So your trade routes changed, and this place wasn't needed anymore?"

"Exactly, my lady," Mekel said. "This is the main house, and there are outbuildings we can convert into lodgings for your staff. The people who serve you," he added.

"It's not much better than a warehouse," Rokshan said.

"We will clean and refurbish it, paint the outside and inside, and enlarge the left-hand offices into a kitchen and dining hall," Mekel said.

Rokshan turned in a slow circle with his head tilted back, looking at the ceiling. "I think those windows should be removed. This place will be stuffy come full summer."

"As you command, your highness."

Lamprophyre couldn't tell what Rokshan was looking at, but he was right about the stuffiness. It was comfortably warm now, which meant it could become unbearably hot. "What is this?" she asked, tapping the archway covered with wood.

"The back door, my lady," Mekel said. He pushed on the wood and it split down the middle, one half swinging outward to reveal more packed earth and two lines of smaller buildings facing one another. "Those used to be storage for trade goods. It will take very little to turn them into housing."

Rokshan pushed the other sheet of wood, making it swing open, and disappeared around the corner to the left. "Come look at this, Lamprophyre," he said, his voice muffled.

Lamprophyre fit herself through the door and followed Rokshan. He'd entered another building, this one with a roof too low for Lamprophyre to pass under. She crouched to look inside. It was the oddest building she'd yet seen, with poles holding up the roof rather than walls, and it was round rather than oblong. Unlike the customs house, it had a floor of stone slabs fitted closely together that smelled like granite. "What is it?"

"The counting floor," Mekel said. "For larger trade items. We will elevate the roof to a proper height and build walls here—" He paced off one side— "and here, for a kitchen."

"It's close to the abattoir," Rokshan said.

"Indeed, your highness, and that was part of my consideration," Mekel said with a bow. "If my lady wishes, we can install a stone floor in the customs house, but it will extend the time of the reconstruction."

"No, I'd rather earth," Lamprophyre said. She liked the softness of the earth in the coliseum and felt a little guilty about that preference, as if she were somehow rejecting her rocky home. "I think this will work. Rokshan, what do you think?"

Rokshan returned to her side. "It's not bad," he said. "Properly altered, it will be ideal. Excellent work, Mekel."

Mekel bowed. "Thank you, your highness. I believe my lady ambassador will be able to move in five days from now."

Rokshan whistled. "Very fast work. I can't imagine—that is, did my father order it?"

Mekel smiled. "His majesty left everything entirely to me," he said, bowing to Lamprophyre, "and I judged it important to show courtesy to our draconic guest."

Lamprophyre managed not to smile. Mekel's thoughts were unexpectedly clear: any concern for her well-being came entirely from him and not because the king had ordered him to wait on her. It was just as clear he felt he was putting one over on Ekanath. Lamprophyre didn't understand the subtleties of his emotion, because no dragon felt that strange mix of respect and disdain for Hyaloclast, but she guessed Mekel knew as well as Rokshan what the king was like.

Rokshan extended his hand to Mekel, who clasped it briefly. Lamprophyre reminded herself to ask about the gesture, in case it was something she needed to learn. "Thank you, Mekel," Rokshan said. "We won't forget this."

"It's my pleasure to serve," Mekel said. *Imagine what a dragon might do for me,* he thought, surprising Lamprophyre. It didn't feel like a completely selfish thought, but it lacked the pure altruism of Akarshan's desires to serve her. It might be a good idea to watch Mekel carefully, in case his motivations became darker. On the other hand, someone motivated by self-interest was fairly easy to control, and Lamprophyre much preferred Mekel's desire for an exchange of favors over Manishi's greed.

She crouched to let Rokshan up, waved at Mekel, and took to the skies. Thinking of Manishi reminded her that the princess would arrive that day to make an exchange. With luck, Lamprophyre would get more than coin out of her—would learn things that might lead her to the creator of that horrible wand.

CHAPTER THIRTEEN

Her successful encounter with the humans gave Lamprophyre confidence enough not to return to the coliseum immediately. Instead, she flew over Tanajital, keeping well above the highest buildings, just in case. Rokshan didn't say anything, so she felt she'd chosen right.

She glided past the tall buildings that formed the center of the eastern half of the city and was startled to see another winged shape pass between her and the white towers, one that disappeared when the buildings were past. "Another dragon!" she exclaimed, searching the sky for the telltale signs of concealment.

Rokshan laughed. "No, that was your reflection," he said. "The glass works like a mirror in some lights—you know what a mirror is?"

"Yes, but our mirrors are obsidian, not bright like that glass." Lamprophyre swung around and took another pass around the same tower, more slowly. This time, it was obvious the "other dragon" was herself, not just because she was the only bright blue dragon in the flight, but because Rokshan was reflected in the glass as well. "But that can't be why you put glass in your buildings."

"No, it's like I said, the glass lets us see out without the wind blowing dust inside."

The wind at this height wasn't terribly strong, but in a storm, it would be unbearable. "That's very clever," Lamprophyre said. "It's interesting how you build your caves to meet human needs."

"I think it's a human trait to alter our environment," Rokshan said. "Do dragons build their own caves, or do you use natural ones?"

"We mostly use natural ones, but we hollow them out to suit our tastes. So I guess we are more like humans than I thought." Lamprophyre dove, drawing a shout of excitement from Rokshan. She laughed in pleasure. "I think you love flying more than I do."

"It's *amazing*. And—don't take this the wrong way, but we really do fit well together. I know you said dragons aren't human servants, but don't you think it's odd that this notch makes the perfect seat for me?"

Lamprophyre was so used to Rokshan's presence she barely felt his weight anymore. "I suppose it is odd. That notch—it doesn't really serve a purpose other than to give our wings added flexibility. So the fact that it works perfectly as a seat for you is strange. But I don't believe Mother Stone created us with that purpose in mind."

"There are scholars who think it's possible to tell for what purpose things came into being based on their shape. Like, a plant with leaves like a foot is good for healing feet. But I don't believe that applies to thinking creatures. Besides, I can't imagine humans being capable of forcing dragons to let them ride them."

The idea should have made Lamprophyre laugh, but she remembered the sapphire wand and it didn't seem so funny. "On the other hand," she said, "maybe humans and dragons used to take advantage of the coincidence the way you and I do."

"I like that idea," Rokshan said. "I asked Anchala what she knew about dragons and humans living together, and she said there are records describing the mountain heights beyond where any human could go. Meaning that the humans who wrote them either talked to dragons, or went with dragons to those places. So that's some evidence."

"Our stories don't say much about humans and practically nothing about humans and dragons together. They're..."

"They're what?"

"It's odd, but I've just realized all the stories I can think of about humans are...I'm not sure I can explain it. They're all sort of unreal. Like, if you heard them in isolation, you'd think they were about mythical creatures. Except dragons definitely knew humans were real before you showed up all over our lands."

Rokshan's hand brushed the tender spot at the back of her head. "Does that mean something?"

"I don't know. Probably not. It's just strange, don't you think? That we have no memories of humans in relation to dragons even though you do?"

"I'm still getting used to the idea that dragons don't read and write. That, to me, is strange."

Lamprophyre banked to follow the line of the Green River. It looked so cool and comfortable. "I wonder if I could learn to read."

"I don't see why not. I can find someone to teach you."

"Not you?" The thought made Lamprophyre feel hollow, a feeling she suppressed as irrational. Just because Rokshan was her friend didn't mean they had to do everything together.

Rokshan laughed. "I'm a terrible teacher. I've got no patience and even less tact. Dharan used to say it was a good thing our roles weren't reversed, because if I'd been his tutor I'd have driven him crazy and he, as a prince, would have had me executed."

"It's too bad Dharan doesn't live in Tanajital. He sounds like the perfect teacher. And we'd be able to meet."

Rokshan said nothing for a moment. "I wonder," he finally said. "Maybe it's not a bad idea, bringing Dharan here."

"You could do that?"

"Well, no. It would be up to Dharan. But I can ask. Like I said before, he would love to be able to discuss ancient legends with you. Just comparing our versions of the same stories would give him something to write about for years."

Lamprophyre flew lower until she was skimming the surface of the river. She lowered a toe to dip into the water, sending up a wave of spray that cooled her leg. "I would like that. If it's not inconvenient."

"We'll leave it to Dharan. Too bad we can't fly to Kolmira right now, but we'd just start another riot."

Kolmira. Lamprophyre remembered Rokshan saying that was where the egg thieves had fled. "Yes, that's too bad," she said. A flash of guilt struck her, and she buried it deep. She'd promised Hyaloclast to keep her true intentions secret, and suppose she was wrong about Rokshan and he was involved? The idea felt wrong, deep inside, but she had her orders, and obeying her queen was as ingrained in her as her ability to fly. Even so, it didn't feel right.

She swung away from the river and headed back to Tanajital. "I'll need a bath soon," she said.

"We could go for a night swim tonight, or during the day tomorrow," Rokshan said.

"You don't think it would frighten the humans on the boats?"

"I think they might be more frightened if they come upon us at night, actually. Humans don't see in the dark as well as you do, and you'd seem more—forgive me—like a monster at night."

That made sense. "Tomorrow, then," Lamprophyre said.

"Let's go back to the coliseum, and I'll send a message to Dharan," Rokshan said, "and then I'll be back before Manishi comes. Though if she arrives before I do—"

"I won't make any trades with her, don't worry," Lamprophyre said. "She'd just try to cheat me."

"I'm sorry she's so avaricious. But I'm sure she'll honor her agreements."

Lamprophyre settled down on the coliseum floor and crouched to let Rokshan off. The stones lay in their piles, undisturbed. Lamprophyre squatted next to them and took a bite of quartz, smooth and savory. "I feel so decadent, eating in the middle of the day," she murmured around her mouthful.

Rokshan chuckled. "Many humans eat three times a day," he said. "You can say you're acclimatizing to the culture."

Lamprophyre took another bite. "If I turn too human, I'll never hear the end of it from Hyaloclast."

"It can be our secret," Rokshan said. He waved and trotted away out of the coliseum.

Lamprophyre settled on the earthen floor, chewing peacefully. She needed to do something ambassadorial soon or she'd feel she'd come to Tanajital under false pretenses. Well. She *had* come under false pretenses, but she was really only trying to fool the egg thieves and the maker of that wand, and they were her enemies, so that was all right.

Even so, it was time she worked out a plan to fulfil Hyaloclast's instructions. She felt certain the dragons only had one enemy—or, rather, they might have several enemies, but the theft of Opal's egg had been planned by one human or group of humans working together. So she had two ways to approach finding that enemy. One was to track down the bandits who'd stolen the egg. The other was to find the human who'd created the wand. It sounded so simple.

Lamprophyre scowled. Sounded simple, but was actually difficult. Rokshan was sure the bandits had gone to Kolmira, which ought to be a definitive direction, but as he'd pointed out, if she went there, she'd just start a riot. That would make it nearly impossible for her to question humans about the bandits.

And finding out who'd made the wand was even more complicated, given that she didn't know who might be capable of creating such a weapon, or where that person might be, or even if the person had known what they were doing. Suppose they'd made it at the behest of someone else? She blew an impatient cloud of smoke from her nostrils and propped her chin in her hands. She needed more information, and she didn't know how to get it.

"It looks like you were successful," someone said, startling Lamprophyre out of her reverie. Manishi came toward her, looking exactly as she had the day before, as if she'd slept in her clothes. Lamprophyre knew from observation that humans didn't generally do this, but she couldn't draw any conclusions about Manishi from this fact. "Can I see?"

Lamprophyre got to her feet. "I brought back things I thought were interesting. You'll have to tell me if you agree."

Manishi crouched beside the piles. "This is just granite," she said with distaste.

"That's for me. The other piles are the ones you might like."

Manishi picked up the chunk of emerald and turned it over to examine all its sides. "Is there more where this came from?"

"Of course. It's not a large seam, though."

"Unfortunate." She picked over the other stones, made a pleased noise when she found the turquoise, and actually licked a small nugget of quartz. It was an unsettling action for a human.

Then she stilled so completely Lamprophyre wondered if she'd had a seizure—did humans have seizures? She reached out to Manishi, but the woman twitched away before Lamprophyre could touch her. Manishi gently touched the kyanite crystal with a trembling hand. "Where did you find this?"

"It wouldn't mean anything to you. High in the mountains." Lamprophyre examined Manishi's face, but her expression still meant nothing to a dragon, and the woman's thoughts remained an incomprehensible blur.

"I've never seen so much kyanite in one place." Manishi stroked the crystal as if the sensation gave her pleasure. "What do you want for it?"

"I—nothing. I mean, it's for me to eat. I don't want to exchange it for coin."

"Then half of it. You can always fetch more, right?" Manishi sniffed her fingers, then sucked on one of them as if she were a dragon enjoying a pinch of stone after a meal.

"Um, I suppose—"

Manishi stood and dug in the pouch at her waist. "Five vahas for the lot," she said, showing Lamprophyre a handful of square gold coins. "It's more than fair."

Lamprophyre drew back, resisting the urge to put her hands behind her. "I think we should wait for Rokshan. He will know the value of the stones." If he could even put a price to the kyanite, which neither of them had thought to investigate.

"Are you saying you don't trust me?"

Manishi sounded angry, and Lamprophyre nearly gave in. She made herself stand upright, which let her tower over Manishi. Manishi stood her ground, which would have impressed Lamprophyre if she'd liked the female at all.

"I'm saying you're awfully quick to make me an offer, and we agreed Rokshan would be the one to put a price on this exchange," she said. "Or I could take this stone to the marketplace and see what I'm offered. Even dragons know humans like to bargain with each other, and I'm sure there are many people who want stone enough to pay more to keep it out of their rivals' hands."

She wasn't actually sure. All of what she'd said came from an old story about a human selling a stone called a pearl, and she'd always believed that one more fictional than most, given that there was no such stone, but with Rokshan not there, she needed to say something to keep Manishi occupied.

Manishi continued to stand firm, her head tilted back so she could match gazes with Lamprophyre. "That won't be necessary," she said, and now her voice was smooth and lilting, almost musical. "You're right, we had an agreement that you would sell only to me at a fair price determined by Rokshan. We should wait for him."

Lamprophyre didn't remember agreeing to an exclusive bargain, but it didn't matter, because there was Rokshan, running toward them. "I hope you didn't try to cheat Lamprophyre," he said, breathing heavily.

"Of course not," Manishi said. Her voice was full of perfect wounded sorrow. Lamprophyre laughed.

"I think she did," she told Rokshan, "but I don't hold it against her that she wanted a good bargain for her coin."

"I do. Manishi, don't try that again or we'll do business with someone else. Devara, maybe?"

Manishi sucked in a sharp breath. "You wouldn't."

Rokshan smiled. "So, which stones would you like to buy?"

Manishi stared at him a moment longer, her eyebrows drawn together over her nose, the corners of her mouth turned down. Then she crouched and pointed at the different piles. "All of those," she said, "and half the kyanite crystal."

Rokshan knelt to count, ticking off stones one at a time. "Fifteen vahas for everything except the crystal," he said. "I don't know how much to value it at."

"I'll give you ten for it," Manishi said.

"Excuse me?" Rokshan stood swiftly and dusted off his hands. "You expect me to trust you to put a value on it?"

"That's twice the going rate," Manishi said. "Market rate, not whole-sale. The price is so you won't go asking around the marketplace and reveal that I'm interested."

Rokshan glanced at Lamprophyre. She didn't even hesitate to listen in on his thoughts: *not sure we can trust her, but that's the devil of a value for a chunk of crystal no longer than her open hand.*

"All right," Lamprophyre said. "You've bought your privacy. But if I find out—"

"You'd better not ask around," Manishi said.

"If I find out *some other way* that you've cheated us, I'll never trade with you again," Lamprophyre said. "And you can believe I know where to get more kyanite."

"I wouldn't jeopardize that possibility," Manishi said. She took more coin out of her pouch and handed it to Rokshan, who made a show of counting it. Then she removed an empty sack made of lumpy woven fabric from where it was tucked into her waistband and crouched to collect the stones. Lamprophyre snapped the kyanite in half and after some thought gave Manishi the slightly smaller piece.

"What is it for?" she asked.

Manishi gently set the crystal inside the sack as if she feared it might shatter. "It wouldn't mean anything to you."

"But I know you use different stones for different magical effects," Lamprophyre said. "Surely that's not so complicated that I won't understand." She wished more than ever that she could hear Manishi's thoughts, because she was sure Manishi would lie to her if the princess benefited by it.

Manishi set the sack down. "Most of them enhance human qualities. Turquoise can make someone more eloquent, for example. A little emerald worn as a ring or pendant makes someone luckier in gaining wealth, or shaped a different way can open them up to finding love."

"That's amazing." Lamprophyre hoped she sounded appropriately amazed. She didn't want Manishi thinking this mattered to her beyond the abstract. "But I've heard humans like certain stones for their decorative value. Like emeralds, or sapphires. Are they more valuable as gems, or as magical objects?"

"The stones humans prefer as jewelry are all ones that passively absorb magical energy," Manishi said, "so they convey benefits without being altered by an adept. Though an adept can make a stone far more powerful than it is naturally. An emerald this size will produce five smaller cut stones, each of which has more power than the original uncut stone."

"So you wouldn't use it in its natural state," Lamprophyre said, remembering the size of the uncut sapphire in the wand.

"I might, depending on what I wanted it for." Manishi seemed to be relaxing. Lamprophyre wondered if she liked talking about magic so long as it was to two people who weren't rivals. "The benefit of a larger stone is its magic has a longer range. An emerald's magic is personal, so there's no point in not cutting it down."

"So are there popular stones you *would* leave uncut?" Rokshan was being very quiet, and Lamprophyre thought about listening to his thoughts to see why, but she felt on edge, trying to guide Manishi to give her information, and didn't want to be distracted.

"I don't care for most precious stones." Manishi rubbed her finger over the rough surface of the sodalite in her ring. "It's the unusual ones that have more interesting effects. But amethyst produces a calming effect— that one, you'd want in a large crystal to magnify its power. It's really the only one I can think of. Sapphire, or ruby, those are both more localized effects."

Lamprophyre clasped her hands loosely to still their trembling. "What do those do?"

"Ruby gives you physical energy, vitality, maybe. Sapphire enhances your mental focus. Scholars like it for that reason."

Mental focus. That wasn't the effect it had had on Lamprophyre and Nephrite. "And each stone does only one thing?"

Manishi's eyes narrowed. "You planning to become an adept?"

"No," Lamprophyre said, trying for a casual tone, "but I'm a creature of magic, and your magic is so different from mine, I'm curious. What will you use the quartz for?"

Manishi lifted the sack. "Quartz enhances other stones' magic. Let me know when you intend to make another trip. I'll have some requests." She turned and walked away, the sack bobbing over her shoulder.

Lamprophyre let out a deep sigh. "She's very strange."

"And oddly resistant to answering certain questions," Rokshan said. "You wanted to know about the sapphire wand, didn't you?"

She didn't have to tell him the whole truth, that it was why Hyaloclast had sent her. "Of course. But I don't know much more than I did before. Why do you think she stopped talking when I asked if stones did more than one thing?"

"She might just have felt pressured. I told you Manishi is secretive about her magic. We're not adepts, but she might not care about that when it comes to keeping her secrets." Rokshan picked up the kyanite crystal. "You didn't ask what she meant to do with this."

"Stones! I forgot." Lamprophyre looked at the kyanite. "Now I'm worried. She was really excited about it."

"And I promised I wouldn't ask around. I wish I hadn't."

"You said Manishi isn't evil. So we shouldn't worry too much about what she has in mind." So sapphire had mind-focusing powers, and Manishi wouldn't say whether that was the only property it had. It wasn't all that much of a leap from mind-focusing to mind-confusing. "Though I think maybe I shouldn't bring her any more until we're certain she isn't plotting something," Lamprophyre continued. "I think—" No, she shouldn't tell Rokshan she suspected his sister of being involved in the plot against the dragons, particularly since she had nothing but a suspicion. "I think she will want to squeeze every drop of value out of this arrangement."

"I agree," Rokshan said. "Maybe she's not evil, but she's certainly opportunistic. And I think I can find out why she wanted the kyanite so badly. Without asking at the market."

"Really? How?"

"Manishi's not the only adept in Gonjiri," Rokshan said.

CHAPTER FOURTEEN

Lamprophyre poked at the square gold coins in Rokshan's hand, keeping her claw sheathed. "How odd," she said. "Why is there a dragon on your coin?" Something else was strange about the shape, but she couldn't figure out what.

"I think it's because we associate dragons with gold," Rokshan said. "That's supposed to be Katayan. The picture on the other side is my father, though you can sometimes find older money with his father's face on it."

Lamprophyre flipped over a couple of coins. "It doesn't look much like him."

"Well, there's only so much a die press can do. It's amazing the dragon looks anything like real dragons." Rokshan closed his hand over the coins and put them into a pouch at his side—a second pouch, hanging next to the first.

Lamprophyre settled back on her haunches and rested her hands on her knees. For every question she had answered, five more took its place. Die press? "And that's enough money to pay for what I need? Servants, and food?"

"More than enough. Though we won't need to hire servants until you move into the new embassy, and the palace will feed you until then." Rokshan absently patted the pouch. "I'll be back soon."

"You're leaving?" Even as the words left her mouth, Lamprophyre felt ashamed. Rokshan had to be so bored, waiting on her all day.

"I'm going to send a message to the academy, asking for a moment of the adept-scholar Lector Sabarna's time. It's tempting to fly right in there, but that would be disruptive, and I want Sabarna to be cooperative. Though she'll be curious enough about you she might not mind."

"This is someone who knows about magic?"

"About magic, and the history of magic. She isn't a practicing adept like Manishi, but she has experience creating artifacts and probably understands the theory better than most. Which makes her an ideal choice for asking these questions, because she won't care why we want to know."

"Be careful," Lamprophyre said, alarmed. "What if she's involved?"

"I doubt it, but you're right, we shouldn't take chances. I'll just tell her you're interested in a conversation." Rokshan gripped Lamprophyre's hand briefly. His was cool to the touch. Hesitantly, feeling like a terrible friend, Lamprophyre listened briefly to Rokshan's thoughts. He was thinking about Sabarna: *not sure what kind of mood she's in, might be testy no matter what I tell her.*

Relieved, Lamprophyre watched him trot away toward one of the exits. She didn't actually think Rokshan would deceive her, or that he had only pretended to help her retrieve the egg, but she knew what Hyaloclast would say: humans, however honorable among their own kind, had no responsibility to dragons, and vice versa.

She settled herself into the strip of shadow and tried to sleep. The day was hotter than yesterday, the sun a white disk in the sky that heated her skin unbearably, the air thick with moisture, and she remembered the customs house with longing. Five days. She could survive five days, particularly if one of them included a cool swim in the river.

She thought about Rokshan's willingness to help her, someone not even of his species, and decided it was impossible that Hyaloclast could be right about him. He was so unlike her friends and clutchmates—well, obviously, none of them were human—but it was more than the difference between human and dragon. Except for Coquina, she liked all her clutchmates, but she was always aware that they were looking at her as a potential mate, and she just didn't feel an attraction to anyone. Not even Flint, who despite his boring name was extremely handsome.

Rokshan, on the other hand, couldn't be her mate, and maybe that was the difference. Maybe being free of the pressure to choose among her friends made it easier for her to relax around Rokshan. Or maybe it was something entirely different. Rokshan never seemed bored even when he had a right to be; he never grew tired of answering her questions; he was as curious about her as she was about him. She'd never had a friend she felt so happy to see, and that, more than anything, convinced her he was innocent of conspiring against dragons. She was young, but she wasn't stupid, and she wasn't easily deceived.

So that meant she could trust him—but did trusting him include telling him her true mission in Gonjiri? Hyaloclast would be furious if she did, but Hyaloclast didn't know Rokshan and, more to the point, Hyaloclast wasn't in Tanajital to find out. And Lamprophyre was increasingly certain she needed a human ally if she was going to find the egg thieves.

She rolled onto her side and let out a puff of smoke. It was too hot for her to sleep. She got to her feet and flapped her wings to create a cooling breeze. She didn't dare go far if Rokshan might return at any moment, but he'd said the city knew about her, and didn't that mean she could at least go flying for a few hundred beats?

With a few strong strokes of her wings, she was aloft, surging into the sky with the wind caressing her scales. She spiraled up until she was higher than the tallest tower, then hovered briefly, enjoying the sight of the city spread out beneath her. It really was beautiful in an alien way.

She glided downward, watching to see if she'd been noticed. Very few humans looked up, and those few either stopped and stared or pointed and shouted things she was too distant to make out, either with her ears or her mind. She flew over the customs house, which bustled with activity she didn't understand. Hopefully, it was activity that would turn the place into a suitable home for her.

High, thin clouds began to cover the sky as she glided back to the coliseum, cooling the air and blunting the sun's rays. Lamprophyre settled into her strip of shade and managed to nap, waking when Rokshan said her name. Blinking, she sat up and said, "I never used to sleep this much. It's this lowland heat and humidity. It's like sleeping in soup."

"I suppose—you know what soup is?" Rokshan settled cross-legged beside her.

"Of course. We sometimes make soup out of older animals that aren't very tender. Usually that happens during the winter. Why, is soup a thing you have?"

Rokshan nodded. "I never thought of dragons cooking the way humans do. You don't seem to use tools."

"We don't, in general. Teeth and claws are enough for most of what we need. We don't use fabric and we don't build with wood, but we can refine metal. Of course, we do that because it tastes better pure. That's not why you do it."

"No." Rokshan leaned back to prop himself on his hands and tilted his head back to look at the sky. "So many differences, and yet we both eat soup."

"That is a strange thing to have in common." Lamprophyre got into a more comfortable position and said, "Did you deliver the message?"

"Yes, and asked for a reply to come here. I'm sorry it took so long, but Sajan caught me as I was leaving the palace and had a few tasks for me."

That irritated Lamprophyre. "I thought you were my liaison."

"Yes, but I have a position of responsibility in the military, and some of my tasks didn't go away when my father assigned me to you. And Sajan isn't happy to lose me. He only has so many competent commanders."

"I don't understand. Does that mean there are commanders who aren't competent? Why would General Sajan choose incompetent leaders?"

Rokshan chuckled. "An excellent question with a difficult answer. The military isn't free from political maneuvering. Some noble families send their superfluous sons into the military, and they pay money for them to have military rank regardless of experience or qualifications. Half of what Sajan does is organizing his officers to keep the useless ones out of positions of real responsibility."

"But you were a...a superfluous son, weren't you? And you said you were good at command."

"Sometimes we get lucky. Most of the nobles who join the Army in that way are at least teachable. Some of them turn out to have real skills. And there are a few who couldn't lead a hungry man to a five-course meal. Those, Sajan finds makework for. Without implying that it's makework." Rokshan sat up and looked past Lamprophyre's shoulder. "There's the messenger. That was fast. Or maybe my duties to Sajan took longer than I thought."

Lamprophyre cast an eye on the sun, closing her nictitating membranes to protect herself from its light. She'd napped longer than she thought; it was late afternoon already, and the sun's rays had lost some of their ferocity. Another couple thousand beats, and the sun would rest on the walls of the coliseum, and then it would be time for a meal. She remembered what Akarshan had said about an experiment, and curiosity stirred.

Rokshan stood and approached the human male who ran toward him. The messenger's eyes were on Lamprophyre, and he stumbled once or twice before coming to a halt in front of Rokshan. "Madama Sabarna asks that you meet her in the Atrium," he panted. "You and the...the dragon."

"That's going to be a tight fit," Rokshan said, mostly to himself. "Right now?"

"She said, at your earliest convenience," the male said. He was much shorter than Rokshan, and Lamprophyre wondered if that meant he was younger.

Rokshan dipped into his pouch—not the one he'd put Lamprophyre's money into—and withdrew a couple of bright copper coins. "Thank you. And—here." A silver coin joined the two copper ones. "Return and let Madama Sabarna know we're on our way."

The male nodded sharply and darted away. Rokshan returned to Lamprophyre's side, but instead of climbing up, regarded her with his hands on his hips. "The Atrium," he said. "You might fit, but getting there will be a problem."

"Let's go, and figure it out when we're there," Lamprophyre said.

THE ACADEMY WAS IN A PART OF TANAJITAL LAMPROPHYRE HADN'T really looked at before, on the southeastern side of the city, well away from the river and the coliseum. What drew her attention was the white roofs, steeply slanting and glittering with an unfamiliar substance that gave off a strong, unfamiliar smell, pungent like chlorite but sweeter. Having swept over many of the roofs of Tanajital and seen how dirty they were, Lamprophyre was amazed at the brilliant cleanliness of the academy roofs.

She coasted past the buildings and wheeled around for another pass. "Where can I land?"

"The Atrium is the one beside that thick patch of trees," Rokshan said. "It looks crowded, but there's actually plenty of space between the trees. Try to set down there."

Lamprophyre eyed the indicated spot. It didn't look crowded, it looked impassable. She reversed course and descended feet first, keeping her wings high and tight and hoping Rokshan was right. The many fat-lobed leaves brushed her skin, tickling the sensitive spots beneath her arms and under her tail, and soon she was surrounded by foliage that smelled of wet growing things. She held her breath against a violent sneeze—she hadn't accidentally set anything on fire with a sneeze since she was a dragonet, but no sense taking chances—and used her arms to fend off branches. Stray, frightened thoughts came to her mind, but she was too preoccupied with her descent to worry about what nearby humans thought of her arrival.

Then her wings tangled in the leaves, and she fell a few handspans, flailing for something to hold onto and hoping Rokshan wouldn't get brushed off. But it was a few handspans only, and then she was beneath the branches and spread her wings wide to catch herself and bear her gently to the ground. She crouched on all fours, breathing heavily from her momentary fear. Rokshan hopped down and put a hand on her arm. "That was tighter than I imagined," he said. "Are you well?"

"I'm fine." She straightened and furled her wings along her back. There was, in fact, a great deal of space beneath the branches; the foliage started half a dragonlength above Lamprophyre's head when she was standing, and because the branches extended horizontally, the trees stood at some distance from each other. She saw no humans other than Rokshan, but could hear their nearby thoughts, some of them frightened, others curious. Turning around would be tight, even in this space, so she held still and listened.

Rokshan was already headed for the far side of the clearing, if you could call it that. "This way," he said, beckoning. "I really don't think you will fit through the Atrium door."

Lamprophyre followed him, and the unseen humans' thoughts intensified so much she had to block them out to hear Rokshan say, "I never thought I'd consider the Atrium too small."

She came out from beneath the trees and saw Rokshan standing next to an arched doorway similar to the one in the customs house, but narrower and with a half-moon of glass set above it. More glass, long, narrow sheets of it, were set into the walls on either side of the doorway. Lamprophyre took a few steps to the side to follow the wall and found more glass sheets, so perfectly clear she would have thought them merely holes in the walls if she hadn't smelled the sharp, cold odor of the glass. The wall curved until it met a second wall, this one blank white with a green and yellow pattern impressed upon it somehow. Lamprophyre sniffed the colors and smelled, very faintly, a nose-tickling, sharp aroma that reminded her of limestone steeped in water.

She turned around and came back to Rokshan's side. "This is the Atrium?"

"Yes. An atrium is a building either open to the elements at the top, or enclosed by glass so you can see outside easily. This is the biggest one in Tanajital." Rokshan eyed Lamprophyre's wings. "It would fit you if you could get through the door—"

"That's all right," Lamprophyre said, though she pictured herself sticking her head through the doorway and had to control a laugh at the image. "Is your friend willing to come to me?"

"Maybe." Rokshan hesitated. "Sabarna is…different. Wait here." He passed through the doorway. Lamprophyre tentatively listened for human thoughts and found they'd retreated somewhat. More of them were curious now than frightened, which was heartening.

She heard Rokshan talking to someone whose replies were high-pitched enough to be unintelligible. Rokshan said, "To the doorway, then. You don't have to—" and the high-pitched twitter cut him off. "You'd rather that than speak to an actual dragon?" Rokshan said. More twittering. "All right, I'll ask," he said, and moments later he appeared in the doorway. His face was flushed in the way that meant either physical exertion or embarrassment.

"Sabarna asks, would you mind entering as far as you're able?" he said.

Lamprophyre suppressed her laughter again. "I don't mind," she said. "But it will look ridiculous."

"That's what I told her. You don't have to—"

"It's all right." Lamprophyre's curiosity about this human who for some reason didn't want to leave the Atrium overcame her desire not to look foolish, as if it mattered what the unseen humans thought of her.

She waited for Rokshan to enter the Atrium, then crouched low and stuck her head and neck inside. Her shoulders would fit as well, but that would leave her arms pinned, and she already felt an unexpected discomfort, not of physical pain but of being trapped in this glass box. She braced herself with her hands and surveyed the Atrium.

CHAPTER FIFTEEN

The tall room felt taller because of the glass filling it and the glass roof Lamprophyre could barely see if she craned her neck. Narrow steps more regular than any she'd seen before circled the Atrium's interior, all the way to the top. Lamprophyre knew what steps were, but the ones she was familiar with were shaped by wind and water, and dragons avoided them because flying was always more convenient. It was obvious these were perfectly sized for human use, and explained why humans could build buildings much taller than they were.

Standing at the foot of the steps was a human female whose long hair, piled more neatly on her head than Manishi's, was as white as the snows on Mother Stone's slopes. Her skin was darker than Rokshan's and very wrinkled. Her clothing was much plainer in design than Rokshan's, being little more than a drape of fabric covering her body loosely, but it was a vivid purple as dark and rich as Lamprophyre remembered Aegirine being. Stones set in rings and strung in a circle around her wrist sent up mingled scents of jade and copper, quartz and chlorite. She regarded Lamprophyre closely, her eyes narrowed. Lamprophyre felt free to stare back. She'd thought all humans had black or dark brown hair, and she wondered if it was polite to ask about it.

"Lector Sabarna, this is Lamprophyre," Rokshan said. "Lamprophyre, this is the scholar-adept Sabarna. Thank you for being willing to accommodate her."

Lamprophyre's back already twinged from the uncomfortable position. "Why didn't you want to come outside?" she asked, not caring if it was rude.

Sabarna didn't move beyond placing a hand on the curving pole that followed the steps up to the top of the Atrium. "You're larger than I expected," she said in that high, twittering voice. "Are all dragons as large as you?"

"Most females are larger. I haven't reached my full adult size yet." Lamprophyre listened for Sabarna's thoughts, but heard only the same strange hum she'd heard from Manishi. Odd. "Are you afraid of the outdoors?"

"And you're very bright, too," Sabarna said. "Our legends suggest dragons blend with their environment, but your coloring would stand out for miles."

Lamprophyre didn't feel compelled to explain about her concealment ability. Why Sabarna wouldn't say anything about her strange refusal to meet Lamprophyre outdoors was a mystery. She looked at Rokshan, who made that gesture with his shoulders she was beginning to understand meant either confusion or an inability to draw a conclusion. So he didn't know, either.

"Dragons don't really need to blend in," she said. "I don't understand. All this glass—you can see through it, so it's almost the same as being outdoors—"

"Lamprophyre and I have some questions about magic," Rokshan said, his tone of voice telling Lamprophyre he intended to head off any more questions about Sabarna's peculiarities. "Lamprophyre has only just learned that stones can be made to convey magical properties, and as she eats stone as part of her diet, she was curious about how we use it."

"Eats stone?" Sabarna came forward until she was nearly nose to nose with Lamprophyre. "What stone?" The hum of her unintelligible thoughts grew more intense, but no clearer.

"Um, most stones," Lamprophyre said, wishing she could back away from the scholar-adept without giving offense. "Granite, quartz, feldspar. As well as stones you would use as gems. They all have different flavors."

"And what part do they play in your diet?"

"They help us digest our food and they fuel our second stomachs. And they taste good."

Sabarna nodded slowly. "Interesting. But you don't gain magical properties from them?"

"No."

"Very interesting." Sabarna turned and took a few paces to the left, then the right, with her hands clasped behind her back. "Our legends say dragons are born of stone and return to stone when they die. Is that true?"

Lamprophyre followed her with her eyes as she paced. "It's partly true. We're born of eggs like anyone else, but when we die, our bones merge with Mother Stone."

"Um, Lamprophyre," Rokshan murmured, "humans aren't born from eggs."

Lamprophyre blinked. "You're not? But you're people!"

"That's an irrelevant aside, Rokshan," Sabarna said. "Dragons must absorb their magical natures from their affinity to stone, whether or not it imparts particular magical properties. Or, more accurately, dragons are themselves the magic stone, and specific gemstones mean nothing to them. You were curious about our magic?"

"Yes," Lamprophyre said, wrenching her astonished gaze from Rokshan. "I heard that human adepts use different stones for different magical effects, and I wanted to know how that works."

"It's not complicated," Sabarna said. "You're a dragon, so you must already know that what makes one stone different from another—what makes quartz different from diamond, for an example—is the way its structure is arranged. As stones emerge from the Immanence, they take certain shapes, and some of those shapes trap magic within their vertices."

Lamprophyre regarded Sabarna closely. So, she was willing to talk so long as Lamprophyre avoided that one topic. She really wished she could hear the female's thoughts. Both Sabarna and Manishi were adepts; maybe being an adept altered their thoughts.

"We heard there are stones that absorb magic passively," Rokshan said.

Sabarna shot him a narrow-eyed look. "Would you like to deliver this lecture, Rokshan?"

"Sorry."

"As I was saying," Sabarna continued, "stones capture magic, either passively or through ritual, and the shape of the stone determines the shape of the magic that emerges. Now, by 'shape' I mean, of course, both the natural structure of the stone and the shape impressed upon a stone by human hands. Faceting, or polishing, or carving all alter the magic a stone can produce."

Sabarna drew a round piece of polished bloodstone, mossy green streaked with crimson set in silver, from around her neck. "I made this years ago," she said, holding it out for Lamprophyre to examine. It was tiny from Lamprophyre's perspective, but it was the size of Sabarna's palm and proportionally very large. "It prevents me from falling ill to various diseases and infections. Bloodstone's magical properties are related to physical health, allowing me to shape this stone to have the effects I described. Had I needed something to heal physical injury, I might have used jade or moonstone."

Lamprophyre waited until it was clear Sabarna was done talking, then asked, "What about the gemstones humans find desirable? Is that because they have powerful magic? Sapphire, or ruby?"

"Most popular precious stones absorb magic at a high natural rate," Sabarna said, "and give benefits without being shaped by an adept. And the current fashion is for stones that sparkle when faceted. But an adept can make a stone far more effective, and thus far more valuable."

"So you wouldn't use, say, an uncut sapphire in a magical item," Rokshan said.

Lamprophyre wished she could warn Rokshan to be careful. Sabarna glanced his way, then returned her attention to Lamprophyre as if she'd been the one to ask the question. "It would be a waste of magical power," she said. "Sapphire focuses mental energy, giving its user better focus, better recall. It takes very little sapphire to accomplish this, and a cut stone provides a greater benefit. An uncut sapphire—you might say it leaks magic, though of course it does nothing of the sort. But it's a useful image. An uncut sapphire, particularly a large one, would provide its magic to anyone within a given radius of the stone, but in an ineffective way. I can't imagine anyone who would do that when they could cut the gem down and provide many people with the full benefit of its power."

"I understand," Lamprophyre said. "So, one kind of stone has one specific effect?"

"No, a stone has general properties that can be altered based on the shape forced upon the stone. For example, a diamond can be cut to radiate a pure light that never dies, or it can be cut differently to create a lens that allows someone to see something at a great distance. Both are related to a diamond's properties of clarity and vision."

"But a magic stone wouldn't work on a dragon, would it?" Rokshan said. "Since dragons are creatures of magic and stone."

Lamprophyre wanted to cheer Rokshan on. It was a good, roundabout way of asking the question they needed to know.

"Of course they would," Sabarna said. "Rokshan, you're not thinking clearly. You should follow the example of your friend Dharan. Now *there* is a young man who reasons well. Dragons are part stone, correct? So they are as easily affected by magic stones as anyone. In fact, absorbing stone through their digestive system ought to grant them the benefits of that stone, if it's been given magical properties. Obviously passive magic isn't enough to affect them, or Lamprophyre would have noticed."

"That's true," Lamprophyre said. "But it would take more magic to affect a dragon, wouldn't it? Because we're bigger?"

"Hmmm." Sabarna fixed her narrow-eyed gaze on Lamprophyre again. "It could go either way. Either you're susceptible because you're made of magic, or you're less susceptible because you're big. We'd have to experiment."

"You're not going to experiment on the ambassador," Rokshan said.

"Then I suppose it's a question with no answer," Sabarna shot back. "Was there anything else you wanted to know? I eat my supper early."

"No—yes," Lamprophyre said. "I was wondering what you'd use kyanite for."

"Kyanite?" Sabarna sounded surprised. "Why kyanite?"

"It's a popular food among dragons," Rokshan said smoothly, "and we discovered it's hard to come by in Tanajital. But no one would say why it was rare or what it was for."

"Kyanite," Sabarna repeated. "Yes, it's rare. Rare enough I'm not sure anyone knows what to use it for."

"But you must know the theory," Rokshan persisted.

"Oh, of course. It boosts mental performance. Not as efficiently as sapphire, though oddly enough they look similar when they're cut and polished." Sabarna eyed Lamprophyre again. "Expensive food, if that's what you use it for. Or do dragons have access to more of it than I think?" Her voice sounded casual—maybe too casual.

Lamprophyre kept a straight face, though she wasn't sure Sabarna could interpret her expressions any better than she could understand human expressions. "No, it's a rare delicacy," she lied. "I'd hoped humans had more of it, but it seems not." Since she suspected Sabarna was lying, she felt not at all guilty doing the same.

"Well, I'm happy to discuss magic any time after classes," Sabarna said. It was a polite dismissal, and Lamprophyre was grateful for it. Her back and hips were in agony from squatting so long.

"Thank you, Lector Sabarna, we appreciate it," Rokshan said. "Lamprophyre?"

"Thank you, Lector Sabarna," Lamprophyre said, and withdrew from the Atrium as rapidly as possible.

Free of that unnatural position, she stretched, flexed her wings as far as possible, and said, "There has to be a better way out of here. I'm sure I can't fit back through those branches."

"This way," Rokshan said.

This time, Lamprophyre saw many humans watching her from the edges of the clearing. None of them approached, but it was easy to hear that most of them were more awestruck than terrified, which suited Lamprophyre. She followed Rokshan beneath the trees, ducking her head occasionally, until they left the clearing behind for a street lined with low buildings. It wasn't wide enough for Lamprophyre to fit, and she said as much.

"It just has to be wide enough for you to leap above the buildings," Rokshan said, pulling himself up into the notch. "Hurry, though, before people stop being amazed and press you too closely."

Lamprophyre nodded. She crouched, furled her wings tightly, and with one powerful leap propelled herself into the sky. She had her wings open before she could fall, and beat the air, sending a gust of wind into the street below. Looking down, she saw a few humans who'd been standing too close had been knocked over by her ascent. She laughed. "I shouldn't find that funny, but it is."

"It gives them something to tell their friends over supper." Rokshan leaned forward. "I don't know if we learned more than we gave away. Sabarna is odd, but brilliant."

"Brilliant enough to create that wand?" Lamprophyre asked.

"Probably, but I don't know why she would. Did you listen to her thoughts?"

"I tried, but I couldn't. It was like listening to four conversations at once and understanding none of them. Manishi's thoughts are the same."

"You didn't mention that before. That's an extraordinary coincidence, if it is coincidence."

Lamprophyre nodded. "It could be that being an adept makes your thoughts hard to understand."

"Or they both have magical artifacts that prevent someone hearing their thoughts."

Lamprophyre hadn't considered that. "But why would they? Humans can't hear thoughts, can they?"

"Unless there are other artifacts that give a human the mind-reading powers of a dragon. I know, you said it's not reading. It's just a figure of speech."

"That would be something people would keep secret, wouldn't it?" Lamprophyre said. "I know it's an advantage I don't want humans to know I have."

"I wonder," Rokshan said. "Sabarna said kyanite was a weak alternative to sapphire, but I've known her for years and I can tell when she's not being completely forthcoming. She knows something about kyanite she wasn't saying. What if that was it? Suppose kyanite is what lets someone hear thoughts?"

Lamprophyre circled the coliseum once, then glided in for a soft landing and let Rokshan down. She stretched her back to ease the aching muscles. "That's a big guess."

"I don't know. She said dragons might absorb the magical properties of a stone, and you said kyanite is popular among dragons. What if it's what lets *dragons* hear thoughts?"

"That's impossible," Lamprophyre said, but as the words left her lips, she wondered if she was wrong. "At least...no, it can't be. If dragons got magic from the stones they eat, we'd have so many abilities."

"Like living for centuries? Being impossible for humans to kill? Those strong bones and teeth and claws?" Rokshan paced before her. "I'm just saying it's possible."

"Yes, but how would anyone prove it?" Lamprophyre settled back on her haunches and let out a puff of smoke from one nostril. "I'm not sure we learned anything new, except that the stone in the dragon-harming wand wasn't a typical use of a sapphire, even an uncut one." She stretched out her aching back again.

"Except that it almost certainly had to be that big to have an effect on a dragon. And remember, it didn't affect me. So whoever made it knew something about dragons, or made a really lucky guess." Rokshan sniffed. "Do you smell steak?"

"What's steak?" She did smell something delicious, hot, juicy cow with a tangy difference. She turned to see Akarshan leading his group of humans trundling the platform along. This time, there was no delicious cow carcass. Instead, heaps and heaps of pieces of meat, steaming even in the warm air, lay piled atop the platform.

"My lady ambassador," Akarshan said, "I hope you don't mind my experiment. I was curious about your method of roasting meat, and wondered if you might not be able to eat meat prepared the human way." He made a sweeping gesture at the platform. "If it's not enough, or if you don't like it, I'll bring you something more conventional, but..."

"Thank you," Lamprophyre said. She picked up a slab of meat half the size of her palm. It was perfectly brown on all sides and steamed with a hot, delicious scent. She bit it in half, causing hot juices to spurt. Oh, it was magnificent, dark pink on the inside and chewy and rich and with an unexpected savory flavor. She devoured the other half and licked her fingers. "That is the best meat I have ever tasted," she said with her mouth full. Akarshan beamed.

"Now I'm hungry," Rokshan said. "I'm going to have my own supper, and I'll see you in the morning, yes? We'll discuss the problem further then." He waved and headed for the exit.

"I wish I'd thought to provide for his highness," Akarshan said. Lamprophyre waved his concern away, her mouth too full for speech. It was strange, having her cow cut up for her as if she were a child, but it was obvious the only way to cook the meat in this manner was to have it carved up before it was roasted. Such a simple idea. She would have to try it herself sometime, though it would take forever to prepare.

She ate until she was full, then waved goodbye to Akarshan and his helpers as they removed the wheeled platform. Full, warm, comfortable...

there was no question she'd sleep well that night, concerns about Manishi's use of the kyanite aside. Tomorrow she'd tell Rokshan the truth about Hyaloclast's instructions, and together they would figure out a plan.

She curled up next to the inner wall and traced the curves and lines Rokshan had said were her written name until she drifted off to sleep.

CHAPTER SIXTEEN

The Green River's name made more sense when you were right up close to it. Thick-bladed green grass grew all the way to the banks, with trees Lamprophyre didn't recognize dipping long, flexible branches laden with leaves into the shallows. She lay on her stomach and dipped a finger into the water, which reflected all that green so intensely she was almost surprised when her finger came away dripping clear water.

The sound of running footsteps made her turn in time to see Rokshan dash past her and leap into the water. He landed far from shore, disappearing beneath the river's surface before she could duck away from the spray his body threw up. She shook droplets from her head and pushed herself up. "I shouldn't do that," she told Rokshan as he emerged, tossing his head back so his wet hair flung more droplets her way.

"No, you'd send up a wave the likes of which no boatman has ever seen," Rokshan agreed. "Come on in." He was bobbing up and down without being pulled away by the current, which wasn't swift at this point in the river's course.

Lamprophyre gingerly slid off the bank into the water. It was cool and smooth, and the weeds growing in the shallows tickled her feet pleasantly. She took a few more steps until the water covered her hips, then lowered her tail beneath the water and sighed with pleasure. "It's not very deep."

"It's deeper where I am," Rokshan said. He splashed water at her face. "Go on, show me dragons can swim."

She batted away the water. "Dragons are very awkward swimmers. Mostly we paddle."

"Then do that. Or do you not like to get your wings wet?" He splashed her again.

"I do not. Why do you keep splashing me?"

"It's a human game." Another splash. Lamprophyre flicked water out of her eyes and splashed Rokshan in return. The wave of water churned up by her hand swept over his head and dunked him, making him cough and gasp.

"All right," he said when he'd recovered, "so that's not a game I can play with a dragon and win."

"I should think not," Lamprophyre said smugly. She walked a few more paces, keeping her wings well out of the water, until she was standing next to Rokshan. "You're not touching bottom? How are you keeping your head above water?"

"I learned to swim when I was young. This is a swimming stroke that keeps me in one place. Though the current wants to drag me away." Rokshan grabbed Lamprophyre's arm and pulled himself up. Supported by the water as he was, he weighed practically nothing. Lamprophyre took the opportunity to observe his chest and upper arms. His muscles were less well-defined than a dragon's were, but they were nicely shaped and didn't bulge like the king's guards. Lamprophyre decided she liked them better than the amusingly bulgy ones. Though she would never tell him this, because he would be embarrassed.

Rokshan held Lamprophyre's arm and lay back so he was floating. "I don't know why I haven't been swimming in a while, because this is wonderful."

Lamprophyre moved her arm to drag him back and forth in the water, making him laugh. "Now let go so I can try to float," she said.

Rokshan released her and watched as she bent backward, dipping her wings into the water. The sensation of cool, moving water over her membranes made her shiver. "That doesn't hurt, does it?" Rokshan asked.

"No, it tickles. But this is the only way I can lie on my back. My wings are too rigid for lying supine to be comfortable on land, even when they're fully spread." She kicked off the riverbed and flung out her arms for balance as she brought her legs up. Carefully, she wrapped her tail as far around her waist as it would go, which wasn't very. Floating on her back took concentration, and for a few beats, all her thoughts focused on keeping herself from dipping below the water.

Rokshan dove, reappearing on her other side, then floated with her. "The current is carrying us away."

"It can't take us so far I can't get us back to Tanajital in no time." She wobbled, flung out her arms again for balance, and tried to relax.

"I feel almost guilty," Rokshan said. "I know my father intended this liaison assignment as a chore, but here I am in the middle of the day, swimming with a friend. It's not even close to being work."

A friend. His casual words warmed Lamprophyre's heart. "We are friends," she agreed. "And I have something I need to tell you, as a friend. Something you can't tell anyone else."

"That sounds dire."

"It isn't. Well, it might be. It's just that Hyaloclast gave me instructions and told me to keep them secret. But I don't want to keep secrets from you."

Rokshan popped upright and began doing that swimming stroke that made him bob up and down. "If it's diplomatic business, you shouldn't tell me, Lamprophyre. You and I may be friends, but we're still representatives of different countries. If we were to go to war, we couldn't share information."

"Diplomatic business?" Lamprophyre considered this. "I don't think that's what it is. It's just that Hyaloclast instructed me to find out who stole the egg, and who made that wand. And I need your help if I'm to do that."

"Oh. Weren't we already doing that?"

"Yes, but the secret is that finding that out matters more to Hyaloclast than anything I might do as an ambassador. So it's more important than just idle curiosity."

Rokshan was silent. Lamprophyre uncurled her tail and stood, digging her toes into the soft muck of the riverbed. "It's almost like you're here under false pretenses," he said.

It was so like what Lamprophyre had thought herself that a chill passed through her, as if clouds had suddenly covered the sun. "I'm not, though. I'm an ambassador, and I intend to do that as best I can. I just also have other instructions."

"What's to stop Hyaloclast from ordering you back to the mountains once those instructions are fulfilled?"

Lamprophyre realized her wings were still half-submerged in the river and lifted them, shaking them out gently. "I—she wouldn't do that." But her words sounded weak in her ears, and she knew it was a lie.

Rokshan shook his head. "And you need me to help you in this task."

"The more I see of the human world, the more I realize I don't know. I can't even fit in all the places you can go. I don't think I can do this without you."

He tilted his head back to look her in the eye. "Even though my helping you will lead directly to never seeing you again."

"No! Even if Hyaloclast stops me being the ambassador, she can't keep me from going where I want. And I don't abandon my friends."

"Huh." Rokshan swam for the riverbank and pulled himself out. He wore very short pants of tan fabric that clung to his body in loose, wet folds. Lamprophyre wanted to ask him about them, but felt as if speaking might make Rokshan decide helping her was a bad idea. She waded after him, holding her breath in anticipation.

"I wonder what the egg thieves had in mind," he finally said. He took a seat beneath one of the strange, drooping trees, crossing his legs beneath him. Lamprophyre ducked her head beneath the branches and settled down nearby. "Why would anyone steal a dragon egg?"

"I don't know. It doesn't make sense. Why would humans want to raise a dragonet?" Lamprophyre slowly flapped her wings to dry them. Between the water and the shade of the tree, she felt cool for the first time since coming to the lowlands, but wet wings were uncomfortable and difficult to fly with.

"Maybe they wanted a dragon ally. Someone who would do their bidding."

"That's a very long-term plan. Dragons aren't adults until they're fifty-five, and they don't have their full growth until they're about seventy. That plan would take up more than one human lifetime."

"Good point." Rokshan rested his elbows on his knees and propped his chin in one hand. "And there's no other use for a dragon egg?"

"I don't understand."

He waved his hand in a funny gesture Lamprophyre didn't recognize. "I mean, the egg shell isn't valuable, or anything like that?"

"Not to us. Who knows what humans might find valuable?" She leaned forward to air out the creases at the base of her wings. "The only thing I know for sure stealing an egg would do is make all of us very angry. Well, and break the parents' hearts."

"Huh," Rokshan said again. "What if that was the point?"

"Making dragons angry? Why would anyone do that?"

"I don't know. Maybe it's a foolish idea. But it's the only thing we can say for sure would result from stealing a dragon's egg."

"Unless there's some use for an egg we don't know about." Lamprophyre thought about young Opal, about something terrible happening to her, and her mind came up blank. "Gonjiri already angered us by settling in our territory without permission. Do you suppose some Gonjirians thought that wasn't enough?"

"We don't want dragons to be angry with us, though," Rokshan said. "We need their goodwill."

"Unless it was someone not a part of your government. But that doesn't make sense, either, because why would some of your people want to hurt their country?"

"Countries aren't as unified as you might think," Rokshan said. "Aren't there any dragons who are opposed to Hyaloclast?"

"No. She's our queen. She's part of what makes us dragons. Opposing Hyaloclast would be like your fingers staging a revolt against your hand."

Rokshan laughed. "That's quite the image. Well, it doesn't work like that for humans. Most Gonjirians respect and obey my father, and most of them are in agreement about what Gonjiri should do. But there are always people who think the king is doing things wrong, or who feel they'd benefit personally from a change in government. Maybe one of these groups wants to weaken Gonjiri so they can take over."

Lamprophyre gasped. "Would that work?"

"Not really. The government is complicated enough that even if the country was weakened from fighting dragons, no antagonistic faction has enough power to take over. They'd need to control the military, for one, and General Sajan is too clever to let that happen."

"But someone might *believe* it's possible, right?"

"And try it anyway?" Rokshan nodded. "That could happen. So we could start by looking for groups who would like to see Gonjiri fall."

Lamprophyre cast a casual glance at the ground near Rokshan's feet. "We?"

Rokshan laughed, a single sharp syllable. "You certainly can't do it alone. Besides, I feel personally involved, having helped you recover the egg."

She raised her gaze to his face. He was smiling. She smiled back. "Naturally. And having involved you, I couldn't let you hunt alone."

Rokshan got to his feet and dusted himself off. Dirt clung to his wet garment, so all he succeeded in doing was spread it around. Curiosity got the better of Lamprophyre. "Why do you wear clothes to bathe? Isn't that uncomfortable?"

"A little, but it's more uncomfortable to reveal my, um, male parts in public. Especially to a female."

"You mean me? I told you, Rokshan, it's not as if I'm human. I don't care about your male parts." Though now she was even more curious about what they might look like, whether he was embarrassed because they were ugly. "Dragons keep their male and female parts inside," she added.

"Convenient," Rokshan said. His face was flushed with embarrassment. "Men—human males—have their male parts on the outside, so we have to protect them by keeping them covered. They're sensitive."

Lamprophyre eyed the tan fabric again. "I don't see how that light cloth is much protection. I can almost see—"

"Could we talk about something else?" Rokshan said in a pleading tone.

CHAPTER SEVENTEEN

M ekel was wrong about it taking five days to make the customs house suitable for Lamprophyre. It was only four days later that Lamprophyre returned to the blue-roofed building and winged down to the bare circle before it. Mekel waited there, shielding his eyes against the dusty wind her flight kicked up. "My lady ambassador, welcome," he said when she'd furled her wings. "I hope you are satisfied with the results."

Lamprophyre examined the building in wonder. Where before the walls had been a dull cream color, marred with dirt, they were now a brilliant white. Blue patterns of lines and curves and dots made the white seem even brighter. "How does the color stay on?" she asked.

"That is paint, my lady," Mekel said. "It is a thin colored liquid that sticks to surfaces and dries quickly. The blue is to match the roof and to reflect your own lovely color."

He was flattering her—she could hear it in his thoughts—but she didn't mind. "I like it," she said. "Is Rokshan here? He said he would meet me."

"His highness has not yet arrived. May I show you the interior while we wait for him?" Mekel bowed and gestured at the entrance.

Lamprophyre entered, and found to her surprise it was easier than before. Someone had widened the entrance. It was such a thoughtful touch, given that the entrance had been wide enough before, that excitement thrilled through her again. This was even more pleasant than choosing her first cave as an adult.

The lanterns were already lit, and the light was brighter than before. The interior was the same bright white color as the outside, and when Lamprophyre sniffed the lanterns, she discovered the glass was clean of dirt. The dirty patches near the ceiling were gone, with square holes where they had been letting in sunlight and a crisp breeze that smelled of fruit and meat and the scent of thousands of humans, pleasant from a distance.

The small sheets of brass were gone, but the slabs of wood—Lamprophyre wondered now if they were doors—were painted a bright red that made the room feel even more cheerful. "Where do these doors go?" she asked, pointing.

"They open on very small rooms where the customs officials used to sit. Far too small for your use. We considered walling them off, but that would have taken more time, so we decided instead to simply lock the doors and paint them." Mekel walked to the back door, which was also painted red, and pushed it open. "My lady?"

Lamprophyre fit herself through the door, which had not been widened, and saw the small buildings were now clean, their roofs repaired and washed free of dirt, and holes had been cut into their faces next to their doors. "Housing for your staff," Mekel said.

"Staff—you mean servants?"

"Indeed, my lady."

That was something she would need Rokshan's help with. Where was he, anyway?

She rounded the corner of the customs house to the left and stopped, astonished. The changes here were even grander than putting paint on the walls. The poles holding up the counting floor roof were gone, replaced by tall stone piles faced with some hard, smooth substance that smelled bitter. The new roof, much more shallowly peaked than its neighbor's, rose well above Lamprophyre's head and cast a dark shadow over the interior. The flat granite stones paving the floor hadn't changed, though they'd been scrubbed clean, and walls half the height of the stone piles isolated about a third of the space. Lamprophyre crossed to the first wall and peered over. Several flat horizontal surfaces sized for humans filled the walled enclosure, along with a long, shallow trough Lamprophyre couldn't see a use for.

"That is the kitchen, my lady ambassador," Mekel said. "Your servants will prepare your meals there."

"I see," Lamprophyre said. "I've never seen a kitchen before. Is there a human name for a room where someone eats?"

"This would be a dining pavilion, my lady."

"Dining pavilion." It sounded so grand.

"If you're satisfied, my lady," Mekel said, "I'm afraid I must leave you. Other responsibilities, you understand."

"Of course." Lamprophyre returned his bow and controlled a laugh at how Mekel preened inwardly at receiving her respect. She watched him walk away, passing humans who stared at him as if he and not Lamprophyre were the exotic stranger.

The dining pavilion opened on the empty circle in front of the customs house, and Lamprophyre settled herself on the stones and imagined what it would be like to eat there. Humans had once more gathered at the mouth of the street, now staring at her. They would stare even more at her eating habits, she was sure.

She listened idly to their thoughts and was surprised to hear an ugly, dark tone to them. Though there were too many minds for her to make out any one clearly, she caught snatches of words: *vicious* and *intruder* and *fire*, the last one repeated from mind to mind as if it were contagious. She left the dining pavilion and walked toward the crowd. "Hello," she said.

Fear surged, and the watching humans backed away. "You don't have anything to fear from me," she added, smiling for reassurance. She hoped. But the noise of their tangled thoughts built until she stopped, swaying with confusion, and blocked them all. A murmur, this one audible to her ears and not her mind, rose above the normal background sound of the city. And the crowd broke and ran, cries of panic threading through the murmur.

"Stop!" Lamprophyre exclaimed, taking a few steps after the fleeing humans before coming to her senses. It made no sense. She hadn't done anything but say hello, and they'd clearly been terrified of her. Her chest ached with sorrow and embarrassment and a little anger. Stupid humans being afraid of someone just because she was big and indestructible and could breathe fire. It wasn't as if she'd done the last within the city. All right, a few times, but just to cook meat, and no one had seen that.

She entered the embassy—how easily she'd come to think of it that way—and flopped down in the center, curling up with her wings spread over herself for comfort. If humans couldn't learn not to fear her, there was no point in remaining in Tanajital. Except there was, because she'd promised Hyaloclast she'd find the egg thieves. How could she do that if every human she met ran screaming?

She went over the humans she'd met who *hadn't* fled from her. The king, Ekanath. Rokshan's sisters Tekentriya and Manishi. Akarshan—she probably wouldn't see him again, since the palace kitchens would no longer provide her food. Some of Akarshan's associates. Mekel. General Sajan. And Sabarna. It was a tiny handful of people, all of whom had reason to understand she wasn't dangerous. She couldn't exactly introduce herself personally to every human in Tanajital.

Someone outside called her name, and she lifted her head to see Rokshan run through the entrance. "Are you all right?" he said. "The streets have gone mad. It's not a riot, but I sent word to Sajan to be prepared to keep the peace."

"It's all my fault," Lamprophyre muttered. "I didn't even do anything, but they were afraid anyway."

"It's not your fault, it's this." Rokshan waved a thin sheet of something pale cream that fluttered like a giant leaf. "I can't believe it. It's pure stupidity—criminal stupidity, if it starts a riot and gets people killed."

"I don't understand. How can a leaf do that?"

"This is paper, Lamprophyre. We write on it, or print on it." He held it still so she could see the curving and straight lines of writing on both sides. "This is a handbill—that just means a short piece of writing to be handed out in the street. It's full of...I shouldn't tell you, it will make you angry."

Lamprophyre sat up. "Now you *have* to tell me."

Rokshan sighed. "Leaving out the details, it's a bunch of lies about dragons and you in particular. How you're here to investigate the city so the rest of the dragons can attack it and kill all the people. How dragons only pretend to be friendly so they can lull humans into complacency and make them easier to kill."

Infuriated, Lamprophyre rose to her full height and snapped her wings open. "That's ridiculous! Why would anyone believe that?"

"Because humans are afraid of things they don't understand. So much in this world is dangerous to us, it's safer to assume anything new is a threat." Rokshan crumpled the handbill and dropped it on the floor. "What matters more is that someone went to the trouble of spreading these rumors, and I would like to know who. And why they did it."

Lamprophyre realized she was towering over Rokshan and settled back down, furling her wings. "So would I. Why would anyone care about making humans afraid of dragons?"

"Someone who doesn't want Gonjiri to make common cause with them," Rokshan said. "Like those disaffected Gonjirians we thought might exist. Or Fanishkor."

"You said tensions were high between your country and theirs."

"Yes, and Fanishkor might be afraid of Gonjiri negotiating an agreement with the dragons that would have dragons attacking Fanishkor on Gonjiri's behalf."

"We wouldn't do that. We aren't interested in getting involved in human wars."

"Fanishkor wouldn't believe that. King Damen is paranoid and suspicious and believes everyone thinks the way he does. I'll wager he's kicking himself right now that he didn't think to approach dragons first."

"Wait. Just—wait." Lamprophyre lowered her head until it was even with Rokshan's. "If Fanishkor is worried about Gonjiri having dragons on their side, wouldn't they want to make us angry with Gonjiri so we wouldn't join you?"

"You mean they could be the egg thieves? But those were definitely Gonjirian bandits." Rokshan closed his eyes and said that unfamiliar curt word. "Who might have been disguised to look that way, to fool us. And you."

"We don't know the difference between human kingdoms, so that ruse wouldn't have mattered," Lamprophyre said, "except that we would have assumed the egg thieves and the humans moving into our territory came from the same place. So it would have worked if not for you insisting on helping me."

"And if you hadn't been willing to stand up to Hyaloclast so she'd listen to my proposal," Rokshan said.

Lamprophyre shivered despite the heat. "I don't think your father realizes how close he came to having Tanajital razed by dragon fire."

"It's even more frightening to think it's still a possibility," Rokshan said. "What would Hyaloclast do if you were attacked by humans?"

"They can't hurt me."

"I know, but attacking you is aggression against dragons. How would Hyaloclast respond?"

"I suppose I would go home and tell her, and she would probably evict the humans from dragon territory and forbid dragons to go anywhere near human lands." The thought of never seeing Rokshan again sent a pang of sorrow through her chest.

"Well, if the people of Tanajital attacked the Fanishkorite embassy, it would be an excuse for Fanishkor to go to war against us. Whoever spread these rumors probably thinks dragons would behave the same. That humans attacking you would bring dragons down on the city."

Lamprophyre shook her head. "I'm not that important. If they attacked *Hyaloclast*, maybe, but not me. But what matters is what those humans believe."

"Right." Rokshan started pacing in front of the door. "We can't let them succeed. There has to be some way to show people the truth so they don't believe the lies."

"What can I do to prove I'm not violent? Since the fact that I haven't attacked *anyone* in the half-dozen days I've been here isn't enough."

Rokshan stopped to look her up and down, then resumed pacing. "You've been isolated for all that time, which in hindsight was a bad idea. It let people build up a monster in their minds because they never saw the real thing. I think you need to show yourself, and I think you need allies. People to interact with you to show you're not dangerous."

"I don't know how to get that. I know practically no one in the city, and half the people I know are members of the royal family and have better things to do with their time than talk to strange commoners."

"You leave that to me," Rokshan said. "For now, let's fly."

CHAPTER EIGHTEEN

amprophyre peered at the paper in Rokshan's hand. The clear light filling the embassy made the marks stand out against the creamy background. "I wish I could read," she said. "What do the marks mean?"

"It's an invitation," Rokshan said. "The front side says Tanajital is invited to meet the dragon ambassador at her embassy tonight. It's short notice for a diplomatic gathering, but this gives our enemy no time to plan a counterattack. And it's not a typical diplomatic gathering, either. Those are for nobles and foreign dignitaries."

"What is on the back side?"

"Things about you that are interesting. Who your mother is. Where you're from. Anything I could think of that made you sound like an ordinary person with ordinary interests. Insofar as that's possible." Rokshan folded the paper and tucked it inside his shirt. "And I've spent the last two days having my own handbills spread throughout the city. One of them counters, point by point, the one our enemy produced. The other is a poem I found in the palace archives—"

"Humans compose poems?"

"Yes—I take it so do dragons?"

"I love poetry. I know hundreds of poems and I'm very good at recitation."

Rokshan grimaced. "I wish I'd known that, it could have gone on the invitation. Also, I want—no, there's no time now. At any rate, I found a poem about dragons written by a human some three hundred years ago. It's not very accurate, because the woman lived in a time when we all thought dragons were dead and she'd never seen one, but it's very complimentary. I hope it reminds people that we weren't always afraid of you."

"That's interesting. Can I hear the poem?"

"I didn't memorize it, but I'll bring you a copy."

Movement by the embassy door drew Lamprophyre's attention. She sat up as a human male entered. His thoughts showed no fear of her, which surprised her; she hadn't stayed hidden in the embassy for the last two days, had made herself as visible as she could by flying over the city, but she hadn't approached any humans either. Being feared and shunned hurt her feelings.

Rokshan strode across the floor to greet the newcomer. "You got my message."

"All three of them," the male said. "Did you think I'd forgotten how to read, or were you just afraid your incentives weren't enough?"

Rokshan laughed and clapped the male on his shoulder. The male was a little taller than Rokshan and broader in the shoulders, and his hair was a lighter brown than Lamprophyre had yet seen on a human. "Come and meet the dragon ambassador," Rokshan said. "Lamprophyre, this is my friend Dharan. Dharan, this is Lamprophyre."

Lamprophyre sat up straight and examined this male Rokshan had called the most brilliant mind of his generation. He looked like any other human male, though his clothes were more colorful than Rokshan's. If he was intelligent, it didn't show on the outside any more than a dragon's intelligence did.

Dharan gazed at Lamprophyre curiously. "Already I can see how our stories are wrong," he said. "The pictures show you as much, much bigger, with scales the size of a human hand. And no records indicate how brightly colored you are. Or are you unique among dragons?"

"I'm not full-sized—I'll add another half dozen handspans to my length in the next fifteen years," Lamprophyre said. "And all dragons have some bright color about them. Even Hyaloclast, our queen, isn't pure black."

"Astonishing," Dharan said. "Rokshan said dragons don't have a written language. Do you know why not?"

Lamprophyre shook her head. "It could be that we live long enough, and have memories good enough, that we don't need to write things down to remember them. Though we have art—we draw on our cave walls, and in places in the heights, and we carve sculptures."

Dharan let out a quiet groan and ran his fingers through his hair. "Dragon art. I have to see it."

"We don't want humans in our homes, sorry. I suppose I could draw for you, but I'm not an outstanding artist."

"That would be nice. But I understand you want to learn to read and write?"

"And share stories," Rokshan said.

"I would, yes," Lamprophyre said. "It's such an interesting concept, that lines and curves could mean something other than pictures."

Dharan glared at Rokshan. "You waited three days before sending word. I have to question whether our friendship means anything to you."

Lamprophyre drew in a breath to protest, but Rokshan laughed and slapped Dharan on the back. "It was a busy three days. Lamprophyre, would you mind letting Dharan fly with you?"

"I don't mind." That wasn't entirely true. Dharan wasn't her friend yet, and flying with Rokshan felt like an extension of their friendship in a very personal way. Still, she could be polite.

But Dharan was shaking his head. "Don't be offended, Lamprophyre, but I'm terrible with heights," he said. "I get dizzy at the top of stairs. Flying—that sounds like a nightmare."

"It's perfectly safe, but I understand," Lamprophyre said.

"Your loss," Rokshan said. "Do you want to take rooms at the palace?"

Dharan shook his head again. "Not if Anchala is living there," he said. "I realize she's your sister, but she's convinced I'm her true love and no amount of reasoning can change her mind."

"Yet another one of your many conquests. How many women has your mother dangled in front of you this year?"

"Too many." Dharan glanced at Lamprophyre. "Is it true dragons mate for life?"

Lamprophyre had had trouble following their conversation, so she jumped on this uncomplicated question gratefully. "We are pair-bonded for life, yes."

"Did you leave your mate behind when you came to Gonjiri?"

Lamprophyre laughed. "No, I'm young enough nobody expects me to choose a partner for a few more years. I hope by then I'll be attracted to someone in the flight. They're all friends, but I don't feel interested in any of the available males."

Dharan nodded. "I'm in exactly your position, except my mother thinks I'm past old enough to marry. I'm only twenty-six, for Jiwanyil's sake!"

"So you could, um, marry, but you don't want to?"

"Dharan is waiting for the perfect woman," Rokshan said. "Intelligent, beautiful, well-spoken, and strong-willed enough to stand up to his mother. I keep telling him he's expecting a miracle, but he's stubborn."

"As if your mother doesn't despair of you ever settling down," Dharan said. "Let's go to the Hidden Ivy and get me a room, and then I'd love to talk more with you, Lamprophyre. It will give me a sense of how to teach you."

"I'd like that," Lamprophyre said. "Will there be enough time before the reception?"

"I have people coming to prepare food late this afternoon," Rokshan said, "and more people to hang lights and do other things to make the embassy even more attractive. But you don't have to worry about that."

"People—that sounds like many servants. Do I have enough coin?"

"Don't worry about that, either."

Lamprophyre put her head low enough to stare Rokshan in the face. He returned her regard placidly. "That makes me worried. I know we already used some of Manishi's coin to hire the humans who keep the embassy clean and cook my food, but it must take a lot of food if we plan to feed all of Tanajital. Where did I get more coin?"

"It's all right, Lamprophyre. You borrowed money from me." Rokshan gripped her hand briefly. "We'll have to make another flight to the mountains, that's all. I promise not to be an importunate lender."

Lamprophyre felt skeptical of this. She knew enough about how humans felt about coin to be certain loaning it out to others was a sensitive subject. But she also knew Rokshan well enough to recognize when arguing with him was pointless. "Tomorrow night," she said. "Maybe there will be garnet available."

"Garnet?" Dharan said.

"I'll explain as we go," Rokshan said. "Try and rest, Lamprophyre. It's going to be a long, busy night."

When the two males were gone, Lamprophyre settled comfortably on the earth floor and rested her head on her arms. She wasn't at all certain Rokshan's plan would work. On the other hand, it wasn't as if she had any other options. If she wanted humans to like her, she had to prove she was likeable. Even her servants were nervous around her, though none of them were outright afraid. She hoped with time that would change.

She also worried about the hidden enemy behind the stolen egg. Everything she and Rokshan had discussed made sense, but it was still all guesswork. She had no proof. Hyaloclast might accept guesswork, but Lamprophyre wanted to be sure, if dragons were going to attack someone, that it was the right someone. And she didn't know how to turn guesswork into proof, short of listening to the thoughts of everyone who might have been involved and hoping one of them would incriminate herself.

Lamprophyre sighed, sending up a puff of smoke, and closed her eyes. Time enough to worry about that when she wasn't at odds with everyone in Tanajital. She hoped Rokshan's efforts would matter.

CHAPTER NINETEEN

Lamprophyre sat on her haunches in the circle outside the embassy, what Rokshan had called a courtyard, and stared in amazement. Thousands of tiny lights like stars fallen to earth winked at her, outlining the steep blue roof and the walls. More lights sparkled around the dining pavilion, winding around the pillars and dangling from the roof. When it was full dark, the effect would be even more amazing.

Servants were putting up lanterns as well, flanking the entrance and attached to the pavilion to shed a warm, bright glow over the colorful walls. In the lantern light, the walls were more yellow than white, and the blue paint took on a greenish tinge, but the embassy was still beautiful in that alien, human way. The smells of roasted meat and fresh green things emanated from the pavilion, which was now full of tables—those were the odd horizontal surfaces she'd seen in her kitchen. Flat stones contained piles of food, all of it human food, hopefully appetizing. More servants bustled back and forth from the kitchen carrying those flat, thin stones or large sheets of metal, all of which smelled of food.

She stepped closer to the pavilion and gingerly touched one of the twinkling lights. It didn't fall down or go out. Looking closer, she realized it was tied to a thin string that was invisible in the twilight. Staring at the light gave her a headache, even as small as the thing was, so she turned her back on it and surveyed the street. It was empty. Lamprophyre had grown accustomed to humans filling the street, their thoughts angry or afraid, and she didn't know what to make of this new development, whether it was good or bad. Though if it was time for the event to begin and no one was here, that suggested bad.

She sighed, and settled herself where she could watch the street. Maybe if she hid...but no, the point of this was for her to meet people and prove how harmless she was, and if humans only came because they wouldn't have to encounter her, what a waste. Even so, she felt stupid sitting here like a deer waiting to be picked off by a hunting dragon.

Something moved in the street. Lamprophyre sat up. A handful of human males emerged, walking slowly in her direction. They had longish, unkempt hair, and she caught a whiff of their body odor, stronger than usual. She politely refrained from pinching her nose shut and said, when they were close enough, "Welcome. I'm Lamprophyre. Would you like something to eat?"

Their minds were full of fear-tinged awe, of images of her much larger than she actually was, but overlaying that was a terrible gnawing hunger, as if they hadn't eaten all day. Curious, Lamprophyre stepped closer to them. "You came for the food, didn't you?" she said, disappointment filling her. Well, it was a start, though it worried her that anyone could be so hungry it overcame fear. Maybe they didn't have coin for food, but she couldn't imagine that was true.

"It said, the dragon says come and see and eat," one of the men said. His voice was gruff and he wouldn't meet her eyes. The other two were silent. Unexpected compassion filled Lamprophyre, and she decided she didn't care if their motives were mercenary.

"Please have something to eat, and I'd like to talk to you while you do," she said.

The three men walked with some hesitation into the dining pavilion and collected food off some of the metal sheets. One of the servants emerged from the kitchen, saw the men, and hurried toward them, her thoughts angry. "You get on out of here," she said, setting her stone slab on a table and gesturing in a shooing manner. "This isn't for the likes of you."

"What are they like?" Lamprophyre asked.

The servant paused in her shooing to look at Lamprophyre. "No better than beggars, they are," she said. "You shouldn't mingle with them, my lady ambassador."

"They're hungry," Lamprophyre said, "and we have all this food. And it looks like no one is coming. So why shouldn't we share with them?"

The men stared at her, their thoughts confused. One of them had his mouth full as if he was afraid someone would try to take the food from him if he didn't gobble it. "I want to know more about Tanajital, and I don't know what beggars are, so they can eat and tell me about themselves," Lamprophyre added. "Please come over here while you eat."

The men hesitated again. Then the one with his mouth full walked to where Lamprophyre sat and swallowed quickly. "You don't want to eat us?" he said.

"Of course not! That's disgusting. Who told you that?"

He glanced at his friends. "Offer food so we'll come near enough for you to snatch. Dragons hunt their prey, right?"

"Yes, but we don't eat people. How horrible." Lamprophyre gestured to the others. "What are beggars? Is that a kind of work?"

The man's confusion deepened. "Don't know beggars?"

"I don't know much about humans, even though Rokshan has answered all my questions. But sometimes I don't know what to ask."

The man took another, smaller bite of his food and chewed it thoroughly before swallowing. His thoughts said *is it playing with us? God's breath, I haven't had anything this good in years, like to die of satisfaction, but at least I'd die full.* "Beggars beg," he said. "Can't find regular work, so we ask money of those who can."

"Oh. So people give you coin for nothing?"

The man nodded. His friends drifted closer, intent on the conversation.

"That seems very nice of them. But you seem—forgive me, but I can see you're hungry, as if you haven't eaten for a while. Do they not give you enough coin for food?"

The man made the noncommittal jerking motion with his shoulders. "Sometimes. Sometimes not."

It seemed to Lamprophyre a very uncertain way to make a living. "Why can't you find regular work? Or is that a rude question?"

Now the man's thoughts were embarrassed. He said, "I get sick, can't get out of bed, and they won't pay me for that. So I can't keep a job. Same as them." He indicated his two friends with a jab of his thumb. One of the others was staring at her with his mouth open, thinking *never thought I'd see such a beast up close,* but he meant nothing cruel by "beast," so she let it go.

"I'm sorry," she said. "That seems very hard." Then, startled, she looked past the men and saw more humans approaching, all of them filled with curiosity rather than fear, with Rokshan at their head. "Please excuse me," she said. "But eat as much as you want, and I would like to speak with you again before you leave."

She walked toward the crowd, who slowed at her approach. "Thank you for coming," she said. "Please have something to eat, and I'd like to talk to anyone who's willing. I want to know more about you."

Rokshan came to her side as the rest of the humans passed into the dining pavilion. "I'm afraid most of them are here for the food," he murmured. "But it's a start."

"I know," she said. "I need some of my coin."

"Right now? Why?"

"Because I want to give it to those males." She indicated the three beggars, who had withdrawn to the far side of the courtyard and alternated taking bites of food with staring at her.

Rokshan followed her gesture. "Beggars," he said. "I should have considered. Lamprophyre, you shouldn't give money to everyone who asks."

"They didn't ask. They told me about what begging means and that they can't do regular work. I want to help."

"Yes, but where does that end? You can't afford to support every beggar in Tanajital."

Lamprophyre blew out an impatient puff of smoke. "I don't think helping three males means I have to do the same for everyone. I know what they were thinking, and they were only brave enough to face me because they were starving. Starving enough that they didn't care I might try to eat them. I think that's deserving of something. And it's my coin to give."

"They're taking advantage of you. You don't know if they were telling the truth. Suppose they're just lazy?"

Lamprophyre glared at Rokshan. "Of course I know they were telling the truth, Rokshan. They felt so embarrassed about not being able to work. I can't fix that, but I can help for now."

Rokshan looked at the beggars again. "I guess you would know," he said. "Let me talk to them, and you go greet your guests. We'll figure out something." He laughed. "I didn't realize how cynical I'd become. You're a good influence."

Lamprophyre blushed faintly purple. "I don't like seeing people go hungry, that's all."

"That makes you a better person than half of Tanajital. Go. Talk. Be friendly." He walked away toward the beggars.

Lamprophyre took a few steps toward the dining pavilion. More people were approaching from the street, enough that their thoughts were a tangled mass impossible to interpret. She blocked them out and faced them with a smile. "I'm Lamprophyre," she said. "Welcome to my home."

Most people arrived, took food, and left again without saying a word to her. Lamprophyre tried not to feel discouraged by this. She focused her efforts on the ones who were willing to talk. Most of them had questions she answered as best she could. She didn't react angrily at the questions about whether she meant to eat humans or burn Tanajital to the ground. If she were to be angry at anyone over those questions, it should be the unknown enemy who'd planted those thoughts in the people's heads with his horrible papers.

"I always thought humans were born from eggs," she told one female who held a small child in her arms. "That's how dragons are born. How does it work for humans?"

The female's skin reddened the way Rokshan's did when he was embarrassed. "I, uh, it's complicated," she said. "Babies grow inside their mother's body."

Lamprophyre's mouth fell open. "*Inside?* How do you get them out? Do you expel them the way dragons do their eggs?"

"Well..."

Lamprophyre realized she'd stumbled on a taboo topic, or at least not one for polite conversation in public between strangers. How she wished she could listen to this female's thoughts without being overwhelmed by those of everyone around her. "Never mind, I'll ask Rokshan," she said. "I'm sorry, I didn't realize it was an embarrassing question."

"Thank you," the female said, sounding relieved. "You said dragons hatch from eggs? How many eggs does a dragon lay at one time?"

"Only one. And she won't lay another egg until the first dragonet is at least thirty, so she can give her child her full attention. I've heard humans are the same, though you mature faster than we do."

"Excuse me, my lady ambassador," another female said, "but I heard you are sixty years old and that makes you barely an adult. Why were you chosen as ambassador? Humans wouldn't give that responsibility to someone only sixteen."

She could hardly tell them what Hyaloclast had instructed her to do. "The dragon queen gave me the assignment because Rokshan is my friend, and he and I work well together. And I care about humans and dragons living together in harmony."

"That doesn't match with what we've been hearing from the frontier," a male with thick gray hair on his chin said. "Humans herded into camps, forbidden to spread out...that sounds more like dragons want to see humans subservient. That's why the Army is there, to protect them."

"I don't know what's going on in dragon territory," Lamprophyre said, "but I'm sure it's more complicated than that. Think about what humans would want if our positions were reversed. If dragons wanted to settle in Gonjiri, wouldn't you want there to be rules about where they could go to hunt, or where they could live? I know Hyaloclast said humans would be restricted to certain areas, but I doubt they're being herded like animals."

To her surprise, the man nodded like he agreed with her. In relief, Lamprophyre added, "I hope someday humans and dragons will live closer together, as they did centuries ago. We each have so much to offer each other."

"Like what?" the male said.

"Oh." Lamprophyre's mind momentarily blanked. "Knowledge about the world. I've only just learned how humans use stone for magic—that's not something dragons do. History, because humans have lost some of that information since the Great Cataclysm. Humans have writing, which dragons don't, which means you have records that outlast your short lives. I want to learn to read so I can learn from those records. Art and poetry."

"What is dragon poetry like?" the female with the child said.

"I don't know how it compares to human poetry," Lamprophyre said, "because I still haven't heard any. Our poetry has changed many times over the years as people come up with new ideas and techniques. This is one of my favorites." She cleared her throat and said:

"The new moon cradled in the old moon's arms

Turns the snow blue
And the stone gray
While the hidden sun behind the earth warms
The lands no dragon has ever flown above.
The snow melts
And the stone wears
But our Mother is forever, and her love
Lives in the snow and the endless stone
And in the voice that finally calls us home."

The stillness that followed her words told her everyone had stopped talking to listen. Embarrassed, she said, "It's an old poem about Mother Stone. You call her Nirinatan. When a dragon is too old or too sick to take care of herself, she flies up to the highest slopes of Mother Stone, and her bones return to the mountain."

"That's beautiful," the female with the child said.

"Thank you." Lamprophyre wished everyone would stop staring at her. She cleared her throat again and said, "Has everyone had enough to eat? Please, help yourselves."

She ducked into the embassy for a moment's peace and found Rokshan there, talking to Dharan. She hadn't seen Dharan arrive, and said, "It's good to see you, Dharan."

"I hope you don't mind that I hid in here," Dharan said. "I don't really like crowds."

"For all you're good at conversation," Rokshan said. "I think things are going well, Lamprophyre. No one's fled in terror or tried to attack you, and you seem to be getting along well with your guests."

"It's actually fun," Lamprophyre said. "Humans are interesting, or at least they are when you know nothing about them so every question is new."

Dharan chuckled. "That's wisdom. Lamprophyre, why don't I meet with you tomorrow morning? We can start reading lessons, and you can come up with more questions about humanity."

"I'd like that," Lamprophyre said.

Dharan and Rokshan clasped each other's wrists. "In the morning, then," Dharan said. "Rokshan, supper tomorrow?"

"What, I can't be part of the reading lessons?"

"Not unless you've spontaneously developed patience and tact." Dharan waved at Lamprophyre and left the embassy.

"You can come if you want," Lamprophyre said.

"No, he's right, I'd just be impatient," Rokshan said. "Let's go out and see if anyone else has arrived. And I haven't had anything to eat yet."

"Neither have I," Lamprophyre said, "but it might scare people if I tear into half a cow in public."

"You have the makings of a wise diplomat," Rokshan said with a smile.

CHAPTER TWENTY

The full moon cast its bright light over the courtyard and the roofs of the embassy and the many, many humans filling the space. It couldn't be all of Tanajital, but enough people had arrived that Lamprophyre felt satisfied at the success of Rokshan's plan. She sat outside the embassy door and smiled at people, but it seemed no one was interested in conversation at the moment. That satisfied her, too. She could understand Dharan's disinclination to be crowded.

She heard, over the noise of the people, distant music, though not from human voices. And yet it was clearly music, a sequence of high-pitched notes repeated every couple of beats. She stood and looked off down the street, which still had a few humans wandering in her direction. All of them were too close to be the source of the music.

"Do you hear that?" she asked Rokshan.

Rokshan bit into a chunk of meat threaded onto a stick. "Hear what?"

"Music."

"Lamprophyre, I'm lucky I can hear *you* over this din. What music?"

Lamprophyre hummed the passage of notes. Rokshan fell still. Then he said a handful of words she didn't know. "That's the last thing I expect-ed," he added. "This could ruin everything."

"Who is it?" Lamprophyre asked, alarmed.

"The ecclesiasts," Rokshan said. "My brother Khadar, to be specific.

That's the Song of the Fifth Ecclesiast, which is Khadar's rank. Wonderful." He spoke with such bitterness Lamprophyre's disquiet grew.

"Why are you so upset?" she asked. "Let me guess. You don't get along with Khadar, either."

"I don't, but that's not why I'm upset," Rokshan said. "Khadar will make this evening all about him. I'll wager he intends to make a huge production out of welcoming you to Tanajital, even though you've been here a week and the ecclesiasts haven't bothered to notice you in all that time. He'll have all sorts of questions for you that you won't be able to answer, and he'll turn that into denigrating you and all dragons as less than humans."

"How do you know all that?"

"Because I know how he thinks. He's always jockeying for position and power. I don't know why he was chosen as Fifth Ecclesiast, since I doubt he really cares about religion. All the other High Ecclesiasts are nothing like him." He gripped Lamprophyre's hand. "Look, you need to be really alert now, all right? Keep him answering your questions so he can't ask any of his own, and let me do as much of the talking as possible."

"All right, but I'm not sure why it matters."

"It matters," Rokshan said, "because you have an audience in all these people, all of whom will be overwhelmed by his magnificence enough that they'll let him shape their opinions. It could destroy all the good work you've done tonight. If you and I can keep him off balance, everything will be fine."

Lamprophyre clasped Rokshan's hand in return. "All right, but I'm nervous."

"Just be yourself and ask a million questions, and you'll be fine." Rokshan released her and walked across the courtyard to stand at the end of the street, watching.

Lamprophyre paced from one side of the courtyard to the other until she realized her nerves were getting the better of her, and stopped. She wondered if humans had nervous gestures too, and what they might be. Too bad Dharan couldn't give her lessons in interpreting human body language as well as interpreting those written marks.

She spoke to a few people, distractedly, until the music was loud enough that even the humans could hear it. One by one, the conversations ceased, and each human turned to face where the street ended at the courtyard. Now Lamprophyre could hear other voices in harmony with the high-pitched notes—except they didn't sound like voices, not even human ones. They sounded more like the wind chasing through hollow reeds, or birds whistling, or the low O sound of air rushing across a hollow stump. She watched the street, too curious now to be nervous, until the first humans came into view.

At first, they were too distant and too close together to be more than a mass of moving yellow, lit by torches. Then they neared, and Lamprophyre could distinguish six humans, all of them dressed in yellow robes that obscured their figures, all of them with a peculiar short haircut she'd never seen before, like an upside-down bowl. Granted, there were many human grooming fashions she was unfamiliar with, but the fact that all of them wore their hair the same way suggested that this was a religious thing.

Behind the six robed humans came two—no, four very large males bearing the same kind of cage King Ekanath had been conveyed in. These were dressed in robes like the others, but white instead of yellow and gathered at the waist by a red cord. The smell of human sweat drifted to Lamprophyre's nose, making her wonder how heavy the cage was that carrying it was such an exertion.

The cage, unlike the king's, had fluttering green fabric hanging down on all sides, obscuring its contents. Lamprophyre stood at her full height to look beyond it. More yellow-robed humans with the same bowl-shaped haircut walked behind the cage. They all held sticks of varying lengths to their lips and appeared to be blowing into them. She realized that was the source of the music—hollow sticks or reeds, not voices or birds. Humans were so clever to adapt a natural phenomenon to make music. It was something she needed to tell the flight about, because there was no reason dragons might not do the same.

When the first six humans reached the end of the street, they spread out around the courtyard, their torches adding to the light but dimming the brightness of the twinkling stars. Irritation took the place of Lamprophyre's nervousness. Whoever they were, they had some nerve distracting her guests from the beautiful display Rokshan had arranged.

The males carrying the cage walked past the robed figures into the center of the courtyard and set the cage down on its legs. The music-making humans came to a halt just where the street met the courtyard, and the music swelled until it was impossible to hear speech over it, if anyone had been talking. Lamprophyre waited, watching the cage. The music built to a magnificent crescendo, then cut off mid-phrase—or at least what a dragon would consider incomplete.

The green fabric twitched, and a human male emerged. His hair was cut in a more familiar fashion, much like Rokshan's, and he wore a long green robe that shone with gold and silver threads over black shirt and trousers. The thread made pictures, but the only one Lamprophyre recognized was a tree like the ones beside the river, with drooping branches. The male shook out his robe and advanced on Lamprophyre, taking slow, measured steps that in a dragon would indicate a willingness to fight.

When he was less than half a dragonlength from her, he opened his mouth—and Lamprophyre said, "Welcome! It's Khadar, isn't it? Rokshan mentioned you. I'm sorry if I don't address you properly, but I don't know much about human religion. Thank you for coming!"

Khadar shut his mouth and blinked at her. He smelled strongly of flowers, not one type of flower but a whole field of mingled blossoms, mixed with a sharp, pungent scent as if those flowers were on fire. Lamprophyre's nose tickled, and she held her breath, wishing she dared pinch her nose shut—but that was one gesture she'd learned was offensive to both humans and dragons. Finally, Khadar opened his mouth and got as far as, "Oh, great Katayan's child—"

"I'm sorry to correct you, it's very rude in dragon culture to correct someone, but I feel it's important to let you know there's no such person as Katayan," Lamprophyre said. "Dragons worship Mother Stone. Maybe you and I could discuss our religious faiths sometime." This was fun.

"No Katayan—" Khadar once again stopped mid-sentence. Lamprophyre risked listening to his thoughts and caught only a fragment, *challenge me on my faith, monster*, before the rest of the crowd drowned him out with their mingled excitement, awe, and residual fear and she had to block them again.

"My lady ambassador," Khadar finally said, "on behalf of the Archprelate of Gonjiri, I welcome you to Tanajital." He took a few steps closer, bringing his terrible scent with him. She wished he smelled of stale sweat like the cage carriers instead. "Legend falls far short of the truth."

"That's very kind," Lamprophyre said, overriding him before he could go into more detail. The itching had become painful, and her nictitating membranes slid shut involuntarily, blurring Khadar's form. "Please, have something to eat, and I'd love to converse further." She took a step backward, hoping to escape the smell.

Khadar followed her. "We eat only food that has been prepared to the glory of Jiwanyil," he said, "but I would like to discuss our faith. Clearly you are in need of religious guidance."

"I'm sure Lamprophyre would be happy to teach you what dragons actually worship," Rokshan said, startling Lamprophyre; he was standing practically on her left flank, and a wrong step by her would have flattened him.

Khadar didn't stop chasing Lamprophyre, though he did turn his attention to Rokshan. "Good evening, little brother," he said, his voice smooth and bland. "I understand you're assigned to serve the ambassador. Fitting, don't you think?"

Lamprophyre could tell it was an insult, though it made no sense to her. She was walking practically blind now, circling the courtyard trying to get away from Khadar. "Rokshan and I work well together," she managed, breathing shallowly through her mouth, "and I...I...oh, *Stones.*"

With that expletive, the sneeze that had been building within her for the last several beats rolled down from between her eyes and through her nostrils and emerged in an explosive blast that echoed off the nearest buildings. Another sneeze, and another, rocked her on her tail. Nothing she did could contain them, and they gradually deepened until she felt she might sneeze her insides out.

As a final tremendous sneeze built within her, she felt to her horror the burning sensation that said more than a spray of liquid was coming. Unable to speak, she waved her arms wildly, hoping the humans would know to get out of the way, and then put her hands over her nose in a gesture she knew was futile. She drew in a deep breath, sneezed from the very depths of her soul, and expelled burning hot fluid in a cataclysmic jet. Most of it clung to her fingers, but some spurted past her hands to strike the green fabric of Khadar's cage.

The cage went up in flames.

CHAPTER TWENTY-ONE

S creams and hoarse exclamations rose from the watching crowd, and humans fled, shoving each other in their desperation to escape. "No, it's all right!" Lamprophyre shouted. She dove for the burning cage and tried to wrap her wings around the fire, but the cage's shape was awkward, and the more she snatched at the flames, the more they spread.

Khadar was shouting things she couldn't understand over the roar of the fire. Lamprophyre looked around for a solution and found nothing, no convenient stream, no bowl for catching rainfall, not even a container of soup that might drench the flames. She tried once more to stifle them, but halfheartedly, because she knew futility when she saw it.

"—uncontrolled, ravening *beast!*" she finally heard Khadar say. She couldn't bring herself to look at him. All that work wasted because she couldn't hold in a sneeze.

"Watch your mouth," Rokshan said in a low, harsh voice. "Lamprophyre is a person, not a beast, and it's your own damn fault she sneezed. Would it kill you not to bathe in that scent for once?"

"People don't breathe fire when they sneeze, Rokshan," Khadar snarled. "It's a dangerous creature, and I'm going to tell Father to have it expelled."

"Call her 'it' again, and one of us is going to need that litter to get home."

Lamprophyre turned to regard the brothers, who stood face to face with barely half a handspan between them. "I'm sorry," she said. "But it was an accident."

Khadar glanced at her before going back to glaring at Rokshan. "Was it?" he said. "Or was this your plan—gather the people together, lull them into security, and then attack?"

"God's breath, Khadar, are you really that stupid?" Rokshan shouted. "You've ruined everything we worked for, and you want that to be Lamprophyre's fault?"

"It's my duty to protect this city——"

Rokshan laughed bitterly. "Your duty. As if you cared about duty when you could live in luxury instead. When's the last time you delivered a prophecy?"

Lamprophyre focused on Khadar, listening to his thoughts now that he and his companions were the only ones in the courtyard. "You have no right to criticize me," Khadar said, and thought *even better than I'd planned, easy to get rid of it now.*

"Somebody has to," Rokshan began.

"Stop," Lamprophyre said in her deepest, most sonorous voice that wasn't a shout. She couldn't give away her ability to hear thoughts to Khadar, not when he was clearly her enemy. "Khadar, I don't know what you believe about dragons or why you came here tonight, but I want you to leave now. This is dragon territory and you don't belong here. What happened was an accident on both our parts, and among dragons, that would be enough for both parties to forgive. Clearly it's not like that with humans, but I'm not going to pretend you weren't partly responsible just because that's a human tradition."

She drew in a deep breath and regretted it when her nose began to tickle again. She pinched it shut, not caring how it looked, and said, "Rokshan, please don't attack your brother. Unless he won't leave, in which case I think you're entitled." She turned her back on both of them and trudged into the embassy.

She settled on the floor, curled around herself, and rested her head on her arms. Khadar wanted her gone and she didn't know why. More to the point, she didn't know if he was involved with the egg thieves. Fanishkor, disaffected Gonjirians, the ecclesiasts; it was too much to believe they were all part of a single conspiracy, but if they weren't, that meant she had more enemies than just the one. She sighed, wreathing her head in smoke. She should have kept Khadar there, kept him talking so she could hear his thoughts, but she was miserable and overwhelmed and not in the mood to do the rational thing.

She didn't hear the sounds of a fight breaking out, just shuffling and murmuring, and after a few dozen beats, Rokshan sat down beside her. "He's gone," he said. "Without a fight, unfortunately. I dearly wanted to punch his smug face."

"I know, but it wouldn't have helped anything." Lamprophyre let out another puff of smoke. "He wants me gone from Tanajital. Probably from Gonjiri entirely."

"You challenged his faith. Maybe that was inevitable."

"No, I mean he wanted me gone before I said anything. He was thinking how it would be easy to get rid of me, and how he'd had a plan to do it, but me setting random things on fire was even better."

"What plan?"

"I didn't hear that part, just that he had one. Could he be behind the egg thieves?"

Rokshan propped his chin in his hand. "I don't know. I don't think so. If he wants you gone, that's the opposite of wanting dragons to attack Gonjiri. He'd be more likely to be behind a plot to keep dragons away from us entirely."

"So I have a second enemy."

"I'm sorry."

"It's all right. Maybe this was too much to ask of Tanajital's people. I'm big and frightening and that's all some of them will ever see."

Rokshan put a hand on hers. "You were making progress with some of them. And eventually they'll realize that you didn't burn anything important and that you tried to put out the fire."

"Maybe." She sighed again. "I'm going to sleep now, and when I wake up, all this will have gone away."

"We can only hope," Rokshan said, and stood. "I'll come by around noon, after your lesson. I'll spend the morning trying to reverse some of the damage that idiot Khadar did. Did you hear anything else from his thoughts?"

"Just that he was very upset about me telling him his religious beliefs are false, some of them, anyway. That was a mistake. Nobody likes being challenged on things they hold dear."

"True. But it's not as if Khadar actually believes them. More likely he was angry because you indirectly challenged his power and prestige. The ecclesiasts can't afford having people doubt their teachings in one respect, because what's to stop them doubting everything else?" He waved, said "Good night," and was gone.

Lamprophyre tucked herself into a more comfortable position and closed her eyes. Things would look better in the morning, they usually did, but at the moment, it was hard to imagine how that could be true.

She dreamed of flying, as she often did, of soaring over the uplands and the mountain heights, though they were strangely warm instead of bitingly, beautifully cold. Then she was curled up in her cave, and birds were walking over her, chirping to each other in a language she almost understood. Straining to comprehend, she woke to find there *were* creatures climbing across her body, sliding down her back and tail and then clambering up her thigh to do it again.

She almost rose up and brushed herself free of the creatures when she realized she could understand their language and their thoughts. Human children, climbing on her as if she were made of stone. "I'm going to attack the dragon!" one of them shrieked.

"No, me!" said another.

Someone else's thoughts were incoherent laughter—that was the one sliding down her tail. She held her breath and remained as still as she could manage. One of the children was thumping her chest, an oddly pleasant feeling just short of a tickle. Then someone touched her wing membranes, and that really did tickle. She let out a gasp, and the children all screamed.

"Wait!" she cried out, but they were gone—no, one remained, lying on the floor and clutching his ankle. Lamprophyre rolled to a sitting position and examined the child. "Are you hurt?"

The child nodded. Water streamed down its face—tears, Lamprophyre had heard of tears, something creatures with no nictitating membranes did to protect their eyes. They also meant sadness or pain, she remembered. "You hurt your ankle?" she said.

The child nodded again. Its thoughts were a blur of pain and fear.

Sorrow struck Lamprophyre's heart, but she pushed it away and said, "Let me see."

She wasn't sure what she could do for the child, but to her surprise it sat up and extended its leg to her. Its ankle was so tiny. She gently felt along the bones and watched its face screw up in pain. "Did that hurt?"

The child paused, then shook its head. That was a gesture that meant the same whether you were dragon or human. Lamprophyre released it and said, "What were you children doing in here?"

The child hugged its knees to its chest. "Fight the dragon," it said. "Are you going to eat me?"

Again Lamprophyre reflected in exasperation on the human assumption that everything wanted to eat them. "Of course not," she said. "Why, are you delicious?"

The child giggled. "No!"

"Then obviously eating you would be stupid." Lamprophyre heard more thoughts approaching, filled with fear and determination and a couple of odd snatches of words: *fight him* and *save Rojital*. Pitching her voice to carry beyond the entrance, she said, "Your friends must be cowards, to leave you in my clutches. I didn't think humans abandoned their kind to save their own skins."

"I'm no coward!" shouted another child who darted through the entrance. "I'll fight you!" The child was followed by two others, all of whom took up aggressive stances, fists raised, legs akimbo. Lamprophyre regarded them with amusement.

"There, that's better," she said. "Now, which of you would like to fight me first?"

The fists lowered. The first child said, "We're not afraid of you!" but its voice lacked the confidence it had had moments before.

"I'm so glad," Lamprophyre said. "It seems everyone else is, and I haven't done anything to hurt anyone."

"You started the fire that tried to burn the Fifth Ecclesiast alive," one of the other children said.

Lamprophyre groaned inwardly. It didn't matter whether Khadar had started that rumor, or it had grown up spontaneously; either way, she now looked like she'd started a religious war. "That's not what happened—were you here to see it?"

The children shook their heads.

"Well, for the moment let's not talk about how foolish it is to make assumptions based on hearsay. I sneezed. A lot. The Fifth Ecclesiast has a really disgusting scent." The children giggled, and Lamprophyre smiled. "And sometimes when dragons sneeze, their second stomachs expel matter. Fire, or acid. I'm really embarrassed because I haven't set anything on fire with a sneeze since I was a dragonet. I accidentally sneezed on Khadar's carrying cage, and it caught fire. I tried to put it out, but I couldn't. And I feel terrible about it, mostly because I thought people were getting used to me and it frightened them. Haven't you ever done anything you wish you hadn't?"

The children exchanged glances. Then the one in the lead, the tallest of them, approached Lamprophyre. "So you wouldn't set things on fire on purpose?" it asked.

"Not to hurt anyone, no. I use my fire mostly to cook my meals. Isn't that how your parents do it? So you know fire doesn't have to hurt people."

The child nodded. "My name is Anamika. Do you have a name?"

"Of course. It's Lamprophyre."

"That's a really big name."

"I know. My mother liked the sound of it."

Anamika smiled. "Are there many dragons where you come from?"

Lamprophyre sat up, making Anamika's eyes go wide. "Very many. Not as many as there are humans in Tanajital."

One of the other children crouched beside the wounded one. "Oh, get up, you big baby, it's not that bad," the child said. The wounded one stood, wobbled a little, but got its balance. The child continued, "I'm Ohar. This is my brother Rojital. Anamika and her brother Varnak live next door to us."

"It's nice to meet you, Ohar. Do you live near here?"

Ohar pointed. "Right down the street. Very close."

Lamprophyre heard more thoughts, these much more agitated, and her heart sank. "Close enough that your parents might be looking for you?"

The children groaned. "Hide us!" Anamika urged. "We'll get in trouble if they find us!"

"Not as much trouble as I'll be in for hiding you," Lamprophyre said. "I guess you sneaked out when you were supposed to be sleeping, right?"

Ohar nodded. He picked up Rojital and said, "How do we get out of here?"

Now the thoughts were joined by footsteps, loud but tentative, and humans approached the embassy. Torches shed a warm orange light over the courtyard. "Let them go, monster!" someone shouted. "We'll burn this place to the ground if you don't!"

Lamprophyre sighed. "You realize there are children in here, right?" she shouted back. "You'll hurt them if you set the embassy on fire."

Anamika laughed. "That's right!" she called out. "That was a stupid thing to say."

"Anamika!" someone else said. "Anamika, are you all right? Is Varnak with you?"

"We're fine. Come in and meet the dragon," Anamika said.

Lamprophyre, alarmed, said, "Oh, Anamika, that's not a good—"

"Let them go, monster!" the first voice shouted.

"He's not a monster, he's a dragon, and he doesn't want to hurt anyone," Anamika said. "So you should come inside and say hello, because we're not coming out until you do."

"That is *not* my idea," Lamprophyre said, deciding not to address the issue of her sex. "Children, go to your parents."

"It's not fair that they all think you're a monster," Anamika said. "Or that they're blaming you for an accident. Besides, my mam says it would do the ecclesiasts good to walk on their own two feet as Jiwanyil intended, so I don't know why they're all so upset about his litter burning."

Lamprophyre drew a deep breath. "Anamika, Ohar, you—"

"Anamika?" someone said from the entrance. A human male stood there, his hand on the edge of the entrance. His gaze fell on Anamika, and he said, "You're well. Thank Jiwanyil. And Varnak—both of you come home this instant!"

"The dragon is friendly, Papa," Anamika said. "I forgot his name, because it's long, but he's nice and he wouldn't ever burn anything on purpose."

"My name is Lamprophyre," Lamprophyre said. "And I'm female."

Papa took a few steps into the embassy, looking like a deer creeping up on a pond that might contain predators. "Lamprophyre?" he said. "But you —that is, you look dangerous."

"I'm not. I haven't hurt these children, have I?" Lamprophyre gestured at the children. "I want humans and dragons to live together peacefully. And I don't understand why humans are so terrified of me. What kind of awful stories do you tell about us?"

"I don't know," Papa said. Behind him, two more human males appeared in the doorway. "You burned the Fifth Ecclesiast's litter."

"Not on purpose. Stones, haven't any of you humans sneezed before? It's not exactly a controllable reflex."

Anamika laughed. Papa's lips twitched in a smile. "I guess it's not," he said. "How uncomfortable that must be for you."

"Fire doesn't hurt me, so it's only uncomfortable and not worse," Lamprophyre said. "I was just telling your children they should go home. I hope you weren't too worried. They were just playing here."

"They're not getting away with this without punishment," Papa said. "Anything might have happened to them. It's good fortune nothing did."

"Well, I would never hurt them. Though I think Rojital landed wrong on his ankle when he was running. It doesn't seem broken, but you might look at it, just in case."

"We will." One of the other males came forward and took Rojital from Ohar. The child yawned and laid his head down on the male's shoulder.

"We can come back to play with the dragon, can't we, Papa?" Anamika said.

"Not any time soon. You're restricted to the house for the next three days," Papa said. He glanced at Lamprophyre, and added, "After that, we'll see."

"I'd love for them to visit again," Lamprophyre said. "Though I understand about punishment. I used to go storm flying as an adolescent, against my mother's command, and I was in so much trouble when she found out—but then I got older and realized how dangerous it was. So it was hard to stay angry when she only wanted to protect me."

Papa's eyes widened. "Yes, exactly. I didn't know—but of course you have a mother, everyone has a mother. I just didn't realize how similar we are."

Lamprophyre chose not to drive this point home. He'd already figured it out.

After the humans left, she settled back down in the quiet darkness of the embassy. Someone had removed the twinkling lights while she was asleep the first time, and the moon had set, making everything peaceful and soft-edged. She'd always liked the darkness, probably why she'd loved storm flying so much, and Tanajital at night was warm and comforting. Or maybe it was just having reclaimed her good name even to such a small extent. Sweet hopefulness carried her off into sleep again.

CHAPTER TWENTY-TWO

"In writing, we assign sounds to letters," Dharan said. "Some letters make more than one sound, which can make reading confusing. But for the most part, it's one letter, one sound." He picked up the long pointed stick he'd brought with him on a cart containing several mysterious objects and drew an elongated shape in the packed earth of the courtyard. "This letter represents the 'L' sound that begins your name. So when you write your name, this is the first letter you write. You try."

Lamprophyre accepted the stick and awkwardly drew the same elongated shape. "It's not very tidy," she said, trying again.

"Everyone's handwriting is terrible when they're just beginning," Dharan said. "Now I'll write your whole name, and we'll sound out the different letters." He took the stick and wrote a very long string of letters. Lamprophyre, dismayed, copied it as best she could. She'd never thought she'd envy Flint of the boring name, but his had to have fewer letters than hers.

"L, A, M, P," Dharan began.

Lamprophyre moved her lips, committing the symbols to memory. "Is this how you learned to read?"

"Me? No. To hear my parents tell it, I woke up one morning when I was three and asked the meaning of some word in a pamphlet my father had brought home. I have no memory of not being able to read." Dharan made that jerking motion with his shoulders. "But I've never had any success in teaching people to read the way I do, so I'm teaching you the regular way."

"I see. What does this mean?" Lamprophyre moved her shoulders up and down.

"A shrug? You don't ask simple questions, do you?" Dharan said. "Shrugging can mean several things. It can mean you don't know, or you're indifferent—that's if someone has asked for your opinion on two choices —or it can mean disdain for an issue. Just now, I meant it to indicate I didn't know exactly how I learned to read."

Lamprophyre shrugged again. Such a versatile gesture. "What are the other letters?"

"Where were we? R, O...um."

"Um? That's not a sound in my name."

"No, but your name has a complicated spelling. These two letters, when they're written together, make the F sound."

"But you said that one was P."

"It is, by itself. But together with this one, it's F."

Lamprophyre sat back on her haunches. "How do you know it isn't spelled with a F symbol? It's a dragon name!"

"It's also a human word. A lamprophyre is a kind of igneous rock, and this is how that word is spelled. Since you said dragons are named for stones, I'm certain this is how you should spell your name."

"But—" Lamprophyre hesitated. Dragons had given humans language, so the word was really a dragon one, not human. But humans had invented writing, so they were the ones who'd decided to give the rock she was named for a complicated, confusing sequence of letters. On a third hand, it would be impossible to learn to read human writing if she insisted on putting letters together the way they made sense to her. "All right. P and that other letter make the F sound. Why is that?"

"I can't explain that now. It's a long explanation and it would sidetrack this lesson. Better you concentrate on reading." He returned to pointing at her name. "This letter means more than one sound. In your name, it sounds like the word 'eye'. R again. And this one—God's breath, I should have started with 'cat' and 'run'—this one is the letter E, but in your name, it doesn't make its own sound, it's what makes the letter Y sound like 'eye'. I'm sorry it's confusing. Does it help to know you have a beautiful name?"

"I do?" Lamprophyre was startled into looking at Dharan. He had his attention on the letters.

"Yes. The sounds are a pleasing combination, and the letters look nice together. And in no time, this will all be natural to you, and you'll look back and be amazed there was a time when you couldn't read."

Lamprophyre traced the letters of her name again. "I look forward to that."

"All right. So your first assignment is to practice writing your name." He walked over to the cart and dragged a large, smooth piece of slate nearly half a dragonlength long and wide out of it with some effort. Lamprophyre took it from him and looked at it closely. It didn't look entirely natural, as it was missing the smooth ridges that showed where a slate was cut from the stone. She ran her palm over it and marveled at how even the surface was.

Dharan held out a cloth sack the size of her fist and withdrew a chunk of white chalk from it. "Do dragons use chalk in their art?"

"Sometimes. We prefer a more permanent medium. Sculpture, mostly."

"Well, the point of this is that it's impermanent. You'll do your writing practice on the slate using the chalk. Write until the slate is full, then clean it off and do it again." He took his own piece of chalk and wrote her name neatly at the top of the slate, then used a cloth to wipe away the letters. Lamprophyre set the slate down, propping it against the wall of the embassy, and accepted the cloth from him. So much tidier than using your hand.

Dharan wrote her name again. "That's for you to refer to. Don't erase that until you're comfortable writing your name. Now." He tugged on another large slate until Lamprophyre pulled it off the cart for him. "Thank you. I brought the biggest slates I could find and could barely manage them. Until Rokshan gets here with the books I need, we're going to learn the alphabet."

"What's that?"

Dharan swiftly wrote letters across the slate. "I told you letters repre-sent sounds. Well, each letter also has a name. Mostly the names are similar to the sounds they make. When we write the letters in a certain order, that's called the alphabet. It helps us remember the letter names and sounds, and it's useful for organizing writing."

"Alphabet. Why do letters have names if they have sounds?"

"Because of what I said about some letters making more than one sound. If I were to tell someone how to spell my name—that is, what letters make my name—I would tell them the names of the letters in order, D-H-A-R-A-N, and not the sounds."

"I understand. Because they can hear the sounds, but that doesn't tell them which letters were used. Like how my name has P and that other letter instead of F."

"Right!" Dharan smiled. "You're going to learn this quickly, I predict. Now, the first letter in the alphabet is A..."

The sun was high in the eastern sky when Rokshan appeared, bearing an oblong sack slung over his shoulder. "Has Lamprophyre learned to read yet?" he asked.

"It's no joke. She's a very quick study," Dharan said.

"I've memorized your alphabet and most of the sounds the letters make, and I can read some words," Lamprophyre added. "But dragons have very long memories, and compared to all the poems and histories I know, this isn't too hard. It's remembering all the words that will be complicated."

"There's no rush," Dharan said. "Did you bring the books, Rokshan?"

"Just don't let anyone know you have them," Rokshan said, setting the sack carefully on the ground. "It's not likely anyone will notice they're missing, and they're not valuable enough for anyone to care, but you know how librarians get about their responsibility to the wisdom of the ages."

Dharan's face squinched up in a funny way. "I know. You should have told them you wanted them so you could make history teaching a dragon to read."

"Sneaking them out was more fun." He opened the sack and withdrew a book, then two more, handing them to Dharan. Lamprophyre regarded them curiously. Dharan had explained briefly that humans wrote words on scrolls or books to preserve them, but somehow she'd thought something so important would be bigger, or at least decorated with gold or something. These were just plain fat squares that smelled of animal skins and dust. The biggest was the size of Dharan's chest, and the smallest was half the size of Lamprophyre's palm.

"These are for you to use," Dharan said to Lamprophyre. "The big one is a kind of abecedary. Usually that just means the alphabet written out, like we did on the slate, but the ones made for beginning readers have lists of words beginning with each letter of the alphabet. This one is special because each word is illustrated." He opened the book, awkwardly due to its size, and pointed. "This word is 'apple'—see the picture?"

Lamprophyre squinted. It was very small, but clearly an apple. "What a clever idea!"

Dharan closed the book and set it on the ground. "This other book is for you to practice your reading. It's a story—I'm afraid it's a religious text, but it's the simplest and clearest book I know. And you'll learn about our religion, which has some good stories."

That didn't sound as interesting, but Lamprophyre nodded.

"Finally, I asked Rokshan to bring...what *is* this?" Dharan said.

"You said get a history from the catastrophe to now," Rokshan said.

"Yes, but I meant something scholarly. Not this watered-down popular nonsense."

"It's not nonsense. It's accurate and complete while still being readable. And since I'm the one who'll be reading it, I decided that was more important."

Dharan shook his head. "Fine. Lamprophyre, this one is too complicated for your skills, so Rokshan will read it to you. It's like I said, a human history from the time we started keeping records as opposed to legends. And Rokshan's probably right that you'll find it more interesting than a scholarly text."

"Rokshan will read it? Not you?"

"I came to Tanajital to meet you, but I can only afford to stay if I take work with the academy as a visiting lector." Dharan shrugged. "So Rokshan will read to you in the afternoons, when you're not busy being an ambassador."

"Don't worry, Lamprophyre, I may not have patience as an instructor, but I'm a very good reader," Rokshan said. He walked over to the slate and tapped Lamprophyre's name in Dharan's handwriting. "Is this how it's spelled? I thought there was an F."

"See?" Lamprophyre said triumphantly.

"Rokshan, don't you dare confuse her," Dharan said. "Lamprophyre, *don't*, for the love of Jiwanyil, ask him to spell things for you. He's terrible at it."

"You're going to convince her I'm bad at everything," Rokshan complained.

"You are not," Lamprophyre said with some heat. "You're good at flying and explaining things clearly, and I'm sure you could have beaten Khadar to a pulp if it had come to that."

"Yes, I heard about Lamprophyre's accident," Dharan said. "Did you really set Khadar's robes on fire?"

"No, I didn't. Is that what people are saying?" Lamprophyre wished she could sink into the ground.

"People are saying a lot of things, all of them false, and I've spent the morning countering them," Rokshan said. "The good news is that someone else is countering them too. I think you made friends last night, and they're speaking in your defense."

That made her feel better. "So it's not too bad?"

"It's bad, but it won't stay that way, and that's good." Rokshan prodded the abecedary with his toe. "Aren't these going to be hard for Lamprophyre to read? They're so small compared to her."

"I have a solution for that," Dharan said. He climbed into the cart and picked up a wrapped bundle that was nearly as tall as he was. "Where will you do most of your reading and writing, Lamprophyre?"

"Inside, I think. I don't want anyone staring at me."

Dharan maneuvered the bundle through the door and set it to one side of the cave—the hall, Rokshan called the big empty space. "This is very valuable, so it's better you keep it indoors, anyway," he said. He untied the ropes holding the cloth around the bundle and gathered cloth and ropes into his arms, revealing something Lamprophyre had never seen before. It was a piece of curved glass set in a metal oval, fastened to two wooden supports on its skinny ends. The supports held it up like legs and were themselves connected by another piece of wood that attached at a perpendicular angle to their bases. Lamprophyre could see how that would keep the thing steady.

She prodded the glass carefully with her finger, and it rotated just a bit. "What is this?" she asked.

"It's a magnifying lens, the biggest in Tanajital. A former academy student made it as part of her work on optics, though knowing her I think she did it just to prove she could. The academy doesn't have a use for it, but it's too valuable to destroy, so it was easy for me to convince them I deserved to borrow it." Dharan held the abecedary open beneath the glass. "Take a look."

Lamprophyre looked through the glass, and gasped. The letters that had formerly been almost too small to read now were as long as her finger and clearly visible. "That's amazing. How does it work?"

Dharan looked at Rokshan. "Maybe she should enroll at the academy, if that's the kind of question she usually asks," he said. "Lamprophyre, the curve of the glass alters how the light strikes the page, which changes the appearance of whatever's behind the glass. Humans know how to create curved glass that makes letters—anything, really—as big or as small as we want."

"I had no idea humans were so smart," Lamprophyre said. She took the book from Dharan and, still holding it beneath the glass, turned the pages. The pictures were vividly colored and as enlarged as the letters.

"If it's almost noon, I need to get to my lectures," Dharan said. "I'll see you tomorrow, Lamprophyre. You really are learning astonishingly fast. Rokshan, don't forget supper tonight."

"I won't." Rokshan saluted Dharan with that wrist-gripping gesture, then watched him disappear down the street. "So, it was a good morning?" he asked.

"It was. But I think I've had enough reading and writing. On my own, that is. I don't mind if you want to read to me." She stepped outside to bring the slates indoors, and stopped. A man stood at the far side of the courtyard, staring at her. She recognized him as one of the beggars from the night before. "Hello," she said. "Excuse me for one moment."

She leaned the slates against the wall opposite the magnifying lens. "That man is here again," she told Rokshan. "The beggar you didn't want me to give coin to. Didn't you say you'd help him?"

Rokshan looked out the entrance. "I did," he said. "That's why he's here." He walked across the courtyard to greet the man. Lamprophyre followed. She felt a little foolish. Rokshan had warned her the man might be lazy, and that he would just keep asking for help if she gave him coin, and he was right.

"I guess you were serious about wanting work," Rokshan was saying as she approached. "Lamprophyre, this is Depik. He's a cook and he needs a job. I told him, if he meant what he said about being willing to work, that he should come here today to speak with you."

Lamprophyre looked down at the man. In the daylight, he looked even scruffier than he had the previous night. "Don't I already have a cook?"

"You've had two," Rokshan said, "but they were both timid, and neither one wanted to stay."

Lamprophyre remembered their fearful thoughts. "And Depik—you're not afraid." That was clear. Depik looked back at her with no trace of fear, at least not of her. He was afraid, she realized, but his emotions were a confusing tangle, fear mixed with resignation and despair, and all she understood was that he was afraid of failing yet again.

Depik shook his head. "You didn't eat me, wonder what you do eat," he said.

"I like cow. Actually, I love steak. Akarshan at the palace cooked it different ways, and it was always delicious. Can you cook steak?"

"I can. What about chicken? Only you might need a mort o' chickens." She heard him think *feathers and all, no more than a mouthful.*

"I've never had chicken," she said. "They're a kind of bird, aren't they? I eat birds as a snack, but if there were enough of them, it could be a meal."

Depik nodded. "I can see how much you'd need in a meal, my lady." To her surprise, his thoughts went from fearful to discouraged. "But you shouldn't hire me. Can't depend on me."

"I don't understand. Why not? You sound as if you know what you're doing, and that's all I really care about."

Depik looked at his feet. "Some days I can't get out of bed. I try, but it's like I ache all over, only it's on the inside. Can't explain. Other bosses, they say I'm lazy, but it's not like I want to lie there thinking dark thoughts. I just can't beat it."

Rokshan said, "Well, Lamprophyre? What do you *think*?"

His peculiar emphasis on *think* confused her only for a beat or two. Then she listened to Depik's thoughts: *don't know why I got my hopes up, dragon could be different but no reason to think so, curse me for a lazy fool.*

"I think you're honest, Depik," she said. "I want to hire you. And when you have one of those days, well, if you're a good enough cook all the rest of the days, I can fend for myself when I have to."

Depik raised his head. There was so much hope filling his thoughts Lamprophyre drew in a breath and held it, waiting for his response. "You mean it?" he said. "I told you I'll disappoint you."

"I don't think you will," Lamprophyre said. "You're responsible for buying my food and preparing it. I eat twice a day, morning and evening, so you should get to work immediately. There are little houses behind the embassy—you can choose one for yourself. Rokshan, give him some coin so he can buy food. Also something for his first wages."

"As my lady commands," Rokshan said with a grin. She nudged him with her elbow, making him stagger.

Depik's eyes widened as Rokshan pressed several silver coins into his palm. "But—I might run off with this, never come back!" he exclaimed.

"I trust you," Lamprophyre said. "Also, I can hunt you down if you do. But I don't think I'll need to. And I'm sorry if this is rude, but you really need a bath."

Depik nodded. His mouth had fallen open and was now as wide as his eyes. "God's breath," he said, "I swear I won't cheat you."

"I believe you. I'll see you at supper." She was learning all sorts of new words for meals. Breakfast. Lunch. Dinner. Supper. She waved at Depik, who didn't wave back, just stumbled away down the street. "I hope he takes me seriously about the bath," she told Rokshan.

"So do I. You're taking a real chance on him," Rokshan said.

"I know, but you didn't hear how terrible he feels about himself. No one should be that discouraged."

Rokshan was silent. She glanced his way and saw he was looking at her with a strange expression. Well, all his expressions were strange to her, but this one she'd never seen before. "You know," he said, "for someone who isn't human, you have an extraordinary capacity for compassion for us."

Lamprophyre blushed faint purple. "You think dragons can't care about humans?"

"I think it's a trait of any rational creature to care primarily about its own kind. Hyaloclast certainly doesn't give a damn what happens to humans. And you already know most humans think you're a monster. Yet you treat humans the way you would members of your flight. I think that's extraordinary."

She blushed harder. "It's nothing you wouldn't do for dragons," she pointed out. "Maybe that makes us both unique."

"Maybe it does." Rokshan held up the small book. "Ready for some stories? You can tell me what we got wrong."

"I don't know," Lamprophyre said as she went back into the embassy. "Maybe you got things right, instead."

CHAPTER TWENTY-THREE

Lamprophyre crouched as low as she could, coiling her tail around her left flank and furling her wings close along her back. With her eyes closed, she counted aloud, "...forty-eight, forty-nine, fifty! I hope you hid better than last time, because I'm coming for you!" She rose to her full height and stomped out of the embassy's back door, making plenty of noise so the giggles were drowned out. She already knew where all the children were, but finding them immediately would spoil the game.

She made a show of scanning the rear of the embassy, shielding her eyes from the sun with her hand rather than closing the nictitating membranes. Ohar crouched inside one of the unoccupied servants' houses; she clearly heard him think *she'll find Rojital first, he's too little to hide well.* Lamprophyre controlled a smile. Ohar was in for a surprise.

She stomped away from the little houses—let Ohar think his ploy was working—and passed the kitchen where Rojital hid under one of the tables. There really weren't many hiding places around the embassy, but Lamprophyre had promised the children's parents they wouldn't stray far from home. Varnak had gone to ground outside the kitchen, on its far side, and Anamika—she was clever; once Lamprophyre left by the back door, she'd moved from her exposed position by the entrance to hide inside the embassy itself, behind one of the slates propped against the wall. If Lamprophyre hadn't already decided to let Rojital win, she might have given the honor to Anamika.

As it was, she decided to worry Anamika some by passing through the embassy slowly, making a great show of sniffing. The children believed it was how she found them, and she saw no reason to reveal the truth. She went out the back door, still sniffing, and walked slowly along the row of houses, bent over to peer inside.

"I've got you!" she exclaimed, throwing the door open and revealing Ohar.

Ohar groaned. "No fair," he said. "I bathed!"

"And now you smell sweet and clean," Lamprophyre said. Ohar scowled.

She "found" Varnak and then Anamika, then made a big show of searching for Rojital. Finally, she said, "I give up. Where are you, Rojital?"

"I'm here!" Rojital exclaimed, popping up from his hiding place. Lamprophyre laughed.

"I guess I'm too tall to see down there," she said. "Though you have a wonderful scent." She brought her face close to Rojital's belly and drew in a long breath. Rojital giggled.

"Let's do it again," Anamika said.

"All right," Lamprophyre said, "one more time." She sniffed Rojital to make him laugh again. He did smell like a human that had had a bath recently, of the sweet, crisp scent of the soap his mother used, but also of dirt—Rojital got dirty faster than any human Lamprophyre knew—and, more distantly...but that wasn't Rojital.

Lamprophyre lifted her head and scented the air. Wood smoke, dark and bitter and not far away. Something big was on fire nearby.

"Stay here, children," she said, and took to the sky.

She saw it immediately: a column of dark smoke rising into the air about a dozen dragonlengths away. As she flew toward it, the background hum of the city became louder, sharper, more terrified. She saw the building clearly now, one of the tall ones humans lived in as opposed to the ones where they sold each other things they made. Humans clustered around the base of it, and fear tangled their thoughts.

Lamprophyre landed in the street a dragonlength from the building. She couldn't approach any closer without trampling humans. The fire consumed the top of the building; she knew from asking Rokshan that buildings like this had levels called floors stacked on each other, and this was the top floor. She risked listening to hear if there were humans still within, but the noise of the flames and the noise of terrified humans on the street made that impossible.

No one seemed aware of her presence. She reflected briefly that all she needed to be accepted in Tanajital was half a dozen disasters, and leaped into the sky again. From there, she saw a line of humans snaking their way from the community well to the building, and the glint of water in containers they passed from one to another. That was clever, but point-less, because getting through the building to the fire would be fatal. And by the time the fire reached a point where their water could quench it, it would be too large to quench.

She dropped lower and hovered near the western corner of the roof, where the fire burned brightest. Carefully, she clung to the ragged side of the building, eaten away by fire, and wrapped her wings around the nearest flames.

Some of them, deprived of the air they desperately needed, flickered and died. But more flames took their place. Lamprophyre ducked her head and soaked in the heat for a few beats. This wasn't something her body could contain. She needed some way to bring water to the roof. Too bad it wasn't the rainy season yet, which Rokshan had told her drenched the city and kept most fires from devastating it. Then, people spent all their time trying to *stop* things getting soaked. The opposite of what she needed now.

That gave her an idea. She took to the sky again, scanning for what she needed. Surely they'd be in use, if only because they shielded people from the sun as well as the rain. Two streets away, she saw it: a bright pink splotch of heavy fabric Rokshan called a canopy. Big as her arms could encompass, and rigid like an upside down bowl.

Lamprophyre flew down to the canopy and examined it. It was held up by sticks at its six corners, and she could smell more sticks on its under-side. She yanked on the canopy and freed it from two of the sticks, but it stayed rigid. Good. She'd guessed right. The sticks on the underside kept it from sagging and would help it maintain its bowl shape. And if she'd understood correctly, it was watertight.

Tugging harder, she freed the canopy from the rest of the sticks and flew with it to the well. Amid screams from the people desperately drawing water, she set the canopy down bowl side up and shouted, "Fill that! I'll be back!"

A second canopy, this one yellow like a chirping bird, was easier to retrieve. She flew with it to the river, struggling to keep it from catching the wind and knocking her off course. When she reached the river, she dove, inhaling its fresh damp scent, and tipped the canopy so it scooped up water as she skimmed the river's surface. The full canopy was heavy and awkward, but she gripped it along its sides as far as her arms could reach and flew back to the burning building.

The fire had spread while she was gone, flames leaping to the next building, and there were humans atop that one, beating at the flames with heavy cloth. "Stand back," Lamprophyre shouted, and tipped the canopy just enough to let a trickle of water overflow it. The canopy fought her, wanting to upend all at once, and Lamprophyre gritted her teeth and forced it to obey. The fire hissed and spat and sent up great clouds of steam, and then it was out. Lamprophyre turned her attention to the doomed building—well, maybe not so doomed, if the humans at the well had listened to her. With the rest of the water, she extinguished some of the fire, drenching the wood so the flames couldn't spread further.

Breathing heavily, her arms aching from the weight of the full canopy, she flew back to the well and found the humans had listened, after all. The second canopy was nearly full of water. She decided not to waste time waiting for it to be completely full, set the first canopy down to be refilled, and took off with the second.

This time, it felt like the water went farther, or maybe the fire had seen the futility of fighting a dragon and was giving up. After the second canopy's burden was shed, only a few fires burned, here and there, and it took very little of a third load of water to extinguish them. Lamprophyre hovered over the blackened, soaked roof, her arms shaking, and thought about dropping the empty canopy to give herself some relief. Then she remembered it belonged to someone who would likely want it back, and flew slowly to where she'd found it. A male and a female stood gaping at her as she descended. "Sorry," she said. "I didn't have time to ask permission. Should I put it back? I'm not sure how it goes on the sticks."

"We'll do it," the female said.

Lamprophyre nodded, too tired to listen to their thoughts. She shook out her arms as she flew away, wishing she could return to the embassy for a nap, but there was the other canopy to deal with, and she should probably check the burned building to see if any of it might fall down. It would be terrible if the falling wood crushed someone.

Having returned the canopy and examined the building, she finally headed for the embassy. As she descended toward the courtyard, she heard Rokshan calling her name. Dully, she landed and waited for him to run to her.

"Lamprophyre, what did you do?" he said.

Fear shot through her. "I put out the fire," she said. "Was that a mistake? I had to borrow those canopies, and I'm sure the humans were afraid of me—Rokshan, I couldn't let it burn. It would have taken so many other buildings with it!"

"Of course you couldn't," Rokshan said. He put a hand on her arm. "You're shaking. Are you all right?"

"Just tired. Water is heavy—I don't think people appreciate that."

Rokshan nodded. "The streets are full of people arguing about you. Some of them say you caused the fire—"

"*What?*"

He waved her to silence. "Most of them are talking about how you put out the fire, and why would you do that if you'd wanted to burn that building to the ground. And everyone's listening to them."

"Where did you go?" Anamika exclaimed. The four children raced around the corner of the embassy, jumping in their agitation. "Was there a fire? You can't breathe water, can you?"

"No, and I think that would be uncomfortable, fire and water that close together," Lamprophyre said. "Rokshan, are you saying I'm *not* being criticized?"

"Only by a few people, and they're being shouted down." Rokshan gripped her arm more tightly. "This is good."

"Very good," Lamprophyre agreed. "And now I need a nap. Children, we can play another day."

As the four children ran off toward home, Rokshan said, "I'm not happy about that calamity, but if we can take advantage of it, so much the better for us."

"I made sure the building wouldn't come down on them." Lamprophyre slouched into the embassy and settled on the comfortable floor. "I wonder if there are any other things I can do to convince people I'm a hero?"

"I can't guarantee other convenient fires." Rokshan settled down beside her and leaned against her flank. "So I don't think we should look for those opportunities, because we have other things we need to do. Like find the thieves."

"I'm discouraged. All our theories seem unprovable. Either it's Gonjirians who hate your father, or it's Fanishkorites who want to start a war, or someone else we haven't even considered. And that's before we include Khadar and the ecclesiasts, who want me gone for some other reason."

"I wouldn't say they're unprovable theories. I've done some investigating—or, rather, I had some of Tekentriya's spy corps investigate."

"I've heard of spies. They sneak around and learn things secretly, right?"

"Right. Some of them spy on the Fanishkorites in Tanajital, so I asked for the information they already have."

Lamprophyre propped her head on her hand. "I'm sorry if this is rude, but Tekentriya doesn't like or respect you. If they're her spies, why would they tell you anything?"

Rokshan laughed. "If I were asking for myself, they'd tell me to whistle for it. But I still have military rank, and they can't refuse an official request from an Army commander. Though if I'd had to ask Tekentriya directly, she'd have turned me down and the devil with the consequences. So I was circumspect."

"I see. Did they know anything useful?"

"First, what we already knew, which is that tensions between Gonjiri and Fanishkor are high. Much of what the spies have been doing recently is countering the Fanishkorite spies embedded in *our* government, if they can find them. I have to admit Tekentriya is good, and they've probably rooted all the enemy spies out, but in times like these, Tekentriya's people have to behave as if their secrets are compromised. Which means laying false trails, and cultivating inside contacts they can feed false information to, that sort of thing."

Lamprophyre felt dizzy just thinking about it. "That's a level of duplicity I can barely understand."

"It's complicated, but it's to our benefit. The second thing I learned is that to the best of our knowledge, Fanishkor isn't making active preparation for war with Gonjiri. That is, they aren't building up troops or stockpiling weapons or any of the other things that have to happen before they can wage war."

"But if their plan is to incite the dragons against Gonjiri, they wouldn't need to, would they?"

"No, they would not," Rokshan said. "That's exactly what occurred to me. If that's their strategy, we should be looking for other signs. Like, for example, if they bought or borrowed a printing press to produce those handbills."

Lamprophyre didn't know what a printing press was, but that seemed an irrelevant question. "Or if we could prove they paid those bandits to steal the egg."

"That would be harder, but yes. It might be easier to find the person who made that wand and follow the trail back to the Fanishkorites."

"That makes sense. And if it's not the Fanishkorites, it would prove that too." She sighed. Rokshan was a warm, comfortable weight against her left side, and she felt increasingly drowsy. "Which means we need to talk to an adept, right? But the ones we know are hiding something as well."

Rokshan yawned. "Let's think about that later. I'm falling asleep."

"So am I," Lamprophyre said.

She closed her eyes, but despite her fatigue, her thoughts kept her awake. How could they find the enemy adept? Well, the sapphire had been unusually large, and maybe someone remembered selling it. That was one possibility. Or if they could find an adept whose thoughts weren't a blur, that might work. Lamprophyre remembered Rokshan's suggestion, that Manishi and Sabarna had artifacts that made their thoughts incomprehensible. An artifact would be made of stone, and Lamprophyre knew more about stone than any adept, she was certain. So what had she smelled?

She cast her mind back to meeting Manishi. She remembered the citrine because it was the first polished stone she'd ever seen. What else? Sodalite, one of her favorite flavors and a rare treat. Aventurine, prettier than it was tasty—Coquina was the color of aventurine and was so proud of that, as if she'd chosen the color instead of it developing as she grew. Lamprophyre shook away thoughts of Coquina and cast her mind back.

Sodalite, citrine, aventurine, and quartz, yes, with that chlorite inclusion. Lamprophyre hadn't scented any other stones on Manishi.

So what had Sabarna worn? There was that bloodstone she said gave her immunity to diseases. If only the dragons had access to that kind of magic, Aegirine might still...but maybe it only worked on humans. She'd also had a string of jade spheres around her wrist and a couple of copper rings, one set with chlorite, one with quartz—oh.

Lamprophyre nearly sat up, but realized she'd wake Rokshan. If it was true that it was an artifact that blurred Manishi and Sabarna's thoughts, she'd discovered something they had in common that might account for it. Quartz, or chlorite, or both.

Rokshan shifted, muttered something she couldn't understand, and fell more deeply asleep. He needed rest as much as she did. So many possibilities to pursue, and this was one of many—one with a low priority compared to everything else. Maybe once they'd solved the mystery of the egg thieves, they could investigate this new one. Or maybe they'd figure it out as they went. As if making this decision had settled her tumultuous thoughts, she closed her eyes and soon drifted off to sleep.

CHAPTER TWENTY-FOUR

Lamprophyre spread the handbill out flat beneath the lens and peered at the tiny writing, which was small enough that even the lens couldn't make it big enough for her comfort. Most of the words were still unintelligible to her, and sounding things out took forever. But she'd found in the three days since Dharan's instruction began that it only took a few beats for her to memorize a word once she knew what it was. She was building quite the vocabulary, even if it was of ordinary words that were no use in reading this handbill.

She heard Rokshan's quick footsteps, unique to him, and looked up. She was learning to interpret his expressions, and he didn't look happy. "What's wrong?" she asked as soon as he was close enough for conversation.

"Nothing." He let out a deep breath. "That is, nothing we can do anything about."

"Is it something to do with this handbill?" She plucked it from beneath the lens and handed it to him.

Rokshan scowled. "I hoped you wouldn't see this. Yes, it's this handbill. Did you read it?"

"I tried. I don't know enough words yet. And most of them are the complicated words that don't fit the basic rules for sounding out."

"It doesn't matter. It's a bunch of nonsense that was clearly written by

Khadar. Nothing specifically targeting you, but reminding people not to have their faith shaken by the appearance of unbelievers in our midst."

"That makes it sound like I'm going around the city telling everyone their religion is false."

"Yes, and that's what's stupid about it." Rokshan crushed the handbill in his grip. "Since you *haven't* done anything like that aside from one time telling Khadar that Katayan isn't real, and almost no one heard that, all this does is make people question their faith when they wouldn't have before."

"Oh. That is pretty stupid."

"Well, it's Khadar. He's not long on brains." Rokshan glanced at the crumpled paper and tossed it aside. "And, like I said, there's nothing we can do about it. It's just irritating."

Lamprophyre shot a short, narrow blast of fire at the ball of paper, incinerating it instantly. "We have more important things to worry about. Did you find the person who sold the sapphire?"

"Sort of," Rokshan said. He sat cross-legged near the lens. "I started by looking for merchants who deal in sapphires regularly. Most of them are lapidaries who sell cut stones, but I found two women who sell the uncut crystals to adepts whose work requires specialized cutting. One of their buyers is Manishi, actually. I described the stone, and neither of them had sold anything like it in the last six months. That's half a year," he said when Lamprophyre gave him a confused look.

"I suppose it's possible whoever did this just happened to have a sapphire that size on hand, but that seems unlikely," she said. "And they told you this without being suspicious?"

"I told them I was looking to buy one and asked how common they were. I also slipped them a few rupyas to loosen their tongues." Rokshan grinned. "And I didn't tell them who I was. Sometimes it's good not to be so public a figure as Tekentriya or Khadar."

"All right, so you know none of the sellers in the market have handled that stone," Lamprophyre said. "What about other markets? Or other countries? If it's Fanishkor behind the egg theft, wouldn't the wand maker be a Fanishkorite?"

"Let's not borrow trouble. We're starting here because Tanajital has the biggest market in Gonjiri, and it's bigger than anything Fanishkor has. It's not unlikely for a Fanishkorite adept to buy stones here. But the important thing is that it's the closest source for stones we have. We'll eliminate all the possibilities in Tanajital and move outward from there afterward."

Lamprophyre nodded. She couldn't help thinking of all the many, many humans there were in Gonjiri alone, not to mention in other countries like Fanishkor and Sachetan and more she wasn't aware of. But Rokshan was right; they needed to start somewhere.

"Anyway," Rokshan said, "those two sellers didn't know about the stone, but they told me about the rock sniffer who supplies both of them. He specializes in precious stones and is apparently the only supplier of raw sapphire in Gonjiri. He's mostly independent, but has been known to hire out his services on an exclusive basis. So if our mystery adept hired him, he could have found that sapphire and delivered it directly to the adept, and no one would know."

"That sounds promising," Lamprophyre said, sitting up tall. "How do we find him?"

"That's where it gets tricky," Rokshan said. "The rock sniffer, Mendesk, is a real loner, and he's known to be fiercely independent and prickly about not sharing information with anyone. So he's unlikely to give up the name of his buyer."

"Oh," Lamprophyre said, feeling deflated. "And I was so hopeful."

"I should say, unlikely to give up the name to another human," Rokshan said. "I'm counting on his being sufficiently intimidated by a dragon to be more forthcoming."

Lamprophyre smiled. "So I get to talk to him? Where does he live?"

"He lives in Tanajital, but he's in the field right now, so no worries about not fitting into his house." Rokshan stood. "When would you like to go?"

Lamprophyre checked the sky. "That depends on how far away he is. It's still early afternoon, so if he's not that far, we could be there and back before sunset."

"I don't know exactly where he is. Somewhere in the Kresetni Hills, which is south of Tanajital a couple hundred miles. They're about as far south as the Parama Mountains are north."

Human distances still made no sense to Lamprophyre, but she knew how long the trip from Tanajital to her home took. "We can do that. I don't suppose there are wild cows there? It will be suppertime before we return."

Rokshan laughed. "No such thing as wild cows, unfortunately, but there are deer all over the hills. Father has a retreat near there—a smaller home he can go to for a rest—and I used to hunt them when I was younger."

"Not any more?"

"I haven't been to the retreat in years." Rokshan followed Lamprophyre into the courtyard. "Not since it became increasingly obvious I was a disappointment to my father for not being interested in a life of politics."

He sounded bitter enough that Lamprophyre decided to drop the subject. She poked her head around the dining pavilion to the kitchen, where Depik was working. "I won't be here for supper, so don't prepare anything," she said.

Depik nodded. "Meat's already here, but it will keep until morning."

"Thank you." The meat smelled good, and Lamprophyre took a long sniff before returning to the courtyard. She leaned down to let Rokshan climb up. "South—can you give me more direction than that?"

"I'll point out the Kresetni Hills when we're close. Then we'll have to search for him. There are quite a few mines there, so it could take a while, but lots of mines means lots of miners who could point us in the right direction."

"Makes sense." She leaped skyward, and in a few dozen beats, she was high above Tanajital and headed south.

She hadn't taken a long flight in a twelveday, not since gathering stone for Manishi, and it felt so good to properly stretch her wings. Gonjiri south of Tanajital was a mass of colors, every shade of yellow and brown and green imaginable. The colors lay below her in squares so regular they had to be human made, misty with distance but still lush and fertile. She watched them slide past until she left them behind for the mingled green-gray-tan of the plains, similar to the foothills south of her mountain home. Humans had spread much farther than she'd guessed.

She gradually rose higher until the air was crisp and cool and not as damp as at ground level. "You're not too cold, are you?" she asked Rokshan.

"I'm comfortable, thanks. I like the wind rushing over me." He leaned forward, pressing against the sensitive spot on the back of her head and making her twitch. "Did I hurt you?"

"No. There's a spot just where you're leaning that's sensitive to pressure. It just feels odd, not painful."

"I'll be more careful. Sorry." He shifted his weight. "We should probably discuss having another reception."

Lamprophyre groaned. "Another one? Because the first wasn't catastrophic enough?"

"This one will be a more typical diplomatic event. It's to introduce you to the other ambassadors and political figures here in Tanajital. My father won't come, but Tekentriya will, and maybe my mother—she's not political, but I know she's curious about you."

Lamprophyre wanted to meet Rokshan's mother, if only because she was starting to wonder if there really was anyone he was related to that he got along with. "Is it a good idea to have it at the embassy? Because I know now it's not the best neighborhood. Not that I'm complaining, because I think I'd be uncomfortable among the wealthy. They have so many strange expectations."

"I was thinking of having it in the parkland outside the palace. It's nice and open with plenty of room for guests."

"You're sure the king won't mind?"

"Just so long as I don't expect him to attend, he wouldn't care if we held it in the Great Hall. Though that would send the wrong message, that Gonjiri directly supports the dragons."

"I thought we were friendly with each other. Not quite allies, but mutually supportive." She caught an updraft and let it boost her a few dragonlengths.

"There's supportive, and then there's supportive," Rokshan said. "Gonjiri is actually in an inferior position with regard to the dragons, because we had to petition you for the right to live in your territory. My father would prefer nobody know this, so he's behaving as if Gonjiri is more of an equal partner. Pandering to dragons by hosting a reception for you would ruin that impression, because it would look like we're begging for your approval."

"I think I understand. Though doesn't Gonjiri already benefit by having a diplomatic relationship with dragons when no other country does?"

"We would if my father took advantage of that, but he's angry enough about our subordinate position that he's not thinking clearly. Or so my mother tells me. I hope he comes to his senses soon. He has to know allying with dragons would keep Fanishkor from attacking."

"You understand politics well for someone who wants no part of them," Lamprophyre said.

Rokshan chuckled. "It was part of my instruction, growing up. It's easier to stay out of politics if you understand the ways in which you might get sucked in. And I find it interesting in the abstract, all the ways people interact with each other."

"I don't know if I'm capable of that kind of thinking. It worries me, in terms of interacting with other ambassadors, I mean. You make it sound like everyone's thinking on at least three different layers all the time."

"They are, but that actually gives you an advantage. You're straightforward and honest, and you aren't easily sidetracked. So if an ambassador wants to trick you into giving something away, instead of trying to match them at their verbal game, you're more likely to push through to the heart of what they want—especially since you have the advantage of hearing their thoughts. Diplomats aren't used to that level of discourse."

Lamprophyre thought about that for a few beats. "That's interesting. It makes me feel more comfortable."

"Besides," Rokshan added, "most of those diplomats are going to be so overawed by you they won't try to trick you or make you look foolish."

"I'll try to think of that as a good thing. I prefer humans not to look at me with their mouths hanging open like flycatchers."

"You know what flycatchers are?"

Lamprophyre chuckled. "They're predators, sort of—that's interesting enough even to a dragon who doesn't normally care about plants."

They flew in silence for a while. Lamprophyre thought about the possibility of an actual alliance between dragons and humans and concluded it was extremely unlikely so long as Hyaloclast believed there was nothing humans could give them. Lamprophyre had to agree that was true as far as military might went. There were enough adult dragons in the flight to raze Tanajital to the ground in less than half a day, and humans had no weapons to stop them. The thought made Lamprophyre uncomfortable, as if in considering it, she'd made a plan she intended to execute.

But there were other ways in which humans had the advantage of dragons. Cooking, for one. Reading, for another. Lamprophyre could already see some benefits of reading over recitation; you couldn't read in the dark, true, but suppose you wanted a story and no one felt like telling it? Books didn't care what kind of mood you were in. And humans were so clever with their construction, they might be able to advise dragons on how to build more efficiently. With glass, even. It wasn't so impossible to imagine a trade alliance, stones for human ingenuity.

Even so, that kind of alliance required dragons to see for themselves what humans could do, and *that* was the unlikely thing, that dragons might travel south to investigate these alien creatures. Feelings of despondency crept over Lamprophyre. She and Rokshan would find the egg thieves, she would report to Hyaloclast—

"You just tensed up. Is something wrong?" Rokshan said.

"I was thinking about what would happen when Hyaloclast learns who stole the egg. She's not temperate in her responses. She might want to burn a city to the ground to avenge us on the thieves. That's not fair."

"You can't convince her otherwise?"

"I can try. She's rational and listens to logical arguments. The trouble is, she might think it's logical to make an example so no one ever tries egg theft again. But whoever this is, it can't be a whole city that's behind it. Even if it's the Fanishkorite king, his country shouldn't suffer for his greed and foolishness."

Rokshan was silent. "Maybe we're doing the wrong thing," he finally said. "I don't want to see innocents suffer either. And yet..."

"We can't let people believe dragons are vulnerable in that way," Lamprophyre said. "I think we have to see this through, and figure out a solution that doesn't end in a city burning to the ground later."

"How long until the next clutch is laid?"

"Five or six years. You're thinking at least we have some time?"

"Yes. Maybe Hyaloclast's anger will subside."

Lamprophyre considered what she knew of her mother. "I think," she said, "that's not something we can count on."

~

IT WAS LATE AFTERNOON BEFORE LAMPROPHYRE SPOTTED THE SMUDGE of hills stretching across the horizon. "Is that it?"

"Yes. They look so small from up here. You'll want to land on the western slopes. You'll see the town as you get closer, Southslope. We don't want to land there, but the largest mine is just east and south of the town, so you can use it as a guide."

Lamprophyre followed his directions. The hills were a ruddy streak across the greenish-brown, though as she descended, more green was visible as splotches here and there on the lower slopes. From the air, the hills were foreshortened, but that amount of exposed stone suggested they were higher than they seemed.

The town of Southslope was nothing like Tanajital with its white walls and golden roofs. It looked like dull clumps of mud, its short buildings huddling together as if intimidated by the hills overlooking it. The hills were more like short mountains, Lamprophyre decided as she swept lower, nothing a dragon would find comfortable, but high enough to be a challenge for human miners.

She turned east and south and soon saw a gash in the rock that was clearly the opening of a sizable mine. Humans moved in and out of it and around the flat area surrounding it. "Set down over there," Rokshan said, "far enough away not to scare them, and I'll see what I can learn."

Very few humans noticed her arrival, but the ones who did alerted others. Lamprophyre landed where Rokshan had suggested and furled her wings to make herself seem smaller. They were afraid, but not panicked, which was good even as it was frustrating. She reminded herself that they'd never seen a living dragon and their fear was natural. Dharan had refused to provide her with human stories of dragons, saying only, "You don't need to be hurt by human stupidity and ignorance, and most of these stories exist specifically to frighten humans in a safe way."

"You mean tales of horror," Lamprophyre had said. "We have those too, but none of them feature real creatures. Why would anyone want to confuse people by lying about real creatures?"

"We thought you were imaginary," Dharan had said, "but that doesn't change how maligned your people are in our writing. Hearing about it will only make you sad and angry."

Now Lamprophyre wondered if Dharan had been correct. Not in his assertion; he was smart enough to know what he was talking about. But maybe Lamprophyre should endure a little pain and anger if it meant understanding exactly what humans feared dragons might do to them, so she could counter those misunderstandings directly.

She watched Rokshan run toward a couple of tiny buildings and talk to a human who emerged from one of them. They were at the limits of her mental perception, and she didn't want to eavesdrop on Rokshan anyway, so she sat and waited impatiently until Rokshan ran back toward her and pulled himself up. "That's going to give them stories to tell their grandchildren, the dragon who carries a human," he said. "We're going east."

"Did that human know where our rock sniffer is?"

Rokshan laughed. "Mendesk is famous in these parts. Some people respect him because he's successful. Others hate him because he's abrasive and arrogant. All of them wish they had his luck. His claim is east of here, and I hope it's easy to find from the air because the mine foreman's directions were hazy. I gathered Mendesk would like its location to be a secret, but of course the government knows where it is."

"Why is that?"

Rokshan stretched out along her neck. "Stay close to the ground if you can. All of this is Gonjirian territory, which means the king owns it. But the government can only exploit so much—it doesn't have the resources to mine the whole hills. So private citizens are allowed to stake a claim, to take charge of a certain area, and pay the treasury for the right to do so."

"I see. So the king's government still makes money and doesn't have to put in the work."

"Precisely. Plus, the miners have to pay a small fee for anything they find, in case someone strikes it rich. The government wants to benefit from that, too."

"I'm a little disturbed that this all makes sense to me, given that dragons don't do it that way at all."

"You're starting to understand the human mind. Turn left. Just a little."

Lamprophyre turned left. She saw no signs of human presence on the hills, though she did see furtive movement that might indicate small prey animals. She cast her gaze southward— "There," she said, pointing. "I don't know if that's Mendesk, but it's a mine." A hole big enough to fit a dragon was carved into the nearly vertical face of the hills, almost perfectly round.

"It's in the right area, and the mine foreman told me Mendesk's claim isn't near anyone else's. Or, more accurately, he claimed the land surrounding the part he's actually working so no one could get close enough to poach. He's got to be successful if he can afford that." Rokshan leaned out far enough Lamprophyre worried he might slip. "I don't see any movement."

"Then I guess we have to wait for him," Lamprophyre said. She checked the position of the sun. "I hope he doesn't take long."

"I can go in after him."

"If he's as paranoid as we're told, isn't it likely he'd attack you for trespassing?" She set down a dozen dragonlengths from the mine entrance and crouched to let Rokshan off.

"Good point," Rokshan said. "Let's find a place to wait."

Now that they were on the ground, Lamprophyre could make out human made structures: a couple of low, sloping buildings made of canopy canvas, but dull green that looked like a blotch against the red ground, and a taller structure also covered in tan canvas that was open on three sides. Beneath that structure lay wooden tables covered with items she didn't recognize and a wooden bucket that even from this distance smelled sweetly of water.

"We probably shouldn't invade his camp," Rokshan said. He lagged behind Lamprophyre as if putting his words into action.

"We're not invading, we're visitors," Lamprophyre said. "And it's not like we're going to touch anything. I'm just curious about how humans extract stone. It's so different from the dragon way."

"How would you mine sapphire?"

Lamprophyre sniffed the water bucket. It roused her thirst after the long flight. "Dig a couple of tunnels. One main tunnel, and one or two more to provide air. Generally it takes ten or twelve dragons to dig a new seam, because it's boring work and we like to keep each other company. Then we sniff out the location of the stone. Usually it's rubies as well as sapphires."

Rokshan walked past her in the direction of the mine entrance. "Interesting. Is that—"

A brilliant flash of golden light erupted from the entrance, followed by a thunderclap that made Lamprophyre's ears ring. The ground shook, knocking her off balance so she dropped to one knee. And Rokshan flew backward as if punched by an invisible fist.

CHAPTER TWENTY-FIVE

"*R*okshan!*" Lamprophyre screamed. She pushed herself to her feet and loped across the ground to where he lay. His eyes were open, and he gasped for air. Lamprophyre got her arm around his shoulders and helped him sit. "Are you hurt?"

Rokshan waved his hands at her and shook his head. "Got...the wind... knocked out...of me," he gasped. Then his eyes widened, and he grabbed Lamprophyre's arm. "*Watch out!*"

Lamprophyre turned to face the mine entrance just as another explosion rocked her backward with its force. Her nictitating membranes closed, not quite fast enough, and spots of light pulsed in front of her eyes, obscuring the figure that ran toward her. She snarled and let go of Rokshan. Shoving off the ground with her powerful legs, she shot toward the figure, gliding low and fast along the ground.

The human raised a glittering chunk of pyrite to the level of her throat, a bizarre gesture that struck Lamprophyre as ominous. She hit the human's midsection, bowling her over and making her lose her grip on the pyrite, which bounced away. With another snarl, she pressed the dull edge of her claw against the human's throat. "Don't move," she said. "How dare you attack us?"

"You invaded my camp," the human replied, her—no, now that the bright flashes were fading, Lamprophyre could see the human had scruffy dark hair growing over his chin and cheeks—his voice surprisingly strong for someone with death poised to tear out his throat.

"Even so..." Lamprophyre realized the male had a point. "Are you Mendesk? We just want to talk."

"I got no reason to talk with you trespassers."

It struck Lamprophyre that Mendesk wasn't at all afraid of her; his thoughts were furious at having his privacy invaded by strangers, but being held captive by a dragon didn't disturb him in the least. "Why aren't you afraid of me?" she asked, removing her claw from his throat.

"Death comes as it does," Mendesk said, pushing himself to a sitting position. "No sense fearing it, whatever form it wears."

"Yes, but most humans are afraid of me when I *don't* threaten them. You don't even seem surprised."

Mendesk stood and brushed red dust from his already filthy trousers. "I get a prophecy every time I leave for the field," he said. "Last one said dragons were in my future. The ecclesiast thought it was symbolic of something, but I knew better."

"So you knew something was coming," Rokshan said. He, too, was covered with rock dust, and Lamprophyre gently brushed off the back of his head. "We're sorry we, um, invaded you."

Lamprophyre picked up the lump of pyrite, which felt unnaturally warm and smelled like an orange. "This is magic," she said.

"Give it back," Mendesk said, his voice going hard and cold.

Lamprophyre didn't move. "Not if you're going to use it on us again."

Mendesk held out his hand. "You want to talk? I don't talk without you give that back. I don't know but that you intend to kill me and take my claim."

"We wouldn't do that."

Mendesk glared at her, his hand unwavering. Lamprophyre hesitated only a beat longer, then put the pyrite into the male's hand. He tucked it away into a pouch hanging from his belt. "Say what you want, then get out of here."

Lamprophyre glanced at Rokshan. Rokshan stepped forward and spread his hands wide, indicating he wasn't a threat. "We're interested in a sapphire you mined a few months back. Specifically, we want to speak to the buyer. We were told by gem buyers in Tanajital that you're the only supplier of sapphire in Gonjiri, and that the stone we're interested in had to have come from you."

Mendesk's posture became aggressive once more. "You think I'm the sort who sells his customers' secrets? Think again, plusher."

Lamprophyre listened to the male's thoughts and heard only *I'm going to die here, see if I don't.* She'd hoped to take the knowledge of the buyer from Mendesk's mind. "We know you are very private," she said, "and guessed that might extend to keeping your customers' information private too. But this is a very serious matter. Something more important than concealing that buyer's name."

Mendesk's lip curled. "Important to you. Not important to me. I'd never do business again if it got out I blabbed."

"We're not interested in telling people about your involvement, and we won't let the buyer know you told us," Rokshan said. "But that person used the sapphire to make a weapon, and we intend to bring him or her to justice. We *will* find that buyer, sirrah, with or without your help. It would just be easier and faster if we had your assistance."

"None of my business what my buyers do with my stones," Mendesk said. His voice was strong and certain, but Lamprophyre heard him think *should have known not to trust that man, had weasel written all over him, no surprise he wanted a weapon.*

"Of course not," Rokshan said. "But we were hoping you would care enough about your profession not to want your wares used for evil."

Mendesk chewed on his lower lip briefly. "What weapon?"

Rokshan glanced at Lamprophyre, his eyes wide, and she took the hint. He was thinking *dare we tell him?*

"It drives people mad," she said. There was no way to completely conceal the existence of the weapon, and this man was unlikely to reveal to his clients that such an effect was possible. She could hear his thoughts becoming more uncertain, and hoped being honest with him—a little honest, anyway—might push him over the edge.

"Impossible," Mendesk said. "You're lying."

"You know I'm not," Lamprophyre said. "It's a terrible weapon, and we want its creator stopped before he makes any more of them."

Terrible indecision gripped Mendesk. "Of course, there is the other possibility," Lamprophyre continued. "Everyone knows you're the only local supplier of sapphires, so if knowledge of this weapon becomes public, everyone will also know you were the source of the stone. And I imagine there are people who will want to hold you responsible."

"That's ridiculous," Mendesk said.

"Humans aren't always rational. I know that from personal experience." Lamprophyre took half a step forward. "If we find this person, we'll stop him before his crimes become public knowledge, and you won't have to be involved at all."

Mendesk drew in a deep breath and let it out slowly. "His name is Abhimot," he said. "Lives in Tanajital. Tall fellow with one glass eye. I don't know more than that."

"Thank you," Lamprophyre said.

"That's more than enough. We appreciate your help," Rokshan said. "And we won't let anyone know you were involved in any way."

Mendesk nodded. "Now get out of here. I got work to do."

Rokshan nodded and climbed up Lamprophyre's shoulder to the notch.

"Wait," Mendesk said. "Do you know what 'the skies will burn' means?"

"Why do you ask?" Rokshan said.

Mendesk shrugged. "It was part of the prophecy that said I'd see a dragon."

"It doesn't mean anything to me. Lamprophyre?"

"Not to me either," Lamprophyre said. She hoped it didn't mean what she feared, that the dragons would go to war against Gonjiri. But that was just a fear, nothing she felt confident about telling this male. She waved at Mendesk, whose mouth fell open, and leaped into the sky.

They flew in silence for a while, until Lamprophyre said, "So our wand maker is Gonjirian."

"Seems like it. Though I'm not jumping to conclusions just yet. He may be innocent of anything but coincidence. Even so, it does look like we're looking for a Gonjirian plot."

"Can you find this Abhimot with just a name and a description?"

"Of course," Rokshan said. "Though I'm reluctant to face him on my own. What if he has an artifact like that chunk of gold?"

"That was pyrite, not gold."

"I'm not sure my body cares about the difference, except that I'm guessing gold does something different than knock me on my ass. I wonder if it's what powers the Army's new weapon?"

"You said you weren't hurt!"

"I'm not, just sore." Rokshan shifted as if he were rubbing his thigh. "I suppose I could take a squad of guards, but we're trying to keep this secret and I'm not sure what I'd tell them about why we have to apprehend this man."

"If you can get him out in the open—"

"That would be ideal, but we shouldn't count on it." Rokshan sighed. "Are you hungry?"

"I'm not. It's earlier than I anticipated, so I think I'll just eat at the embassy. I can roast that cow myself."

"I'd rather eat at the palace than find a place where you won't terrify everyone. Sorry."

"It's all right. I'm used to it." She still didn't like knowing how afraid humans were of her, but she no longer took it personally. To them, she was like a terrifying storm, or a flood, or some other natural disaster that was dangerous simply by its existence, and while that was annoying, at least very few of them believed she was evil.

They didn't talk much the rest of the way to Tanajital. Lamprophyre felt the weariness that accompanied not having made many long flights recently; her wings ached, and the long muscles of her flanks felt tight. She would sleep well that night.

It was sunset when they arrived back at the embassy. Someone had lit the lanterns flanking the entrance and on the pillars of the dining pavilion. It warmed Lamprophyre's heart that someone had given consideration to her needs, even if it was likely a servant who was paid to do so. She let Rokshan off and said, "Dharan says tomorrow is a rest day, so there's no reading lesson. Should we wait until the following day to track down Abhimot?"

"No, I can at least find out where he lives," Rokshan said, "and we can make a plan from there. I'll see you tomorrow sometime." He waved and disappeared down the street.

Lamprophyre watched until he was gone, then entered the dining pavilion. It was empty and dark despite the lanterns burning outside, but the cow was still there, half hanging from a hook attached to the ceiling, half lying in the shallow trough she'd learned was intended for that purpose. It didn't smell quite as fresh as it had earlier, but she wasn't picky.

She lifted the partial carcass from the trough and sniffed it all over. There was another scent, something tangy Depik had seasoned it with. She hoped she wasn't ruining some culinary plan of his, but she was definitely hungry now and disinclined to wait until morning. And she felt bad about rousing Depik just to do something she was capable of doing herself.

She laid the carcass back in the trough and breathed out a light fire to touch every exposed part, turning the meat to keep it from burning. She'd learned from Akarshan about letting cooked meat sit for a few dozen beats, and she was in the mood for something very rare, so she let the fire burn only enough to sear it, then sat beside the carcass counting heartbeats and breathing in the delicious aroma. While she waited, she sniffed out the lights and liver and kidneys and ate those raw. The taste honed her already keen appetite and made her count faster.

Finally, when she couldn't stand the waiting any longer, she picked up the carcass and took it to the center of the dining pavilion, where she settled in to eat. The taste wasn't quite as good as either Depik or Akarshan managed. She chastised herself for going soft and tore off another mouthful. She really needed to buy a herd of cows and introduce the flight to the marvelous meat.

Her stomach gave an unexpected rumble. She burped, and tasted something strange, something sweeter than cow meat and almost cloying compared to the tangy seasoning. She sniffed the meat, but smelled nothing out of the ordinary. Another burp rose up within her. This one was sharp and painful, and when it emerged, the sweet taste was so strong she gagged.

She set the carcass down and sat up, hoping to stretch out the gas pain. Her legs refused to respond. Frightened, she twisted to touch her legs, and agony shot through her midsection like claws tearing her insides apart. She collapsed over the carcass, her arms twitching, and cried out as the pain struck her again. One leg shifted, its claws scoring the stone floor, and then lay still. Numbness radiated from her spine down her limbs even as spasms wrung her abdomen and chest. She cried out more loudly, unable to form words. Poison. She'd been poisoned.

Her pain-addled brain focused on this fact and roused her to fight her ravaged body. Poison. What did one do about poison? *Get it out.*

She raised one hand, steadied it with the other, and opened her mouth as wide as she could manage. Shuddering against another spasm of pain, she waited for it to release her, then swiftly jabbed two fingers at the back of her throat. Immediately a different kind of tremor wracked her body, and she fell helplessly to the floor, barely able to support herself on her elbows before both her stomachs turned inside out and she vomited cow and burning matter all over herself and the floor.

When the convulsions ceased, she lay on her side, one wing pinned painfully beneath her, and gasped for air. For a moment, she thought she'd been fast enough, that she'd expelled the poison from her body. Then agony wracked her again, and she clutched her midsection and wished she knew how to weep like a human. They did it so readily, surely it provided some relief.

There's something else. Something easy. She felt dizzy and swollen, and her breathing was loud and ragged like a storm raging over the mountains. When a dragon ate something poisonous, there was—yes. Lamprophyre pushed herself half upright and looked around the dining pavilion. Everything was so dim. Pillars with fuzzy light blotches attached to them, the low walls of the kitchen—

"My lady!"

Someone had heard her screams. Lamprophyre didn't recognize the voice, or the hands trying to support her—so stupid, no human could lift a dragon. It didn't matter. She saw what she'd been looking for: the table and chairs Rokshan and Dharan used when they shared a meal with her. Another seizure gripped her, the sharp agony in her stomach almost overridden by the pains in her muscles, like being wrung by hands bigger than her own. She rolled onto her stomach when it was over, blinked away the fuzziness in her vision, and breathed out fire as hot as she could manage to engulf the table.

In her extremity, control was not something she had much of. Hot liquid splattered the chairs, causing them to catch fire as well, but the table itself fell apart almost instantly into charred black cinders. Lamprophyre grabbed two handfuls of the charcoal and stuffed it into her mouth, nearly gagging again at the horrible bitterness. She swallowed, gulped down more, swallowed again, and had to stop, lying curled in on herself, when another pain struck. Desperate, she stuffed herself until half the table was gone, hoping the poison didn't act so quickly she was simply killing herself faster.

The human beside her hadn't fled when she burned the table. He had dragged her wing out from under her, easing that much smaller pain, and she could barely feel his hands on her arm. If he had thoughts, she was too far gone to hear them. Pain wrung her out again, but more weakly. She continued to lie curled up in a ball, her other wing covering her face. The pain might be lessening because she was dying. She couldn't die so far from home. How would she ever reach Mother Stone in this condition?

"My lady. My lady! What's wrong?"

Depik. She recognized his voice now. She tried to apologize for waking him, but managed only a low moan. The pains weren't nearly so close together. She tried to sit, but her body wouldn't respond more than the merest twitch of her wing tips. Her mouth was dry and tasted bitter, like charcoal—well, that made sense. She ran her tongue around the inside of her mouth, moistening it. "Depik," she whispered. "Poison."

"Poison?" Depik sounded horrified. "Poison, how?"

"In the meat." No, that was wrong. Surely fire would have burned the poison away. But the lights, and the liver and kidneys—she'd gulped those down practically without tasting them. "The offal."

"I left them out," Depik said. "I thought—I was abed, my lady, anyone might have come back here."

His thoughts were starting to be audible, like voices rising up through deep waters: *more careful,* he thought, and *why would anyone do such a thing?*

"I need to get inside," she whispered. She didn't think she could move, but the idea of sleeping outdoors rather than in the comfort of her cave made her feel sick again.

Depik disappeared, making her feel unexpectedly bereft. But he came back in a few beats with a bucket of water he sluiced across her abdomen, washing away her vomit. It steamed and sent up a terrible stench, bitter bile laced with the sweet smell of the poison. He began to swab the mess away with a cloth, but Lamprophyre took it from him. "You'll...burn... yourself," she said, swiping at the remaining splotches of burning stomach matter and then dropping the cloth into the largest puddle of water.

Depik walked around to her front and lifted her arm with some effort. "Can I help, my lady?"

Lamprophyre wanted to laugh, but it would hurt his feelings. "Get... the lantern..." she said. "Light...my...way."

With tremendous effort, she rolled onto her hands and knees and crawled with agonizing slowness out of the dining pavilion and into the embassy, where she collapsed. Her heart was thudding so rapidly it hurt, her stomach still roiled with pain, every muscle ached as if she'd been under a rockfall, but she was alive.

With one final exertion, she dragged her legs beneath her wings and fell into a confused stupor, not quite asleep but unable to move, her brain seizing on moments from the day's journey and running through them in an endless cycle. She watched Rokshan flung backward by the pyrite's magic over and over again, and over and over again she tried to reach him first and failed. If this was the poison's final effect, death might be a release.

CHAPTER TWENTY-SIX

S he must have fallen asleep at some point, because eventually she opened her eyes and it was day, and Anamika was standing beside her, saying, "Lamprophyre? Wake up. Didn't you want to swim?"

Lamprophyre groaned and tried to sit, but she still ached too much for her muscles to respond. "I'm afraid I'm sick," she said. "I'm sorry. We'll have to swim another day."

"I didn't know dragons got sick. Should you have soup? Mam always makes soup for me and Varnak when we're sick."

The idea of food of any kind made Lamprophyre's stomach revolt. "Not now. Maybe later. Now I need to sleep."

"All right. I hope you feel better soon."

The next time Lamprophyre opened her eyes, what felt like a thousand beats later, Anamika was gone. Lamprophyre focused on breathing, in and out through the mouth, filling her lungs with warm, damp air and wishing more than ever she was home in the mountains, where no one had ever tried to poison her.

She tried to sleep again, hoping her body would finish purging itself while she was unconscious, but sleep eluded her, and she lay staring at what was in her line of vision, which was a slate where she'd written a number of words beginning with G: gather, goose, grin, goad, garnet. Her handwriting was still sloppy, but it was intelligible.

She was so used to thinking of herself as indestructible, impervious to any human attack, she hadn't thought of the ways in which she was vulnerable. Now that her body wasn't tearing itself apart, she could think more rationally. It was possible that poison wouldn't have killed her, given how small a portion she'd eaten, but she had to assume whoever had done it had intended her death. But she couldn't make any assumptions about who that human was. It was tempting to think it was the egg thieves, but she and Rokshan hadn't made enough progress for the egg thieves to know they were in danger—or was she wrong? In any case, it was possible this was a random human who hated and feared dragons and wanted her gone, and there was nothing she could do about that.

A shudder ran through her, tinged with pain, the last remnants of the poison. She could still taste it under the charcoal bitterness. She would have to hire guards now, and be more careful with her food; she didn't think Depik was careless in choosing meat, but he needed to be extra cautious now. Too bad he'd been asleep and hadn't seen the poisoner.

She heard Rokshan approaching and managed to lift her head to look at him. "I found—you look terrible. Are you ill?"

"I was poisoned," she said. Rokshan's cheerful expression faded to one of horror.

"*Poisoned?* How?" he demanded.

"In the meat. The offal. Depik left it all out in readiness for today, and someone poisoned it."

Rokshan gripped her hand as well as his small one would allow. "But you didn't die."

"It wasn't fast-acting enough, and I got most of it out of my system. But I ache all over and I feel I could never eat again." Lamprophyre put her other hand atop their joined ones. "And I don't know what to do. If I have to defend against this kind of attack..."

"We'll post guards. Maybe they can alter the kitchen to be more secure. Didn't any of your servants see or hear anything?"

"Depik only heard me making noise after it happened. I haven't seen anyone else this morning." It occurred to her that she should have seen Depik at breakfast time. "Wouldn't it be nice if it was the egg thieves that did it?"

"Nice? Lamprophyre, you're still lightheaded if you can call being nearly killed 'nice.'"

"True, but at least then I'd only have one enemy to worry about instead of potentially all of Tanajital." She tried and failed to sit up. Rokshan put his other hand on her shoulder.

"Lie here and rest. You should probably eat something if you want to keep your strength up." He hesitated, then said, "You're sure Depik wasn't responsible?"

"Depik? Why the Stones would Depik want me dead?"

"If he was part of a deep-laid plan—"

"That's absurd!"

"Lamprophyre, it's starting to look like we have to consider absurdities, given that anyone might have done this. Depik's sad story might have been calculated to appeal to you, putting him in a position to kill you."

Lamprophyre blew out a fist-sized knot of smoke that made her second stomach ache as if it had been the one poisoned. "I heard his thoughts, Rokshan. It wasn't Depik."

"Oh. Well, that's a relief. I'll go see what he's up to and have him make you some chicken broth or something—is that something dragons eat when they're sick?"

"Meat broth? Sometimes, yes. But I'm not hungry."

"Hungry or not, you need food. I'll be right back."

Lamprophyre closed her eyes and listened to the sound of his retreating footsteps. The city sounded peaceful today, its rumbling higher pitched like birdsong, the muffled murmur of human speech like its quiet breath. It made her feel peaceful, too, despite everything that had happened.

Footsteps, quick and light, and the sound of the back door creaking shut. "Depik's ill," Rokshan said.

Lamprophyre tried to sit up and the world spun around her. "Not more poison?"

"No. It's that illness he told you about, where he can't get out of bed. He just groaned when I prodded him. You ought to fire him if he can't do his job."

"It's not his fault if he's ill. He'll be back to work soon. Besides, I told you I wasn't hungry."

Rokshan scowled. "Looks like I'll have to do it. It's your own fault if the soup is awful. And I'm going to have to send someone for fresh chickens, because there's no way I'm trusting anything that was in your kitchen last night."

Lamprophyre managed to doze while Rokshan bustled around. Servants ran back and forth in front of the entrance, and once she heard a chicken squawk and be instantly silenced. Finally Rokshan was shaking her shoulder and saying, "You'll have to drag yourself out here, because none of us can lift the cauldron."

She groaned, but found she was able to walk on hands and knees to the dining pavilion, where Rokshan had built a fire in the middle of the floor and positioned a cauldron, enormous even by Lamprophyre's standards, over it. It smelled deliciously of cooked bird, and when Lamprophyre's stomachs rumbled, for once it didn't hurt.

Rokshan handed her a hollow glass tube as long as her arm. "Use this to drink the broth," he said, "and we'll bring you the meat when you've regained some strength."

Lamprophyre examined the tube closely, then put it in her mouth and blew through it. "Almost," Rokshan said, and showed her how to put the tube in the cauldron and drink through it. The broth was warm, very comforting, and Lamprophyre discovered she was hungry after all. She slurped up broth until her stomach felt less painful, and then ate shredded, boiled chicken until she was full. Her muscles still ached, but the weakness was mostly gone, and she was able to walk back to the embassy and settle herself comfortably.

Rokshan sat beside her holding a bowl containing some of the chicken meat. "Not too bad," he said, using the strange pronged stick he called a fork to convey meat to his mouth. "I'm good at cooking so long as it's over an open fire. I got used to doing it on maneuvers. The Army," he added when Lamprophyre gave him a confused look.

"I wouldn't think a prince would do any cooking," she said. "In all our stories, princes and princesses have adventures. They don't do anything simple like cooking or...I can't think of anything else."

"Princes and princesses need occupation as much as anyone. Tekentriya is the most active person I know, and she insists everyone around her be active, too. Manishi is obsessed with magic. Even Anchala spends her whole day researching. I guess Khadar is the only one of us who's indolent, and even he can't get away with doing nothing, not as the Fifth Ecclesiast." He took another bite. "Besides, those adventures never sounded like fun to me. Either the prince had some task that earned him a boring reward, or he had to fight monsters that were likely to kill him."

"Well, thank you for cooking for me. I feel better."

"It's my pleasure. Besides, it's selfishness. I need you well so we can catch Abhimot."

Lamprophyre sat up. "You were going to look for him today, weren't you?"

"Yes, and I've tracked him down. He lives in West District, and his neighbors don't like him much, based on how quick they were to tell me about his many unpleasant habits."

"Unpleasant, how?"

"He doesn't keep his part of the street clean and has to be reminded to fuel his lantern—householders in West are legally obligated to maintain a light source along the street. He's not friendly and he's never willing to help when someone moves in or gets sick. A few people told me he has unsavory visitors, though they weren't forthcoming about what 'unsavory' looked like. And two children went into some detail about his glass eye and how he sends it out by itself at night to peer in people's windows."

Lamprophyre gasped. "He can do that?"

Rokshan laughed. "I think that was just the kind of story children tell about anything strange. At any rate, I was going to go back this afternoon and confront him, but if you're not well, I want to put that off until tomorrow."

"Unless he lives in the coliseum, I don't see how I'd be much help with that confrontation."

"I was thinking of the possibility I'd apprehend him and drag him back here. But it can wait." Rokshan put his empty bowl aside and stretched. "I think I'll go back to the palace and arrange for guards for this place."

"You mean, soldiers? I thought that would look too much like pandering, or favoritism, or something," Lamprophyre said. "I can hire private guards."

"It's more important you not be hurt," Rokshan countered. "And Gonjiri has an interest in making sure you aren't. Besides, there aren't any private fighting forces I'd trust with something like this." He rose and picked up his bowl. "I'll come back this evening to check on you. And if Depik isn't up by then, I'll kick him until he is."

"Don't—"

"I was kidding, Lamprophyre. I won't harm him. Now, try to sleep." He waved goodbye and walked out the back door.

Lamprophyre shifted her position until she felt more comfortable, then tucked her wings over herself and closed her eyes. It was fun to imagine frightening the maker of that wand, who couldn't possibly expect a dragon to come after him, but the practicalities kept interfering. What would the rest of the city think if she pounced on a human that as far as everyone else was concerned was a helpless victim of the mad dragon? It would only make them fear her more. And yet she and Rokshan didn't have much choice, if they wanted to learn the truth. She drifted off to sleep hoping Rokshan would find another solution.

Hard, heavy footsteps roused her some time later from dreams of flying backwards and upside down. Confused, she raised her head, blinked at the world not being reversed, and stood. She felt only a little wobbly, and her stomachs had settled.

Then she heard Depik shout, "My lady! Help!"

With a lurch, she propelled her still-awkward self out of the embassy into the courtyard, which was full of uniformed soldiers. Two of them had Depik by the arms and were dragging him toward the street as he kicked and thrashed. "What the *Stones* do you think you're doing?" she roared, bringing every soldier in the courtyard to a halt. She shoved her way to Depik's side and grabbed the arm of the nearest soldier, her fingers wrapping entirely around his arm and overlapping. "Take your hands off him!"

"My lady ambassador," someone said from behind her. She released the soldier and turned. The male who addressed her wore the bright uniform General Sajan had. He tilted his head to look up at her where she towered over him, his thoughts showing only a hint of fear: *can take care of herself, God's breath, no idea who'd try such a thing.*

"What are you doing with my cook?" she said, not quite as loudly.

"My lady ambassador," the uniformed soldier said, "this man is accused of poisoning you. We're taking him into custody."

"What?" Lamprophyre turned to stare at Depik, who shook his head violently. "Depik didn't poison me."

"With all due respect, my lady, he had the most opportunity, and he's a known vagrant," the soldier said. "We'll interrogate him and prove his innocence or guilt."

"But he——" Lamprophyre closed her mouth. She didn't want to reveal her secret ability, certainly not in the middle of the street, but she also couldn't allow them to subject Depik to whatever interrogation they thought necessary. Particularly since the soldier's thoughts about the word "vagrant" weren't complimentary.

She turned on the soldier again. "He's not guilty," she said. "I've already interrogated him and I'm satisfied of his innocence. That should be enough for you."

"My lady, you can't possibly know——"

"*I know*, soldier," Lamprophyre said, taking a few steps in his direction and forcing him to stand with his back arched to meet her gaze. "Depik has my confidence. If he wanted to poison me, he'd be much smarter about it—or do you think he doesn't know he's the first one suspicion would fall on?"

The soldier swallowed, the sharp lump in his throat bobbing up and down. "No, my lady."

"I appreciate that you and your people want to keep me safe. Thank you. But wouldn't it be better to ask around the neighborhood to find out if anyone saw someone skulking around here last night?" Lamprophyre not very gently peeled hands off Depik's arms and prodded Depik in the direction of the kitchen. "And if you do find out who did it, I'd like to know."

The soldier made a complicated gesture, stepped away from Lamprophyre, and shouted, "Form up!" As the soldiers tramped about getting into a regular, square formation, the male said, "I hope you're right, my lady."

"I am," Lamprophyre said.

The soldier shouted again, and all of them marched away down the street.

Lamprophyre let out a long breath. "Well, that was an exciting way to wake up," she said.

Depik was staring at her. "My lady," he said, faintly as if he were out of breath, then more loudly, "You don't know I didn't do it! Why did you protect me?"

Lamprophyre regarded him. "Did you poison me?" she asked.

"Of course not!" His thoughts fiercely matched his words, with a fainter undercurrent of *she shouldn't believe me, I look so guilty, never in a million years would I...*

"I believe you," Lamprophyre said. "And it's like I said: if you were going to poison me, I think you'd be smarter about it. But I gave you a chance when no one else would, and that matters to you."

Depik's mouth fell open. Then he let out a great, sobbing breath, and tears trickled down his face. "Why?" he said. "I'm nothing to you."

His tears made Lamprophyre uncomfortable. "I suppose because you needed help," she said. "And dragons don't give help with an eye to how it might be repaid. I don't know how humans do it."

"Most wouldn't," Depik said. He wiped his eyes and said, "I'm feeling better now, my lady, and whatever you want for supper, I'll do. But no more leaving food here overnight, not even if it's more convenient."

"That's what I was thinking." Lamprophyre considered her stomach. "Something light, I think. And not complicated. I hope Rokshan didn't leave you a huge mess when he made soup."

"My fault he had to," Depik said, but his thoughts weren't nearly so grim and despairing as they usually were when he contemplated his illness. "Go on and rest, my lady. Leave it to me."

"Thank you."

Lamprophyre walked back into the embassy and settled in front of her slate. Practicing her handwriting would keep her from fretting too much about Abhimot and the wand. It occurred to her that someone capable of making such a weapon knew far too much about dragons' weaknesses, more even than dragons did, and that he might have more weapons at hand. He might be more dangerous than they thought.

She'd written a dozen words starting with the letter G a dozen times each when she heard Rokshan's quick footsteps approaching. "I feel better," she began, but fell silent when she saw him, his expression furious. "Is something wrong?"

"It turns out one of Abhimot's neighbors liked him better than I thought," Rokshan said. "Abhimot's fled."

CHAPTER TWENTY-SEVEN

"How do you know?" Lamprophyre exclaimed.

"I had a feeling," Rokshan said, "just a passing instinct that I should check Abhimot's neighborhood again. His house was empty, and the woman across the street told me she'd seen him leave two hours earlier, heavily laden like he was going on a journey. Somebody must have told him I was asking around, and he legged it."

Lamprophyre let out two impatient bursts of smoke. "Well, Stones take him," she said irritably. "How will we ever find him now?"

A shadow fell across the entrance. "My lady, supper's ready, and there's enough for his highness if he wants," Depik said.

"Thank you, Depik, we'll be right there," Lamprophyre said. When he was gone, she said, "Do you want supper?"

"How can you think of food right now?"

"I'm grateful I'm alive to be hungry, that's how. Let's eat, and we can discuss a new plan."

Though the destroyed table had been removed, no one had replaced it, so Rokshan sat cross-legged on the floor next to Lamprophyre and ate crumbling handfuls of ground-up cow meat. "This is surprisingly good," he said. "Maybe hiring Depik wasn't so crazy."

"I told you," Lamprophyre said with her mouth full. She chewed and swallowed and added, "This can't be impossible. Abhimot ran, which makes him look very guilty. So it's essential we find him."

"I can't think how," Rokshan said. "Tanajital's a big place, and Gonjiri is even bigger. Lots of places to hide, even for a man with a glass eye."

"If he were a deer or a boar, I could hunt him by scent, but you humans mostly smell the same to me. He doesn't have that scent Khadar wears, does he?"

"Not to my knowledge. It's unfortunate he doesn't have a more obvious impairment. Something that would stand out."

"Or had strangely colored hair or skin. Then I could skim low over the city, and we could spot him that way." Lamprophyre stopped with her hand halfway to her mouth. "Maybe that's not impossible."

"He looks just like everyone else from above," Rokshan said.

"Yes, but what did Sabarna say about diamonds? That they could be made to see things very far away?"

Rokshan wiped his mouth. "I think those are for viewing known locations, not finding someone."

Lamprophyre waved a dismissive hand at him. "Yes, but what I'm getting at is maybe there's magic for that. Not necessarily a diamond, but some other stone."

"Huh." Rokshan's eyes unfocused as he looked into the distance past Lamprophyre's ear. "That does seem like useful magic. I'll wager there is such a thing."

"So we should ask Sabarna?"

Rokshan shook his head. "She goes to bed early, and rousing her is impossible. I don't think we should wait for morning. That means..."

Lamprophyre scowled. "I don't trust Manishi."

"Neither do I, but in a backwards way, that makes her trustworthy, if only because we can trust her to try to cheat us."

"But suppose Abhimot is a friend of hers?"

"That is *extremely* unlikely. I did mention she doesn't work with others, right? Even if she knows him, she's not likely to care about protecting him. If she learns he's created an artifact no one's ever thought of before, she might actually help us for free if it means being able to steal his work."

Lamprophyre stood. She no longer felt wobbly, her stomachs didn't hurt, and her vision was clear. "Then let's talk to her now, and maybe we can track down Abhimot tonight."

LAMPROPHYRE WAITED IMPATIENTLY IN THE PARKLAND OUTSIDE THE palace for Rokshan. The sun was halfway below the horizon, but the trees in the park blocked her view of it, so all she could see was the sky shading from rose to peach to a blue the exact color of her clutchmate Flint of the boring name and handsome body.

She huddled in on herself, hoping to go unnoticed, and listened to the night birds taking wing. Flint had always been her good friend, but so was the rest of the clutch except for stupid Coquina. Their clutch was so lopsided, with five males and only two females. Most of the males would end up finding mates from the previous clutch, but Lamprophyre couldn't help feeling guilty at not being interested in any of them. There was nothing wrong with pair-bonding outside your clutch, it happened all the time, but Lamprophyre felt as if she'd been offered a delicious cow someone had gone to the trouble of butchering and cooking perfectly and turned it down. At least none of her clutchmates were pining after her. That would make everything so awkward.

She heard Rokshan approaching and unfurled her wings, crouching low for him to mount. "Did she have something?"

"She did," Rokshan said, "and I'm trying not to feel very, very suspicious that she so readily parted with it." He dangled a blue stone hanging from a silver chain in front of her face. Lamprophyre grasped it and turned it to catch the last rays of sunlight. It had been polished, but beneath the almost liquid blue of the surface lay dozens upon dozens of tiny cracks that gave it the appearance of a sheet of ice. As she turned it, color sheeted across it, blue and green and violet like an oil slick.

She sniffed it. "It's just an ordinary feldspar," she said. "Pretty enough, with the polishing, but I don't see anything unusual about it, aside from how it doesn't occur locally."

"Manishi impressed upon me the importance of not losing it," Rokshan said. He retrieved it from Lamprophyre and put it around his neck, then mounted and settled himself securely in the notch. "Its actual purpose is for finding lost things. You hold the image of what you want to find in your thoughts, and the stone resonates with the image to lead you to it."

"But we haven't seen Abhimot."

"Not up close, but I did see him this morning when I was asking around. At least I hope that was him, because if more than one person lives in his house, we might be out of luck. But I've run out of ideas."

Lamprophyre moved away from the trees and spread her wings wide. "If it turns out you're wrong, the stone will at least lead us to someone who knows him."

"I hadn't thought of that. All right, let's head northwest."

The cool night air banished the last of Lamprophyre's queasiness. She flew swiftly in the direction Rokshan indicated, making slight course corrections but mostly staying on the northwest heading. Within a few hundred beats, they were past the great wall of Tanajital and winging across the cultivated plains. "He can't have gotten far," she said.

"No, and the stone is tugging downward. What's down there?"

Lamprophyre scanned the dark ground, sparkling here and there with firelight. "I don't—no, there's a small human city below us. Is that where he is?"

Rokshan leaned far out. "It's where the stone is pointing, at least. Go ahead and circle around, just to be sure."

Lamprophyre made a great sweeping loop around the black blotch of lantern-lit buildings before descending to land some dozen dragonlengths from the city. "Now what?"

"It's dark," Rokshan said. "You could come with me into the city."

"Are you sure that's safe?"

"I've been contemplating all the potential weapons this adept might have, if he created the wand. I'd rather not face him alone."

Lamprophyre nodded. "I thought of that, too. All right. I can conceal myself—it's nearly full dark, but better not take chances."

With her bright blue scales dulled to near-black and her copper membranes faded to charcoal, she glided silently over the rooftops while Rokshan called out directions in a low voice. She'd just swept past a building taller than its neighbors when Rokshan said, "He's in there."

She took another look around. The tall building was surrounded by empty space on both sides. To the west, the space was brightly lit and full of humans, most of whom went in and out by an entrance that was large by human standards. Lamprophyre's head and shoulders would barely fit through it. To the southeast, the space was smaller, but it was also dark, illuminated only by one lantern over an even smaller doorway.

Lamprophyre said, "I'm going to let you off there and then sit on the roof."

"The *roof*? Are you serious?"

"All it takes is one person coming outside at the wrong time to let Abhimot know he's been found. You go inside and get him to come out here, and then I'll pounce on him."

Rokshan slid off down her shoulder and crouched to regain his balance. "And if we start a riot when the dragon attacks the innocent human?"

"Then we start a riot. But I have faith in your ability to make this work."

Rokshan grimaced, but headed for the door. Lamprophyre leaped for the roof's ridge beam, flapping hard to lower herself lightly onto it. It was narrow, forcing her to dig her toe claws into the wood and spread her wings for balance. After a few heart-stopping moments, she relaxed and let her concealment fall. She would be visible if anyone looked up, but Lamprophyre knew from experience that humans very rarely looked up.

She listened to the thoughts of the humans beneath her, but heard only commotion and confusion she had to block out. This would be so much easier if she could listen just to Rokshan, or, better, the thoughts of Abhimot. Maybe there was a magical artifact that could manage it. It was too bad she didn't want anyone to know she could hear thoughts, or she might work with an adept to create such an artifact. Though the only adepts she knew were Manishi and Sabarna, and Manishi was prickly and Sabarna unable to set foot outside. More black marks against the potential project.

She surveyed the entrance on the brightly-lit side. Humans greeted each other and went inside together, or left in pairs or groups of three. None of them were Abhimot or Rokshan. Lamprophyre wobbled again, then froze as someone glanced upward. Whatever had drawn the female's attention was nowhere near Lamprophyre, and the female paused only for a beat before walking on.

Music filtered out of the building into the evening air, rising and falling every time the door opened and closed. Lamprophyre hadn't heard much human music to date, and what she had heard hadn't impressed her much, at least the compositions. But humans used so many different instruments it almost didn't matter that their melodies were repetitive and their harmonies rarely included more than four voices. If Lamprophyre had been at all musical, she might have occupied her time when she wasn't learning to read with learning to play those unusual instruments.

The door opened again, and two figures exited. Lamprophyre was interested enough in the music she didn't at first realize one of the two was Rokshan. He had his hand on the shoulder of the second male, who was taller than he was, and appeared to be directing him across the open space toward the street. The second male carried a walking stick, but didn't lean on it. Lamprophyre disengaged her toe claws from the wood and pushed off, gaining altitude rapidly.

Once Rokshan and Abhimot were on the street, she dared listen to their thoughts. Abhimot was thinking *get him alone, take his things, definitely a rich plusher with clothes like that.* Rokshan's thoughts were much clearer and well-focused, a single repeated line of *Lamprophyre, watch where we go and dive once we're around the corner.*

She did as Rokshan instructed, waiting for her moment. The two turned a corner that put them out of sight of the tall building and the humans hurrying in and out of it. Rokshan immediately lowered himself to one knee and bent his head as if searching for something. Abhimot raised his stick to strike Rokshan. And Lamprophyre plummeted, spreading her wings at the last moment to course past the two of them and pluck Abhimot off the ground and carry him away.

Abhimot screamed, a high, sharp, terrified sound Lamprophyre wished she could muzzle. "Shut up, or I'll drop you," she said. "On purpose."

The male flung his arms around Lamprophyre's arms, his hands scrabbling desperately for something to hold onto. He stopped screaming, but his breathing was ragged and his legs kicked helplessly. Lamprophyre flew a few dozen dragonlengths more, leaving the city behind, before descending. When she was near enough the ground that falling wouldn't injure Abhimot, she dropped him, shaking his grip free of her arms. He hit the ground with an *oof* and lay sprawled there for a few beats, then tried to rise. Lamprophyre landed beside him and put her foot on his chest, pressing down gently and digging in her toe claws just enough that he could feel them through his clothing. He started to scream again, but Lamprophyre pressed harder, and the sound cut off.

"So, you were going to beat and rob my friend, were you?" she said, not really caring about the answer. She didn't want to interrogate this male until Rokshan was there, and Stones knew how long that would take.

"Let me go," Abhimot said, his voice weak and breathless. "I swear I'll never do anything bad again. Please." One eye was wide and terrified. The other rolled independent of the first, never settling on anything.

"So you *have* done bad things. We thought so. Thanks for confirming that."

Abhimot's mouth closed in a tight, thin line. His hands groped at Lamprophyre's ankle as if he could make her let him up. "I've never hurt you," he finally said. "Never seen you before. We can make a deal."

"That's true, you haven't seen me before," Lamprophyre said, "but you have hurt me, if indirectly."

"Don't know what you mean. Please, let me go. I'll do anything—I know where valuable magical items are—"

She heard Rokshan running toward them and said nothing until he drew up even with her and bent over with his hands on his knees, breathing heavily. "I take flying for granted," he said when he'd mostly recovered. "Did he tell you anything?"

"That he's a bad man, that he's never hurt me, and that he can make it worth our while if we let him go." Lamprophyre pressed down just a little more and enjoyed seeing the male gasp. "Also that he meant to beat you and take your things."

"Interesting." Rokshan dropped to one knee beside Abhimot and looked him over. "I wondered why he was so ready to follow me outside. Well, Abhimot, this is your lucky day. Answer our questions honestly, and we'll let you go."

Abhimot stared at him. "Questions?"

"You made an artifact whose sole purpose is to incapacitate a dragon. Why?"

Abhimot's expression became one Lamprophyre couldn't read. It was clearly one Rokshan didn't like, because he slapped Abhimot and said, "Now is the wrong time to try to play us, Abhimot. We know what you've done. We just want the details. Who asked you to make that wand?"

Lamprophyre thought this might be a bad line of inquiry, since for all they knew, Abhimot had done it on his own. But his thoughts were going like mad, almost too fast for her to hear, thinking *how did they know? Damn dragon should have gone mad for weeks, no way they could trace it to me.*

"Some man," Abhimot said. "Came to me with a proposal. A theory he wanted proved. Said I was the one to do it." He swallowed, licked his lips, and continued, "I didn't know if it worked, but he paid me anyway."

"That's not true," Lamprophyre said, listening to the adept's thoughts. "You're experienced enough you knew it would work even if you couldn't test it on account of there being no dragons around. Don't try to make yourself look less guilty."

Abhimot nodded. "It's true, it worked. But I swear I never used it on no dragon. You want vengeance, you find that man."

"Did he tell you why he wanted it?" Rokshan asked.

"Never said, and I never asked." Abhimot swallowed again. "He was the sort you can picture getting a thrill out of torturing kittens, you know? I was just glad he never came back. Wish I'd never done business with him, but the money was too good."

"What did he look like?"

"A man." Lamprophyre pressed harder, and Abhimot gasped. "I swear! Dark hair maybe a little longer than normal, lighter skinned than you, brown eyes like most of Tanajital. Had a mole on his upper lip and his eyebrows grew together in the middle. Said his name was Harshod, but that was probably a lie."

"Gonjirian?"

"I guess so. Never asked. He didn't have an accent, so probably."

Rokshan glanced at Lamprophyre, his eyes wide in a now-familiar expression. She listened, and heard him think *I don't know what else to ask.*

"Who else knows how to make that artifact?" she asked.

Abhimot actually tried to shrug. "Nobody but me," he said. "I swear I'll never tell anyone about it. Please don't kill me." *I'm never coming back to Tanajital if I live through this, Jiwanyil help me.*

Rokshan's expression changed. "Where did you meet this Harshod? At your home?"

"No. In South District, in a house by the old academy. I always went to him. But I doubt he's still there."

Rokshan nodded and stood. "Well, what do you think?" he said.

"I think I should eat him," Lamprophyre said mischievously. Abhimot squeaked. The scent of urine wafted through the air, making Lamprophyre's nose wrinkle.

"He's too thin to be good eating," Rokshan said with a straight face. "He's answered our questions, I think we should let him go."

"Well, if we have to," Lamprophyre said. She didn't feel as casual as she sounded. Hyaloclast wanted vengeance on this man, but Lamprophyre couldn't kill another person in cold blood. She didn't care if that made her weak. Besides, he was only indirectly responsible, because Lamprophyre was sure what Hyaloclast really wanted was the person behind the plan. She didn't let herself think too hard about whether she was making excuses.

She leaned down until she was a handspan from Abhimot's face. "If it turns out you lied to us," she said, expelling a gust of burning air from her second stomach, "I'll be back. And I won't care how stringy you are. Now, get out of here, and don't tell anyone you spoke with us. In fact, you might want to go into another line of work, because if the rest of the dragons find out what you did, being eaten will be the least of your worries."

She released him, but Abhimot didn't rise. Rokshan pulled himself up, and she flew away, not looking back.

"He *was* telling the truth, right?" Rokshan said when they were well away from the stricken male.

"Yes, as far as he knew. He's right that Harshod might not be a real name."

"It's a clue, anyway. And he confirmed we're looking for a Gonjirian conspiracy." Rokshan sighed. "I'm exhausted. Let's worry about this tomorrow. I have no idea how we'll track Abhimot's employer, whatever his name actually is."

"We got this far," Lamprophyre said. "We'll figure something out."

CHAPTER TWENTY-EIGHT

The park at noon was cooler than the open spaces near the palace or the city streets, but that still made it warmer than Lamprophyre liked. She didn't want to think about how hot it would be when spring became summer.

She sprawled beneath a tree whose branches spread out horizontally, brushing up against its neighbor so between the two of them there was enough shade for her to fit into, and watched the humans setting up canopies. The brightly colored canvases had fluttering strings hanging down on all sides that reminded her of the drooping branches of the trees near the river, trees Rokshan called willows. The strings moved in the scant breeze Lamprophyre could barely feel. She wished for the first time in her life she could be blasted by the northern winds, her skin chilled until it tingled.

"I still think this is a mistake," she told Rokshan, who lay beside her with his arms folded back behind his head, staring up at the trees. "Half these people will only come to see what disastrous thing I'll do next."

"They're diplomats," Rokshan said. "They'd never say that to your face."

"Isn't it worse if they say it where I can't hear? Then I don't know who to trust. Or I wouldn't, if I couldn't...you know." There were too many servants around for her to mention being able to hear thoughts.

"Superficial politeness is better than hostility. Besides, the other half will genuinely want to know you better, and isn't half better than none? And you'll only get that if we host a reception."

Lamprophyre blew a jet of smoke through one nostril. "You make sense." She wearily got to her feet and lumbered over to the nearest canopy. No servants remained near it, so she was able to get up close. She'd fit beneath it if she crouched, though her wings might be a problem. Better to leave the canopies for her guests, though if it rained as it looked like it would—the reason for the canopies in the first place—she might get very wet. There was nothing she could do about that.

"Akarshan was very generous in letting us use his kitchens," she said over her shoulder. "Though I suppose it's reasonable he didn't want Depik taking over."

Rokshan let out a grunt that might have meant anything. She turned to see he'd closed his eyes and settled in to sleep. Grimacing, she walked back over to him and prodded his shoulder. "Rokshan. Don't fall asleep. We still have planning to do."

Rokshan grunted again, but he opened his eyes. "We've done all the planning we can, and now it's up to other people to implement those plans."

"I meant the other plan."

"Oh." Rokshan sat up and finger-combed his hair back into order. "No one's approached the house Abhimot told us about in the last three days, or gone to Abhimot's house. Whoever this Harshod is—"

"If that's his name."

"Right. He's gone to ground thoroughly. I'm not sure what else we can do to find him."

Lamprophyre settled beside Rokshan again. "Let's think about what he must have done. He bought the wand from Abhimot. He gathered a bunch of humans to help him. And he traveled with his companions into dragon territory and attacked Nephrite without anyone else seeing him."

"That's not entirely true," Rokshan said, "or, rather, there's a possibility someone did see him. If he and his men looked like bandits, which they did when we caught up with them, they could have moved through dragon territory without standing out. Also, we don't know that he was with those men. Someone else was their leader, after all—that bandit you dropped on his head didn't resemble Abhimot's description of Harshod."

"True, but do you think he would have trusted the wand to someone else? It's both powerful and valuable."

"I don't know. I know nothing about him to make that guess. I mean, it could go either way—either he didn't want to let the wand out of his sight, or he didn't want to risk being caught." He sighed. "Maybe it's time for drastic measures."

"What does that mean?"

"I mean," Rokshan said, "we should pursue the bandits directly."

"You mean, follow their trail down the river to Kolmira? Didn't you and your soldiers do that already?"

"We chased the bandits as far as the river, but I wasn't in a position to go farther than that, given that I had to report about my encounter with you dragons. So my men and I didn't really investigate or go into Kolmira."

"Can we do that? I thought we didn't want to start a riot."

"We don't, but isn't finding the egg thieves worth scaring a few people? It's been long enough that news of your presence here has spread throughout most of Gonjiri, so you won't be that much of a surprise." Rokshan stood. "Besides, like I said, there's nothing more we can do here, and Kolmira isn't far. We can get there, ask around, and be back before the reception starts."

Lamprophyre stood as well, hunched over so her head barely brushed the branches. "All right. Flying has to be cooler, anyway."

Storm clouds gathered as they made their way westward, adding to the coolness of flying, though the air was heavier and muggier than usual in anticipation of the coming storm. "You know," Lamprophyre said, "if Harshod wasn't with those bandits, he must have been so frustrated when they returned with no wand and no egg."

Rokshan laughed. "I wish I could have seen his face."

"Me too." She twisted her long neck to try to look at Rokshan. "It was his best chance to incite the dragons. Everything else he's done has been so small by comparison."

"I wouldn't call poisoning you small."

"I'm only one person. It's small scale, at least." She watched the ground roll past beneath her. "Where should I go?"

"Let's start where we attacked the bandits and go downstream from there. There might be settlements that saw them. Damn, but I wish we could have done this immediately."

"There was no way to do that. It was a twelveday before you returned to the flight, and we couldn't have gone before that."

"I know. It's just going to be difficult, searching for them nearly a month later. But it shouldn't be impossible." Rokshan leaned forward. "I think it's down there."

Lamprophyre didn't know how he could be so sure, given that all the clumps of trees along the wide river looked the same to her, but he was the experienced one. She swooped down to alight on the west bank of the river. "Here?"

"Close enough." Rokshan slid down and walked a few paces southward. "It doesn't matter if we find the exact location, so long as we don't miss any settlements they might have passed. Are you ready?"

"To possibly scare people? I've been ready for that for the last couple of twelvedays." She crouched for Rokshan to mount up again, then took to the skies.

She rose high enough to get a good look at the river. Three clots of dark, angular growth clung to the riverbanks, two of them much smaller than the most distant one. "That's Kolmira," Rokshan said when she pointed. "I hope we learn what we need from those other two settlements, but I have a feeling we're going to need to enter the city."

Lamprophyre suppressed a sigh and glided southward to the first settlement. She swept over it, circled around to find a landing spot, and set down south of the farthest buildings. "Is this close enough?"

"It's not bad. I'll be back." Rokshan ran toward the settlement, heading for the shore and the wooden platforms sticking out into the river. There were no boats visible, and no people running and screaming. If this was going to be their pattern, Lamprophyre landing well away from human buildings and Rokshan doing all the talking, it was going to be a very boring day.

After about a hundred beats that in her boredom felt more like a thousand, Rokshan returned. "A fisherman remembered seeing a boat with a scorch mark down its side pass about a month ago," he said, pulling himself up. "They don't get a lot of traffic in either direction, as far north as they are, so it stood out. He said the boat didn't stop."

"Then we move on?"

"Right."

The second settlement proved disappointing. Rokshan couldn't find anyone who remembered seeing the bandits' boat. Discouraged, Lamprophyre said, "Does that mean they stopped somewhere upstream?"

"No, or we would have seen the boat tied up along the shore," Rokshan said. "They came through, probably without stopping, and I'll wager they stopped in Kolmira. Finding them there might be impossible, but we have to try."

Lamprophyre nodded, and took to the sky once more.

Kolmira looked nothing like Tanajital, though both cities were bisected by their rivers and both were packed with buildings set close to one another. Unlike Tanajital, Kolmira sprawled, its buildings rarely taller than a couple of dragonlengths and unchecked by a city wall. Its two halves were about the same size, and both were darker than Tanajital, with roofs that were either dirty or made of some dark material and walls that didn't gleam with whiteness. Lamprophyre saw very little glass, just empty window holes. The place depressed her, and she couldn't believe she'd gotten so used to anything human she could think of Tanajital fondly by comparison.

The riverbank was wide, with the nearest buildings set well back from the edge, and Lamprophyre was actually able to set down near the largest one. It couldn't be more than one story tall, but it was more than two dragonlengths on each side and had several doors Lamprophyre could fit head and neck and shoulders through. This one did have glass windows, which Lamprophyre suspected meant its owner was prosperous.

Humans gathered around the building, some emerging from within, and while their thoughts were fearful, none of them screamed or fled. She crouched to let Rokshan off and furled her wings to make herself look smaller and, she hoped, less threatening. "This isn't so bad," she said.

"Wait here. I'll talk to the dock master. If we're lucky, he knows the names and faces of every bandit on that boat and will think them clearly enough for you to hear."

"Wait!" Lamprophyre said. "If they're bandits, would they really stop here like legitimate sailors?"

"The line between bandit and legal is very fine," Rokshan said. "A legitimate sailor might become a bandit by sailing beyond a certain point. And I can't think where else to start. I'll be right back."

Lamprophyre settled in to wait. The humans watched her warily. She amused herself by trying to pick out individual thoughts from the mass, but most of them were either frightened or uncomplimentary, so she stopped doing that after a few dozen beats. At least no one had attacked her.

She realized the crowd had shifted just as a female detached herself from the crowd and made her way down the bank to Lamprophyre. Lamprophyre sat up and regarded her as warily as the humans had her. "Hello," she said when the female was close enough for speech. "Can I help you?"

"What are you doing here?" the female said. Her tone was aggressive, but her thoughts were uncertain: *had a rider, wonder what it wants, knowledge I can sell.* She wore her long, light brown hair gathered high, fountaining out from the crown of her head like a muddy waterfall.

"My friend and I are searching for sailors who came here about a...a month ago," Lamprophyre said, reaching for the word Rokshan had used. "They had a boat with a big burn mark on its right side. I don't suppose you saw it?"

That boat, the female thought, and said, "Can't say as I recall."

Lamprophyre remembered what Rokshan had said about paying the sapphire merchants to be more forthcoming and wished he hadn't left with the coin pouch. Though he might need it to convince whoever he was talking to, so maybe it was just as well. Now, how should she push? "It was full of sailors," she said, "and one of them had black hair on his face, very thick and long."

The image of the bandit captain rose up within the female's thoughts. "Lots of men grow beards," she said. "Could be anyone."

"I suppose, but this was a specific person. He had a head injury."

The female's thoughts were coming more quickly now, mostly images of the charred boat and the bandit captain and a building Lamprophyre had never seen before. It looked like a Kolmiran building, with dark roof and walls, but there was nothing to say where in Kolmira it was. "Doesn't sound familiar," the female said.

"I see," Lamprophyre said. "Well, that's all right. We'll ask someone else. Thank you for your time."

The female stared at her, her head cocked to look Lamprophyre in the eye. "You're polite," she said. "Thought you'd burn the city."

"Really? Why would I do that?" Polite, she could hang on to polite.

"'S what dragons do, yes? Burn things?"

"Not really," Lamprophyre said. "Just because we can doesn't mean we will. You could..." Her eye fell on the blade sheathed at the female's left hip. "You could kill everyone you meet with that weapon, but you don't, do you? You use it to defend yourself."

The female's eyes widened. "I—" she said, then fell silent.

"I don't know why you humans assume dragons are interested in hurting you and destroying your cities," Lamprophyre said, pitching her voice so the humans watching this interchange could hear. "My friend Dharan won't let me read the stories you tell because he says they will just upset me. But if those stories say dragons are evil monsters, they're not true. And I think you should want to know the truth rather than believing lies."

She saw Rokshan emerge from the building, followed by a short, plump male with no hair on his head and black hair covering his face as if compensating. "This is my friend Rokshan. I let him ride on my shoulders when I fly. You can ask him if he feels at all frightened by me."

Rokshan watched her curiously as he approached. "Should I be worried about this crowd?" he murmured.

"No," Lamprophyre said, listening to their thoughts. They were still afraid, but more of them were curious, and a few actually felt ashamed.

"Well, this is Alok, and he asked to meet you." Rokshan's eyes widened in the signal Lamprophyre was now used to. She listened, and heard Rokshan think *He doesn't know anything, but good will is good will.* Alok's thoughts were more jumbled, but she clearly heard *dragon, dragon, dragon* and *like the legends but God's breath she's blue.*

"Hello, Alok," she said. Alok's thoughts grew even less coherent with excitement, making her smile. "Are you the dock master?"

"His assistant," Alok said. "Never thought I'd meet a real dragon. And he's allowed to ride?" He nodded at Rokshan.

"He is." She could hear Alok working up to ask if he could ride as well, and cut off that embarrassing line of conversation with, "He's the only human I will allow to ride on my shoulders. Otherwise it's uncomfortable."

Alok's disappointment didn't make it into his speech. "That must be magnificent. Always thought those were the glory days, humans and dragons together."

"What glory days?" the female said. Lamprophyre hadn't noticed her still standing there.

"Don't know your history?" Alok scoffed. "Back before the catastrophe, humans and dragons lived together. Humans riding dragons, dragons teaching humans. My nan told me the old stories, but I never thought I'd see those days come again."

The female eyed him closely, her lips pursed as if in thought. "Never heard of that," she said, but her thoughts were more curious than dismissive.

"We have to be on our way, but thank you, Alok," Rokshan said, extending a hand. Alok took it, his eyes never leaving Lamprophyre. "We'll ask at the southern docks."

"Good luck finding those bastards," Alok said.

The female's eyes narrowed, but she said nothing. *Wonder why they want Harshod's stooge?* she thought.

Lamprophyre's heart leaped.

She contained her impatience long enough for Rokshan to climb up and for the two of them to rise high above Kolmira. "That female," she said.

"Which one?"

"The one standing next to me. She knew the bandits, and she recognized their leader. And she knows he's got something to do with Harshod! Though I don't know what a stooge is."

"It's someone who works for someone else, usually doing unpleasant or thankless work. You got more than I did. Though I got the feeling from talking to Alok and his superior that they don't know about bandit activity because they don't want to. So they deliberately avoid noticing the less than legal business that passes through here. Did she know where the bandit's leader lives?"

"I don't know. She kept thinking about a particular building in connection with him, but it might just be a place he goes to often. Unfortunately, I couldn't tell where the building was, except that I think it was Kolmiran. I guess we could sweep the city. I'd know it when I saw it."

"Or we could take a more direct route," Rokshan said. "But you might want to conceal yourself."

"Why?"

"Because I'll wager anything you like that that woman is going straight to that man, or to Harshod himself, to tell him strangers are asking after him."

Lamprophyre craned her neck. "That's really clever."

"We'd better hurry, though, if we don't want to lose her." Rokshan leaned out. "We're too high for me to see her."

"I'm not. But I can't conceal you."

"I doubt anyone will look up and notice me, but you stand out."

Lamprophyre nodded. She scanned the streets below, looking for the woman, but despite her words to Rokshan, the streets were nothing but rivers of people, flowing in all directions. She cast an eye on the stormy sky, concentrated, and smoky gray spread across her scales, mottled to match the clouds. "Stay well behind my neck, if you can," she told Rokshan, and dropped.

She started from the dock master's house and followed the main streets, looking for her prey. It took a few beats to find her, swimming upstream against the current of bodies filling one of the narrower streets. Her hair, lighter than most of those around her and waving in the breeze the storm had kicked up, drew Lamprophyre like a beacon. Having identified her, Lamprophyre rose higher and made several spirals so as not to outpace her. "I think I see where she's going," she said. "At least, I recognize the building. Should we get there ahead of her?"

"Which one is it?"

"The one with the round, short tower on one side."

"I see it." Rokshan leaned out again, then pulled back as if he'd just remembered she was concealed. "I don't dare go in there alone, and you won't fit. I think we need to wait for her to give her warning so our prey will flee, and then we can grab him."

"All right. But I can't keep up this concealment for much longer."

Rokshan leaned forward and pointed. "Why don't you land on that building there? The tall one? It's near enough to our target we'll see if anyone bolts."

Lamprophyre nodded and descended. The building Rokshan had chosen had a steeply sloped roof like the embassy, but with a wider ridge beam. She settled lightly onto it, digging in her toe claws for stability, and let her concealment fall. No one looked up, no one screamed, and she relaxed.

Shortly afterward, the female walked up to the door of the building Lamprophyre had seen and let herself in. "Interesting," Rokshan said. "So either it's a public place, or she's closer to the bandits than we thought."

They waited. Rokshan's shoes dug uncomfortably into Lamprophyre's side, but she was afraid to ask him to shift for fear he'd fall off. Neither of them spoke; Lamprophyre didn't have anything to say, and she was preoccupied with listening to the thoughts of the humans in the building. They were close enough, but there were many humans and their thoughts faded into a mingled hum from which random fragments emerged, none distinguishable as belonging to a particular person.

After about three hundred beats, the door opened, and the female emerged. Lamprophyre opened her mind to its fullest, and heard her think *should've gotten paid for that news, not sure where he went.*

She spread her wings and took off, startling Rokshan, who grabbed hold of her ruff for security. "Where are we going? He's still in there."

"I don't think he is. I need to stay close enough to hear that female's thoughts." She concealed herself again and glided along, hovering barely a dragonlength above the female's head. More thoughts drifted to her mind: *why a dragon* and *dare attack such a creature, balls of solid brass* and *maybe better he's gone but God's breath do I need the money.*

"We're going to talk to her again," Lamprophyre said, dropping her concealment and swooping low. It took only a few beats for the humans filling the street to notice her and panic. Lamprophyre kept her attention on the female, who alone hadn't tried to flee, but had drawn her blade and stood holding it defensively in front of her. She landed in front of the female and spread her wings. This time, looking big could help.

"I know you know who Harshod is," she said, speaking loudly, though the din of the panicked humans had grown distant as they fled. "We want to speak with him."

The female shook her head. "I don't know what you're talking about."

Rokshan jumped down. "You went to warn him, or his flunky, but he was gone," he said. "Where?"

The female didn't move. Lamprophyre said, "We can make it worth your while."

She heard the female think *more money, could use a few rupyas.* "Rokshan, a few rupyas?" she said, hoping he'd go along with the half-formed plan she'd come up with.

Rokshan dug in his pouch and came up with some silver coins he handed to the female, who took them with one hand while the other kept the blade raised high. He glanced at Lamprophyre with that wide-eyed look, and she heard *go ahead, hope you know what you're doing.* So did she.

"You wanted to sell the information that we were asking around after Harshod, but he wasn't there," Lamprophyre said. "So now you're going to sell information to us."

The woman's thoughts became fearful, and Lamprophyre quickly said, "We won't let anyone know about this conversation. We just want to know about Harshod. He did have a boat full of bandits that came here about a month ago, right?"

The woman glanced at the rupyas in her hand. "He did," she said. "The boat was scorched all down one side—was that you?"

"Does he live in Kolmira?" Lamprophyre chose not to answer the female's question.

"Never saw him before three months ago. We all thought he came from Tanajital or Suwedhi to take over Kolmira's crime. I don't know what he did to piss you off, dragon, but it's not like him. Or not like we thought he was, anyway."

Lamprophyre didn't know what it meant to take over a city's crime, but she said, "So you thought he was a criminal leader? He didn't do anything else related to dragons?"

"Not a thing. He'd leave for a few days, but he always came back. Guess he's gone again now."

"And you have no idea where he went?" Rokshan said.

The female shrugged. "His henchmen wouldn't tell me. But you watch that building, and you'll find him. He always comes back."

Rokshan nodded. He handed her a few more rupyas, making her eyes go wide. "That's for you to forget we had this conversation."

"Sure. But I don't think it will matter," the female said. "Everyone saw the dragon land. If Harshod has something going about dragons, that will tip him off for sure."

"We'll take that chance," Lamprophyre said. "Thank you."

Rokshan hauled himself up, and Lamprophyre beat her wings until she was once more high above Kolmira. "Was that a stupid thing to do?" she asked. "Letting Harshod know we were there?"

"I'll have soldiers watching that house by tomorrow," Rokshan said. "They'll pick up Harshod before he's warned."

"So we have to hope he doesn't come back tonight."

"Try not to be so optimistic," Rokshan said, but he sounded amused.

CHAPTER TWENTY-NINE

They flew back to Tanajital in silence and landed on the training grounds outside the palace. Rokshan jumped down and said, "I'm going to change for the reception. I'll see you here at sunset, yes?"

"I don't know if I can stand still for a reception when I'm worried about Harshod escaping," Lamprophyre said.

"I'll send a detachment of soldiers immediately. We'll catch him, Lamprophyre. Now try to enjoy the evening." Rokshan waved and trotted away toward the low, dirt-colored buildings where the soldiers lived.

When he was out of sight within the buildings, she took to the air and flew a couple of passes around the city. Flying calmed her, as did the lack of frightened thoughts, and she dared go downstream a ways to bathe before returning to the embassy. The air was muggy and still as if the world was holding its breath, waiting for the storm. Lamprophyre understood the weather well enough to know the storm wouldn't reach Tanajital until nearly midnight, but she couldn't help watching the skies and hoping she hadn't made a mistake. An early storm would definitely ruin the reception.

She took a short nap, waking when the last rays of the sun slanted through the embassy doorway. Sleeping and her bath had relaxed her further, and she felt she could face whatever the humans might bring to bear on her.

Servants were lighting lanterns when she arrived at the park. The nearest ones glanced at her warily, but she heard nothing more fearful from them than one female thinking *hope the dragon doesn't wreck anything, big as a house, can't possibly be graceful.* It irritated Lamprophyre more because she was conscious of not being very agile on land, and she shared the servant's worry.

Keeping her wings furled close to her side, she made her way between the canopies, which Rokshan had instructed the servants to set out well spaced apart. The smell of human food, which included green things and the biting scent of cheese, tantalized her even though a dragon couldn't digest most of it. She stuck her head beneath a canopy and was relieved to find Akarshan there, supervising the arrangement of tiny bits of food that were surely too small a bite even for humans. "Akarshan," she said. "It smells wonderful."

"Thank you, my lady," Akarshan said. "I admit this is the most unusual reception I have ever served."

"Oh? Why is that?"

Akarshan gestured at the round metal sheets. "We do not normally display all the food at once," he said, "but bringing it from the kitchens, it's quite a distance. So the initial serving has been set up here, to save time."

Lamprophyre examined the metal sheets again. "You make it look so pretty, like flowers," she said.

"Thank you." Akarshan twitched one of the tiny morsels into a more regular arrangement. "Do dragons drink wine? Spirits?"

"I've heard of those things, but no. That is, we might, but we don't make them ourselves."

Akarshan removed a bottle from a wooden stand and removed its top. He offered it to Lamprophyre. "Sniff this, my lady."

Lamprophyre sniffed. She'd smelled grapes before, and this smelled slightly of grapes, but even more of woody, resinous aromas that weren't very pleasant. She refrained from making a face, though she didn't think Akarshan would understand the expression, and said, "It's not very nice, is it? Is that wine?"

"It is, my lady. Alcohol is an acquired taste, and not one you should try to acquire at a public gathering. Though I imagine it would take a barrel of wine or more to get you drunk." Akarshan poured dark red wine from the bottle into finely shaped glass cups. Lamprophyre looked at them in fascination. She was capable of making glass herself, but humans found the most intriguing shapes for it.

She heard Rokshan approaching and withdrew from beneath the canopy. Rokshan wore a white shirt that made his brown skin look darker and white trousers that came to just below his knee. Over all that, he wore a robe of some dark blue fabric that shimmered when it caught the light and was stitched all over with designs in silver thread. It reminded her once more of Flint. She'd thought of him frequently in the last few days, hadn't she? Maybe that meant something.

"I should have a robe made that matches your colors," Rokshan said. "It would look so dramatic."

"I agree. Are you nervous? I'm getting nervous again."

"Of course not. They're just people, Lamprophyre, and they can't hurt you."

"Not physically. But Khadar, for example, spread all those lies about me, and that's a kind of hurt."

"True, but I promise you no one who comes tonight will try anything like that." Rokshan gripped her hand briefly. "Just be straightforward and honest, and everything will be fine."

"Her Excellency the Lady Tanura, ambassador from Sachetan," someone shouted. Lamprophyre tensed.

"Perfect. Lady Tanura is nicer than most of the ambassadors. You'll like her," Rokshan said. "But let's meet her away from the canopies, all right? Give yourself room to move." He walked away in the direction of the unseen voice.

Lamprophyre came out from between the brightly colored canopies to a spot where the trees grew sparsely. Rokshan joined her after a few beats, bringing with him an unusually dark human wearing clothes similar to his. If Lamprophyre had still been depending on hair length to tell male from female, she would have been confused, because this female wore her black hair cut very close to her scalp. But recent observation had taught Lamprophyre that human females' chests bulged symmetrically in two places, and though those bulges varied in size, they were always distinct from males' flat chests. It was a more reliable indicator of sex than hair length.

This female's very short hair showed off the curve of her skull, which

Lamprophyre found intriguing and attractive. She also had a well-defined facial structure and large brown eyes that at the moment regarded Lamprophyre with as much curiosity as Lamprophyre felt.

"Lamprophyre," Rokshan said, "may I introduce Lady Tanura of Sachetan, your counterpart."

Lady Tanura bowed, a graceful, flowing motion Lamprophyre envied. "My lady," she said, her voice high, like birdsong, "thank you for the invitation. I am most interested in meeting you." She spoke with an accent unlike Rokshan's, stretching out the vowels.

"Thank you, my lady," Lamprophyre said, returning the bow much more awkwardly. "Sachetan is south of Gonjiri, yes?"

"It is. Far enough south that we do not abut upon dragon territory. But we would like to know your people better." Lady Tanura nodded to Rokshan, who had vanished briefly and returned holding a glass of wine he offered to the ambassador. She sipped, and added, "I think you will find our people much less antagonistic than those of Gonjiri."

Lamprophyre heard her think *that idiot Ekanath, wasting his chance,* and said, "I'm afraid the people of Gonjiri were influenced by our first unfortunate interactions and some false old stories. The ones I've met who overcame those fears have been very nice."

"Sachetan does not have a tradition of wicked, terrifying dragons," Lady Tanura said. "It's unfortunate you can't visit my country to see for yourself. I wonder, would your people be interested in an exchange of ambassadors?"

"An *exchange?*" Lamprophyre hoped she hadn't sounded too startled. "Ah, where dragons live isn't very hospitable to humans. So probably not. But I'm sure if you were to approach Hyaloclast, she could make that decision." It would almost certainly be "no," but maybe if enough humans pestered the dragon queen, she'd grow tired of it and agree to negotiations.

"Hyaloclast."

"She's our queen. She's the one who sent me to Gonjiri."

"Of course. She is also your mother?" Lady Tanura sipped her wine again.

"She is, but that doesn't really matter when it comes to politics."

"I see." Lady Tanura's thoughts remained placid, if calculating; *too far away, but that's a small thing* and *trade items, do dragons make things?* "I understand dragons control the Parama Mountains, is that correct?"

"That's our home, yes."

"Have dragons found precious stones there? I've heard you eat stone."

Lamprophyre glanced at Rokshan. Was that public knowledge? She couldn't remember who knew what anymore. Though it didn't matter, did it, because it wasn't as if that was a dangerous secret. "We do eat stone, and we've found deposits of minerals you humans find valuable, yes."

"Sachetan is famous for its garnet. We'd be interested in opening trade relations with dragons. Garnet for, well, it would depend on what you have. But I'm sure we could come to an arrangement."

Lamprophyre wished she didn't feel like she was teetering on the edge of a precipice, her wings frozen and unable to take her to safety. Lady Tanura's thoughts remained calm but curious, but there was an edge to them Lamprophyre didn't like. Hyaloclast had specifically instructed her not to enter into any agreements, but did that mean concealing those instructions as well?

"We would have to see," she said. "At the moment, I'm just here to spread the word about dragons' existence and learn more about human countries and customs. Hyaloclast would prefer not to interfere until we understand you better." That sounded nice and noncommittal.

"I see," said Lady Tanura. "How interesting." *They're hiding something,* she thought. Lamprophyre's heart sank.

"Excuse me, Lady Tanura," Rokshan said, "but my mother is here, and I'd like to introduce Lamprophyre to her."

"Of course." Lady Tanura smiled and bowed. "I look forward to speaking with you again, my lady. Perhaps in a less public situation?"

That sounded more ominous than Lady Tanura meant. Lamprophyre bowed and smiled without saying anything.

"See? That wasn't so bad," Rokshan said once they were away from the Sachetan ambassador.

"She thinks it's suspicious that I won't agree to trade," Lamprophyre whispered. "I think I made a mistake."

"She's an ambassador. They're suspicious of everything. Don't worry about it." Rokshan came to a halt in front of the canopies. "Bow, and let her speak first," he murmured.

"What?" Lamprophyre said. Rokshan shook his head and bowed, so

Lamprophyre did too, though she wasn't sure whom she was bowing to. There didn't appear to be anyone near enough to justify a bow.

Beautiful creature, someone thought. Lamprophyre tried to hold her bow a little longer, wobbled, and stood rather than fall over. A group of females approached, five of them surrounding a much smaller female whose skin was unusually fair for a Gonjirian. That female wore a multicolored robe over the same kind of white clothing Rokshan wore, and her footwear exposed her blunt, bare toes. Her hair was arranged in an elaborate display of loops and curls atop her head, giving her the appearance of a flower in full bloom. She smiled as she drew near. "Rokshan, you didn't say she was beautiful," she said in a soft voice Lamprophyre had to strain to hear.

"Mother, may I introduce Princess Lamprophyre, ambassador of the dragons," Rokshan said, rising from his bow. "Lamprophyre, may I present you to her majesty Satiya, queen of Gonjiri."

"Your majesty," Lamprophyre said, bowing again. "It's nice to meet you."

Satiya said nothing, but walked closer and began to circle Lamprophyre, gazing at her steadily. "That notch seems designed for a human rider," she said.

Lamprophyre controlled her first response, which was to give the queen an angry set-down. "It's just coincidence," she said instead. "Though I'm sure humans and dragons used to take advantage of it all the time."

"Yes, the old stories. Anchala has been full of nothing else these last few months." Satiya completed her circuit and came to a halt near Lamprophyre's head. "Are all dragons as colorful as you?"

"More or less."

"Well, it's not as if you'd need to conceal yourself. I can't imagine any creature capable of attacking you." Satiya tilted her head like an inquisitive bird. "And you and my son are friends."

"We are."

"Astonishing. That a human and a dragon could have enough in common to become friends, I mean. But Rokshan has a gift for making friends, so perhaps it's not so astonishing."

Lamprophyre looked at Rokshan, whose cheeks reddened. "It's our differences that make us friends, I think," she said. "We never run out of things to talk about, or to teach each other."

"That's wonderful." To Lamprophyre's surprise, Satiya laid a hand on her forearm and drew close. "Watch out for him, will you?" she said in a voice pitched so low only Lamprophyre could hear it, and that with difficulty. "He's still finding his place in the world, and I think you may be part of that."

"I...all right," Lamprophyre said in the same low voice, though she was sure hers carried farther. Satiya smiled and patted Lamprophyre's arm.

"I'm so pleased to have met you," she said. "I hope more dragons find their way to Tanajital. You are all very welcome here." The queen's thoughts echoed her words with such sincerity Lamprophyre stifled an impulse to say something sarcastic about the welcome she'd had.

She watched the queen walk away, surrounded by her attendants, and said, "She's very nice. I can see why you get along with her."

"Mother has always believed the best of me. I'm not sure why," Rokshan said. "Come. Let's see who else you can meet. My father's not here, of course, but neither are Khadar or Tekentriya, so this might turn out to be a good event after all."

Three of her least favorite people, not attending. "I already feel more cheerful," she said.

CHAPTER THIRTY

Lamprophyre followed Rokshan back and forth between the canopies, watching humans eat those tiny morsels of food and drink wine. It was fascinating, actually, how they made food and drink part of the ritual. Dragons had no such traditions; they ate when they were hungry, and their gatherings for storytelling or art display or races were never diminished by the inclusion of food. But humans seemed to like it that way. She eavesdropped on their thoughts and learned most of them saw the food as a way to lessen tensions between themselves and other humans they were usually at odds with. Fascinating.

She spoke with a number of other ambassadors and Gonjirian nobles, all of whom were wary of her, but not frightened. All the ambassadors wanted some kind of negotiation with dragons, and Lamprophyre's tactful refusals strained nerves otherwise soothed by knowing they didn't see her as a threat. After the fifth time she had to gently refuse a very reasonable suggestion, she was cursing Hyaloclast's name and wishing the queen were here to manage things, if she was so hot on not building relations with humans.

It took her several of these meetings to wonder when she would meet the Fanishkorite ambassador. But when she asked Rokshan about it, he shook his head. "Recalled," he said in a low voice. "That means his king summoned him home. There's no diplomatic contact between our countries right now—another reason to suspect they intend to come to war against us."

"Wouldn't it make more sense for them to keep their ambassador here, to make you believe relations are more cordial than they are?"

"Yes, and no. My understanding is that the ambassador's withdrawal was the result of *our* ambassador to Fanishkor being recalled. All very polite, nothing anyone could take offense at, but it's the first moves in anticipation of hostilities. I think, once we discovered how many spies they had in Tanajital, we couldn't pretend any longer that things were normal."

"That's more complicated than I think I can handle."

"Like I said, forthrightness is as much a weapon as duplicity," Rokshan said. Lamprophyre hoped he was right.

After nearly a thousand beats, she felt comfortable enough to leave Rokshan's side and strike out on her own. Talking to people made her thirsty, and she wished she'd arranged for some cool, fresh water for herself rather than the nasty wine in those tiny glasses she couldn't fit her mouth around. At one point, she reached the end of the canopies and took a moment to sit and look back over the display. From there, the background hum of many voices talking quietly mingled with the hum of many thoughts, a soothing effect. She checked the sky. Another thousand beats, and the event would be over. Nothing bad could happen in such a relatively short time.

As if summoned by her thoughts, a trill of notes rang out over the gathering, causing the humans nearest Lamprophyre to turn and look at the far end of the park. Lamprophyre cursed herself for her optimism. Of course something bad could happen in that time. Something bad named Khadar. Why he'd decided to come, she had no idea, and she wished she'd insisted on not inviting him—but Rokshan had, with a grimace, said it would be unforgivably rude not to invite the High Ecclesiasts, and that included Khadar.

The space between the canopies was crowded with people, so she made her way around them, following the sound of the music. There were paths through the park paved with tiny, round-edged stones, and Khadar and his entourage approached along one of them from the direction of the city. Instead of the green-curtained litter, Khadar sat on a chair painted gold—not real gold, Lamprophyre smelled—carried by the same four males who'd carried the litter before. This time, he wore a strange peaked hat on his short, dark hair, a hat whose green color matched his formal robe with all the pictures on it. None of the pictures were visible while he was sitting, but Lamprophyre remembered them well. She wished she could ask him if the pictures meant anything, but that was too civilized a conversation to expect out of the Fifth Ecclesiast.

Lamprophyre found Rokshan under a green canopy, standing next to a female whose black hair cascaded past her waist unchecked. "What do I do?" Lamprophyre pleaded.

"Don't get close to him. There are a lot of flammable things around here. Sorry," Rokshan said.

"It would serve him right if you sneezed on him," the female said. "He's so full of himself it's no wonder there's no room for God."

Lamprophyre, startled at the female's casual words, looked at her more closely. She wasn't watching Lamprophyre; her attention was on the approaching procession. "I don't think we've met," she said.

"I'm Anchala," the female said, still not looking at Lamprophyre. "I was hoping we could talk, but it seems Khadar has made that impossible."

Anchala. Rokshan's sister whom he did get along with. "Maybe later," Lamprophyre said. "Once Khadar has done his worst."

Anchala laughed. It was a lovely sound not similar to her voice, which was rather rough, as if she'd been coughing. "Let's hope it doesn't come to that."

Rokshan said that unfamiliar, curt word whose meaning he refused to tell Lamprophyre. "I'm going to talk to him," he said. "We should find out what he wants before he does something stupid." He strode away in the direction of the procession. Lamprophyre settled on her haunches and strained to hear their thoughts. Anchala, right next to her, was easy: *wonder if she has a mate, beautiful color, how many stories she must know.* Rokshan wasn't thinking anything coherent, but his irritation with his brother was clear. And Khadar's thoughts were surprisingly not fearful. If anything, Khadar was filled with self-righteous indignation and the words *bring the creature to the knowledge of the true God.*

Lamprophyre groaned inwardly. So Khadar wanted to convert her. That was a conversation that could not end well for either of them.

Rokshan had reached the procession, which came to a halt as if he'd been the size of Lamprophyre instead of a slightly taller than average

Gonjirian male. Khadar's thoughts became too agitated for her to hear clearly, though his anger at being confronted by Rokshan was very clear.

"Can you hear them?" Anchala asked.

Lamprophyre shook her head. "They're too far away."

"I meant their thoughts," Anchala said.

Lamprophyre jerked, startled. "How—why would you—"

"I've made a thorough study of our oldest records," Anchala said. "None of them come out and say dragons can hear thoughts, but the implications are clear. It's true, isn't it?"

Lamprophyre decided she didn't want to lie to the only one of Rokshan's siblings he liked. "It is. But I'd rather no one knew."

"Yes, that would be quite the advantage." Anchala stopped speaking again, but she was thinking *you don't need to be afraid of me, I won't tell.* Feeling awkward, Lamprophyre blocked her thoughts. Somehow it felt like more of an intrusion when the person knew you could listen in.

With Anchala's thoughts blocked, Lamprophyre couldn't listen to Rokshan and Khadar either, but it didn't matter, because the procession had resumed its steady pace toward the canopies. Rokshan walked beside Khadar's chair. His face was set and angry, and Lamprophyre didn't need to hear what he was thinking. Khadar's expression was unfamiliar to Lamprophyre, though she'd become better at interpreting human facial expressions. She guessed, though, that he still felt that horrible self-righteousness.

Carefully sniffing the air, she walked toward the procession. If she were going to set anything on fire, better it be well away from her guests. But Khadar didn't stink of flowers on fire this time, just soap, as if he'd scrubbed well before arriving. Maybe she was wrong about him not fearing her.

"My lady ambassador," Khadar said before Lamprophyre could speak, "thank you for the invitation. May Jiwanyil's grace fall upon all in attendance here."

"Jiwanyil's grace," came the murmur from behind Lamprophyre as the humans repeated Khadar's words, somewhat raggedly as the sound reached those who were farther away.

"Thank you for coming, Khadar," Lamprophyre said. "I'm glad we have no hard feelings over the accident."

Khadar's bearers set the chair down, and Khadar stood. "You should address me as 'your Holiness,'" he said. "It's all right, I know you weren't to know."

Lamprophyre glanced at Rokshan, who gave the tiniest nod of assent. So it wasn't a lie, meant to throw her off balance. "Thank you for the correction, your Holiness," she said, though she didn't bow. "Is that how all ecclesiasts are addressed, or just you?"

"All ecclesiasts except the Archprelate, who is addressed as Most Holy One," Khadar said. "But you aren't likely to meet him. He lives a life of pure simplicity, isolated from the crudity and darkness of this world."

Lamprophyre thought this was a bad way for someone supposedly responsible for the spiritual well-being of an entire country to live, isolating himself so he didn't know anything about the people, but it was none of her business. "I'll remember that, your Holiness," she said. "I remember you said you don't eat food unless it's been specially prepared, but please join the gathering."

"Actually, I came only to speak with you," Khadar said with a smile. "I have been troubled ever since our first encounter. You seem terribly misinformed about the nature of God, and I feel it's my duty to instruct you."

"This isn't the time, Khadar," Rokshan said. "If you want an interview with the ambassador, you can come to the embassy."

Khadar ignored him. "Of course, you dragons have been isolated from the world for so long, it's no wonder your religious beliefs are so confused. We believed you were all destroyed, leaving Katayan alone with no worshippers, but perhaps he was more lost than we imagined."

"Khadar," Rokshan said, sounding angrier than before.

Lamprophyre blew out an involuntary puff of smoke. "Your Holiness," she said as calmly as she could manage, "I'm fascinated by the differences in our religions. But surely you can see that human worship would have to be different from dragon worship? We live in the shadow of Mother Stone, who guides and protects us, and when we die we return to her. I assure you, dragons have never heard of Katayan—that's not even a dragon name."

"You see?" Khadar exclaimed, spreading his arms and almost shouting the words. "Your ignorance is truly touching—"

"Ignorance?" Lamprophyre growled.

"Khadar, shut up and leave now," Rokshan said, "before you anger the ambassador."

"Threats will not stop me from preaching the truth," Khadar said, and now he really was shouting. "I will not allow false doctrine to pollute the minds and hearts of honest Gonjirians!"

"I am *not* preaching false doctrine, you imbecile," Lamprophyre shouted, "and if you can't see that our two faiths don't have to be at odds, I don't think much of you as an ecclesiast!"

Gasps rose up from behind her, and murmured conversations began. Khadar looked surprisingly pleased, and Lamprophyre had a sinking feeling she'd put herself into his hands. "Exactly the response I would expect from an apostate," he said, "but I do not hold your attitude against you. I intend—"

Rokshan grabbed Khadar's shoulder. "Get out. Now."

"Get your hands off me." Khadar tried to wrench away, but Rokshan held him fast.

The noise behind Lamprophyre had grown, filling the air with words spoken and unspoken. Lamprophyre blocked out the thoughts, but the noise lessened only slightly. "You're not entitled to be rude to me no matter what you believe about religion," she shouted, "and Rokshan's right, you need to leave."

"I will not abandon my religious duty," Khadar said.

The noise had grown deafening. Lamprophyre opened her mouth to shout at Khadar again, then saw Rokshan's expression. He no longer looked angry; he looked confused. "What's wrong?" she asked.

Rokshan shook his head and let go of Khadar. "Those are soldiers," he said, stepping toward Lamprophyre. "Why soldiers?"

Lamprophyre turned. From where she stood, she had a clear view of the training ground, where the noise came from. Soldiers filled it completely, more soldiers than she'd ever seen in one place. They were converging on the canopies. They weren't moving very fast, and Lamprophyre immediately saw why: marching beside General Sajan at the head of the company was Tekentriya, lurching along as fast as she could, which wasn't very.

She watched curiously as the soldiers approached within a dragonlength of the canopies and stopped. They hadn't drawn their swords, but they looked close to doing so. General Sajan and Tekentriya came forward together. The general's expression was concealed by his beard. Tekentriya's expression was impossible for Lamprophyre to understand.

She risked listening for their thoughts, but the rest of the people were such a muddled buzz she had to stop or be overwhelmed.

Tekentriya stopped near Lamprophyre and stood in that awkward, leg-thrust-out position, but showed no sign of discomfort. "My lady ambassador," she said, "you stand accused of murder."

CHAPTER THIRTY-ONE

"*Murder?*" Lamprophyre exclaimed.

"Tekentriya, what are you talking about?" Rokshan said. "That's impossible."

Tekentriya kept her gaze fixed on Lamprophyre. "This afternoon, a village ten miles north of Tanajital was burned to the ground. No survivors. Witnesses report—"

"If there were no survivors, how are there witnesses?" Rokshan demanded.

Tekentriya flicked a sharp glance his way. "Travelers came upon the village after the incident. They say every building in the village was utterly destroyed, and the streets were covered with bodies reduced to ash and splintered bone. What they described resembles no earthly fire. My lady ambassador, where were you this afternoon?"

Stunned, Lamprophyre said, "I was with Rokshan—we flew to Kolmira."

"And you returned when?"

"I don't know human time measurements. The sun was still high in the western sky. Early afternoon."

"Where were you after that?"

"In the embassy." Lamprophyre shook her head. "No, I also went swimming. You can't possibly believe I'd do such a horrible thing!"

"Did anyone see you this afternoon? During your swim?"

Lamprophyre's heart sank. "No. I flew far downstream so I wouldn't disturb anyone."

"Tekentriya, this is insane. Lamprophyre would never hurt anyone." Rokshan stepped forward and put himself between Lamprophyre and his sister. "Why couldn't magic be involved? A magical fire—"

"Rokshan, this is none of your business."

"Of course it's my business. I'm the ambassador's liaison, and I'm also her friend. My word should count for something, even with you."

Tekentriya glared at him. "What's that supposed to mean?"

Rokshan stood his ground. "I know you don't think much of me, but you don't believe I'd be complicit in covering up Lamprophyre's involvement in this disaster if she were responsible? I'm willing to stake my own reputation on her being innocent."

Tekentriya's dark, unexpectedly delicate eyebrows rose. "An entire village is dead," she said. "Several hundred people, including children. Your reputation is irrelevant compared to the fact that we have a dangerous creature in our midst and no guarantee she won't do this again."

"But I didn't!" Lamprophyre said. "Why would I? I've lived among you for a couple of twelvedays and I've never done anything to hurt anyone. I don't even know what village you're talking about—I've been out of Tanajital exactly four times, and I certainly have no reason to want to destroy an entire human settlement!"

"No?" Tekentriya said. "Then you deny being upset by the handbills that circulated a few weeks ago, spreading rumors about dragons?"

"No—I mean, yes, of course I was upset, but that's irrelevant."

"It's relevant because the handbills were produced in that village." Tekentriya took a lurching step forward, pushing Rokshan to one side. "You decided to take your revenge in a rather dramatic way, didn't you?"

"But I didn't know that!"

"And she wouldn't have burned the village if she had," Rokshan said. "Tekentriya, see sense. Lamprophyre isn't the only one who can create that kind of fire."

"Stay out of this, Rokshan," Tekentriya said. "My lady ambassador, General Sajan is here to take you into custody. We can't have you free to escape justice or burn another village. Will you go quietly? Because I warn you, refusing to go or fighting our soldiers will suggest your guilt."

"You'd risk war with the dragons by forcibly confining an ambassador?" Rokshan exclaimed. "You're out of your mind."

"Which is why I'm asking the ambassador to go with General Sajan voluntarily," Tekentriya said, not taking her eyes of Lamprophyre. "As a courtesy to Gonjiri and as a gesture of good faith."

"Lamprophyre," Rokshan said in a low, intense voice, "you don't have to do this. They have no proof."

Lamprophyre looked from Rokshan to Tekentriya and then to General Sajan. "You have no way to confine me," she said.

"That had better not be a threat," Tekentriya said. Lamprophyre risked listening to her thoughts, and over the confusing background hum of the assembled humans, Tekentriya's thoughts were a tangle of fear and determination. Despite her dislike of the woman, Lamprophyre respected her courage.

"It's not," she said. "It's just—you ought to see that if I were really dangerous, I wouldn't care about proving my innocence. I'd just burn you all where you stood."

"Lamprophyre," Rokshan muttered, "you're not helping."

"I haven't killed anyone, and I didn't burn that village," Lamprophyre declared in a loud voice. "And I say you need more proof than the fact that I'm capable of doing so. You don't take General Sajan into custody every time someone in Tanajital is killed with a sword, do you? And yet I'd wager he's capable of that act. I'm innocent, and I'm not going to act like I'm guilty just to calm your fears of me." Anger fueled by days of hearing humans' fear and suspicion boiled up inside her.

"You're the only one who benefited from destroying that village," Tekentriya said. "That and the manner of its destruction is proof enough for me."

"How did she benefit—" Rokshan stopped. "Wait," he said. "What village?"

"That's irrelevant," Tekentriya said.

"Bindusk," General Sajan said at the same time. Tekentriya glared at him.

"Bindusk has—had—maybe seven hundred people," Rokshan said. "It was barely a dot on a map. There's no way they had a printing press to produce those handbills. And how did you know that's where they came from?"

"My people investigated the handbills in case their writer decided to move beyond simple calumny to inciting riot," Tekentriya said. "They traced their origin to Bindusk." Uncertainty crept over her fear and determination.

"How sure are you that someone didn't try to deceive you?" Rokshan asked.

"Don't you dare suggest my people are incompetent," Tekentriya said, taking a couple of awkward steps forward to put herself within striking distance of Rokshan. "The trail was clear."

"And you were keeping an eye on Bindusk after that, weren't you?" Rokshan wasn't at all intimidated by Tekentriya's threat. "If anything else came out of that town, you were ready to identify the culprit. Except somebody burned it to the ground, making it impossible for you to find the author of those handbills. And impossible to discover that there never was a printing press in Bindusk." Rokshan turned to Lamprophyre, his eyes wide. "What do you *think*, Lamprophyre?"

She listened. Rokshan was thinking *this is the work of our enemy Harshod, can't tell her because she'll want to know why we care, up to you now if we reveal our intention.*

She almost spoke up then. Revealing the existence of a group plotting against Gonjiri and the dragons—that was something Tekentriya should know. Except Tekentriya was definitely intent on proving Lamprophyre guilty of a terrible crime, and while she wasn't conveniently thinking about what she would do to Lamprophyre as a result, Lamprophyre was certain she had something in mind. What if *Tekentriya* was involved in the plot? She had the resources to burn a village, she hated and feared Lamprophyre, and she was heir to the throne. Maybe she wanted the kingdom sooner than nature and her father's eventual death would provide.

"I think an adept could find traces of a printing press, if there was one," she said, wishing Rokshan were a dragon to hear her own thoughts in response. "I don't know what presses are made of, but your adepts are clever."

"They're made of wood and metal. A lot of metal," Rokshan said. "Can dragon fire make metal disappear?"

"No. It would liquefy the metal, but the metal would all still be there."

"Have someone search the ruins, then," Rokshan said. "It's unlikely there was more than one thing in Bindusk made of that much metal. If the printing press wasn't there, then someone laid a false trail."

"You don't tell me what to do, boy," Tekentriya snarled. "But I intend to discover the truth. I still want this monster confined. Ambassador or not."

"She's not a monster, and you had better give her the respect you would any other ambassador—most of whom are listening to this and having second thoughts about their relationship with Gonjiri," Rokshan said. "And I told you I'll stake my reputation on her innocence. I'll take responsibility for any destruction she causes."

"Don't be a fool. It doesn't work like that."

"Rokshan, you can't," Lamprophyre said.

He cast a glance back at her, then returned his attention to Tekentriya. "Lamprophyre isn't dangerous," he said, "and I think you're a fool for fearing her. I'm so certain she won't hurt anyone I'm willing to take her punishment if she does."

"Rokshan!" Lamprophyre exclaimed.

He looked back at her again. "Why are you worried? You won't commit any crimes, so I won't suffer any punishments."

"Yes, but—"

"You're willing to sacrifice your life for this creature? Which of us is the fool?" Tekentriya snarled. "Very well. But don't leave Tanajital. I want her where my people can watch her."

"All right." Rokshan turned to General Sajan. "Tell your men to stand down," he said. "You're frightening our guests."

Lamprophyre could hear the thoughts of everyone in attendance, and while she couldn't make out more individual thoughts than those of the few humans nearest her, none of the others sounded frightened. They actually sounded excited. Well, the prospect of witnessing an ambassador being taken into custody, giving them a thrilling story to tell their friends, was exciting. Khadar was the only sour note, and he sounded frustrated: *beast should suffer for her apostasy, foolish beliefs going to contaminate all of Tanajital.* Well, Tekentriya *had* stolen his audience and his moment.

General Sajan's expression was hidden by his facial hair, but Lamprophyre heard him think *Rokshan's gained confidence, good for him standing up to that harridan Tekentriya.* "Don't think this is resolved," he said, but it sounded like a warning rather than a threat. He gestured, and the soldiers flanking him shouted orders that made every soldier in the formation turn on his heel. A few of them felt nervous of turning their back on Lampro-phyre, but it was a distant feeling, and Lamprophyre didn't worry about it. General Sajan saluted Rokshan, turned, and with the rest of the soldiers marched back the way they'd come.

This left Tekentriya alone facing Rokshan and Lamprophyre. Again, determination and anger overlaid her fear. "She makes one wrong move," she said, "and I will bring every weapon I possess against you both."

"Find the truth," Lamprophyre said.

Tekentriya glared at her. Then she turned and lurched off toward the palace, avoiding the area with the canopies and Lamprophyre's guests. Lamprophyre let out twin bursts of relieved smoke before thinking they might make people nervous.

"Now what?" she asked Rokshan, pitching her voice low to keep the others from hearing.

"We have to find Harshod," Rokshan said in similarly low tones. "Why didn't you tell Tekentriya about him?"

"Because it occurred to me that a plot by disaffected Gonjirians might have the heir to the throne at its head."

"Oh. Good point." Rokshan rubbed his face and pinched the bridge of his nose, squinching up his eyes into narrow slits. "We'll have to discuss it tomorrow. Tonight, we still have guests."

"I'm not sure I can endure making polite and meaningless conversation after that."

Rokshan gripped her forearm briefly. "Think of it like this. Khadar is going to have trouble regaining momentum after that interruption. If you avoid him for the rest of the evening, it will be a peaceful night."

"That's true," Lamprophyre said with pleasure.

CHAPTER THIRTY-TWO

L amprophyre woke late the following morning. She hadn't realized how hard it would be to get some of her guests to leave. From comments she overheard both audibly and mentally, she learned the wine was particularly good and there was plenty of it. Something to remember to change if she had to do this again.

She stretched every muscle, from her legs to her wings. Stretching felt good. So did inhaling the aroma of freshly-cooked pig, something new Depik had offered her a few days ago. It wasn't quite as delicious as cow, but it was still better than horse. She couldn't believe she'd ever settled for horse. Rokshan had warned her not to tell humans about that part of her diet, saying that many upper-class Gonjirians owned horses for riding and they could be sensitive about the possibility someone might eat their beloved animals. That struck Lamprophyre as odd, but what could you expect from people who allowed animals to live inside their caves?

Rokshan arrived just as she was finishing off her pig. "Your generosity gained you a remarkable benefit," he said, settling on the floor beside her. "Depik is as good a cook as anyone in the palace kitchens."

"I like to think generosity is its own reward, but I won't refuse other benefits," Lamprophyre said. She covered her mouth and burped. That was another human custom, pretending they weren't passing gas in any way. Dragons never did that. Lamprophyre didn't like holding in a burp, because that meant she could taste it, and pig or cow or chicken mingled with her stomachs' contents tasted nasty. But she tried to show politeness by human standards.

"So. Exciting night," Rokshan said. "Our friend Harshod seems to have gotten ahead of us."

"It worries me that he knew to attack that village when I was off where no one could see me," Lamprophyre said. "How could he possibly know we're on his trail? He wasn't in Kolmira to find out—do you think he did go back before you sent soldiers?"

"I think this is just the next step in his plan. Except it doesn't fit with everything else he's done." Rokshan did his contemplative monkey pose. "Burning a village is likely to make Gonjiri angry with dragons, not the other way around."

"You don't suppose he's trying a new strategy? Given that we've countered all the other attacks he's made?" How Rokshan could sit like that, Lamprophyre couldn't understand. Just thinking about crossing her legs made her hips hurt.

"Maybe. I suppose he might believe humans attacking you for destroying a village would bring the dragons down on Tanajital."

They sat in silence for a few beats. The still air, muggy and hot the way it got before a storm, clung to Lamprophyre like a second skin, though one soft and fragile like human skin instead of hard like dragon scales. It had rained briefly around midnight, but the respite from the humidity had lasted only a thousand beats. She flexed her wings to create a breeze, but the air shifted only slightly and then settled back over her. Flying would be a relief, but she'd have to stay close to Tanajital or risk Rokshan being punished for her so-called crime.

"What worries me," Rokshan said, "is if Harshod isn't in Tanajital, we have no way of capturing him. You promised not to leave."

"And you can't capture him by yourself. Could you bring soldiers?"

"Maybe, but I think, after last night, Sajan won't be cooperative, if only because he doesn't want to fight with Tekentriya. I had to talk fast to justify sending soldiers to Kolmira."

"Do you think she'll actually try to find what's left of the printing press that isn't actually in that village?"

Rokshan blew out his breath. "I don't know. I thought she was fair, for all her other faults, but last night it seemed she was acting out of fear."

"She was afraid, but she was also convinced she was doing the right thing," Lamprophyre said. "Maybe that's a good thing."

"Maybe." Rokshan shifted position to lean back. "But it still leaves us with two problems instead of one. Keeping the dragons from attacking Gonjiri, and proving you innocent of murder."

"Both of those problems would be solved if we could find Harshod," Lamprophyre said. "I think it's time we asked for help."

"Help?" Rokshan's eyes narrowed. "You don't mean—"

"We can't leave Tanajital, we can't get help from the soldiers, and we can't go from building to building searching for Harshod," Lamprophyre said. "We need magic."

"I was afraid that's what you had in mind," Rokshan said. "Who should we go to? Sabarna is easier to work with, but she doesn't have the right kind of knowledge. And Manishi isn't trustworthy."

"What kind of knowledge do we need?"

"Sabarna would understand the theory of how to find someone whose appearance you don't know, but Manishi would be more likely to already have an artifact that would do it." Rokshan sighed. "And I have to return the pendant we used to find Abhimot, anyway. It concerns me that she hasn't demanded its return yet."

Lamprophyre nodded. "We'll just have to keep our eyes on her."

"Right. And in truth, I'm more worried about her cheating us out of money than I am about her being one of Harshod's people. Particularly if Tekentriya is involved. Manishi gets along with her even less well than she does me." Rokshan got to his feet. "I'll send a message asking Manishi to meet us here. Do you mind if I promise her more stone as an incentive?"

"I don't know when I'll be in a position to get it, but all right."

She washed her hands and face with water from the rain barrel, which was low despite the midnight rain, and went into the embassy to wait. Waiting was hard. She was used to taking action, to making a decision and then doing it, whatever it was. Having to depend on humans to be her hands and legs, so to speak, frustrated her even as she was grateful for Rokshan and Depik and her servants. She lay on the floor and pillowed her head on her arms, closing her eyes and listening to the voice of the city.

Footsteps roused her from her doze—so embarrassing, to fall asleep in the morning, but the city was hot and the air was saturated with water and she was used to the cool, crisp mountain breezes stirring her blood. She blinked at Dharan. "I forgot you were coming," she said.

"I brought some new books," Dharan said, "and more chalk. This approaching storm is enough to make anyone sleepy."

Lamprophyre yawned and got to her feet. "I love a good hard rain," she said, "though flying through a storm is dangerous."

"But you've done it."

"Naturally." Lamprophyre smiled. "What books did you bring?"

"Another epic poem," Dharan said, "by Ganghir, since you liked the first. A history of Tanajital. And—" He withdrew a large, awkward tome from the satchel— "a book about the constellations and their stories, with pictures."

Lamprophyre accepted it from him and turned the pages. "It's beautiful," she breathed, "and so colorful." The pictures glowed bright as dragons, and gold accented the large capitals heading each page.

"Be careful with it. There aren't many copies in existence." Dharan set the other books in a pile next to the ones she'd already read and liked enough to keep.

"This looks like it would take a long time to copy, if someone had to write it all out," Lamprophyre said.

"They don't. Here." Dharan gently took the book from her. "Notice how each letter is identical to all the others like it? This is printing. The pictures are drawn once, then duplicated by magic and bound into the text. The only thing done by hand is the gilding on the capitals."

"That's amazing." Lamprophyre extended a hand to touch a picture, but withdrew it before making contact. "Why aren't there more copies?"

"The magic that duplicates the pictures is extremely expensive. There's another, more common edition made without them, with just the writing. But I liked the illustrations enough I bought this copy for myself."

"Thank you for loaning it to me. It's so beautiful." Lamprophyre accepted it back from him. "Though I suspect you're trying to convert me, with all these stories of Jiwanyil."

Dharan laughed. "I can see how it might look that way. But to me, these are just stories. I'm not sure I believe in God."

Lamprophyre closed the book more abruptly than she'd intended. "Not believe in God? How is that possible?"

"There's too much randomness and evil in the world," Dharan said, "and the ecclesiasts who claim to speak for Jiwanyil are mostly corrupt, selfish, and lacking in the kind of wisdom I'd expect from people supposedly close to God. There's never been a prophecy that couldn't be explained by coincidence."

"What about the flood Rokshan told me about? The one where your people ignored the prophecy, and thousands died?"

Dharan shrugged. "No one ever mentions that the dam in question was old, and its caretakers had warned the king more than once that it needed repair. It's not as if its breaking was a huge surprise."

"Oh. I didn't know that." Lamprophyre felt uncomfortable. "I don't know that I believe in your God, either. At least, I suppose he could exist alongside Mother Stone, but I'm not sure how."

"People believe in God because they don't believe in themselves," Dharan said. "And, not to be offensive, but I think that applies to dragons, too."

Lamprophyre stiffened. "That *is* offensive."

"Sorry. Like I said, it's not something I'm sure of—it's just a possibility."

"Don't listen to him," Rokshan said as he entered the embassy. "He's a known heathen. The reverends are afraid of him, and more than one ecclesiast has declared him apostate."

"What's a reverend?"

Rokshan took the bag of chalk from Dharan and extracted a lump. "Reverends are ordinary people who preach the doctrine of Immanence," he said, drawing a large, lopsided oval on Lamprophyre's slate and chalking the word REVEREND inside. "Anyone can be a reverend so long as he sticks to revealed doctrine and doesn't preach anything new. They also perform weddings and funerals."

He drew a smaller oval above the first, with a different word. "Ecclesiasts speak for Jiwanyil in prophecy and proclaiming new doctrine. They have to prove they have the capacity to hear the word of God spoken to their hearts and minds. There aren't as many ecclesiasts, obviously."

"So Khadar can prophesy?" Lamprophyre had trouble imagining any deity willing to share their wisdom with Khadar.

"Technically, yes. Though I've sometimes wondered if he pulled some kind of trick to get around that requirement." Rokshan drew a very small oval above the other two. "Then there are the High Ecclesiasts, one for each way in which the Immanence took shape within the world. Meyari, God of the Living World. Nirinatan, God of the Living Stone. Vrelok, God of Beasts. Katayan, God of Dragons. And Jiwanyil, God of Humans." He chalked tiny pictures around the oval Lamprophyre could barely make out. Rokshan had a dragon's eye for detail; each picture was surprisingly recognizable despite being sketched with only a few sure strokes.

"So is the Archprelate one of the High Ecclesiasts?" she asked.

"No, he's at the top." Rokshan drew a tiny human form above the ovals. "He's responsible for receiving revelation for all of Gonjiri."

"If that's what he's doing," Dharan muttered. Rokshan shot him an irritated look.

"But what about other countries?" Lamprophyre asked. "Don't all humans have the same religion? Why isn't he Archprelate for the world?"

"Yes, Rokshan, why not?" Dharan said with a smile.

"Shut up, Dharan, you're a heathen," Rokshan said without malice. "No country wants to be dictated to by religious prophecies from another country. So every country has its own Archprelate, who guides that country and receives revelation solely for it. Personally, I don't think there's anything wrong with the idea that God's word might be different for different countries, but there are a lot of people in Gonjiri who'd like to believe ours is the only true Archprelate. Same for Fanishkor and Sachetan and so forth."

"And this is why Rokshan and I get along despite differences of religious opinion," Dharan said, clapping his friend on the shoulder. "He's got a flexible mind and a willingness to hear the other side."

"I just think it's hubris to imagine humans have it all figured out," Rokshan said. "Lamprophyre, I sent a message to Manishi, asking her to come here when it's convenient. I hope that doesn't mean midnight."

"Manishi? Why do you want to talk to her?" Dharan asked, making a sour face Lamprophyre had no trouble interpreting.

"Trade," Rokshan said. "Lamprophyre brings her stone and she pays us for it."

Lamprophyre felt uncomfortable about lying to Dharan, even indirectly. It wasn't likely he'd tell anyone the truth about their search, and even less likely he was somehow involved with Harshod. But it was an old dragon saying that three could keep a secret if two of them were dead, and she didn't intend to take chances, even with a friend.

"I can practice reading until then," she said.

Rokshan cleaned off the slate. "I can't believe you've only been reading for a few days. I had no idea dragons were geniuses."

"She has a phenomenal memory," Dharan said. "She's learning the words as pictures of themselves rather than as collections of sounds. I wish I could teach a few more dragons to see if Lamprophyre is unusual."

"Maybe, if humans stop being afraid of us, more dragons will come south," Lamprophyre said, but she knew as she spoke it was a vain hope. She settled her new book with the vibrant illustrations under the lens and hoped Manishi would come soon.

CHAPTER THIRTY-THREE

Manishi arrived before noon, just as Dharan was preparing to leave. "I remember you," she said. "You're one of Rokshan's academy friends. Whatever happened to the one I rejected as my apprentice?"

"Baleran returned to Sachetan, and *he* rejected *you*, if you'll recall," Rokshan said.

Manishi shrugged. "All I know is he was a terrible apprentice and I was glad to be rid of him. Mother must have been mad to think it was a good idea."

Dharan and Rokshan exchanged glances, their faces expressionless. Lamprophyre thought about listening to their thoughts, but she'd promised herself not to eavesdrop on her friends, however tempting it might be.

"I'll see you in two days, Lamprophyre," Dharan said. "That should give you time to read those books for us to discuss them. I'd also like to take down some dragon poetry, if you're willing to recite."

"That would be nice, yes. I'd like to be able to share our poetry with humans."

Dharan nodded, clasped wrists with Rokshan, and left. Manishi watched him go. "Handsome fellow," she said. "And not stupid. If I intended to marry again, I might choose him."

"How very generous of you," Rokshan said. "Thanks for coming. We have a proposition for you." He'd dragged the chairs in from the dining pavilion and now gestured to one of them, inviting Manishi to sit.

"A proposition?" Manishi settled herself on the chair with the air of someone prepared to stay for a while. "I haven't exhausted my stores of the last stone I bought from you, but I'm always interested in more."

"We need to find someone we've never seen," Rokshan said. "And we think you know how to do that." He sat in the other chair, which he'd placed opposite Manishi's, next to Lamprophyre.

Manishi looked from Rokshan to Lamprophyre and back again. "Really," she said. "I'm flattered. But that sort of thing is very difficult."

Lamprophyre tried once more to hear Manishi's thoughts, but got only that dull hum. "Difficult. Not impossible," she said.

"Exactly," Manishi said. "It's resource-heavy and very expensive. That sort of thing—"

Lamprophyre rolled her eyes. "How much kyanite do you want?"

Rokshan jerked in surprise. Manishi's lips curled in a slow smile. "Either you're desperate, or you're as disinclined to bandy words as I am," she said. "I like that. So you know my price. I want another crystal the size of the one you had before. The whole crystal. Get me that, and I'll help you find anyone you like."

"There's a catch," Rokshan said, recovering himself. "Lamprophyre has been accused of destroying a village. She's agreed to be confined in Tanajital until her innocence is proven."

Manishi frowned. "So why did you waste my time?"

"Because you want the kyanite, and you don't want anyone to know you have it," Lamprophyre said. "That means I'm the only one who can supply it to you. And unless we find this person, I'm not leaving here any time soon. So we both benefit from you helping us now."

"You're asking me to take a big risk."

"Not so big, considering you know we're trustworthy," Rokshan said. "Which is more than we can say for you."

"You wound me, Rokshan," Manishi said with a smile. "All right. You give me the kyanite, and a double handful of the same quality emerald you found before, and I'll provide you with what you want in advance of payment. The emerald," she added, holding up a hand to forestall Rokshan's objection, "is the fee to cover my working for you without the usual retainer. Don't tell me you aren't good for it."

Rokshan scowled. Lamprophyre didn't need to hear his thoughts to know he believed they were being cheated. But they didn't have much choice. "Agreed," she said. "How soon can you do it?"

Manishi smiled. "I've already started," she said.

"OBSIDIAN," LAMPROPHYRE SAID. SHE BREATHED ON THE FLAT FACE OF the stone and watched mist spread across it and then fade. "Didn't you say you'd pay extra if I could find obsidian?"

"I did," Manishi said. "But that's not relevant now. Step back."

Lamprophyre took a step backward, and her tail came up against the rough wooden wall behind her. What Manishi had called her workshop was a wooden structure barely large enough to fit Lamprophyre, with a double door almost as wide as the wall it was set in, thank the Stones, and no windows. Tall wooden boxes with tiny metal knobs in regular patterns along their fronts lined two of the four walls, with chunks of topaz and quartz with that same chlorite inclusion sitting atop them. Also atop the boxes were a few smaller pieces of obsidian, jagged and sharp where they'd broken off from a larger piece, and a purple cyclosilicate stone the size of Lamprophyre's fist that smelled rich and sweet. Too bad she and Manishi weren't friends, because she might have asked for a taste.

Lanterns glowed dully at all four corners of the ceiling like tired stars, adding the smell of burning oil to the scent of damp wood and sawdust, which coated the floor and clung unpleasantly to Lamprophyre's feet. She pinched her nose against a sneeze, which in this place could be catastrophic, and pressed herself even more firmly against the back wall.

Beside her, Rokshan stepped back as well, though not as far as she had. His eyes were intent on the slab of obsidian twice as long as her arm, mounted in a metal frame that could swivel to turn the stone horizontal or vertical. "It looks like a mirror," he said.

Manishi rotated the stone so it reflected all of them, Manishi clearly, the more distant Rokshan and Lamprophyre as dull blurs. "In a sense, yes," she said. "It cost a fortune to create."

"And yet you keep it in an unlocked, unprotected shed in the slums of Tanajital," Rokshan said.

Manishi laughed. "If you'd tried to enter without me, you'd find out how unprotected this place is," she said. "Don't worry about me. Now, who is it you want to find?"

Lamprophyre exchanged glances with Rokshan. She didn't need to eavesdrop to know what he was thinking: if they'd guessed wrong, and Manishi was complicit with the egg thieves, telling her what they'd learned could be dangerous. But Lamprophyre didn't see that they had much choice. "A man," she said. "He took up residence in Kolmira three months ago. He's an enemy to dragons."

Manishi's eyes widened, but the curl of her lip suggested she was about to mock them. "An enemy to dragons? That's dramatic. Who would be so stupid?"

"This man would," Rokshan said. "We need to find him. We think he's left Kolmira temporarily, but we don't know where he went."

"You're not giving me much to work with," Manishi said. "Is there anything else? You said you've never seen him—what about personal habits? Known associates? Has he done anything to hurt dragons, or is his enmity theoretical?"

Rokshan shot a look at Lamprophyre. Lamprophyre hesitated, cast a brief and semi-sincere mental apology Hyaloclast's way, and said, "He ordered the theft of a dragon egg."

Manishi went perfectly still. Her hand closed tightly on the obsidian mirror's frame. "Did he," she said, inflecting her words as a statement rather than a question. "Was he successful?"

"No. We recovered the egg. But we didn't capture the thieves."

"How unfortunate," Manishi said. She was gradually relaxing. "Do you know if he ever had contact with the egg?"

"We don't think so. We believe it was his stooge who did it." Lamprophyre felt proud of remembering the word.

"Hmm. Was it your egg?"

"Of course not!" Lamprophyre's outrage immediately faded as she remembered Manishi couldn't know Lamprophyre wasn't pair-bonded. "Except in the sense that all dragons, all eggs, belong to the flight."

"That might be enough." Manishi let go of the mirror, which canted backwards, and walked to one of the boxes. She took hold of a metal knob and pulled. To Lamprophyre's fascination, the knob and a square of wood attached to it separated from the box, revealing a smaller box with no top that was full of smoothly polished citrines in every shape from round to irregularly bumpy. Lamprophyre stepped closer to get a better look and received a fierce glare from Manishi. "Stay back," she said. "These aren't for eating."

"I would never—" Lamprophyre began hotly.

"She's just curious," Rokshan said. "I don't understand why you don't keep all this in your rooms at the palace. If all those drawers are full of stones, this place represents tens of thousands of vahas' worth of magical material."

"Because the defenses on this place are powerful, and Father refused to let me set them up anywhere that might destroy the palace if they were triggered," Manishi said. She scooped up a handful of citrines and returned to the mirror. Pushing down on it until it was horizontal, she shifted parts of the frame to lock the mirror in place, then set the citrines on it. Some were cloudy; others were clear. All of them were varying shades of orange-yellow, from translucent to dragon-bright. Their dull reflections glimmered from within the obsidian surface.

"This is going to be complicated, and I'm not interested in explaining the magic," Manishi said. "Do as I say, without questions, and we'll find your man." She pushed the citrines around with her forefinger while Lamprophyre waited impatiently for her to do something magical. But all she did was select a stone that was a flattened oval the color of winter sunrise and push the others to one end of the mirror. She handed the stone to Lamprophyre. "Hold that in your non-dominant hand."

Lamprophyre closed her left hand over the tiny stone. It was cool for only a beat or two before warming with her body heat. Manishi returned to the wooden box and pulled open another drawer. Lamprophyre smelled the warm, spicy odor of powdered azurite coming from the coarsely woven bag Manishi removed. Manishi took a metal bowl with a complicated handle and poured the azurite into it, then held it over the mirror and shifted the handle. Azurite drifted onto the polished surface from tiny holes that had been concealed until the handle moved, as if it had shifted the holes into alignment. Fascinated, Lamprophyre watched a thin layer of bright blue stone dust build up on the mirror until its surface was invisible.

Manishi worked the handle again, stopping the sifting dust, and set the contraption aside. She drew a series of symbols in the dust with her finger, starting at the narrow end of the oval and working her way around. Though some of the symbols were letters, Lamprophyre didn't recognize words, and sounding them out produced nothing coherent. If they were magical, they didn't make the room feel any different.

Manishi finished writing and dusted off her hand. "Put the stone here," she said, pointing at a semi-circular symbol at the top of the oval. "Don't disturb the dust."

Lamprophyre gingerly lowered the citrine onto the surface so it appeared the semicircle cradled it. Almost as soon as it left her fingers, it lit up with a soft glow that looked even more like a sunrise. Lamprophyre backed away, holding her breath so she wouldn't blow the dust around.

Manishi picked up another citrine, this one nearly orange and clear enough to see through, and touched it lightly to the glowing stone. The glow bled upward into the second stone, reddening her fingertips. She set the stone down carefully a short distance from the first within another semicircle. A trail of orange light traced a path through the symbols to connect the two stones. Manishi laughed, a low, throaty sound that wasn't entirely pleasant. "The dragon, and the egg," she said. "Let's see how many steps it takes to reach our man."

She repeated the steps again, first with a pale stone barely tinged with yellow, then with one mottled yellow and orange and shaped like a knucklebone. The path of orange light extended farther with each new stone. Finally, Manishi picked up a flattened sphere the color of a dying fire and touched it to the knucklebone. Light flared, making Lamprophyre involuntarily close her nictitating membranes and causing Rokshan to exclaim in pain. "It's just light," Manishi said, somewhat impatiently. "Don't be a baby."

Lamprophyre squinted at the bright speck in Manishi's hand. "Does that mean you found him?"

"It means I have a link to him I can use as I want," Manishi said. "But yes, he's in Tanajital. Do you want him dead?"

"Of course not!"

"I don't see why it's 'of course not.' If he tried to steal a dragon egg, I could see your people wanting revenge." Manishi closed her hand over the stone, making her fist glow faintly. "If it's not death, what do you want from him?"

"Answers," Rokshan said. "We need to get him where we can question him."

"That's harder. Manipulating people to obey you isn't simple."

Manishi's eyes were distant, as if she were lost in thought. "I can give him nudges in the right direction, but I can't force him to do anything. Where do you want him to go?"

"Hmm. The coliseum is empty today. Better make it there," Rokshan said.

"Then let's see where he is now."

Manishi gathered up the citrines she hadn't used and put them back in their drawer, then carefully swept the azurite dust off the mirror, not disturbing the glowing symbols or the stones powering them. She tapped the citrine in her hand against the mirror's surface twice, then set it down at the center of the cleared space. The glow redoubled, reflected by the mirror until the little room was bright as day and Rokshan and Manishi's faces were almost pale. Lamprophyre's hands were faintly green like new grass. Green like Coquina—for once, the comparison didn't anger her.

"Show him to me," Manishi said, tapping the stone with one finger and then jerking it away as if she'd been burned. The mirror's surface rippled like a pond disturbed by a rock, then flashed brightly enough that Lamprophyre flinched again. This time, the brightness was only that of a cloudy sky, reflected in a mirror of metal rather than obsidian. A man visible from the waist up stood silhouetted against the reflected sky, his face lit by an unseen sun.

He looked just as Abhimot had described him: longish dark hair, light brown skin, brown eyes the same color as Rokshan's surmounted by eyebrows that grew together in the middle. A dark spot on his upper lip that looked like a small round insect made Lamprophyre's lip itch in sympathy. His image was perfectly still, but the background bobbed slightly, suggesting that they were watching him in motion. Since they would have to be facing him and walking backwards to have this perspective, Lamprophyre was just as happy it was magic and not reality.

"This doesn't tell us where he is," Rokshan said.

"Have patience. I did mention this is difficult, right? I don't know if I'm getting paid enough for this."

"That had better not be a sideways demand for more stone," Lamprophyre said.

"It's not. I'm better off putting you in my debt for later. Now, be quiet so I can think." Manishi stared at the image of Harshod, who turned his head as if watching someone else go by. Lamprophyre observed him, too.

He didn't look like someone who might torture kittens, but Lamprophyre still had trouble interpreting human expressions and he could well be a hardened criminal.

"That's it," Manishi said. She plucked the central stone from the mirror, and the surface once more turned to glimmering black glass. Bouncing the stone in her hand as if it were a live coal, she hurried to a different wooden box and opened a larger drawer. She withdrew a mass of silver that Lamprophyre realized was a lot of very thin wire. She'd seen wire used in jewelry, but never so much of it in one place.

Manishi tucked the spool of wire under the arm holding the stone and pulled the loose end, unlooping several handspans of silver to dangle free. She began wrapping the stone in wire, not smoothly, but irregularly until the stone was a lumpy ball of silver, completely invisible. Manishi dropped the spool, which bounced a couple of times and rolled away, and rapidly dug through another drawer until she found a sharp double-bladed tool with which she cut the wire. She threw the tool back into the drawer and bent the cut end of the wire until it was tucked away inside the rest.

Rokshan had moved closer, watching Manishi with the expression of someone who was bursting with questions. Manishi rolled the silver ball in her fingers, then handed it to Rokshan. "That binds his body and soul in one, rooted in the stone," she said. "He'll be drawn to it over time. So I suggest you figure out where you want to meet him and be prepared for his arrival."

"Amazing," Rokshan said. "If this works—"

"'If,' what 'if'?" Manishi said, sounding offended. "Of course it will work. But get out of here. I don't like the look of him, and I don't want him coming here."

"Thank you," Lamprophyre said. "I promise to have your payment soon."

"You'd better," Manishi said.

CHAPTER THIRTY-FOUR

Out on the street, Lamprophyre looked at the tiny ball of silver in Rokshan's hand. "Is the coliseum really the best place?" she asked. "It's rather public."

"We can't have him drawn to the embassy, if Manishi's right about not being able to override his free will. If he knows what it is, there's no way he'd go there no matter what magic we use on him." Rokshan put the ball into his money pouch and climbed up. "Let's go, and decide how we'll confront him."

Lamprophyre leaped into the sky and rose until she could see all of Tanajital spread out beneath her. She wished Harshod were visible in some way, maybe glowing with the orange light that had tracked him, but the city looked as peaceful and busy as ever, with no sign that their prey was somewhere in those streets.

She spiraled down to land within the coliseum and ducked to let Rokshan off. "If I know he's coming, I can conceal myself," she said.

"We don't know what direction he'll come from. We have to assume we won't see him until he's here," Rokshan said. "Damn, but I wish I had soldiers. Though they're not good at concealing themselves, and they'd just warn Harshod off. What I *need* are Tekentriya's spies, but that's a waste of a wish."

"Let's get up high," Lamprophyre suggested. "We can watch from above, and chase him down if he runs." She hoped he'd run.

Rokshan nodded and climbed back into the notch. Lamprophyre flapped slowly until she reached the nearest arch and settled herself carefully on it. Only a few people noticed her, and when she concealed herself, they soon stopped looking for her. After a few dozen beats, she let color bleed back across her scales and wings. No one looked up. They almost never looked up.

Rokshan sighed and settled himself more comfortably. "And now," he said, "we wait."

Nothing happened. The sun slipped inexorably across the sky, broiling the city beneath. Lamprophyre immediately regretted her position, which had very little shade. Rokshan, pressed against her body that was much warmer than a human's, must be miserable. "Maybe we should go somewhere else," she suggested. "I could fit inside that box you said your family uses."

"It would be cramped, and I doubt you could get out quickly enough to surprise Harshod," Rokshan said. "I wish this stone had some kind of signal attached to it to indicate when the target is near. Then we could go anywhere we liked."

Lamprophyre flexed her wings to make a breeze that cooled the back of her neck and not much else. "Are you watching the west? I'll watch the east."

"All right."

More time passed. Lamprophyre's legs ached from holding position on the arch. She continued to scan the crowds even as despair crept over her. This was a stupid idea. How many thousands or even tens of thousands of humans lived in Tanajital? And they were searching for one human in all that crowd. It was ridiculous to believe they could be successful with such odds as those.

She looked almost directly down at the wide space surrounding the coliseum. The shadows— She gasped. "My shadow," she said. "It's starting to show."

Rokshan shifted to her other side. "It doesn't look like a dragon."

"Not now, but give it a thousand beats and it will stand out to anyone who walks past. Including Harshod."

"Then maybe—wait. I see him. I think." Rokshan shifted again and pointed. Lamprophyre followed the line of his arm, barely visible to the left of her face. The crowd still looked like a faceless mass.

"It's definitely him. And he's headed this way," Rokshan said.

"I don't—" Lamprophyre stopped and focused on a group of males walking together past the coliseum. One of them wasn't as dark-skinned as the others, and his hair was untidy and brushed his collarbone. Instantly Lamprophyre concealed herself against the arch. Harshod didn't appear to have seen them, but there was no sense taking chances.

She felt Rokshan shifting position again, this time hunching down behind her neck. "I can't see him from here," he whispered, though there was no way Harshod could hear them at such a distance. "Tell me what he's doing."

"Walking in this direction," Lamprophyre whispered back. It was contagious. "He's left the other males behind, but he's not coming directly here. He keeps stopping and looking behind him like he thinks he's being followed."

"I wonder if he can tell the magic is affecting him. Maybe it translates to the sense of being followed."

"I don't know. There, he's moving again." Lamprophyre rose up, stretching her legs. "Hold on." She stepped off the arch and dropped to the ground, spreading her wings to catch herself at the last moment.

"What are you doing?" Rokshan exclaimed, as loudly as he could without raising his voice. "Now we really can't see him."

Lamprophyre shuddered and turned blue again. "I know, but I was about to lose my concealment, and that might have drawn his attention. Besides, we know he's coming here, so we might as well wait for him inside the coliseum." She drew in a breath and concealed herself once more, blue and copper turning rust-red and dusty tan.

Rokshan nodded and put her between himself and the side of the coliseum Harshod had been approaching by. Lamprophyre spread her wings to give him as much cover as possible. Her heart beat rapidly in anticipation of facing Harshod, even though she still didn't know what to do with him once she caught him. If he wouldn't tell her who his commander was, assuming he had a commander, she wasn't sure she could torture the information out of him. Maybe Hyaloclast should have sent someone more cold-blooded.

Over the hum of the city's pulse, she heard footsteps approaching. Her heart sped up until it beat nearly as fast as a human's, painful and hard. Her skin vibrated with the need to maintain concealment. The footsteps grew louder, but also more tentative, slowing until the pauses between each step were at least a beat apart, maybe two. The waiting would drive her mad.

A figure stepped through one of the arched entrances. The sunlight fell fully on him, revealing that his clothing was smudged with dirt and his disordered hair was shiny with grease. He took a few more steps forward. Shielding his eyes with one hand, he said, "I know you're there, dragon. Show yourself."

Lamprophyre's carefully maintained concealment shivered and fell apart. She stared at Harshod, her mind teeming with questions. He didn't sound afraid, or angry, just tired. She listened for his thoughts and heard the echo of the words he'd just said.

Rokshan walked out from behind her and took a position on her right side. "You knew we were here," he said. "And you came anyway."

Harshod shrugged. "You went to a lot of trouble to find me, I figured, why not say hello?" He didn't move any closer, but it didn't matter; he was within pouncing distance, and that was all Lamprophyre cared about. His thoughts were still focused on his speech. That kind of single-mindedness was rare even in dragons, and she'd never encountered it in humans before.

"How did you know?" Lamprophyre asked.

"I don't think that's information you need," Harshod said. Now he did step forward just a few paces. The breeze brought his conflicting scents to Lamprophyre's nostrils. He smelled of unwashed human and grease, but more importantly, he *reeked* of stone, at least half a dozen different stones big enough to catch Lamprophyre's attention. If it was a stone that was protecting his thoughts, she couldn't work out which one.

"It doesn't matter," Rokshan said. "Tell us who told you to steal that egg and start a war."

Harshod smiled. One of his teeth gleamed gold. "You figured it out. Good for you! Then you must also know I'm not going to answer that question."

"So you do have a superior," Rokshan said. "We wondered about that. Thanks."

Harshod's smile faltered briefly. "It's already too late," he said. "Gonjiri will go to war against the dragons, and it will be decimated."

269

"Leaving Tekentriya in a position to take over," Lamprophyre said.

Harshod's thick eyebrows drew even more closely together. "Tekentriya?" he said, sounding surprised. "Yes, of course."

Rokshan said that curt mystery word. "It's not Gonjiri," he said. "Are you even Gonjirian?"

"I told you I'm not interested in answering your questions." Harshod shifted his weight as if preparing to run. Lamprophyre smiled and blew out a puff of smoke that drifted away on the light breeze. Harshod's gaze never left Lamprophyre's face. "So maybe you should ask yourselves," he continued, "if I didn't come to talk, why *did* I let you lure me in?"

"Are you working for Fanishkor? Or does Gonjiri have an enemy we don't know about?" Rokshan persisted.

"I don't care about your motives," Lamprophyre said. "You're going to answer my questions, or I'll peel the skin from your flesh until you do."

"I'm terrified. See how I'm shaking?" Harshod extended a hand that was perfectly steady. On his middle finger he wore a ring set with an oversized lump of what Lamprophyre realized was erythronite crystal, sparkling like a cut ruby but paler and gaudier. A bracelet set with aquamarines dangled around his wrist. "No, I think you'll find Gonjiri only has one true enemy."

"And who's that?" Rokshan said.

Harshod's hand closed into a fist. "Dragons," he said.

A blast of bright yellow fire streaked from Harshod's clenched hand to strike Rokshan full in the chest. Rokshan screamed as fire engulfed him, blazing hot enough that even Lamprophyre felt it.

Her own scream came less than a beat after his. Rokshan threw himself on the ground and rolled madly, trying to extinguish the flames, but the fire burned as if no human agency could put it out.

Lamprophyre picked up Rokshan and wrapped her left wing around him, beating the flames licking at his head and face with her opposite hand. Distantly, she felt someone grab her right leg and climb up her body. Harshod. He *dared* touch her—! She twisted, trying to dislodge him, but he'd gotten hold of her ruff and was hanging on as if his life were in the balance. The fire was nearly out, but Rokshan was disturbingly limp in her arm, and her terror for him outweighed her concern for what Harshod was doing.

Then something struck the back of her head, exactly at the sensitive spot, sending sharp agony shooting through her whole body. Her vision blurred and darkened, but instead of the sweet release of unconsciousness, the pain increased until she screamed and flung Rokshan away. Seizures racked her, and she vomited her last meal all down her side. Desperately, she sucked in air in great harsh breaths, unable to control any part of her body but her lungs. She'd never felt pain like it before. She needed to recover so she could capture Harshod, because if he could do this to her, if he had another dragon-hurting weapon, no dragon anywhere was safe.

Gradually, the seizures stopped, and she lay numb and barely conscious on the floor of the coliseum. Part of her mind was screaming at her to get up and find Rokshan, to see how badly hurt he was, but movement was beyond her. She practiced breathing, which was still all she could control, until the black haze in front of her vision disappeared and she could see the ruddy ground and a segment of the wall of the coliseum. Rokshan wasn't there. She hoped that meant she wasn't looking the right way.

"Rokshan?" she called out. Her thin, reedy voice didn't carry beyond her own ears. "Rokshan!" she tried again. She heard nothing but the distant sounds of the city. Nobody cared about the screaming. If Harshod—

Fear jolted through her, and she managed to lift her head and one arm before collapsing. Harshod couldn't still be here, but what if he was finishing Rokshan off? With a tremendous effort, she got her arms beneath her and pushed herself to a crouching position. Immediately, she saw Rokshan lying on the ground about a dragonlength away, his back to her.

She dragged herself to his side. The dragonlength felt more like a thousand as she crept along, hauling her still-inert legs and drooping wings behind her. When she reached him, she gently turned him onto his back. His face was streaked with burns from the chin up, his clothes were nearly burned away, and his chest was blackened where Harshod's fire had first struck.

"Get away from him!"

Startled, Lamprophyre twisted to see where the voice had come from. Soldiers poured through the eastern entrances, swords and pikes held ready to attack. They surrounded her and Rokshan, their thoughts filled with fear and anger. Lamprophyre turned her attention back to Rokshan, leaning her face close to his mouth. "I said get back!" the same voice shouted, but she ignored it.

"He's still breathing," she said. "Isn't there someone—a healer, or a physician, or something? I know humans take—"

"Step away from the prince," a new voice said, one she recognized. General Sajan entered the coliseum and pushed through the soldiers to the front of their ranks. "Back up," he added, "or by Jiwanyil we will find a way to kill a dragon."

Lamprophyre took three steps back, raising her hands the way she'd seen Rokshan do to indicate harmlessness, as if she wasn't herself a weapon. "Harshod did it," she said. "He had a ring that blasts fire. If we go now, we can still catch him."

"We saw no one else leave this place," General Sajan said, "and found only you standing over the burned body of Prince Rokshan. I hope you have a better explanation than that."

Lamprophyre's heart sped up once again. "It's true," she said. "We were trying to find Harshod—he's part of a plot to set Gonjiri against the dragons—"

"Because a dragon attacking a prince of Gonjiri wouldn't do that itself," General Sajan said. "You're coming with us. If you're innocent, you have nothing to fear."

"I can't! Harshod is getting away, and we'll never know who was behind the plot!"

General Sajan motioned to his soldiers. She heard him think *we're all going to die here, wonder what Rokshan thought when she attacked him,* and then soldiers advanced on her, hemming her in with their weapons. "Why are you here?" she asked, struck by a sudden thought.

"We were warned there was danger," General Sajan said. "That someone intended to start a riot in the city, trying to get the people to rise up against you. I never thought—" He shook his head. "Come quietly, and no one has to get hurt."

"You have to take care of Rokshan first," Lamprophyre said. "He might be dying."

"You should have thought of that before you burned him," General Sajan said, but his thoughts were less certain: *why care if she meant him dead? Something's wrong.*

"It wasn't me," she insisted. "Rokshan is my friend, and I would never hurt him. *Please*, help him!"

General Sajan approached close enough to look more closely at Rokshan, staying outside Lamprophyre's grabbing distance. The soldiers relaxed slightly, watching their leader, and Lamprophyre took to the skies before any of them could try to stop her.

CHAPTER THIRTY-FIVE

She heard shouts, and twisted to look behind her, but the soldiers hadn't brought archers, and she was well out of their reach. Her heart ached at leaving Rokshan behind. If he died... She didn't know how to end that thought, because he was closer to her than any other person and she couldn't bear the idea of him being gone. The soldiers would take care of him. They had to.

So, the Army had heard there would be a riot? Lamprophyre would wager all her money and Rokshan's, too, that Harshod was behind that rumor. He'd planned all of this, though she had no idea how he'd managed it. All that stone. If it were magical, it might give him all sorts of advantages. If she didn't follow him immediately, she might lose him, but chasing after him could be suicidal depending on what artifacts he had at his command. She needed to know what he was capable of if she wanted to counter him and ultimately capture him.

Soon enough, General Sajan would mobilize more forces, and then nowhere would be safe. She had only a slim advantage in being able to get anywhere within the city faster than a human. She wheeled in the sky and headed for Manishi's workshop.

As she flew, she argued with herself. What was she thinking? If General Sajan believed she had attacked Rokshan, so would the king and everyone else. And Ekanath might not like Rokshan much, but he was still his son, and the king couldn't let his son be attacked and not retaliate. So Gonjiri would go to war against the dragons, the dragons would slaughter the humans, and Harshod's masters would have the war they wanted.

Harshod had been surprised when she brought up Tekentriya, which suggested she wasn't part of his plot. So either it was some other group of Gonjirians, or Rokshan was right and those masters were Fanishkorites. She was tempted to act as if the latter were true, but that might be a mistake, and Lamprophyre didn't like making assumptions, especially since she'd just learned all their earlier assumptions were wrong.

Maybe war was inevitable. She certainly couldn't convince Gonjiri not to attack. But she couldn't stand by and do nothing. And this was the only trail she had: Harshod, and whoever gave him orders.

People screamed and fled when Lamprophyre landed in the narrow street beside Manishi's workshop. Lamprophyre didn't care. The fewer people in the street, the less chance she had of trampling someone accidentally. She turned carefully in the cramped confines, wishing Tanajital had been built for dragons, and tried the door. Manishi's shed was closed tight. Without windows, Lamprophyre couldn't see if Manishi was inside. She thumped the door with her fist, making the rickety structure shake and dust go flying off the roof.

"She left," a small voice said. Lamprophyre turned her head, which was all she could manage, and regarded the tiny human child standing surprisingly close.

"Did you see her go?" Lamprophyre asked.

The child nodded. "We're not supposed to play around here because mam says she's no better than she should be. I don't know what that means."

"Neither do I. Thank you." Lamprophyre squatted, then said, "You should move away. The wind from my wings will knock you over and I'd hate for you to be hurt."

The child nodded again and backed away, probably not far enough, but Lamprophyre was in no mood to be patient. She leaped into the sky and looked back at the child, who had, in fact, fallen on its rump. It tilted its head to stare at her with wide, round eyes, and despite her heartache and sense of urgency, Lamprophyre waved and was heartened when the child waved back.

So. Manishi had likely gone back to the palace. Not somewhere

Lamprophyre was welcome at the moment. She hesitated for only a few beats before winging her way toward the academy and the Atrium.

She crashed through the foliage and startled several humans into screaming and running. Breathing heavily from the speed of her flight, she gasped, "Wait! I need someone to talk to Sabarna! Please!"

No one responded. In despair, Lamprophyre closed her eyes and sagged. This was hopeless. She should go back to the flight and warn them, give Hyaloclast a chance to figure out what to do.

"Excuse me?"

Lamprophyre opened her eyes and regarded the male standing before her. "I'll go," she said dully. "I'm sorry I intruded."

"You want to speak with Lector Sabarna? I can send her a message. You know she won't come outside, right?"

"I know," Lamprophyre said. "Why are you helping me?"

"Why not?" the male said. "Besides, if you're looking for Lector Sabarna, you must be desperate. I've never taken any of her lecture courses, but she terrifies me. Wait here." He turned and headed for the narrow entrance to the Atrium. Lamprophyre watched him go, feeling stunned. She'd become so accustomed to feeling like a dangerous outsider she didn't know what to do with someone willing to help so altruistically. Maybe this quest wasn't so hopeless, after all.

Shortly, the male returned. "She says she'll speak to you where she did before," he said. "How in Jiwanyil's name do you fit inside?"

"Only part of me does, but that's enough." Lamprophyre made her way beneath the branches to the Atrium, crouched, and stuck her head and neck through the entrance. The tall room felt warmer than it had before, and the sunlight flowing through the sheets of glass heated her skin more than was comfortable for a dragon. She tilted her head back and looked far, far up to where the stairs emerged from the wall. No one was present, and she couldn't hear or smell anyone approaching. She sighed, and settled in to wait, hoping the soldiers were too busy helping Rokshan to pursue her.

After almost a hundred beats, footsteps sounded on the stairs, and Lamprophyre once more tilted her head to watch Sabarna descend the steps. She looked irritated. "I hope this is important," she said before Lamprophyre could say anything. "I have a lecture in twenty minutes."

"This won't take long," Lamprophyre said. "Lector Sabarna, Rokshan and I have been trying to find someone who wants to start a war between Gonjiri and the dragons. The human we were chasing attacked Rokshan and made it look like I burned him. He also knew we were following him and arranged for soldiers to try to arrest me. He has a lot of magic at his disposal, and I need your help learning what he's capable of. Please, help me."

Sabarna blinked. "How much magic?" she asked.

"Ah, I don't know. He had six different types of stone on him. I remember the smells."

"Tell me the stones."

"Erythronite—that almost has to be how he created fire, because it was in a ring he pointed at us. Aquamarine in a bracelet. I didn't see the others, but there was agate, chalcedony, pyrite, and sapphire. Sapphire and ruby smell almost the same, but I'm certain it was sapphire."

Sabarna's eyes narrowed. "He burned Rokshan with a stone?"

"Yes. He pointed his fist at him, and fire shot out of the stone and hit him."

"You're right, erythronite is the only thing that will do that. It's very rare and comes from far away—how do you even know what it is? You can't possibly have seen it before."

Lamprophyre wanted to scream at the irrelevant aside, but she was depending on this woman for help, and satisfying her curiosity might make her more cooperative. "It's in our bones," she said. "All dragons have a connection to Mother Stone, who is the source of all stone everywhere. I know what a stone is, even if I've never seen it before, because there is a part of me in it. Or it in me. It's part of our religion."

"Fascinating." Sabarna paced in a tight circle before Lamprophyre. "Erythronite for fire. Pyrite focuses elemental power, either inwardly or outwardly. If this man intends to fight a dragon, I assume that means an outward focus. It will create a blast of force similar in power to the blast of fire."

"I know. I've seen it done. It can't hurt me."

"A large enough stone or concentration of stones might be able to [...] Something small, like a ring or a pendant, probably not. But—don't get its way, just in case." Sabarna tapped one short, stubby finger again[...] lips. "Agate will enhance his strength. You said he knew where [...]

That's probably the aquamarine. It's good for producing the non-religious kind of visions."

"I don't know what that means."

Sabarna waved her hand in the air in a gesture Lamprophyre didn't recognize. "Visions like opening a window on some other location to see what's beyond. Far seeing."

"Oh. I understand."

"Chalcedony. That's an unusual one. It allows two people to communicate at a distance, but it's never been implemented, to my knowledge. The Army might know how. This world is in a sad state if good things only have military uses. If you catch this man, I'd like his chalcedony artifact. Something to study. At any rate, it might be how he receives his orders."

"You said before sapphire is for mental focus. How would that benefit someone like him?" Or was it another dragon-confusing stone? But if he'd attacked her with it, the effect hadn't been anything like what she'd experienced aboard the bandits' boat.

"I admit that's a strange choice. Sapphire gives you the kind of focus you usually only need in performing a difficult task. It might help you block out distractions, for example, or bring important details to mind. Perhaps he just wanted clarity for this attack."

"Maybe." The more she thought about it, the more convinced she was that it was actually a variation on the sapphire wand. "So are there ways to counter his magic? Or do I have to get his artifacts off him?"

"Well, ideally you'd take them from him," Sabarna said, "but..." She looked Lamprophyre up and down as if gauging her size. "Wait here."

Lamprophyre waited impatiently, imagining she could hear the marching steps of soldiers coming to capture her while she was stuck helplessly in this stone and glass cage. Eventually, Sabarna returned. The adept carried a chunk of faceted topaz the size of her fist attached to a slim gold chain. "It hangs to my navel when I wear it," she said, "which means it should be a snug fit for you. This will disperse some of the blow from a physical attack, though as I said, I'm not sure the pyrite will have any effect on someone your size. But—just in case."

"This is so generous," Lamprophyre said. "I don't have a way to pay ."

"ust bring it back when you're done, and don't forget about the chalcedony artifact," Sabarna said. "You said Rokshan was burned? How badly?"

Lamprophyre swallowed, the memory of her friend's ravaged body making her heart hurt again. "Badly. He was still breathing, but I hope they got him help. Is that something human healing can fix?"

"I can't say without seeing him," Sabarna said, "but in principle, there's very little a good healer armed with jade or moonstone can't repair. Don't be afraid. He's a prince—they won't let him die." She set the topaz pendant around Lamprophyre's neck and patted her hand just as if Lamprophyre were her child. "Good luck," she said. "I don't want to see Tanajital in flames."

Lamprophyre suppressed the urge to point out that if Sabarna never left the Atrium, she was unlikely to see that even if it happened. She crawled out backwards, made her way to the edge of the trees, and leaped into the sky once more. Now, to find Harshod.

CHAPTER THIRTY-SIX

She flew in a slow circle above the city, not caring that it made her an obvious target. She doubted General Sajan could get archers in position quickly enough to take advantage of her low flight, and it wasn't as if they could hurt her. The general had said he hadn't seen anyone leaving the coliseum, which might mean Harshod had left out the other side. For a moment, fear shot through her at the idea that he might have magic to make himself invisible, but then she remembered Sabarna's words and felt calmer.

The other side—that meant the west, heading away from the palace and toward the river. Another jolt ran through her. If Harshod reached the river, he could go anywhere. But she was faster than any boat, so Harshod must have counted on the soldiers slowing her down enough to give him a head start—and on the sheer number of people in Tanajital to conceal him from her eyes. He was right, Stones take him. There was nothing distinctive about him—

—or was there? Humans all smelled the same unless they used hadar's noxious scent, but stone...stone was different, varied, and easily extinguishable by any dragon. True, in a city this size there might be thousands of a particular kind of stone, magical or not, but Harshod's collection of artifacts had been a unique blend of scents and was strong enough to leave a trail.

Lamprophyre examined the coliseum. It was empty. Sparing a thought for Rokshan, wherever he was, she swooped down on the west side and inhaled deeply. The smell of stones, particularly the granite and sandstone of the coliseum, cut sharply across the warm, damp scent of human flesh. She sniffed again, teasing out individual scents that normally faded into the background. Her stomachs rumbled, but she ignored them. Bitter chalcedony, the orange tang of pyrite—there. Six scents twined together, making a trail that led west.

She sprang into the sky and followed the trail, slowly. Though the smells were distinctive, it had been several hundred beats since Harshod had passed this way, and the trail was beginning to dissipate. This didn't make the scent weaker, but it did widen its path, and more than once Lamprophyre followed a strand of scent that came to an abrupt end. She was vaguely aware of humans beneath her pointing and exclaiming, but she needed all her concentration to follow the trail and couldn't spare any for listening to their terrified thoughts. So long as no one attacked her, or pointed her out to the soldiers, she didn't care if they were frightened.

The buildings beneath her shrank the nearer she came to the river until they were all short and too small for Lamprophyre to fit into even if their doors had been big enough. The streets between them were similarly narrow, leaving Lamprophyre hoping Harshod hadn't gone to ground there. She was willing to smash an open space for herself, but that seemed hard on the people who owned those tiny, weary-looking houses. Their roofs were dirty and stained with old water marks, and the sour smell of unwashed flesh clung to everything. Here, the humans who saw her ran to hide inside their houses, as if that would protect them. Terrible sadness came over her that she could even think that way. Those humans didn't deserve her anger; that was all for Harshod, and she would make him pay.

Boats lined the riverbank, tied to poles that jutted from the water like branchless, leafless trees. Lamprophyre landed on the bank downstream a bit and surveyed them. They weren't all alike, she realized: some of them had rounded sides that rose high above the water, while others were flat barely platforms floating on the river's surface. She couldn't understa how the tall ones managed not to tip over, but the flat ones made s reminding her of flat, palm-sized leaves that floated in the p dragons had created far north of here.   dn't

She sniffed again. The trail led to the river and stopped.

be right. She walked slowly upstream, ignoring the shouts and cries from the humans on the boats and outside the buildings sticking out over the riverbank. Harshod could be here, on this side of the river, but that made no sense. Surely he knew he had to get away as fast as possible, in case his ploy didn't work and Lamprophyre tracked him as she was doing now?

There. A breeze brought the bitter smell of chalcedony to her nose, mingled with the sweetness of aquamarine. It came from mid-stream, just ahead.

A shout nearly underfoot startled her. She'd just passed one of the flat boats tied up at the bank, and as she turned to see who'd shouted at her, her tail brushed the boat and set it rocking. The female at the far end of the boat shouted again and clung to the pole to keep from falling off. "Stay back!" she exclaimed. "Don't you dare smash my ferry!"

"I'm sorry, I didn't mean to," Lamprophyre began, then sniffed deeply. Harshod's scent tangled around the woman and flowed away into the center of the river. "Did you see a man come this way?" she demanded. "Someone who was on your boat?"

"I see lots of men," the woman said, releasing her grip on the pole.

Lamprophyre racked her brain for a description and settled on the thing she remembered best. "This one had a spot on his lip like a round black insect. Hurry, this is important."

"Why should I tell you?"

Fear for Rokshan and anger at Harshod filled Lamprophyre to bursting. She put a foot on the boat and pressed, tipping the far end up and forcing the woman to grab the pole again. "I'll sink your boat if you don't talk," she said. "I might sink you, too. Just tell me where he went and I'll leave you alone."

The woman gasped and hugged the pole like it was her only salvation. "I took him across!" she said. "Please, go, just leave me alone."

"Took him across. Where?"

The woman stretched out one arm, pointing, then quickly grasped the pole again. "Straight across to the landing. I don't know where he went, I swear."

"Thank you," Lamprophyre said. "You should be more polite." She pushed the boat roughly, making it rock harder, and flew off in the indicated direction.

Once past the river, trailing Harshod became easy again, as if the breezes coming off the water had dissipated his trail more quickly. She'd never been on the west side of Tanajital, and it astonished her how little it resembled the city she knew. There weren't any tall buildings, and from her aerial perspective, what buildings there were looked like oddly geometric bumps arranged along streets that curved and meandered rather than running in straight radial lines emerging from circular plazas the way Tanajital proper had. Even the city wall seemed lower and dingier. She saw no archers, no soldiers of any kind atop it.

She followed the scent all the way to that wall, to an arched entrance not big enough to admit a dragon, though of course with her wings, that didn't matter. Beyond the wall, the city continued, as if it were a water barrel filled to the brim with rainfall that then spilled over the edge. There were no streets, just small, dirty houses of wood and thatching that would burn readily.

Harshod's trail ended at one of these houses. Lamprophyre flapped slowly to hover over it. There was nothing to set it apart from the others; it had the same roof made of dry water reeds from the riverbank, the same wooden walls covered with that strangely scented white material that made a hard crust when it dried. But he had definitely gone inside, and he hadn't left. Lamprophyre considered the roof again. It didn't have a ridge beam, but came to a point at the center with four sides slanting down from that peak. It smelled dusty, and there were a couple of holes in it. Lamprophyre wondered if the reeds were watertight. If not, it would be miserable come the rainy season.

She flew down and landed neatly on the peak. It was sharp enough Lamprophyre shifted her weight to stand on two of the four sides, balancing neatly. The reed surface gave under her weight, but didn't tear. She sat, tense at the possibility her landing might have drawn their attention, and listened to the murmur of indistinct speech coming from within. There were three humans inside, none of them aware of her presence by the lack of fear in their thoughts. One of them had that singleness of thought she associated with Harshod. He was instructing the others, telling them *send word back* and *almost time now*. The other two were listening to him intently, judging by how they weren't thinking about unrelated things. It was the perfect time to attack.

Lamprophyre flapped once, twice, half a dozen times until she was positioned above the building's door. She sucked in a deep breath, let the air mingle with the contents of her second stomach, and blew out a great blast of fire that struck the roof.

CHAPTER THIRTY-SEVEN

Flames sprang up immediately, burning lower than Lamprophyre had expected, so she breathed out again, hotter this time, and rejoiced in how the fire spread. She heard shouts from within, and the door opened.

Lamprophyre pounced on the first human through the door, grabbing her around the waist and flinging her aside to strike the next building over and then fall limp to the ground. She snatched the second human, tossed him from one hand to the other, then launched him into the air, catching him by the ankle and letting him dangle upside down while he screamed.

Something punched her in the chest, rocking her back on her heels slightly but not hurting her. She dropped the second human and made a grab for Harshod, who darted back, seeming unconcerned about the burning roof just handspans above his head. "You," he snarled, and aimed his fist at her again.

"Me," Lamprophyre agreed. "You shouldn't have hurt Rokshan without making sure I was dead."

Another blast struck her with no more force than a gentle slap to the ribs. "I thought you were," Harshod said. "My mistake. It won't happen again."

Lamprophyre grabbed for him again. He darted out of the way, farther into the building. She snatched some of the burning reeds off the roof and flung them at him, making him curse. "Answer my questions, and I won't kill you," she said.

Harshod laughed. "You don't have it in you to kill. I've been watching you. So generous. So ready to find a non-violent solution. How fitting that instead you've incited a war between dragons and humans."

"That was you. Why did you do it? Your masters told you to?"

Harshod turned and ran deeper into the building, out of sight. Lamprophyre grabbed the sides of the door. She would bring the building down on his head if she had to. She pulled, and then felt the other humans climbing up her back, one on each side. She bucked, twisted, and flung one of the humans off just as the second one struck. Once again Lamprophyre felt a blow to the sensitive spot on her neck. This time, all it did was send a twinge of nerveless pain through her spine and arms and legs. "Ow! Stones take you!" she shouted, and slammed herself backward into the nearest building, spreading her wings as flat as she could. The human let out a grunt and slid off.

Lamprophyre went for the building again, this time tearing up the burning roof. It came apart readily in burning chunks of reeds that smoked as if fighting her fire. She tore handfuls of it away from the wooden frame beneath and tossed them through the widening holes, hoping to hit Harshod. She couldn't see him through the smoke and flames. She smashed the thin wood of the frame to make a hole big enough to fit her head and neck inside. The laughing fire boiled up through the opening and through another hole, this one in the wall opposite the entrance. Harshod was nowhere in sight.

She pulled her head out to inhale fresh, clear air and saw movement on the far side of the building. Past the smoke billowing from the house, she saw Harshod fleeing westward. Cursing, she rose into the air and sped after him. He was her prey, and he would not escape.

She ran him down only a few dragonlengths away, plucking him off the ground and carrying him off just as she'd done Rokshan all those days ago. Fleeting worry for Rokshan coursed through her, replaced by fury at the male in her hands. "Talk," she said, "or I'll drop you."

"Drop me, and you'll never learn the truth," Harshod said.

"We'll see," Lamprophyre said, and released him.

He fell screaming less than a dragonlength before Lamprophyre dove and snatched him out of midair. "From this height, a fall might not kill you, but it would hurt worse than anything you can imagine," she said. "That's assuming I don't keep playing with you until I get bored." She dropped him again. "I can do this *all day*," she said when she'd caught him once more. "So it's up to you. Tell me what your masters wanted, and I'll let you go."

"I don't believe you," Harshod said.

"I'm not the untrustworthy one here." She tossed him this time and caught him by the ankle, raising him so his upside-down face was level with hers. "It's true, you hurt my friend, and I want you to suffer. But it's more important that Gonjiri not go to war. I want to know the truth, and I want to stop that happening. So I'm willing to bargain for, let's say, the next twelve beats. After that, I stop caring what happens to you and go back to figuring it out on my own. Your choice."

Harshod was silent briefly. Finally, he said, "Put me down, and I'll talk."

They were almost past the farthest reaches of the city's outskirts, to where a road cut through cultivated fields just showing green with spring growth. Lamprophyre alit on the road and dropped Harshod, not roughly, at her feet. "First, I want your stones. The artifacts," she said.

"That wasn't part of the bargain."

"Of course it was. The bargain was you do whatever I say, and I don't turn you into a greasy pyre and eat your entrails." This bloodthirsty show appealed to her. "You didn't hear those words? I assure you that's what I meant."

Harshod glared at her. Slowly, he removed the erythronite ring, then a similar one with a chunk of pyrite, and tossed both at her feet. The aquamarine bracelet came next, followed by a second bracelet from which dangled a polished oval of agate. Finally, he drew a pendant of chalcedony, so large Lamprophyre had to suppress a sneeze at its strong bitterness, from within the neck of his shirt.

"Where's the sapphire?" she asked.

Harshod's eyes widened slightly. "What sapphire?"

She could smell its sweet odor, like overripe cherries. "Please," she said. "Don't lie to a dragon about stone. The sapphire. What does it do? Is it like the wand?"

His lip curled, making the black dot on his face move like a living insect. He dug into the pouch at his waist and pulled out a chunk of uncut sapphire smaller than his fist. "Here," he said, offering it to her.

Lamprophyre shook her head. "Do you think I'm stupid? Just toss it next to the others." She had no intention of touching it, which made her wonder how she was going to transport it back to Tanajital. Maybe the topaz would protect her from it enough that she could drop it into the river, right at the center where it was deepest.

Harshod shrugged and tossed it into the little pile at Lamprophyre's feet. "Fine. I'm helpless. What do you want to know?"

Lamprophyre hooked the chalcedony pendant's chain with her sixth claw and looped it over her wrist. This could repay Sabarna for her help. "Who wants war between Gonjiri and the dragons?"

"Fanishkor, obviously. Even a dragon ought to understand that." His dismissive tone of voice angered her, but she suppressed her irritation and said nothing. Maybe it was obvious to him, but he clearly hadn't considered all the possibilities she and Rokshan had. "Gonjiri fights the dragons and loses, Fanishkor overruns Gonjiri. Simple."

"Except you didn't count on two people caring about that not happening," Lamprophyre said.

"No. Why would humans and dragons ever make common cause? You and that whelp of a prince turned my every ploy on its head. Stealing the egg, turning Gonjiri against you..." Harshod laughed. "I thought for sure the poison would work. Kill the dragon queen's daughter, and nothing would stop her taking her vengeance."

Lamprophyre decided not to point out why that wouldn't work. "Well, you've failed. And when I tell King Ekanath what you've done, that all of this was a Fanishkorite plot, that will be the end of it. So you can go back to your masters and tell them not to bother anymore."

Harshod laughed again. "Of course it worked. You're here, aren't you?"

"I—what do you mean? I captured you."

"You fled the scene of your attack on the prince. That makes you look even more guilty than his burned body did. Once that's reported to the king, nothing will convince him that dragons aren't evil. He'll order out the troops, they'll march on the mountains, and I'll have the war I wanted." Harshod smiled. "There's nothing you can do about it."

Lamprophyre sucked in a breath. "But Rokshan will tell them what happened when he wakes up."

"*If* he wakes. Even if he survived the blast to receive a healer's attention, the treatment will have him unconscious for at least five days. Long enough to put the Army out of his reach. It's too late."

His deep chuckle pained her more than an evil laugh would have, his eyes mocked her helplessness, and without thinking she balled up her fist and punched him in the stomach. It knocked him off his feet, and she was certain she felt something rupture. She didn't care.

She stood over him, fire roiling in her second stomach, and thought about setting him on fire as he'd done Rokshan. He was responsible for so much evil. She was sure Hyaloclast wouldn't think twice about doing it. But she'd promised to let him go—or was a promise to an evil human anything worth keeping? She felt a pain in her right fist and realized she'd unconsciously let her claws extend just enough to prick her flesh. The pain woke her from her reverie. She should never have promised anything so rash, no matter what the bargain. And yet she had.

She heard running footsteps less than a beat before something slammed into her flank, sending a jolt of pain through her leg. "What—" she said, turning. One of Harshod's companions darted back, brandishing a club with a chunk of jasper bound to its tip by long strands of copper wire. She turned back just as Harshod flung himself between her legs, grabbing the sapphire.

She kicked the other male in the stomach, flinging him away, and then Harshod was clinging to her arm and scrabbling his way up to her shoulder. She tried to grab him, but the pain in her leg dulled her reflexes, and in the space of two beats he was perched in the notch where Rokshan rode. More pain exploded at the back of her head, but it was not as terrible as before, and after a moment's blindness she realized she was still upright and could move.

"That's it," she snarled, and took to the sky.

She sped upward for a dozen beats, with Harshod clinging to her and pressing the sapphire into her vulnerable spot. The pain grew so intense she was afraid of blacking out again, of falling out of the sky and smashing both of them. But that was unacceptable. She swallowed the urge to vomit and dove, nearly vertically, faster and faster. She pulled up at the last possible moment and rose, again nearly vertically. The sapphire fell away from her neck as Harshod gripped her ruff with both hands. Lamprophyre snarled at him. This was only the beginning.

Half-blind, she leveled off twenty dragonlengths above the ground and flew away from Tanajital, faster and faster until she heard Harshod groan with the effort of holding on. Then she banked sideways and rolled. Harshod's weight slipped, one of his hands let go her ruff, and he dangled helplessly from her neck. Lamprophyre shrugged her shoulders, but he clung to her as if he'd bound himself there. Frustrated, Lamprophyre rolled again, and for the briefest moment felt his other hand reach up to grab hold. Then he was gone.

Dizzy from her aerial maneuvers, at first his absence meant nothing to her addled brain. Then she came to herself with a jolt and dove after him. She still couldn't see clearly, and to her Harshod was an oblong shape falling faster than she could fly in that state. She heard him cry out once before hitting the ground, and it struck her to the heart. Slowing her pace, she landed beside him, swaying once before collapsing.

"Help..."

She sat up, astonished. He was still alive? Blood pooled beneath his body, his bones were clearly shattered, but his lips were moving in a soundless plea.

Fury rushed through her. He had tried to kill her and Rokshan both, had attacked her more than once—and he had the nerve to beg her for his life. She pushed herself to her feet. "No," she said in the firmest voice she could manage. "Sparing you would make a mockery of everyone who's suffered for your actions. And you'd never stop trying to hurt me and my people. You don't deserve my pity."

Harshod's eyes met hers. Then the light drained from them, and he sagged, limp and motionless. Lamprophyre closed her eyes and breathed in deeply, trying to control the dizziness. Then she looked around. She'd flown far from Tanajital, far from the cultivated fields, but she needed to leave this place before anyone saw her with Harshod's body. Explaining why his death was earned would be virtually impossible.

The two who'd been with Harshod were gone when she returned, as were the other artifacts. She felt too tired and sick to care about tracking them down. She flew in slow circles, low to the ground, sniffing for the sapphire, and found it some dozen dragonlengths from Harshod's body in a patch of grass whose sweetness clashed horribly with the odor of the sapphire. Gingerly, using just two claws, she picked it up. Nothing happened. Maybe it was designed specifically to affect that strange sensitive spot at the back of her head. She dropped it in the middle of the

Green River anyway. It was not a weapon she wanted to hand over to any adept.

Flying slowly helped clear her head, and once she was past the river, she accelerated until she was flying at full speed over the roofs of Tanajital. She needed to find Rokshan, to wake him up. If a healer could make him unconscious, a healer could rouse him. Then they would convince Ekanath not to go to war. However afraid and angry the king was, surely he wasn't stupid as well.

She approached the palace and flew around it, circling the training grounds. No soldiers filled the space, and Lamprophyre's hopes rose. Rokshan had woken on his own and told everyone the truth. There would be no war. She clung to that as she finished her circle and landed outside the palace's enormous front entrance.

The grand doors were shut, and no human was visible anywhere. Lamprophyre felt the wood all over, looking for a way to open the doors. In the embassy, the back doors had handles that let you pull the doors open when you were on the inside. These doors were flat and blank, and she couldn't tell which direction they were made to open. Aside from smelling faintly of a spicy wood she didn't recognize, they were completely uninteresting and very bland compared to the bright gilt of the palace.

She ran her hands down the center and found a grain too regular and straight to be natural. She sniffed it. This was familiar; it was the place where the two halves of the door joined. Interesting, but not useful to her since she couldn't figure out how to open it.

She pounded on the door with her fist. "Somebody open this door!" she shouted. "I need to see Prince Rokshan. Please, someone help!"

No one answered. She listened, but didn't hear any thoughts nearby. The possibility that the palace was empty passed through her mind, and she dismissed it. The palace was large enough to hold many humans, and there was no way they'd all left it at once. They were just hiding from her. Frustrated, she drummed on the door with both hands and shouted, "I don't want to break this thing down, but I really need to see Prince Rokshan! Let me in!"

Still nothing. The door rattled on its hinges, bouncing slightly and revealing the crack where the doors met. Lamprophyre regarded it more closely. She pushed hard on one half of the door, and the crack appeared again. Carefully, she fitted her claws into the crack and pulled, not very hard so she wouldn't simply tear through the wood. The door moved slightly, then stopped. It felt as if it were caught on something.

Lamprophyre looked farther down. She could barely see past the wider crack, not big enough for her to fit her hand inside, but there was something there, a piece of wood lying perpendicular to the crack. That didn't make sense. If it were there to stop someone opening the door—

Lamprophyre felt stupid. These doors opened inward, not outward, and the thing the door was caught on was its own hinge. She pulled on the door again, once more exposing the inner beam, and slid her claws through the gap. With a slash, she cut a deep groove into the beam, not quite enough to cut it in half, but enough to weaken it. She removed her hand, took a deep breath, and shoved the door as hard as she could. The door burst open, snapping the beam with a loud crack and making Lamprophyre stumble from the sudden lack of opposition. She was in.

The door was easily wide enough to admit her, and the cave—the hall —beyond was even wider. Her toe claws clicked across the hard, flat stones whose glossy surface didn't smell like real stone, and she had to duck her head to avoid a metal web gleaming with fire that lit the hall dimly, as if the king depended on fireflies to provide him light. Staircases wide enough to admit her, if the steps had been deep enough to fit her feet, stood to the left and right, ascending to a couple of doors much too small for her. Another arched entrance lay straight ahead between the staircases. She might be able to fit inside that entrance if she crouched low and kept her wings furled tight. Aside from that, she saw no way for her to exit and no humans to tell her where Rokshan was.

"Hello?" she called out. "Someone? Please, I need to speak with Prince Rokshan."

Distantly, she heard thoughts, mostly terrified ones. Entering the palace was a bad idea if she wanted the humans to trust her, but she was certain they'd brought Rokshan here, and without him, she had no chance of stopping the war. But there were other minds, thinking *invasion* and *no idea what she was thinking* and *Rokshan dying*, and that last one filled her with desperation. "Help me, please!" she shouted.

A female with long black hair appeared at the top of the left-hand staircase. "Calm down," Anchala said. "You can't help him if you scare everyone."

"I'm not *trying* to scare anyone," Lamprophyre said, frustration taking the place of desperation. "Where's Rokshan? Is he—he's not badly hurt, is he?"

"He's alive, but not much more than that. What burned him?"

"An erythronite ring. It's an artifact. A Fanishkorite wanted to make it look like I burned Rokshan so Gonjiri would attack the dragons and leave itself open to Fanishkorite attack." *Now* it sounded so obvious she felt incredibly stupid.

Anchala looked at Lamprophyre without approaching. "And you're here to stop that happening."

"Yes." Lamprophyre didn't like the sound of Anchala's voice, flat and emotionless to match her tired, grieving thoughts.

"It's too late," Anchala said. "The Army's troops crossed the border into dragon territory two hours ago."

CHAPTER THIRTY-EIGHT

"But I've only been gone a few hundred beats!" Lamprophyre said, and realized it had been quite a bit longer than that, however long human hours were. "I have to stop them."

"How?" Anchala said. "My father believes you attacked Rokshan. He sent word to the troops on the border that they were to attack the dragons. If you try to reach them to convince them otherwise, they'll attack you."

"I have an artifact." Lamprophyre tapped the topaz, making a little *tink* noise with her claw. "It protected me against a pyrite blast."

Anchala was shaking her head. "You haven't seen the weapons the Army has," she said. "The pyrite artifacts are huge, easily three feet across and covered in crystals. They were developed to use against Fanishkor, but I'm sure the Army will take advantage of the coincidence."

"But Rokshan said they were intended to attack a human. That they were small."

"He might have believed so, but he's not involved with the weapons development branch of the Army, and I doubt he's aware of the large versions they created. Maybe a blast from those won't kill a dragon outright, but they will certainly incapacitate one. Even an artifact won't be enough."

"Stones," Lamprophyre swore. "Then it will be a real battle when they come up against my people."

"It will. And..." Anchala's gaze drifted sideways. "Even Rokshan telling Father the truth might not be good enough. I think Father fears dragons so much he might want an excuse to get rid of them."

"It doesn't matter. We have to try. Can't anyone wake Rokshan?"

"He was badly burned and his lungs were damaged. If the healer wakes him, it will interrupt the healing process."

Lamprophyre cursed again. "How long will it take?"

"I don't—wait here." Anchala disappeared through the doorway.

Lamprophyre settled on her haunches and waited, thrumming her fingers on the strange not-stone slabs covering the floor. If she'd known the Army had such large versions of the pyrite weapon, she could have demanded they be removed from where they could threaten dragons. Having them so close to the mountains wasn't the act of an ally. She could even have flown north and destroyed them—but it wouldn't have mattered, would it, because she couldn't destroy the knowledge of how to make them, and if they were enemies, eventually humans would use them against dragons no matter what she did.

The sound of many humans approaching from outside roused her from a doze she'd fallen into despite her anxiety, weariness overcoming fear. Soldiers. Of course she should have expected soldiers. As far as they were concerned, she'd attacked the palace and intended to finish off Rokshan or kill the king or some other horrible, stupid act of violence. She turned around and shoved the doors closed, then scooted back so her body's weight kept them shut. That was better than a flimsy wooden bar.

A quiver shuddered through the wood as something thumped on it. Despite her fear and exhaustion, she smiled at the image of dozens of soldiers pounding on the door with their ineffectual fists. It would be less funny if they had a pyrite artifact like Anchala had described, but she didn't care. All that mattered was that they didn't break through and attack her until Rokshan had stopped this whole nightmare.

Eventually, she heard Anchala returning with a companion. The human male who entered beside her was nervous, but not terrified, and his thoughts of *completely believe something her size could burn a man nearly to death* were emotionless, as if he were calculating how many cows he would need to serve fifty guests. She suppressed her urge to set him straight about what had happened and asked, "Is he the healer?"

"I am," the male said. "You have some nerve coming here after what you did to the prince."

"I *didn't*," Lamprophyre exclaimed. "Rokshan is my friend. I would never hurt him. What is *wrong* with all of you humans that you can't understand friendship?"

"I told you, Ishay, it was a Fanishkorite plot," Anchala said. "Lamprophyre needs to know Rokshan's condition. He's the only one who can stop Gonjiri going to war against the dragons."

"Fanishkorite..." Ishay said. He scratched his head. "I suppose that makes sense, in a terrible way. What proof do you have?"

"Does that really matter now?" Lamprophyre demanded. "I need to know how long it will be before Rokshan is healed. If the Army was on the border, we don't have long before it reaches the mountains." She wished she had a better sense for how fast the Army could move, how far it was in human distances to the mountains—she knew so little, and her lack of knowledge might get people killed.

"Oh, it will be weeks before he's fully healed," Ishay said.

"That means at least fourteen days," Anchala said, seeing Lamprophyre's confusion.

"That's too long." Lamprophyre let out an impatient burst of smoke. "Can't you do anything to make it faster?"

"His lungs are healed, so I can wake him at any time," Ishay said, "but the longer he's unconscious, the less the scarring will be. I can't let him be disfigured just because you're impatient."

"I'm impatient," Lamprophyre said through gritted teeth, "because without him, Gonjiri will fight the dragons, be weakened, and be overrun by a Fanishkorite invasion. I think Rokshan would care more about stopping that than how he looks."

"Even so, that's not a decision any of us can make for him. I'm sorry."

She was going to stab him through the heart and she wouldn't even regret it, except he was still the one caring for Rokshan. "Then let's ask him," she said. "You can wake him long enough to find out what he wants to do, and then if he chooses to continue healing, you can make him unconscious again. Right?"

"I suppose..." Ishay didn't sound convinced.

"Of course you can," Anchala said. "Let's go, Ishay."

"But I want to be there," Lamprophyre protested. "And I barely fit inside this hall."

"You'll just have to wait," Ishay said, conviction returning to his voice. "If you're right, Prince Rokshan can make this decision without your prodding him and exerting undue influence."

"It's all right, Lamprophyre, I'll tell him the details," Anchala said. "Go back to the embassy and someone will come for you when the decision's been made." *It will be Rokshan. We both know it,* she thought.

"But—" Another thump, a harder one, rattled the wood and echoed dully off the walls. "I can't leave," she said triumphantly. "The soldiers will attack me if I do."

Anchala looked past Lamprophyre at the doors. "Damn," she said. "They're going to break that door down."

"Not with me sitting in front of it. Go, get Rokshan. He'll convince the king, and the soldiers will stand down if the king tells them to." Lamprophyre settled herself more firmly against the doors.

Ishay was already gone. Anchala gave the doors one last look, then followed him.

The thumping was more regular now. Lamprophyre listened to the soldiers' thoughts. There were enough of them that they should have been incomprehensible, but the nearest ones, at least, were so focused on what they were doing that they all thought the same: *lift, rush, SLAM, down, lift, rush, SLAM.* She wondered what they'd found to beat on the door, because even a hundred soldiers all hitting it with their fists at once couldn't produce such a pounding.

A sharper *crack* sounded above the dull thump, and the left-hand door moved enough that Lamprophyre felt it. She looked over her shoulder, but saw no sign that the door had been damaged. As she watched, the soldiers struck the doors again, and for just a moment, she saw a line of light between the halves of the door. Her earlier confidence faded. She didn't know what she would do if they managed to break through. She certainly couldn't attack them, and they couldn't hurt her. Maybe they would sit in this room staring at each other until Rokshan arrived.

She heard rapid footsteps, and she had just sat up and extended herself to listen to the person's thoughts when Rokshan ran in, his clothes and hair in disarray, his feet bare. "Hurry," he said. "If we—"

"Rokshan!" she shrieked, and leaped to her feet, hurrying toward the stairs. She grabbed him around the waist and hugged him the way humans hugged each other, her embrace swallowing him up. "You look—"

"I don't want to know," Rokshan said. "I wouldn't let them give me a mirror."

"But can't they resume healing you when this is done?"

Rokshan shrugged. "The longer I wait after the injury..." His voice trailed off, and he stepped away from her. "Time enough to worry about my vanity when we've stopped a war."

Lamprophyre nodded and swallowed around the sudden lump in her throat. She wasn't human, to judge human beauty or ugliness, and to her, it didn't look bad. Streaks of livid burn scars extended from the neck of his shirt up his throat to his chin and along one cheek, and if there was more than that—and there almost certainly was—it was hidden by his clothes, fresh and unburned and smelling of linen rather than charred flesh. But she realized his disorderly hair was as much because parts of it were burned off, and the back of his right hand bore more scars, and she finally understood why humans wept for tragedy, because he would never look the same again.

It didn't matter to her. He was still her dearest friend, and he was alive, and they would stop this war.

Rokshan ran his hand through his hair, vainly trying to smooth it. "So what happened?" he said. "The last thing I remember is you picking me up and wrapping me in your wing, and the worst pain of my life. Anchala told me the Army was marching on dragon territory because they believed you were the one who burned me. Harshod did it, didn't he? He started a war with us as proxies."

"He did. It was a Fanishkorite plot all along, Rokshan, Harshod confessed. You have to tell your father the truth so he'll stop the Army before the dragons attack it."

"If he'll listen to me."

Lamprophyre grabbed Rokshan's shoulder and shook him, then released him when he winced. "This is no time to feel insecure! You *have* to convince him. Dragons and humans will die if you don't."

Rokshan nodded. "You're right. Can you—"

With an earsplitting crack, the doors flew open, followed by a handful of soldiers carrying the bole of a giant, limbless tree banded with iron.

They stumbled as if they hadn't expected the door to give way so abruptly. More soldiers poured through the gap and converged on Lamprophyre, swords drawn, faces set with terror. They thrust and swung at Lamprophyre's flanks and tail with great blows that rebounded back at them.

"Stop it!" Lamprophyre said. "You can't hurt me with—hey! You're wasting your time! Stop!"

"Stand down," Rokshan shouted. "I said *stand down!*" He raced down the rest of the stairs to where the soldiers could see him clearly. "God's breath, stand down immediately or you'll all face trial!"

The nearest soldiers stepped back, lowering their weapons. Another voice, one Lamprophyre didn't recognize, joined Rokshan's, shouting more orders for the soldiers to stop attacking. That male, who was dressed in a uniform similar to General Sajan's but without all the markings, pushed forward through the soldiers and saluted Rokshan. "You're alive, sir," he said. "What happened?"

"Lamprophyre and I were attacked by a Fanishkorite spy intent on starting a war between Gonjiri and the dragons," Rokshan said, pitching his voice to go past the broken doors. "He made it look as if Lamprophyre had burned me, but it was a hoax. She's our ally. Captain Garim, take your men to the garrison and prepare to defend Tanajital."

"Defend from what, sir?" Captain Garim said.

"If the worst comes, from dragons," Rokshan said.

Captain Garim eyed Lamprophyre, turned his attention briefly on his soldiers, whose swords showed signs of being battered, and said, "Are you sure, sir?"

"It's a precaution only. I'm confident it won't come to that. But imagine if I'm wrong and we're not prepared." Rokshan saluted Captain Garim, who after a slight hesitation returned the salute. He called out orders, and the soldiers picked up their iron-bound tree and retreated from the palace.

"You know they can't defend against dragons, especially if the border troops have all the giant pyrite artifacts," Lamprophyre said in a low voice.

"Giant *what?*"

"Anchala told me. The Army has pyrite artifacts that might be big enough to hurt or kill a dragon."

Rokshan swore under his breath. "That might make it impossible to convince the dragons we don't mean them harm," he said. "Wait here. I'll—"

"Rokshan!"

Lamprophyre's heart sank. Ekanath. He was angry and afraid and relieved all at once, which puzzled Lamprophyre—why relieved?

Rokshan turned to face his father, who stood at the top of the right-hand stairs with both Anchala and Manishi standing behind him. Lamprophyre listened to Rokshan's thoughts; *he has to listen* and *never good enough for him* were at the top of his awareness, and Lamprophyre's heart felt even lower. If there were ever a time for Rokshan to stand up to his father, it was now.

CHAPTER THIRTY-NINE

E kanath's attention went from Rokshan to Lamprophyre. "What is that beast doing here?" he roared. "Come to finish the rest of us off?"

"I am not," Lamprophyre began indignantly, but Rokshan waved her to silence.

"She's not a beast, Father," he said. "She saved my life. We were attacked by a Fanishkorite spy intent on starting a war that will weaken Gonjiri so Fanishkor can attack."

Lamprophyre was impressed. She'd thought explaining the situation would be much more complex. Ekanath, his mouth open for another roar, jerked backward and closed his mouth. "Impossible," he finally said. "The attack on you proves what we've seen—that dragons want the human threat to their lands eliminated."

"They don't. Why would you believe that?"

"They only allow us in their territory on sufferance. They keep us isolated in tiny settlements. They're afraid we'll encroach on their mountains and take their gems and silver. Attacking you sent the strong message that the rest of us are next."

Rokshan shook his head. "Father, none of that is true. I would wager anything you like that most of that information was spread by Fanishkorite agents. Lamprophyre, tell Father why you were sent to Tanajital. The truth."

Lamprophyre eyed him warily. She didn't think the truth was very reassuring. But she trusted Rokshan to know what he was doing. "Some humans stole a dragon egg," she said. "Hyaloclast sent me to find out who, so we can retaliate and prevent anyone from trying that again. We aren't afraid of humans at all. We just want to decide where humans can go in our lands, the same as you would do if dragons wanted to settle in Gonjiri. I don't believe we're confining humans in settlements, because you're people and that would mean treating you like animals. And if you want our stone, I'm sure we can make arrangements. I've already done that for myself."

She took a deep breath. "Your majesty, humans and dragons used to live together in harmony," she said. "There's no reason we can't do that again. We have so much to offer each other, and I wish you'd see that. I wish Hyaloclast would see it, too."

Ekanath stared at her in silence. Then he transferred his gaze to Rokshan. "You were burned by dragon fire," he finally said.

"No, your majesty, it was an artifact," Lamprophyre said. "A red stone called erythronite. It makes fire, very powerful fire—or maybe it's just that the crystal was large that the fire is so powerful. I don't know. But that's what burned Rokshan, not me, and it's probably what destroyed that village."

"I see no red stone," Ekanath said.

Now Lamprophyre felt stupid for not tracking down Harshod's companions. "The attackers took it with them—"

"You let them escape?"

"No—I was injured, and I was worried about Rokshan—"

"Stop badgering her," Rokshan said. "Father, she's telling the truth. Harshod—the Fanishkorite—set me on fire, and Lamprophyre extinguished it."

"Not soon enough," Ekanath said, in a voice that cut Lamprophyre to the heart.

"I'm sorry I couldn't do more," she said. "Harshod attacked me, too." She decided not to give any more details about that attack. Ekanath wasn't her friend, and she had no intention of revealing her weakness to a potential enemy.

"Lamprophyre and I have been trying to find this enemy ever since Lamprophyre came to Tanajital," Rokshan continued. "Harshod started by trying to anger the dragons so they'd attack us, and when that failed, he made you believe dragons are our enemy so you'd send the Army after them. Which you did."

"You dare criticize my decision?" Ekanath said. "No one attacks the royal family with impunity."

"Which is what he was counting on," Rokshan said. "Father, all of this has been a plot, playing on our fear of dragons. Fanishkor will attack us when we're weakened from fighting the dragons, and Tanajital really will burn. You have to send word to the Army to retreat. It might not be too late."

"We can't retreat," Ekanath said. "That will make us look vulnerable. The dragons will attack."

"Lamprophyre and I can stop them," Rokshan said. "But only if the Army doesn't attack first. Please, Father. I know you don't think much of me, but I swear this is the only way to keep our country safe."

Ekanath's eyes narrowed in the expression Lamprophyre was coming to understand meant deep thought, as it was always accompanied by a narrowing of mental focus. "You disappointed me," he said. "You had a responsibility to this family, a responsibility to serve Gonjiri the way a prince should serve, and you turned your back on it. Sending you to the Army meant making the best of a bad situation. No one was more surprised than I when it turned out you had a gift for command."

The scars on Rokshan's face stood out more sharply for a moment. "Meaning even your useless son was able to make good?"

"God's breath, Rokshan, stop putting words in my mouth!" Ekanath shouted. "You were never useless, and that's why it broke my heart to see you wasting your life, mocking the duties I wanted you to take on. Ruling Gonjiri means responsibility, not reward, and if you could only learn that by joining the Army, well, at least you learned it. Sajan tells me he's never had a better commander, and you're only twenty-five. And then you want to throw it all away to fly around with this creature who isn't even human? Tell me why I should be proud of you for that!"

Lamprophyre stifled the urge to shout at the king. Rokshan was immobile, his face set with anger. "I made an alliance with creatures of legend," he said. "I discovered a plot against this country. Against you. I've learned things no human has known for centuries. How *dare* you dismiss that as 'flying around'?" He turned his head away briefly, controlling a louder outburst. "We have an opportunity to make this kingdom stronger. You were the one who asked for a prophecy about what we should do about Fanishkor, and the ecclesiasts told you to settle northward. That prophecy wanted us to meet the dragons. Can't you see that *they* are the solution? Dragon allies would make even an enemy stronger than Fanishkor hesitate before attacking us."

Lamprophyre had almost forgotten why humans were all over dragon territory. Put that way, if you believed in human religion, Rokshan's words made obvious sense. It was just as obvious from Ekanath's thoughts that he'd never considered the situation in those terms before. It was tempting to think him stupid, but Lamprophyre knew how easy it was to be so focused on a problem you missed the right solution. Hadn't she thought of herself as inferior to Coquina before Rokshan had pointed out everything she'd done to beat her?

Ekanath came down the steps and crossed the floor to Rokshan. "They don't care about us," he said. "What do we have to offer them?"

"Friendship," Rokshan said. "Knowledge. Magical artifacts—they don't use stone for that. Let me and Lamprophyre work that out. But you—call off the Army. Please."

Ekanath nodded slowly. "I'm taking a tremendous chance," he said. "If the Army is attacked, it will be helpless."

"We won't let that happen."

Ekanath's eyes narrowed again. "You know," he said. "I believe you won't." He gripped Rokshan's shoulder. "Let's stop this war. And then I think you and I should talk."

"I look forward to it," Rokshan said. Lamprophyre, eavesdropping again because she couldn't help herself, discovered he was telling the truth.

Ekanath withdrew a blue chalcedony pendant a little smaller than Harshod's from within his shirt. He held it to his lips and let out a puff of breath that misted its smooth surface as if it were obsidian. "General Jossit," he said, "new orders. The Army is to return across the border. Cancel the attack."

There was a pause in which Lamprophyre held her breath, afraid of even that small disturbance ruining the communication. Then an unfamiliar male, his voice as clear as if he were standing next to them, said, "Your majesty? Please confirm those orders."

"Confirmed. The Army is to stand down. Prince Rokshan's attacker was not a dragon, but a Fanishkorite agent intent on starting a war. Return before the dragons take issue with our invasion."

"Understood. I will communicate with you when we've crossed the border." The mist disappeared.

Lamprophyre wished she had some way to hear that male, General Jossit's, thoughts just then. He'd sounded perfectly calm, as if these new orders weren't extraordinary, but she was sure he had all manner of questions he wanted to ask. She should ask Rokshan if not asking questions when you desperately wanted to was part of being a soldier, or a general, or was just General Jossit himself.

"We have to go," Rokshan told her, and Lamprophyre broke out of her reverie and stretched her wings out. "Thank you, Father."

"Thank you, son," Ekanath said. "Good fortune to you."

"Wait," Manishi said, hurrying down the stairs. "Give me that pendant—no, both of them." She took Harshod's chalcedony pendant from Lamprophyre and swiftly removed the king's from around his neck, making him protest. Manishi ignored him. She held both stones together in her left hand and raised that closed fist high. Light flared around her fingers like dancing blue fire, tiny little flickering flames that outlined her fingers. The bitter smell intensified for a beat, then faded. Manishi opened her hand. Now Harshod's larger stone, which had been a light gray, was the same blue as the king's.

"They're attuned to each other," Manishi said. "You saw how Father activated it, Rokshan. Breathe on it, and your words will carry through the stone to this one." She handed back each stone.

Rokshan settled his around his neck. "I'll let you know what happens," he said. "Hurry, Lamprophyre."

Lamprophyre turned carefully, not wanting to end their fragile accord by trampling the king, and squeezed past the doors, one of which hung awkwardly by its upper hinge. Once outside, she crouched to let Rokshan climb up. He moved smoothly, with no sign that his scars pained him. "You know what we have to do," she said.

"The dragons may already know the Army is there," Rokshan said. "We have to convince Hyaloclast not to attack."

"And hope it's not too late," Lamprophyre said.

CHAPTER FORTY

The late afternoon sun slanted across Lamprophyre's left side as she winged northward. Another storm was coming, one that blackened the northeastern skies and made the hot, wet air smell of lightning. That storm could be good news for them, since Hyaloclast wouldn't let the dragons fly through it. Or, if it came on too quickly, it could be bad news, forcing Lamprophyre to land and wait it out while the dragons came ever nearer to attacking the Army. She chose to see it as an ally.

As she flew, she told Rokshan what had happened between Harshod's attack and the events in the palace. She wanted to tell the story quickly, but Rokshan kept interrupting her for details she'd left out.

"You threw away the sapphire?" he said. "Was that smart?"

"If it was a weapon against dragons, especially if it was what nearly killed me, it's too dangerous to let anyone have it," she said. "I don't know that I trust any adept to not use it against us dragons."

Rokshan brushed his fingers across the sensitive spot, sending a tingle through her. "This is quite a weakness," he said. "I'm surprised no one's ever discovered it before."

"It's in a relatively protected spot on my body, and it's not as if dragons go around deliberately hitting each other trying to find weaknesses. Maybe people used to know about it, back when dragons and humans lived closer together. But I think it's mostly a weakness in combination with whatever that sapphire did. Harshod thought the stone had killed me."

"I'm glad it didn't kill you. Though it does raise the question of how *Harshod* knew about this weak spot. How he knew we were looking for him, for that matter."

"And how he knew what to ask Abhimot to make. He knew far too much about exactly what he needed to start a war. I'm glad he died." Lamprophyre banked right and craned her neck. "Though I wish his companions hadn't escaped with the rest of his artifacts."

"Lamprophyre." Rokshan's voice was quiet. "Are you all right?"

"I'm fine." She swallowed to moisten her suddenly dry throat. "I did what Hyaloclast wanted."

"And killed a human. That can't leave you untouched."

"No. But when I start to feel awful at the memory of taking a life, I remind myself of how many people he hurt, directly or indirectly. I should never have agreed to let him go, and I'm glad I didn't have to. Especially since he hurt you so badly. It would have felt like a betrayal of you."

"I feel fine. The scarring is an odd sensation. Like my skin is made of thin leather."

Lamprophyre risked a peek at his thoughts and felt as if her heart would break. "You don't have to be stoic with me," she said. "This is a major change, isn't it?"

Rokshan sighed. "I'm afraid to look at myself. I can feel the burns are everywhere, though mostly on my chest and shoulders. I never realized how vain I was—Lamprophyre, I don't know if I can bear this."

"You're still you," Lamprophyre said. "No one who cares about you will mind your scars. Or are you afraid you won't be able to attract a mate?"

A short, curt laugh burst out of him. "Yes, that had occurred to me. Though I suppose a prince is still a good catch, even a damaged one. As if I didn't already have worries enough on that score."

"I thought, from what you and Dharan said, you weren't ready to be pair-bonded. Married."

"I'm not, but tell that to the hundreds of Gonjirian young women who would love to bear a royal child. It's hard enough finding someone who cares for me as Rokshan and not as the prince. Now I'll always wonder if a girl is suppressing her revulsion—"

"Stop talking like that," Lamprophyre said hotly. "If that really is something that worries you, you can bring any female who seems interested to me, and I'll listen to her thoughts. And if she *is* that shallow, I'll scare her off. You shouldn't have to endure that kind of cruelty."

Rokshan laughed again. This time it was a cheerful, amused sound. "I have such a friend in you," he said. "You're the nicest and most honorable person I know."

Lamprophyre blushed lilac. "Well, *you're* kind and loyal, and that makes me feel better about Harshod's death. Though I feel I won't ever be the same again."

"You did what you had to do. We both did. You sacrificed your innocence, and I sacrificed my dubious good looks."

"I think your sacrifice was bigger."

"I don't know. Will you be in trouble for letting Abhimot go? Even if he was under orders, Hyaloclast might still consider him a villain."

A chill passed through Lamprophyre. "Maybe. Let's worry about stopping the dragons, and then I'll deal with Hyaloclast." Rokshan was right; Hyaloclast had given her instructions, and even though Harshod had been the ultimate villain, she might be upset that Lamprophyre had had their enemy in her hands and not killed Abhimot. That wasn't something Lamprophyre could dwell on, not while so much else was at stake.

They flew on into the growing gloom, the sun setting like a molten orange to the left, the black clouds rolling toward them on the right. Even if the moon hadn't been near dark, it would have given them no benefit that night, not with the skies blackened as they were. The warm, moist air clung to Lamprophyre's wings like a thin caul, slowing her progress. She slipped from updraft to updraft, desperately trying to increase her speed. She tried not to think about the Army crawling like ants back toward the border, of dragons winging easily overhead and unleashing gouts of fire or trails of black acid on the helpless soldiers. And then those soldiers, defending themselves, would turn the pyrite artifacts on the dragons, and it would be a catastrophe.

"Can you see anything?" she asked.

"We're too high," Rokshan replied. "Can you fly lower?"

"I can, but it will slow me down."

"Better that than overshooting the mark. If the dragons have already engaged the Army, we don't want to fly past them."

Lamprophyre nodded and dropped. She knew Rokshan was worried by the way he didn't shout with excitement the way he usually did when she pulled that maneuver.

They soared low across the ground, twelve or fourteen dragonlengths high. The sun had nearly dipped below the horizon when Lamprophyre saw movement, deliberate and large, and smelled masses of pyrite like a forest of orange trees. "It's the Army," she said with relief. "And there aren't any dragons around."

"Can you reach the flight's caves before we lose the light?" Rokshan asked.

"I don't know. I'll try." She rose higher, aiming herself at the distant speck that was Mother Stone. At worst, she could fly mostly blind and trust to her instincts for where her mountain home was.

Twenty beats later, more movement caught her eye, blocking Mother Stone from view. In the dimness, it looked like birds grouped loosely together the way no birds ever flew. "Stones," Lamprophyre swore. "They're on the way."

"We still have time," Rokshan said. "We'll catch them well before they reach the Army."

Lamprophyre nodded. She didn't point out that the dragons might not stop even if Lamprophyre and Rokshan reached them first. No sense borrowing trouble, as Rokshan was fond of saying.

They sped toward the dragons until the oncoming flight was a scattering of bright blotches against the charcoal sky. In the distance, thunder rumbled, and a streak of lightning shot across the clouds. A few raindrops spattered Lamprophyre's wings, cool and refreshing after the muggy heat of the day. The storm would be a comfort for a few beats, and then it would drench her skin and the membranes of her wings and make flying very difficult as well as dangerous. She pushed herself harder, willing the storm to hold off for a hundred beats, fifty beats, even a dozen.

Then lightning ripped through the sky again, much closer, and the rain poured down like a river in full flood. "Hold on!" Lamprophyre shouted, and sped up, water slapping her wings like sharp fingers of stone. She slipped from one gust of wind to another, angling her body to take advantage of the crosswinds and closing her nictitating membranes to keep from flying fully blind. If she hadn't been tense and exhausted with anxiety, she would have thrilled at the sensation of flying with the storm.

The dragons were close enough now to be identifiable as individuals despite the blurs her second eyelids made them. Lamprophyre flapped her wings to slow herself, then hovered in place, not something she could keep up indefinitely in this wind. "Hyaloclast!" she shouted. "Please stop! It's a mistake!"

The wind battered her words and carried them away, hopefully to Hyaloclast's ears. She could barely make out the dragon queen, whose black scales blended with the storm. Her red membranes were the only bright thing about her, and they continued to advance without slowing. "*Please*, Hyaloclast," Lamprophyre shouted again. "Give me just a dozen beats to explain!"

Hyaloclast's bulk loomed up before Lamprophyre. The great dragon slowed and signaled to the others to wait. "You've discovered our enemy as I instructed?" she shouted over the storm. "Because that's the only reason I can think of for you to be here. Though why you still bear this human on your back like you're some kind of beast, I have no idea."

"It's a mistake," Lamprophyre babbled, "a terrible mistake. The ones who stole the egg and made the wand are from Fanishkor—they wanted to start a war—"

"I have no interest in human politics." Hyaloclast's wings stirred up gusts of wind that made Lamprophyre struggle to maintain her position. "Soldiers from Gonjiri have entered our territory, breaking our agreement. We will destroy them, and then we will destroy their king."

"You have to listen!" Lamprophyre screamed. She wiped rain out of her face, a futile gesture, and said, "We need to land. Please, let me explain. Then, if you don't agree, you can do whatever you like to the humans."

Rokshan made a pained noise. Hyaloclast sneered. "I don't need your permission, Lamprophyre," she said, and dropped toward the distant ground. Lamprophyre followed, with the rest of the flight behind. She hoped Rokshan wasn't getting drowned by the downpour, but she had no attention to spare for him.

Hyaloclast landed and settled herself on the soaked ground, arching her wings to give her some shelter. Lamprophyre crouched to let Rokshan hop down, then curved her wing protectively over him. Hyaloclast eyed this, but said nothing. One by one, the other dragons settled themselves around Hyaloclast and Lamprophyre. No one spoke. It took Lamprophyre a few beats to realize this was because they were all waiting for her.

She cleared her throat. "Hyaloclast, you sent me to be an ambassador to the humans," she said. She listened for Hyaloclast's thoughts, looking for guidance—the dragon queen might not want her secret instructions exposed—but Hyaloclast was completely unruffled, a surprise given her antagonistic attitude. Lamprophyre set this mystery aside to be unraveled later. "You wanted me to find out who stole Opal's egg. I did. It was a Fanishkorite male named Harshod, and he was acting under orders from someone in his government. Fanishkor, not Gonjiri."

"I told you human politics are irrelevant to us," Hyaloclast said.

"That's not true. You wanted vengeance on the one who stole the egg, not on innocent humans, so you must care about not attacking the wrong person. And the point of the egg theft was human politics. Fanishkor wanted to use us, Hyaloclast. They intended us to attack Gonjiri and weaken it so they could attack afterward and conquer them easily. We were meant to be their tools."

As she'd hoped, this set the dragons to hissing and growling, their angry thoughts filling Lamprophyre's mind. Hyaloclast sat up. "They dared," she hissed. "We will turn their cities to ash."

"I'm not finished," Lamprophyre said. "Part of the plan was to make Gonjiri believe dragons wanted their royal family dead. Our enemy, Harshod, attacked Rokshan in a way that made it seem I'd done it. And the king, seeking vengeance, sent his Army to attack the dragons."

Hyaloclast looked at Rokshan, who alone among the assembled people wasn't getting steadily wetter. "You are Rokshan," she said. "You realize I could kill you as proxy for your foolish father and no one would stop me."

"But you won't," Rokshan said, regarding her fearlessly, "because you're honorable, and I think you know both Gonjiri and you are pawns in someone else's game."

"Dragons are not pawns, young prince," Hyaloclast said. "So, Lamprophyre, you expect me *not* to defend our territory against human aggression?"

"Once King Ekanath found out the truth, he ordered the Army to turn around and return to Tanajital—the human city. This was all a mistake. You won't destroy people over a mistake, will you?"

"A mistake made by someone who fears us," Hyaloclast said. "Someone who is likely to go on making 'mistakes' of this nature. I'm inclined to make an example of this human Army to prevent it happening again."

Lamprophyre glanced at Rokshan, who nodded. She didn't need to hear his thoughts. "That would be a mistake of a different kind," she said. "The humans have weapons that can hurt or maybe even kill a dragon."

"Impossible."

The thoughts around Lamprophyre became tangled with confusion, and she blocked them out. "It's true. They make a blast of force. The small ones—it's like being punched by a powerful fist. But the Army has enormous ones that can tear a human or a dragon apart, they tell me. We can destroy their Army, but they will kill or injure many of us."

"They tell you? So you haven't seen them work."

"Not the big ones. But the small ones are powerful enough I have a good idea about the power of the big ones."

"So the humans brought dragon-killing weapons," Hyaloclast said. "They planned to attack us. And you expect me *not* to see that as an act of war?"

"They were frightened," Rokshan said. "People do foolish things when they're frightened. They're trying to fix their mistake."

"It's too late for that," Hyaloclast said.

"It's not," Lamprophyre said. "Nobody's attacked anyone else yet. It doesn't have to come to bloodshed. Please, Hyaloclast."

Hyaloclast sat up and regarded her closely. With the rain running down her head and neck and dripping off her wings, she should have looked bedraggled, but she looked every inch a queen.

In desperation, Lamprophyre said, "Look. What is it you want? What do dragons want? Because the humans would like a real alliance. They have so many things we might benefit from, if we can overcome these first misunderstandings."

Hyaloclast said nothing. Lamprophyre stared her down, her heart beating so fast it felt like time was speeding up. Finally, Hyaloclast said, "Why do you care?"

Confused at what felt like a change of subject, Lamprophyre said, "What?"

"Why," Hyaloclast said, enunciating carefully, "do you care, Lamprophyre?"

Lamprophyre looked at Rokshan again. "Because humans are like us, and not like us," she said, "and I think we can make each other stronger. Because we're both people, and as rational beings we have more in common with each other than we do with any other creatures. Because it sounds like we were the answer to their religion's prophecy, and I want to know why that is. And because I've made human friends as dear to me as my own clutch. If that's possible—if humans and dragons can build those kinds of bonds—then I think we should."

Hyaloclast fell silent again. Lamprophyre wondered if, like that day in the heights when Rokshan had faced the dragon queen down, she once more needed a plan to take herself and Rokshan to safety. Then Hyaloclast said, "Will the humans destroy their dragon-killing weapons to show good will?"

"They aren't just for killing dragons. Those weapons are our surety against Fanishkor," Rokshan said, "so I don't think so. But we would never turn weapons of any kind against our allies."

Hyaloclast looked down at Rokshan. "You are asking for a tremendous display of trust on our part."

"As are we," Rokshan countered. "Dragons are capable of breathing fire and spitting acid regardless of whether or not we're allies. We wouldn't ask you to cripple yourselves for our peace of mind. We have to trust each other."

"Fairly said," Hyaloclast said. She glanced up at the sky. The pelting rain had diminished somewhat, and Lamprophyre no longer felt as if she were standing under a waterfall.

"So Gonjiri is not our enemy," Hyaloclast said. "It is Fanishkor that ordered the theft of the egg? We will turn our wrath upon them, and the world will see what happens when dragons are attacked."

Lamprophyre felt sick. "It was someone in the government who ordered it. We don't know any more than that. It might not have been the king, but it doesn't matter. The Fanishkorite people weren't responsible, and they shouldn't have to suffer for their leaders' mistakes."

"They support their rulers, and in so doing support their actions," Hyaloclast said.

"They couldn't!" Lamprophyre exclaimed. "Humans aren't like dragons. Dragons all know each other—they all know you personally, Hyaloclast. Most humans never even see their king, and they don't have a choice in being ruled by him. If dragons destroy Fanishkorite cities, we'll be killing innocent people. And that doesn't show the world anything except that dragons are cruel and vindictive."

Hyaloclast's eye ridges shifted, narrowing her eyes. "You speak to me of justice?"

"If not me," Lamprophyre said, "then who? You sent me to discover the truth. I did. And the human male responsible for taking Opal's egg is dead. Fanishkor knows why he died and they'll never try anything like that again. Let that be enough."

Hyaloclast's eyes narrowed further. "Dead?"

Lamprophyre's heart sank. "I killed him. He attacked me."

"So you killed him in self-defense?"

Hyaloclast's tone of voice was derisive, as if self-defense was the stupidest reason ever for taking a life. Lamprophyre lifted her chin and regarded the dragon queen unflinchingly. "No," she said. "I could have saved his life, maybe. But he hurt too many people, and he would have gone on hurting people—I'm sure dragons are not the only ones he's tried to kill, and who knows how many humans are dead because of him. So I chose to let him die. It was the right choice, but I still wish it hadn't been me who made it. And if that makes me weak, then I'm weak."

Hyaloclast returned her regard, stare for stare. "There's nothing weak about abhorring violence," she said. "Weakness is in letting that abhorrence allow evil to go unpunished. You made the right choice. And I respect that." She shook out her wings, sending a tremendous spray into the air. "We will not attack Fanishkorite cities," she declared, her voice carrying to the farthest reaches of the flight. "But if the opportunity arises, we will avenge ourselves on whoever that man's superiors are."

Lamprophyre felt uncomfortable at this, but it was likely the best she was going to get out of Hyaloclast.

"Can you prove the human Army has retreated?" the dragon queen continued.

"They may have camped due to the storm and nightfall," Rokshan said, "but I give you my word as commander that they will cross the border by no later than noon tomorrow."

"I should ask for more surety than that," Hyaloclast said, "but I'm inclined to take Lamprophyre's assessment of your character to heart. Very well." She flapped her wings again. "In three days, I will arrive at your human city to discuss the future with your king. Alliances aside, I have no desire for humans to encroach on our mountains. It is a holy thing," she told Rokshan, who nodded.

"Lamprophyre," Hyaloclast continued, "a word with you. Alone." She pushed off with her powerful legs and rose into the sky, scattering the last falling raindrops. Lamprophyre followed her. The cool, wet air wrapped around her, slowing her flight nearly as much as her reluctance to hear whatever Hyaloclast had to say did.

They rose a handful of dragonlengths into the sky, far enough to be out of earshot of the flight, before Hyaloclast slowed and hovered. "You have an interesting way of obeying my orders," she said. "I'm certain making friends with humans was not something I told you to do."

"No, but you didn't tell me not to," Lamprophyre dared, "and I didn't make agreements with the humans, even though they might have benefited us."

Hyaloclast's expression didn't change. "You think you understand our needs better than I do?"

"I understand *humans* better than you do, which makes sense, don't you think? Some of them I wouldn't dare treat with, because they're deceptive and I don't think that way. But some of them are honorable, and we could gain by making agreements with them. You have no idea how valuable our stone is, Hyaloclast. And they have *cows*. You really need to taste cow. And there's glass, and even artifacts—"

"Understood," Hyaloclast said with a cutting-off gesture. "All right. Make your agreements. But make them with care. And don't be so enthusiastic. People take advantage of that."

"I understand."

They looked at each other in silence for a few beats, until Hyaloclast said, "You know I expected you to fail."

"I know."

"But not for the reasons you believe."

Surprised, Lamprophyre said, "I—what do you think I believe?"

Hyaloclast sighed. "You think I'm hard and unfeeling and that I don't respect you."

That was more accurate than Lamprophyre felt comfortable with. "I would never say that."

"You don't have to." Hyaloclast fixed her with a bloody gaze that increased Lamprophyre's discomfort. "I've never liked how prone you are to comparing yourself to others," she went on. "Particularly since those comparisons are usually your weaknesses against someone else's strengths.

You think I enjoy watching my daughter pitting herself against that wretch Coquina? Whose only positive features are beauty and a turn of speed? You are far superior to her, and yet you insist on holding her up as a standard you ought to aim for. That disappoints me."

Lamprophyre almost forgot to maintain altitude. "But...you never said..."

"I don't believe in coddling anyone, least of all my own child. You would never learn to fly unaided if I hovered beside you all the time. I wouldn't have mentioned this now if you hadn't just shown me how much you've grown in the last few twelvedays. You don't need to prove yourself to anyone but you, Lamprophyre. Not even me."

"Oh," Lamprophyre said. "But I wanted..." She swallowed. "I think your respect is worth having."

"That's an honor I'm not sure I deserve," Hyaloclast said. "But I appreciate it. And I am proud of what you've accomplished. Now—get back to that human city and warn them I'm coming. I had better not be shot at."

Lamprophyre smiled. "As if you'd feel it."

"It's so undignified. Go on. Get."

Lamprophyre plummeted to the ground and gave Rokshan a leg up. "You ready for a night flight?" she asked.

"I thought you said it was dangerous."

"I did. And?"

Rokshan laughed. "Fly on, then."

CHAPTER FORTY-ONE

Lamprophyre swept past the great southern gate in Tanajital's wall a third time. "I wish she'd get here already," she complained. "I'm sure everyone's sick of watching me fly loops around the city."

"You underestimate how dramatic your appearance is," Rokshan said. She felt him shift as he waved to the soldiers on the wall yet again. "It's not something humans tire of, watching a beautiful, powerful creature in motion. It's why horse racing is so popular."

"I'm not sure whether to be pleased at the compliment or irritated that you just compared me to a draft animal."

Rokshan laughed. "If we could arrange for dragon races, that would make human fear of dragons virtually disappear. Imagine it, Lamprophyre. Humans choosing favorites, cheering on their chosen dragon..."

"That's either brilliant or the worst idea in human history. Though dragons do like to race. I know Bromargyrite and Porphyry of my clutch would take that offer in a heartbeat."

"It's something to consider, anyway. I'm not sure how many of your people are interested in visiting the lowlands for an extended period." Rokshan leaned forward and pointed. "I think that's her. Them. Looks like more than one."

Lamprophyre coasted to a stop and hung hovering above the eastern wall. "It's Hyaloclast," she said, "and Leucite and Heliodor and Flint. She

brought an escort." Why Flint, who was as young as she was, Lamprophyre didn't know, but it was comforting, as if otherwise the dragons
would be antagonistic. Which was foolishness; Hyaloclast was here as a
potential ally, and Leucite and Heliodor were open-minded—probably—
and Flint was smart for all he looked beautiful and dim. Everything would
be fine. Flint's presence was still a relief.

She flew out to meet the dragons above the plains to the north, the
tilled ground making squares of every shade of green beneath them. They
must look so dramatic against the cloudless sky, Hyaloclast and the
midnight-blue Flint a stark contrast to bronze Leucite and Heliodor with
her flame-orange scales and brilliantly gold wing membranes. Lamprophyre, with her scales nearly matching the sky, was the least exotic of the
five.

"The king will meet you on the training ground," she said, pitching her
voice to carry over the wind. "It's where the Army practices military
things. The palace isn't big enough to fit all of us. Actually, it's barely big
enough to fit me in their great hall. So I hope you won't feel insulted."

"Rational people take no offense where none is intended," Hyaloclast
said. "I'm interested in seeing this human city up close. Our legends don't
say how large they are, but even from here I can see it's quite sizable."

"Tanajital is the largest Gonjirian city," Lamprophyre said as their little
group continued flying toward the city.

"It's also the second largest on the continent," Rokshan said, "second
only to Jyotini in Sachetan, which is farther south." His voice didn't carry
as far as Lamprophyre's, but Hyaloclast seemed to have no trouble hearing
him.

"Interesting that you have a wall surrounding the city even though it is
breached by the river in two places," Hyaloclast said. "How does that
affect your defense?"

"The river narrows an enemy's assault so they're forced to attempt an
entry at only two places, both of which are heavily fortified," Rokshan
replied. "We also have several observation points along the river upstream
and down, so an enemy would be hard pressed to sneak inside."

"I see," Hyaloclast said. "And, four gates?"

"You realize you sound like someone assessing Tanajital as a target,"
Rokshan said.

To Lamprophyre's shock, Hyaloclast laughed. "I do, don't I? Don't worry, young prince, I'm simply comparing what I see to our stories of human cities of the past. I'm curious as to how much has changed over the centuries."

"There was a lot I didn't know to expect," Lamprophyre said. "Humans build a wide variety of buildings that all have names beyond 'building.' They create stairs and stack their homes atop each other. And they use materials we don't know, such as glass—I mean, the kind of glass they have is very different from ours."

They swept past the wall and Lamprophyre led the group in the direction of the palace. "The dragon embassy, where I live, is that way," she said, pointing. "Ahead is the coliseum, that's the building with no roof and red arches. They have races there. And the palace is just beyond that."

All the dragons made noises of appreciation when they saw the palace with its gilded roofs. "I didn't realize humans' craftsmanship was so impressive," Leucite rumbled. "It's like piles of crystals dusted with talc, drenched in molten gold."

"It makes me hungry," Flint muttered so Lamprophyre alone could hear. She giggled.

They flew around the side of the palace to where the soldiers had built a wooden structure half a dragonlength tall. Stairs led to the top, which was a platform wide enough that Lamprophyre could have rested on it if she weren't worried about crushing the thing. When she'd looked at it earlier that morning, the platform had been empty. Now, a gilded chair with a high back and a fringed canopy stood opposite the stairs, with a smaller but no less ornate chair beside it to the left. King Ekanath sat in the large chair, his hands gripping the armrests loosely as if he weren't nervous, though Lamprophyre, listening to his thoughts, knew he was barely keeping himself from restlessly tapping his foot in anxiety.

Tekentriya stood to his right, one hand resting on the high back of the chair, her bad leg thrust out in front of her. Her thoughts were angrier and less nervous than Ekanath's: *huge mistake* and *make us their vassals if we're not careful* and *Rokshan thinks he has that beast controlled.* Lamprophyre's dislike of Tekentriya hardened.

Satiya sat in the chair to Ekanath's left, placid and peaceful as her husband was not. As Lamprophyre drew nearer, Satiya put her hand over Ekanath's, and without looking at her, he turned his hand to take hold of hers. It was such a tender gesture it startled Lamprophyre, who'd thought the king incapable of such emotion. Anchala stood behind her mother, her long black hair tangling in the light breeze.

Manishi, at the end of the platform some distance from the little group at its center, was dressed as informally as ever, but Lamprophyre scented stone and guessed she considered herself as well-clad as anyone. Though her position might have been determined not by disdain for her parents but by a hatred of her brother Khadar, who occupied the opposite end. Manishi's expression was disdainful of the Fifth Ecclesiast, which put Lamprophyre in greater charity with the adept.

Khadar's thoughts, she didn't want to listen to, but decided if he was going to attack her again, she ought to be prepared. He was mentally grumbling about having to be there at all and thinking dire thoughts about *heathens in our midst, spreading apostasy and leading people astray.*

Colorful canopies shielded all the members of the royal family except Manishi, who had stepped away from the one intended for her. Lamprophyre landed a respectful two dragonlengths away and to the side, leaving plenty of space for Hyaloclast to alight in front of the stairs. The platform put Ekanath and the other humans face to face with the dragon queen.

No one spoke. Lamprophyre realized neither ruler wanted to be first, probably because that would give up social standing, or usurp it, or something only rulers cared about. She took two steps forward and said, "Hyaloclast, this is Ekanath, king of Gonjiri. Ekanath, this is Hyaloclast, dragon queen. As dragon ambassador to the humans, I want to thank you both for agreeing to meet." She hoped that was sufficient introduction to make them both feel they weren't giving anything up.

Hyaloclast stirred. "Your majesty," she said, her voice deeper than usual, "it's good to meet you. It has been centuries since a human ruler and a dragon queen came face to face."

"Then I am pleased to be part of making history," Ekanath said. He rose and walked forward to the edge of the platform. "And I would like to apologize for the misunderstandings that have plagued our initial encounters."

Lamprophyre kept from falling over in shock. Beside her, Rokshan put a hand on her flank as if he needed its steadying help as well. Ekanath apologizing. What next?

"As would I," Hyaloclast said, and Lamprophyre swallowed an astonished squeak. "I would prefer us to move forward in amity and let those misunderstandings stay in the past."

"Agreed." Ekanath offered his hand to Hyaloclast, who took it in her huge one with barely a breath of hesitation.

"I understand from the ambassador," Hyaloclast said after releasing the king's hand, "that the humans of Gonjiri came north in response to a prophecy, and that you believe the intent of this prophecy was to bring humans and dragons together once more. How will this affect the Gonjirians currently settling in our territory, if the prophecy has been fulfilled?"

"I've given that consideration in the last three days," Ekanath said. "It's true, we might withdraw from dragon territory entirely, but I think we would both benefit from a closer association. If it's acceptable to you, I would like to maintain that Gonjirian settlement, and encourage dragons to visit so we can grow accustomed to one another. And, of course, dragons are welcome within Gonjiri at any time."

Hyaloclast smiled. "That's ambitious. I'm not sure either dragons or humans are quite so civilized as to be that immediately accepting of one another. But I appreciate the offer. And I will send dragons south a few at a time, so as not to overwhelm our new allies."

Lamprophyre was practically bursting with questions, primarily ones about how Ekanath had become so enthusiastically cooperative in only a few days. Hyaloclast turned to her, and she immediately realized the dragon queen had heard her thoughts. "What do you recommend, ambassador?" Hyaloclast said. "How should we proceed, in your experience?"

"Limit the dragons to visiting Tanajital at first," Lamprophyre said. "Gonjiri knows about dragons, but the smaller towns aren't used to seeing them. We can spread out to Kolmira and Suwedhi and farther south and east as time passes. I'm sure the humans here will tell others about us. And dragons should remember how small and fragile humans are, and try to see themselves as humans do. I have some human children friends who think of me as a very large toy, but their parents are always aware that I could hurt those children accidentally, just because I'm so much bigger."

"And humans should remember the same," Rokshan put in. "While we can't hurt dragons, we have any number of things, particularly artifacts, that dragons have no understanding of. We should remember not to take our knowledge for granted."

"Well said," Hyaloclast said. "We will make this a slow process. It's been centuries, after all—we don't need to recover our lost relationship overnight."

"I would also like to discuss a military alliance," Ekanath said. "Though Rokshan and Lamprophyre's efforts have lessened the chance of a Fanishkorite invasion, Fanishkor is still a threat to Gonjiri—and to dragons, if I understand correctly. Something about the theft of an egg?"

Heliodor and Leucite growled. Hyaloclast said, "That will not happen again. But yes, it appears we have a common enemy. We dragons are not interested in starting a war, but by the Stones, we will end one if it comes calling. So if Gonjiri chooses to attack Fanishkor preemptively, we will not join you. But we will enthusiastically support you if Fanishkor attacks. Is that enough alliance for you?"

"That is exactly what I intended to propose," Ekanath said. "I hope it will not be necessary."

Lamprophyre, listening in, found to her surprise that he was telling the truth. He was turning out to be not at all what she'd thought at their first meeting. Whether Hyaloclast considered tracking down Harshod's superiors and killing them an act of war, she didn't know, because Hyaloclast had already moved on to thinking about her next question.

"I hope you will not take offense at our not permitting a human ambassador to live with us," Hyaloclast said. "Our homes are not hospitable to humans, and there are also religious reasons why we do not allow humans to stay there permanently. Is there some compromise we could come to?"

"A human ambassador living among the settlers would be close enough to relay information," Ekanath said. "As to communication, my daughter Manishi has a solution."

Manishi picked up a large sack that looked to be made of the same fabric her shirt was and walked forward to join the king. "It's a new development in magical artifacts," she said, opening the sack.

Hyaloclast and Lamprophyre both wrinkled their noses at the strongly bitter scent that emerged. "Chalcedony," Hyaloclast said. "Very large pieces. I'm afraid I don't understand."

Manishi reached into the sack and withdrew a polished round of white chalcedony bigger than her fist. She handed it to Lamprophyre, then gave Hyaloclast a second piece almost the twin of the first, but half again as large. "These two are attuned to each other. You breathe on it—Lamprophyre knows how—and it allows you to speak to the person holding the other piece, however far apart you are."

"My ambassador will have a similar piece for speaking to me," the king said. "It will cut down on misunderstandings and make coming to an accord much simpler."

"Fascinating," Hyaloclast said. She sniffed the chalcedony, then ducked her head and sneezed. Every human on the platform tensed, but Hyaloclast simply wiped a hand across her nose and said, "Excuse me."

Ekanath relaxed. "I believe there is a banquet prepared—a formal meal," he corrected himself. "If you'd care to join us, your majesty? There are many more things we can discuss, and I believe my daughter Anchala is anxious to speak with your entourage about dragon customs and history."

"Thank you, that would be most welcome," Hyaloclast said. "Mother Stone knows we are happy to share our lost knowledge with you."

Khadar shifted. "Mother Stone," he said, his voice angry and dismissive. "Your majesty, how can you allow these creatures to spread their heresy freely among the people of Gonjiri?"

"Excuse me?" Hyaloclast said. Her words were polite, but Lamprophyre could hear her thinking *heresy? Who is this whelp?*

"That's inappropriate, Khadar," Ekanath said. "Show respect to the dragon queen."

"I refuse to allow dragons and their misguided religion—"

"Shut up, Khadar," Rokshan warned.

"Misguided?" Hyaloclast said. Now she sounded angry. "Mother Stone, misguided?"

"Khadar is overzealous. I apologize for his outburst," Ekanath said. He strode to Khadar's side and grabbed his arm. "Now is not the time—"

Khadar shook him off, causing Rokshan to start up the stairs toward them. "I have a duty to this people that trumps your frightened diplomacy!"

"You do not," Lamprophyre said, following Rokshan. "You don't believe any of that. You just don't want to lose power!"

"Don't challenge an ecclesiast, ambassador," Ekanath said angrily. Lamprophyre, aware that she couldn't reveal she'd heard all of that in Khadar's thoughts, fell silent.

Khadar stepped to the edge of the platform. "Listen to me!" he shouted, raising his arms high. "Jiwanyil will not be mocked! The true—"

He stopped speaking. No one moved. Lamprophyre watched Hyaloclast, fearing Khadar might have started the war she'd worked so hard to avert, but Hyaloclast stood perfectly still, waiting for Khadar's next words.

Khadar licked his lips. His eyes closed, and he swayed as if he were about to faint. Rokshan, halfway up the stairs, hurried to his side, and Lamprophyre put herself beneath Khadar to catch him if he fell. She didn't like him at all, but he was still a person and she didn't want to see him break his neck.

Khadar's eyes opened. Lamprophyre was within only a few handspans of him, so she saw clearly that his eyes, which had been the same brown as Rokshan's, were not only now the green of new leaves, but the color completely covered his eyes, iris and pupil and white and all.

He licked his lips again. "*This shall not stand,*" he said, or, more accurately, someone else said through his mouth; the voice was not Khadar's, but that of a stranger who might have been male or female by its pitch. "*The north cries out, the south pleads, and none shall stand in its path. Fear the ally, and make room for the stranger. The skies will burn.*" White foam collected at the corners of his mouth that he licked away.

Lamprophyre exchanged glances with Rokshan, who was thinking *a true prophecy? Khadar? Sooner think a dog might speak for Jiwanyil than him.*

Movement brought her gaze back to Khadar, whose head twitched. It twitched again, this time bringing his shoulders with it. Then he was jerking helplessly like a fish on a line, and Rokshan dove past the king to grab him, but missed as Khadar's seizure threw him forward, off the platform and into Lamprophyre's hands. She held him tightly, frightened both of dropping him as well as of hurting him with her firm grasp. "What do I do?" she exclaimed.

"Set him down gently," Satiya said. The queen had left her seat and stood at the edge of the platform, watching her son convulse. Lamprophyre did so and stepped back, afraid Khadar might strike her and hurt himself in his thrashing. But the seizure had already begun to pass, and after only a beat or two, Khadar lay limp and unconscious at her feet.

"Send for Ishay," Ekanath said. He hurried down the stairs and knelt beside Khadar. "And send to the Archprelate's palace. They need to know of a new prophecy."

"Prophecy?" Lamprophyre said. "That was a prophecy? Are they all so dramatic?"

"This was mild," Satiya said. "We saw the Second Ecclesiast bleed from the ears after delivering the prophecy that sent our people north."

Lamprophyre stepped back to allow Khadar's parents more room. "He's waking up," she said, before realizing she'd known that from hearing Khadar's thoughts. But no one paid her any attention. Khadar blinked, and his eyes were their usual brown.

"Lie still," Satiya said, putting a hand to his forehead. "You were possessed of a prophecy."

"I—what?" Khadar's eyes were wide and confused. Lamprophyre, listening in, heard him think *not possible, it's a lie* and *me, why me, I've never heard Jiwanyil's voice but once in my life*. She drew in an outraged breath to denounce him as a fraud—how dare he pretend to religious authority and challenge her faith? But Rokshan put a hand atop hers, startling her, and she caught herself before once again almost revealing her ability.

"You won't remember," Ekanath said. "But no one present will ever forget. Now we must pass these words on to the Archprelate and the other ecclesiasts for their interpretation."

"The skies will burn," Rokshan murmured. "Remember, Lamprophyre?"

"No—" Lamprophyre began, then shook her head. "That rock sniffer, Mendesk. It was part of his prophecy. So were dragons."

"What are you saying, Lamprophyre?" Hyaloclast asked.

Lamprophyre shook her head again. "It's nothing. A coincidence." If it wasn't coincidence, Rokshan could tell the ecclesiasts about it, not her. It wasn't her religion, after all. But the idea that Rokshan's faith had now pointed three times to her people made her uncomfortable, as if her skin were the wrong size and someone might expect her to step out of it. It was harder to dismiss human beliefs when she'd seen evidence that their God really did speak to them—if that's what it had been.

Then Ishay was pushing past her and kneeling beside Khadar, examining his eyes and touching his throat and the backs of his hands. "Prophecy?" he said. "I see no ill effects. It's perfectly natural for an ecclesiast to have such a reaction. Help him up."

Khadar got heavily to his feet with Ishay and Rokshan's help, but when they let go of him, he took two steps and had to throw out his hands to keep his balance, grabbing Ishay's shoulder and making the healer stagger. "Perhaps not quite *no* ill effects," Ishay said in a humorous tone. "I'll escort the Fifth Ecclesiast to where he can rest."

"Quite a dramatic ending to this meeting," Ekanath said when Khadar and Ishay had disappeared around the corner of the palace. "If you'll join us, your majesty?"

"I'd like a word with the ambassador first, if you don't mind," Hyaloclast said.

Rokshan waited with Lamprophyre as the rest of the group, dragons and humans, passed beyond the platform to where Lamprophyre could smell the aroma of steak wafting on the breeze. When it was just the three of them, Hyaloclast said, "I would ask the young prince to leave, but you'll just tell him everything I'm about to say later, so I see no point in wasting my breath."

Rokshan smiled. Lamprophyre said, "He's very discreet."

"He's kept your secret, so I imagine he is." Hyaloclast smiled at Lamprophyre's dismay. "Don't think I don't know you haven't told any of these humans that dragons can hear thoughts. You're too intelligent not to keep that secret, and too close to this young man not to have shared it with him. But I wanted to ask about the human who made such an extraordinary display. Why does he challenge our religion?"

"Khadar is—he has high rank in the human religion, which is different from ours." Lamprophyre felt unexpectedly uncomfortable telling the dragon queen this, as if she somehow owed it to Rokshan not to cast doubts on his faith. "They believe there's a god of dragons that's not Mother Stone, for one, and when I told Khadar that, he became angry. He thinks I want to take power from him by tricking humans away from their true religion. But I haven't, aside from saying we've never heard of their dragon god."

"I'm afraid my brother likes having power over people," Rokshan said, "and he uses his calling to gain more of it. I'm stunned that he was possessed of a prophecy. I would have sworn he faked his way into the ranks of the ecclesiasts."

"He thought he did," Lamprophyre said, remembering Khadar's thoughts. "Are you sure he wasn't faking now?"

"Positive. I've seen other prophecies delivered, and they all take the speaker in that way, more or less."

"That is unimportant, at least to dragons," Hyaloclast said. "What concerns me is what he said last. 'The skies will burn.' It sounds as if you've heard that before."

"Someone else received a prophecy containing those words, yes," Rokshan said. "It's a strange coincidence."

"Or not," Hyaloclast said. "Those words are passed on from dragon queen to dragon queen, to be held in confidence against a future day in which they will come true. I never thought to hear them on a human's lips." She looked off past the platform. "It seems we have more in common than I thought."

"But why tell us?" Lamprophyre said. "If it's supposed to be confidential?"

Hyaloclast returned her attention to Lamprophyre. "Because I have a feeling something is coming," she said. "Something dragons and humans will face together. And if that something is as dire as my instincts tell me, confidentiality will not matter. Here in Tanajital, you will be first to know if any more of these ecclesiasts receive such prophecies, and you will tell me what you learn."

More secrets. Lamprophyre's heart felt leaden. "All right," she said.

Hyaloclast laughed. "This is not like my last instructions, Lamprophyre. I see no reason to conceal my interest, though I expect you not to speak of it casually. I intend to search our memories for anything that might shed light on those words, and I will share what I learn with you in exchange. I know too little of humans to judge how useful they might be in this search, but I choose to act as if their knowledge is valuable. And as our fates seem intertwined, keeping secrets might be fatal in the long run. Just...be discreet. Not all humans are our allies."

"I can do that, Hyaloclast." Relief washed over her. She hadn't realized how wearying it was to keep the dragon queen's secrets until she no longer had to do so.

"Excellent. Now, what is that delicious smell? Is that cow? You may be right about that being something humans can do for dragons." Hyaloclast clasped Lamprophyre's hand briefly and walked away.

"I don't know about you," Rokshan said when the dragon queen was out of earshot, "but I've had about all I can take of mysterious revelations for one day. Can we agree to talk of nothing but trivialities until tomorrow?"

"That's acceptable," Lamprophyre said. "Do you think this will make Khadar more insufferable, or less?"

"Since it's not possible for him to be more insufferable, I'll go with the latter." Rokshan strolled beside Lamprophyre as she crossed the training ground to where the food had been arranged under canopies, two of them very large and tall. "But I think maybe we both need more religious instruction."

Lamprophyre made a face. "I'd rather be a heathen like Dharan."

"I mean because it sounds like Khadar's isn't the only prophecy along those lines. I wonder if we could track down other ecclesiasts who've been possessed of that one. I know they're supposed to record all prophecies in the Hall of Visions—that's in the Archprelate's palace—and I think they let people look at them. For a fee."

"Which means selling more stone. And I still haven't gotten Manishi's kyanite." Lamprophyre sighed. "This is coming awfully close to non-trivial, and it's going to spoil my appetite for that delicious steak I smell. Let's eat, and then I want you to meet Flint. Maybe we can convince him to race us around the city. Unless you'd rather walk."

Rokshan laughed. "Walk?" he said. "With you, I'll always choose to fly."

SNEAK PEEK: FAITH IN FLAMES

The oncoming storm that blackened the western skies smelled of lightning and cut grass and fresh warm water, a lake's worth of it. The rainy season in the lowlands had proved to be more uncomfortable than the hot, drier spring had been. Lamprophyre had thought rain would keep the temperature low, but all it had done was saturate the air the sun heated to an unbearable level so it clung to her scales and wings like a caul. On the worst days, the ones where clouds didn't dim the sun and any movement felt like swimming in soup, she napped fitfully in her hall and dreamed of crisp, cold mountain air, of sleeping on chilled stone in a cave warmed by her body heat, and woke to the unpleasant reality of Gonjiri in summer.

Rokshan never seemed disturbed by the weather, but humans were acclimated to the lowlands in a way no dragon could ever be. He wore long-sleeved linen shirts regardless of how hot it was, which made Lamprophyre's heart ache for him because she knew his clothing choice had nothing to do with comfort and everything to do with the burn scars she still had never seen. It wasn't something she could task him with, not even on days like today when there was no one else around and he was perched comfortably in the notch behind her shoulders. Once again, she promised herself she'd find a time to discuss the forbidden subject, and once again she knew she was lying to herself.

Lamprophyre eyed the clouds and calculated how long it would take for the storm to arrive. More than a thousand beats, which was more than long enough for her purposes. The wind blowing those clouds in her direction buffeted her, prompting her to put her back to the wind so she didn't have to close the nictitating membranes over her eyes. She wanted to see this through to the end, even though it had been Rokshan's idea and she wasn't totally sure it was a good one.

"I'm not sure this was a good idea," Rokshan shouted over the wind. "The soldiers are all distracted." He shifted his weight so he was leaning over her left shoulder, putting more of her body between himself and the wind. Below them, the great granite wall of Tanajital loomed dully, its usual sparkle dimmed by the overcast. Soldiers thronged its wooden wall-walk, all of them intent not on potential enemies approaching from the north, but on the colorful specks speeding along the southern wall, on the far side of the city. Lamprophyre decided not to say she'd told him this might happen.

"Too late now," she said instead. The specks were moving fast enough around the curve of the wall that already they were visible as colored blotches, red and midnight blue and tarnished silver and, ugh, grass-green. In another beat or so, they were recognizable as dragons.

Despite herself, Lamprophyre's heart raced with excitement. Rokshan had been right about one thing for sure: there was nothing in the world to beat the sight of a magnificent, powerful creature in motion. She wasn't racing because she feared her rider losing his seat, and also because the dragon ambassador losing might look bad, but watching was almost as good. Now, if only Porphyry would pull ahead...

The dragons were headed directly for her. Lamprophyre resisted the urge to fly backward, out of their path. Dragons never collided with each other intentionally, and moving would just make her look stupid. Rokshan clutched her ruff more securely, but gave no other sign that he felt nervous in the face of four dragons barreling down upon them. Closer, closer... Porphyry was right on Coquina's flank—

—and the dragons swept past, four streaks of color that separated to fly in all directions as they shed momentum. Lamprophyre ground her back teeth together. She'd promised not to compare herself to Coquina anymore, not after the illuminating conversation she'd had with Hyaloclast about Coquina's true merits or lack thereof, but old reactions died hard, and seeing Coquina fly past head and neck in front of Porphyry irritated her. She put on a pleasant smile and flew upward to where her clutchmates had gathered, their eyes dilated and their breathing heavy from their exertions.

"Coquina wins again," she said. "That's three out of five."

"I'm just lucky," Coquina said with a laugh and a flutter of her wings that pretended to humility. Lamprophyre resisted the urge to grind her teeth again. Coquina was pretty and fast, both of which qualities Coquina had Mother Stone to thank for rather than her own perseverance in developing them, though Coquina persisted in acting as if possessing them made her superior.

"I don't know why we bother," Orthoclase said, flapping his wings in a leisurely fashion at odds with his breathless voice. "Only Chrysoprase can beat her every time, and she thinks it's beneath her dignity to race younglings."

"As if Chrysoprase weren't only twenty-seven years older than us," Flint said. He stretched, showing off his shapely, muscular torso, a move that on anyone else would have indicated vanity. "She thinks being a mother means she has to protect her dignity."

"What does a dragon mother do to raise her child?" Rokshan asked. "I thought dragons didn't care as much about parentage as they do about their clutch or their respect for Hyaloclast."

"That's when we're adults," Porphyry said. His scales, red as ripening cherries, were darker in the light from the oncoming storm and became even darker as he did a slow loop in midair. "Dragons can't fly until they're fifteen, so they need to be watched before that so they don't venture into places they can't get out of, or might fall off of."

"And they need feeding," Flint added, "particularly the males, who can't cook their own food. So mothers and fathers take care of their physical needs, and they also tell stories so the dragonets learn their history."

"Chrysoprase is overprotective," Coquina said. "Pyrope is eighteen, but her mother still keeps her close to the nest. It's ridiculous."

"There's nothing ridiculous about caring about your child's safety," Lamprophyre said. "And Pyrope is accident-prone. Remember when she climbed up to that ledge looking for garnet and got stuck? It was almost two thousand beats before anyone figured out where she'd gone."

"That was when she was ten, Lamprophyre," Coquina said. "And

Chrysoprase has been overprotective ever since. I know if *I* had a child, I wouldn't want it to grow up frightened and stunted." She cast a quick glance at Flint, who was looking back at the city wall and missed her coquettish look. Lamprophyre, who hadn't missed it at all, wondered once more if Flint knew Coquina was pursuing him. He was too smart to be ignorant of her flirtation, but he'd never once acknowledged it, and Lamprophyre couldn't tell if maybe he really was ignorant, after all.

"We should go," Rokshan said. "The soldiers are still staring. They're supposed to be alert to threats, not watching dragons. Sorry. I didn't realize, when I suggested racing, that it would draw their attention so thoroughly."

"But it proves you were right, Rokshan," Orthoclase said, "about humans being interested in dragon races. I haven't heard a single frightened thought the whole time we've been up here. Though I wasn't really listening. Too busy eating Coquina's dust."

Coquina laughed again. This time, it was a more brittle sound, and to her surprise Lamprophyre felt sorry for her clutchmate. She was almost certain Coquina had only set her sights on Flint because he was gorgeous, but if she felt genuine affection for him, how terrible if he really didn't care for her. Lamprophyre almost listened to Coquina's thoughts, but eavesdropping was bad manners, and she didn't want to fall into old habits of being obsessed with Coquina.

They flew lazily back to the warehouse district, not needing to race the storm, though Lamprophyre suspected she and Rokshan would get a little wet returning to the embassy after seeing the others to guest quarters. Humans thronged the streets below, heading for shelter. None of them looked up or pointed in amazement; none of them gave the dragons more than a passing thought. That was another thing Rokshan had been right about. Nine twelvedays before, when they'd arranged to rent these warehouses as temporary homes for dragons visiting Tanajital, he'd said, "Humans don't stay amazed at the extraordinary long. Soon enough, extraordinary becomes normal, and then normal becomes taken for granted. You'll see." Based on the thoughts she overheard from below, dragons—at least these dragons—were definitely taken for granted.

The streets surrounding the warehouses were wide enough for dragons to land on, and once humans had become accustomed to their draconic neighbors, they'd stopped using those streets entirely. Lamprophyre never feared stepping on humans in these streets. Even so, today she hovered rather than landing, saying, "Are any of you going home this evening?"

"I have business with a stone supplier," Orthoclase said. "He has some stone I've never tasted. You'll all love it once I've worked out what else to pair it with."

His clutchmates laughed. "We eat better than anyone in the flight thanks to you," Porphyry said. "I'm staying the night. Don't feel like flying as late as that storm will require." Flint nodded agreement. Coquina just shrugged and went into her warehouse.

"All right, then I'll see you in the morning," Lamprophyre said, flapping hard to propel herself skyward. She felt Rokshan wave at her clutchmates, and then the two of them were high over Tanajital and headed for the embassy.

Fat drops of rain had begun to fall when she descended to the court-yard in front of the embassy and hurried inside before crouching to let Rokshan dismount. She turned so she could watch the rain fall and settled herself comfortably on her stomach. "It's still pretty," she said, "even though I'm ready for the rainy season to be over."

"We have another couple of months before that happens," Rokshan said. He settled himself in the cross-legged position that always made Lamprophyre's hips ache just looking at it. "That's five twelvedays."

"I'm getting used to human time measurements, too," Lamprophyre said. "Though I still have to count it out in my head. Maybe someday it will be more natural."

Rokshan nodded. "Odd," he said. "I smell cooking. Isn't it a little early for Depik to make supper?"

"It's not supper, it's soup," Lamprophyre said. "It's for the beggars."

Rokshan's eyebrows went up in an expression of disbelief. "Soup for beggars? Why is Depik making soup for beggars?"

"He wanted to help our neighborhood," Lamprophyre explained. "Because he needed help for so long, and now he's in a position to help others. I don't always use all the meat from a cow or a pig, and he asked if I minded him using the scraps and the bones to feed the hungry. Though it's not always just the hungry. Anamika and Varnak sometimes get permis-sion from their parents to eat here. But mostly it's beggars."

"Lamprophyre," Rokshan began, then went silent. She turned to look at him and recognized the expression he got when she came up with a question that had a complicated, human answer. "Lamprophyre," he went on, "you're an ambassador. I'm not sure you should be feeding beggars out of the embassy. No human ambassador would do such a thing."

"I'm not human," she pointed out, "and I don't see why not. Maybe Tanajital is welcoming of dragons now, but it can't hurt to build goodwill, just in case. And Depik was so excited about his idea, I didn't want to turn him down. He's had fewer bad days in the last month, I think, and while I don't think his illness is cured, this certainly seems to have made a difference."

Rokshan shook his head slowly. "I can't argue with your logic. It's just an unusual idea most humans wouldn't have—but you're not human, yes, I'm aware." He chuckled. "I don't know why I'm objecting. This plan of Depik's will probably end up having unexpected and positive side effects, just like everything you do."

"I'm glad you can see sense." She settled herself more comfortably on the floor and closed her eyes. The rain rattled the roof tiles and occasionally blew through the window holes near the ceiling, spattering her hindquarters in a not-unpleasant way. Beside her, Rokshan leaned against her side, tucking himself into the crease of her shoulder. It was so restful, sitting and napping with a friend.

She'd almost drifted off to sleep when she heard Rokshan say, "There's someone I want you to meet. A friend of mine. A...female friend."

She blinked and shifted a little, not enough to dislodge Rokshan. "A female friend? Or do you mean more than a friend?"

"I'm not sure yet." Rokshan laughed, a little self-consciously. "Nevrita's attractive, she's intelligent and funny, so I'm not sure what she sees in me—"

"Don't be derogatory of yourself. That makes you look weak and stupid, and you're neither of those things."

This time, his laugh was amused and unforced. "Sorry. I meant that as a joke, but...anyway. I met her at a concert hosted by Lady Tanura, where it turned out we both like the same composers, and then she was a guest at the reception for the new Rezmish ambassador, so we talked some more, and I've seen her several times since then. She's interesting, and I like her, and I think it might be more than just liking."

"I was at that reception, and I don't remember meeting anyone named Nevrita."

"You didn't. Remember, you left early? She arrived after that."

An unexpected pang of jealousy stabbed through Lamprophyre. "And you're just now telling me about her?"

"Why are you upset? I wasn't sure this was anything more than casual acquaintance, and I didn't see the point of doing something so dramatic as introducing her to my best friend until I knew she was someone I wanted you to meet."

"Best friend" comforted Lamprophyre and made her feel stupid about her reaction. "You're right. I'm sorry. I'd like to meet her, if she's as interesting as you make her sound."

"She is. She's never met a dragon before, and she seemed excited when I suggested I introduce you. Maybe in a few days?"

"I look forward to it." She closed her eyes again and felt Rokshan relax into her side. So. Rokshan hadn't had any romantic relationships since she'd met him last spring, and after he'd been burned so badly by a Fanishkorite spy wielding a fire-blasting artifact, she'd wondered if he felt uncomfortable getting close to a female human. He'd said something along those lines that day, but they hadn't discussed it since. If he liked this Nevrita, and Nevrita liked him, she was happy for him. And she wasn't going to let a stupid irrational jealousy affect how she treated the female. It wasn't as if Rokshan would stop being her friend just because he started a new and different relationship.

She let the pounding of the rain lull her to sleep, and woke to find the noise had ceased and the air was cool and fresh. It was the only thing about lowland weather she enjoyed, the pause after the storm before the sun could once again heat the air hotter than dragon's breath. They didn't have anything like it in the mountains.

Beside her, Rokshan stretched and got to his feet. "That soup smells amazing," he said. "I'm almost tempted to become a beggar."

"You can have some without being a beggar," Lamprophyre said. "Though aren't you supposed to attend a banquet at the palace tonight?"

Rokshan groaned. "It's Khadar's birthday. I wish I could gracefully break my leg or something to get out of it. He's always so insufferable, as if birthdays were invented solely to benefit him."

"I'm too big to fit into the banquet hall," Lamprophyre said, not concealing her relief.

"I wish I could ask Nevrita to accompany me, but singling her out like that would have my parents all over me, wanting to know when we're getting married. So I'll have to suffer alone." Rokshan stretched, making his joints pop in a way Lamprophyre hated. Humans were so fragile, she always expected him to snap his bones or pop his arms from their sockets. "Have a nice meal, and I'll see you tomorrow."

Lamprophyre followed him out into the courtyard and watched until he disappeared up the street. The earth of the courtyard, hard-packed from generations of human feet, always had its top layer stirred up by heavy rains, and the mud clung unpleasantly to Lamprophyre's feet and tail when she incautiously let it sweep the ground. She tried wiping off the dirt, but it just clung to her hand instead. Irritated, she scooped water from the brim-full rain barrel and washed her hand, then entered the dining pavilion and settled herself in her accustomed place near the kitchen.

Depik came around the corner and bowed. "If you're ready, supper's near done," he said. "And the soup is ready."

"It really is a lot of work, making the soup and then washing all those bowls," Lamprophyre said, remembering Rokshan's dubiousness. "Are you sure this is a good idea?"

"My lady," Depik said with a frown, "you've never been hungry, truly hungry. I have. I remember how it feels. I'd wash a thousand bowls if it meant sending these people away full."

"I understand, a little," Lamprophyre said, feeling abashed. "And I agree that it's satisfying to help." She stood until she towered over the kitchen wall, which was taller than Depik but still only half as tall as she was at full height. "Let me handle the soup cauldron, and you can carry the bowls and spoons."

The cauldron wasn't very big, not nearly the size of the one Depik used to cook soup for her, and she lifted it easily and set it down near the entrance to the pavilion, opposite the rain barrel. Depik set down a stack of wooden bowls as the first of the evening's beggars approached. She and Depik had been providing soup for almost a twelveday, but those who came for a meal were still timid, even the ones Lamprophyre recognized as repeat visitors. She watched as they filled their bowls and retreated into the courtyard to eat. Some of them brought their own bowls, but even they stayed to eat, watching Lamprophyre as if they expected her to do something interesting.

Depik rolled out the trolley containing the evening's half a cow, expertly butchered and cooked to perfection, and Lamprophyre tore happily into the meat and idly listened to the thoughts of her "guests." The ones she saw regularly interested her, like the woman with two children in tow—all right, that was less interesting and more heartbreaking. The woman's thoughts were always focused on her children, but Lamprophyre wished she knew her story, why she had no mate—or maybe she did, and he wasn't capable of helping to provide for his family. It wasn't something Lamprophyre felt comfortable asking.

There was the young man with only one leg; Lamprophyre tried not to stare, but that wasn't something that ever happened to dragons and she almost couldn't help herself. There was the old man whose wispy white hair flew in all directions like one of those flowers that broke apart into a thousand fluffy seeds. His thoughts were chaotic, unintelligible except for the occasional snatch of coherent language, *can't find my way* or *it speaks like thunder*, and his constant smile and vacant eyes reminded her of the dragon Gabbro, who'd needed help to find his way to Mother Stone when his madness took him completely.

And there was the odd woman who didn't look like a beggar at all. Her clothes were finely stitched and dyed a rich purple and blue, and she wore a faceted garnet the width of Lamprophyre's thumb in a setting of gold wire wrapped around her upper left arm. That alone told Lamprophyre she was wealthy, or had wealthy friends. Her thoughts were always amused, as if she were laughing at the people around her, and Lamprophyre couldn't decide if she disliked her or not.

Depik came to supervise serving the soup, and Lamprophyre ate and watched the humans. Dragons took care of each other, and this was a way in which humans did the same, but she knew it wasn't a universal trait. For every human they fed that night, a dozen or more elsewhere in Tanajital or in the other cities of Gonjiri would go hungry. She understood why Rokshan was so skeptical of Depik's efforts; when she thought about how many humans were in need, she knew it was impossible to help them all. And yet not helping when she was capable felt wrong. She could only do her best, and hope it made a difference to some.

She finished her meal before the last of the soup was served, so she sat and watched the beggars in silence until they'd all departed, the wealthy woman with a nod and a smile for Lamprophyre as if she knew what

Lamprophyre thought of her. Then Lamprophyre hauled the cauldron into the kitchen to be washed, waved good night to Depik, and went into the embassy. Rokshan was probably still at supper, listening to Khadar talk about how wonderful he was. Much as she enjoyed being with Rokshan, she didn't envy him his supper companion tonight. Khadar, the Fifth Ecclesiast and a powerful religious figure, didn't like her any more than she liked him, and since he always found a way to steer conversations around to how she was a heretic for not believing in his religion, she was just as happy to have been excluded from the birthday celebration.

She settled in to sleep, watching the lazy evening sunlight slant across the courtyard and illuminate the end of the street that terminated there. Maybe she should make an effort to get to know the people they fed, now that they had regulars. She fell asleep imagining a conversation with the old man, whose thoughts floated as madly as his hair, and who told her a secret she couldn't remember come the morning.

ABOUT THE AUTHOR

In addition to the Dragons of Mother Stone series, Melissa McShane is the author of many other fantasy novels, including the novels of Tremontane, the first of which is *Servant of the Crown;* the Extraordinaries series, beginning with *Burning Bright;* and *The Book of Secrets,* first book in The Last Oracle series.

She lives in the shelter of the mountains out West with her husband, three children and a niece, and three very needy cats. She wrote reviews and critical essays for many years before turning to fiction, which is much more fun than anyone ought to be allowed to have. You can visit her at her website **www.melissamcshanewrites.com** for more information on other books and upcoming releases.

For news on upcoming releases, bonus material, and other fun stuff, sign up for Melissa's newsletter **here.**

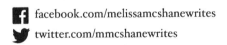

facebook.com/melissamcshanewrites

twitter.com/mmcshanewrites

ALSO BY MELISSA MCSHANE

THE DRAGONS OF MOTHER STONE

Spark the Fire

Faith in Flames (forthcoming)

THE CROWN OF TREMONTANE

Servant of the Crown

Exile of the Crown

Rider of the Crown

Agent of the Crown

Voyager of the Crown

Tales of the Crown

THE SAGA OF WILLOW NORTH

Pretender to the Crown

Guardian of the Crown

Champion of the Crown

THE HEIRS OF WILLOW NORTH

Ally of the Crown

Stranger to the Crown

Scholar of the Crown

THE EXTRAORDINARIES

Burning Bright

Wondering Sight

Abounding Might

Whispering Twilight

Liberating Fight

Beguiling Birthright (forthcoming)

THE LAST ORACLE

The Book of Secrets

The Book of Peril

The Book of Mayhem

The Book of Lies

The Book of Betrayal

The Book of Havoc

The Book of Harmony

The Book of War

The Book of Destiny

COMPANY OF STRANGERS

Company of Strangers

Stone of Inheritance

Mortal Rites

Shifting Loyalties

Sands of Memory

Call of Wizardry

THE CONVERGENCE TRILOGY

The Summoned Mage

The Wandering Mage

The Unconquered Mage

THE BOOKS OF DALANINE

The Smoke-Scented Girl

The God-Touched Man

Emissary

Warts and All: A Fairy Tale Collection

The View from Castle Always

Made in the USA
Middletown, DE
16 October 2023

40879499R00195